0   20   40   60   80 miles

River Terek

C A S P I A N   S E A

D A G H E S T A N

M O U N T A I N S

Baku

A Z E R B A I J A N

NAGORNO
KARABAKH

A R M E N I A

A Z E R B A I J A N

I R A N

OUR GAME

OUR GAME

A NOVEL BY

JOHN LE CARRÉ

ALFRED A. KNOPF   *New York*   1995

He who thinks of the consequences
cannot be brave.
Ingush proverb

Who gathers knowledge
gathers pain.
Ecclesiastes 1:18

If I were living in the Caucasus,
I would be writing fairy tales there.
Chekhov, 1888

OUR GAME

I

LARRY went officially missing from the world on the second Monday of October, at ten minutes past eleven, when he failed to deliver his opening lecture of the new academic year.

I am able to set the scene exactly because it was not so very long ago, in the same dreary Bath weather, that I had dragged Larry down to see the wretched place for the first time. To this day I have the most accusing memory of the brutalist slab barracks closing in on him like the walls of his new confinement. And of Larry's ever youthful back walking reproachfully away from me down the concrete canyon like a man going to his nemesis. If I had had a son, I thought as I stared after him, this was how it would feel to be dumping him at his first boarding school.

"Hey, Timbo," he whispers over his shoulder, the way Larry can speak to you from miles away.

"Yes, Larry."

"This is it, is it?"

"This is what?"

"The future. Where it all ends. Leftover life."

"It's a new beginning," I say loyally.

But loyal to whom? To him? To me? To the Office?

"We have to scale down," I say. "Both of us do."

The day of his disappearance was by all accounts equally depressing. A cloying mist envelops the hideous grey university campus and breathes a sticky pall over the alloy-framed windows of Larry's grimy lecture room. Twenty students sit at desks facing the empty lectern, which is of a particularly violent yellow pitch pine, very scratched. The subject of his lecture has been chalked on the blackboard by a mysterious hand, probably a doting pupil's. *Karl Marx in the Supermarket: Revolution and Modern Materialism.* There is a bit of laughter. Students are the same everywhere. On the first day of term they will laugh at anything. But gradually they fall quiet and content themselves with smirking at each other, peering at the door, and listening for Larry's footsteps. Until, having allowed him the full ten minutes' grace, they self-consciously put away their pens and notebooks and clank along the rocking concrete pavement to the canteen.

Over coffee, the freshers are duly appalled by this first experience of Larry's unpredictability. This *never* happened to us at school! *How* will we catch up? Will we be given *notes?* Oh, *God!* But the hardened ones, Larry's fans, only laugh. That's Larry for you, they explain happily; next time round he'll bat on for three hours and you'll be so hooked you'll forget lunch. They speculate about what might have kept him: a bumper hangover, or an outrageous love affair, of which they ascribe any number to him, for in his mid-forties Larry is still a lover just to look at: he has the lost-boy appeal of a poet who never grew up.

The university authorities took an equally relaxed view of Larry's reluctance to appear. Common Room colleagues, not all from the friendliest of motives, had reported the offence within the hour. Nonetheless the administrators waited for another Monday, and another no-show, before mustering the energy to telephone his landlady and, on receiving no satisfaction from her, the Bath police. It was a further six days before the police called on me: a Sunday, if you can believe it, ten o'clock at night. I had spent a wearisome afternoon escorting a coachload of our village elderlies on a trip to Longleat, and a frustrating evening in the winery wrestling with a German grape press, which my late uncle Bob had christened The Sulky Hun. Nevertheless, when I heard their ring my heart leapt while I pretended to myself that it was Larry, hovering on my doorstep with his accusing brown eyes and dependent smile: "Come on, Timbo, fix us a bloody big Scotch, and who gives a damn about women anyway?"

· · ·

TWO MEN.

It was pelting rain, so they had huddled themselves into the porch while they waited for me to open up. Plain clothes of the deliberately recognisable kind. Parked their car in my drive, a Peugeot 306 diesel, very shiny under the downpour, marked POLICE and fitted out with the usual array of mirrors and aerials. As I peered through the fish-eye, their hatless faces stared back at me like bloated corpses: the elder man coarse and moustached, the younger goatish, with a long, sloped head like a coffin and small, round eyes like bullet holes shot through it.

Wait, I told myself. Add a beat. That's what being calm is all about. This is your own house, late at night. Only then did I consent to unchain the door to them. Seventeenth-century, iron-bound, and weighs a ton. The night sky restless. A capricious wind snapping at the trees. The crows still shifting and complaining, despite the darkness. During the day we had had a crazy fall of snow. Ghostly grey lines of it lay on the drive.

"Hullo," I said. "Don't stand there freezing. Come on in."

My entrance lobby is a late addition by my grandfather, a glass-and-mahogany box like a vast elevator that serves as an antechamber to the Great Hall. For a moment, there we stood, all three, under the brass lantern, going neither up nor down while we looked each other over.

"This is Honeybrook Manor, is it, sir?" said the moustache, a smiler. "Only we didn't seem to see a sign at all."

"We call it the Vineyard these days," I said. "What can I do for you?" But if my words were polite, my tone was not. I was speaking the way I speak to trespassers: Excuse me. Can I help you?

"Then you would be Mr. Cranmer, am I correct, sir?" the moustache suggested, still with his smile. Why I say smile, I don't know, for his expression, though technically benign, was devoid of humour or of semblance of goodwill.

"Yes, I'm Cranmer," I replied, but preserving the note of question in my voice.

"Mr. Timothy Cranmer? Just routine, sir, if you don't mind. Not disturbing you, I trust?" His moustache hid a vertical white scar, I guessed a harelip operation. Or perhaps someone had smashed a broken bottle into him, for he had a patchy, reconstructed complexion.

"Routine?" I echoed, in open disbelief. "At *this* time of night? Don't tell me my car licence is out of date."

"No, sir, it's not about your car licence. We're enquiring about a Dr. Lawrence Pettifer, of Bath University."

I allowed myself a chastened pause, then a frown midway between amusement and vexation. "You mean Larry? Oh my Lord. What's he been up to now?" And when I received no answer but the stare: "Nothing *bad*, is it, I trust?"

"We're given to understand you're an acquaintance of the Doctor's, not to say close friend. Or isn't that correct?"

It's a little too correct, I thought.

"*Close?*" I repeated, as if the notion of proximity were new to me. "I don't think I'd go *that* far."

As one man, they handed me their coats and watched me while I hung them up, then watched me again while I opened the inner door for them. Most first-time visitors to Honeybrook make a reverent pause at this point while they take in the minstrels' gallery, the great fireplace, the portraits, and the wagon roof with its armorial bearings. Not the moustache. And not the coffinhead, who, having until now lugubriously observed our exchanges from behind his older colleague's shoulder, elected to address me in a deprived and snappish monotone:

"*We* heard you and Pettifer were bosom pals," he objected. "Winchester College was what we heard, no less. You were schoolmates."

"There were three years between us. For schoolboys that's a lifetime."

"Nonetheless, in public school circles, *as* we hear, such things make a bond. *Plus* you were students together at Oxford," he added accusingly.

"What's happened to Larry?" I said.

My question drew an insolent silence from both of them. They seemed to be deliberating whether I rated an answer. It fell to the elder man, as their official spokesman, to reply. His technique, I decided, was to play himself in caricature. And in slow motion too.

"Yes, well, your doctor friend has gone a bit *missing*, to tell you the truth, Mr. Cranmer, sir," he confessed, in the tones of a reluctant Inspector Plod. "No foul play suspected, not at this stage. However, he's missing from his lodgings and his place of work. And so far as we can *gauge*"—how he loved that word; his frown said so—"he's not written anybody a goodbye billy-doo. Unless he wrote you one, of course. He's not here, is he, by any chance, sir? Upstairs, sleeping it off, so to speak?"

"Of course not. Don't be ridiculous."

His scarred moustache abruptly widened, revealing anger and bad teeth. "Oh? Now, why am I being ridiculous, Mr. Cranmer, sir?"

"I would have told you at once. I'd have said, He's upstairs. Why should I waste your time, or mine, pretending he isn't here if he is?"

Again he didn't answer me. He was clever in that way. I was beginning to suspect he was clever in other ways as well. I had a prejudiced view of policemen that I was trying to unlearn at the same time that he was deliberately playing on it. Partly it was a class thing; partly it stemmed from my former profession, which treated them as poor relations. And partly it was Larry agitating in me, because, as we used to say in the Office, Larry only had to be in the same borough as a policeman to be arrested for obstructing him in his lawful duties.

"Only you see, sir, the Doctor doesn't appear to have a wife, a companion, a significant other, nobody," the moustache was lamenting. "He is highly popular with the students, who regard him as a card, but ask his colleagues in the Common Room about him, you meet what I call a blank wall, be it contempt, be it envy."

"He's a free spirit," I said. "Academics aren't used to that."

"Pardon me, sir?"

"He's used to speaking his mind. Particularly on the subject of academics."

"Of which body, however, the Doctor himself happens to be a member," said the moustache, with a cocky lift of his eyebrow.

"He was a parson's son," I said unthinkingly.

"Was, sir?"

"Was. His father's dead."

"He's still his father's son, though, sir," said the moustache in reproof.

His phoney unction was beginning to act like an insult on me. This is the way you think we ignorant coppers should be, he was telling me, so this is the way I am.

A long passage hung with nineteenth-century watercolours leads to my drawing room. I went ahead, listening to the clip of their shoes behind me. I had been playing Shostakovich on my stereo, but without conviction. I switched him off and in a show of hospitality poured three glasses of our '93 Honeybrook Rouge. The moustache murmured, "Good health," drank, and said amazing to think it had been grown right here in this house, as you might say, sir. But his angular sidekick prodded his glass at the fire in order to examine the colour. Then shoved his long nose into it and sniffed. Then took an expert bite and chewed while he peered at the exquisite baby Bechstein piano that in my madness I had bought for Emma.

"Do I detect a certain hint of a Pinot in here somewhere?" he demanded. "There's a lot of tannin, that's for sure."

"It *is* a Pinot," I retorted, through gritted teeth.

"I didn't know a Pinot could be ripened in England."

"It can't. Not unless you have an exceptional site."

"Is your site exceptional?"

"No."

"Then why do you plant it?"

"I don't. My predecessor did. He was an incurable optimist."

"What makes you say that, then?"

I mastered myself. Barely. "Several reasons. The soil is too rich, it is poorly drained and too high above sea level. My uncle was determined to ignore these problems. When other local vineyards thrived and his did not, he blamed his luck and tried again next year." I turned to the moustache. "Perhaps I might be allowed to know your names."

With a due show of embarrassment, they pushed their passes at me, but I waved them away. I too had flourished passes in my day, most of them fakes. The moustache had tried to telephone me in advance, he said, but discovered I had gone ex-directory. So happening to be in the area on an unrelated matter, sir, they decided to take a liberty and ring the bell. I didn't believe them. Their Peugeot had a London registration. They wore city shoes. Their complexions lacked the country glow. Their names, they said, were Oliver Luck and Percy Bryant. Luck, the coffinhead, was a sergeant. Bryant, the moustache, was an inspector.

Luck was taking stock of my drawing room: my family miniatures, my eighteenth-century Gothic furniture, my books—Herzen's memoirs, Clausewitz on war.

"You read a lot, then," he said.

"When I can."

"The languages, they're not a barrier?"

"Some are, some aren't."

"Which aren't?"

"I have some German. Russian."

"French?"

"Written."

Their eyes on me, all four of them, all the time. Do policemen spot us for what we are? Do they recognise something in us that reminds them of themselves? My months of retirement were rolling away. I was Operational Man again and wondering whether it showed and where the Office was in this. Emma, I was thinking, have they found you? Grilled you? Made you say things?

It is four in the morning. She is seated in her attic studio, at her rosewood kneehole desk, another extravagant gift I have bought for her. She is typing. She has been typing all night long, a pianist who has formed an addiction to the typewriter.

"Emma," I entreat her from the doorway. "What's it all for?" No answer. "You're wearing yourself out. Get some sleep, *please.*"

Inspector Bryant was rubbing his hands straight up and down between his knees, like a man separating wheat. "So then, Mr. Cranmer, sir," he said, his smile set to invade, "when did we last see or hear from our doctor friend, if I may make so bold?"

Which was the question for which I had been preparing myself day and night these last five weeks.

BUT I didn't answer him. Not yet. Determined to deny him the interrogator's rhythm, I favoured a leisured tone in keeping with the fireside atmosphere we were sharing.

"Now, when you say he had no *companion* . . . ," I objected.

"Yes, sir?"

"Well, for heaven's sake"—I laughed—"Larry always had someone on the go, surely."

Luck cut in. Rudely. He was a stop-or-sprint man, no middle gear. "You mean a *woman?*" he blurted.

"Whenever *I* knew him he had a stable of them," I said. "Don't tell me he's turned celibate in his old age."

Bryant weighed my words.

"Such was the reputation that preceded him to Bath, Mr. Cranmer, sir. But the truth, we find, is somewhat different, isn't it, Oliver?" Luck went on glowering at the fire. "We have quizzed his landlady thoroughly, and we have quizzed his academic colleagues. Confidentially. Not wishing to stir up a mare's nest at this early stage of our enquiries, naturally." He drew a breath, and I was moved to wonder how much his lugubrious behaviour was modelled on his absurdly successful television counterparts. "To begin with, immediately subsequent to his taking up his appointment in Bath, he was all that you imply. He had his drinking haunts, he had an eye for the pretty girl student, and it appears that more than one succumbed. Gradually, however, we see a change. He goes serious. He doesn't do the parties anymore. Many evenings are spent away from his diggings. Sometimes whole nights. Less drink is taken. *Subdued* is a word that crops up quite a lot. *Purposeful* is another. There's a secretiveness in the Doctor's recent habits, not to put it too finely, that we seem unable to crack."

It's called tradecraft, I thought. "Perhaps he was growing up at last," I suggested airily, but evidently with more feeling than I intended, for Luck's long head turned to stare at me while the firelight played red and orange on the strings of his neck.

"His only occasional visitor we're aware of in the last twelve months is an overseas gentleman known as the Professor," Bryant went on. "Professor of what or where is anybody's guess. The Professor never stayed long; he seemed to turn up unannounced, but the Doctor was always glad to see him. They'd have a take-in curry and a pack of beer, some Scotch was popular and laughter was heard. The Professor was clearly a wit in his own right, according to our source. He would sleep on the sofa and leave next day. Just a light bag, he had, very self-sufficient. A cat that walked by himself, she called him. He never had a name, not as far as the landlady was concerned, just Professor: This is the Professor. Him and the Doctor spoke in a very foreign language too, quite often into the small hours."

I nodded, trying to display a polite interest rather than the fascination he was kindling in me.

"It wasn't Russian, or the landlady would have recognised it. Her late husband was a naval officer who'd done a Russian course, so she knows what Russian sounds like. We've checked with the university. None of their official guests fit the bill. The Professor came privately and left privately."

I am walking on Hampstead Heath, five years ago, Larry at my side. We walk too fast. Together, we always do. In London parks, on our weekend retreats to the Office's safe house in Norfolk, we walk like two athletes competing even in their leisure.

"Checheyev's become a curry convert," Larry announces. "For six bloody months he's been telling me a lamb's a lamb and sauces are decadent. Last night we go to the Viceroy of India, he wolfs a chicken vindaloo and discovers God."

"A small, sturdy type of person he was in build, apparently," Bryant was saying. "Late forties, she puts him at, black hair swept back. Sideburns, a full moustache, drooping at the corners. Usually wore a bomber jacket and the track shoes. Complexion *brownish* but still *white*, she says. Pitted. Like he'd had spots when he was a kid. Dry type of humour, a lot of twinkle. Not like some professors she knows. I don't know if that rings a bell at all?"

"I'm afraid it doesn't," I said, refusing to allow the bell to ring— or, more accurately, to acknowledge its deafening chimes.

"Went so far as to say *sparkling*, didn't she, Oliver? We thought she might have the hots for him."

Instead of answering, Luck brusquely addressed himself to me. "Which languages does Pettifer speak, precisely, apart from Russian?"

"*Precisely*, I don't know." He didn't like that. "He's a Slavonic scholar. Languages are his forte, minority languages particularly. I had the impression he picked them up as he went along. He's something of a philologist too, I believe."

"In his blood, is it?"

"Not to my knowledge. He has the flair."

"Like you, then."

"I have application."

"And Pettifer hasn't?"

"He doesn't need it. I told you. He has flair."

"When did he last travel abroad, to your knowledge?"

"Travel? Good heavens, he travelled all the time. Used to. It was his passion. The more unsavoury a place, the better he liked it."

"When was his *last* time?"

September 18, I thought. *When else? His last time, his last clandestine meeting, his absolute last laugh.* "The last time he *travelled*, you mean?" I said. "I'm afraid I've really no idea at all. If I ventured a guess I should simply mislead you. Can't you check flight lists and things? I thought that sort of information was computerised these days."

Luck glanced at Bryant. Bryant glanced at me, his smile stretched to the limits of its patience.

"Well now, Mr. Cranmer, sir, if I could just go back to my original question," he said with terminal courtesy. "*When's* the problem, that's for sure. And it would be very nice of you if you would finally let us into the secret and tell us *when* you last had contact with the missing man."

For the second time, truth almost intruded. *Contact?* I wanted to say. *Contact, Mr. Bryant? Five weeks ago on September 18 at Priddy Pool, Mr. Bryant! Contact on a scale you'd never imagine!*

"I guess it must have been sometime after the university offered him permanent employment," I replied. "He was ecstatic. He was sick of short-term lectureships and scrabbling for a living as a journalist. Bath offered him the security he was looking for. He grabbed it with both hands."

"And?" said Luck, for whom gracelessness was clearly a sign of virtue.

"And he wrote to me. He was a compulsive note scribbler. That was our last contact."

"Saying what, exactly?" Luck demanded.

Saying that Bath University was exactly what it was when I brought him there: grey, bloody cold, and smelled of cat piss, I retorted in my mind as the truth again welled up in me. *Saying that he was rotting from the head down, in a world without faith or antifaith. Saying that Bath University was the Lubyanka without the laughs and that, as ever, he held me personally to blame. Signed, Larry.*

"Saying he had received his official letter of appointment, that he was overjoyed, and that we should all share his happiness," I replied blandly.

"*When* is this, exactly?"

"I'm not good at dates, I'm afraid. As I keep telling you. Not unless they're vintages."

"Have you got his letter?"

"I never keep old correspondence."

"But you wrote back to him."

"Straight away. If I get a personal letter, that's what I do. I can't stand having anything in my in tray."

"That's the former civil servant in you, I expect."

"I expect it is."

"Still, you're retired now."

"I am anything but retired, thank you, Mr. Luck. I have never been busier in my life."

Bryant was back with his smile and his scarred moustache. "I expect that's your varied and useful community work you're referring to there. They tell me Mr. Cranmer-sir is the regular saint of the neighbourhood."

"Not neighbourhood. Village," I replied equably.

"Save our church. Help the aged. Country holidays for our disadvantaged children from the inner cities. Open up the house and grounds to the peasantry for the benefit of the local hospice. I was impressed, wasn't I, Oliver?"

"Very," said Luck.

"So when was the last time we *met* with the Doctor, sir, face-to-face—forgetting our compulsive letter writing?" Bryant resumed.

I hesitated. Intentionally. "Three months? Four? Five?" I was inviting him to choose.

"Was that here, sir? At Honeybrook?"

"He's been here, yes."

"How often, would you say?"

"Oh my goodness. With Larry, you sort of don't log it: he drops in, you give him an egg in the kitchen, kick him out. . . . In the last couple of years, oh, half a dozen times. Say eight."

"And the *very* last time, sir?"

"I've been trying to think. July, probably. We'd decided to give the wine vats an early scrub. The best way to get rid of Larry is put him to work. He scrubbed for an hour, ate some bread and cheese, drank four gin and tonics, and pushed off."

"July, then," said Bryant.

"I said. July."

"Got a date at all? A day of the week, say? A weekend, was it?"

"Yes, it must have been."

"Why?"

"No staff."

"I thought you said we, sir."

"Some children from the housing estate were helping me for a pound an hour," I replied, again delicately avoiding any mention of Emma.

"And are we talking here of the middle of July or the beginning or more the end of it?"

"The middle. It must have been." I stood up, perhaps to indicate how relaxed I was, and made a show of studying a bottlemakers' calendar that Emma had hung beside the telephone. "Here we are. Aunt Madeline, twelfth to nineteenth. I had my ancient aunt staying with me. Larry must have dropped in that weekend. He chatted her up."

I had not set eyes on Aunt Madeline for twenty years. But if they intended to go looking for witnesses, I had rather they went after Aunt Madeline than Emma.

"Now, they do *say*, Mr. Cranmer," Bryant proposed archly, "that Dr. Pettifer also made quite copious use of the *telephone*."

I gave a sprightly laugh. We were entering another dark area, and I needed all the self-assurance I could muster. "I'm sure they do. And with reason."

"Something come back to you, does it, sir?"

"Well, dear me, yes, I suppose it does. There were times when Larry with a telephone could make one's life utter hell. Ring you up all hours of the day or night. He wasn't singling you out; he rang everyone in his phone book."

I laughed again, and Bryant laughed with me, while Luck the puritan went on brooding at the flames.

"We all know one of those, don't we, sir?" Bryant said. "Drama merchants, I call them, no disrespect. They get themselves a problem—a fight with the boyfriend or girlfriend; should they buy this incredible house they've just seen from the top of a bus?—and they're not happy till they've sucked you in. I think it's my wife who attracts them in our household, to be frank. I haven't the patience myself. When was the last time Dr. Pettifer came up with one, then, sir?"

"With one what?"

"A drama, sir. A what I call a wobbly."

"Oh, way back."

"Months again, was it?"

I again affected to rummage in my memory. There are two golden rules to being interrogated, and I had already flouted both of them. The first is never volunteer extraneous detail. The second is never tell a direct lie unless you are able to stick it out to the bitter end.

"Perhaps if you could describe to us the nature of the drama, sir, that might enable us to put a date on it, mightn't it?" he suggested in the tone of somebody proposing a family game.

My dilemma was acute. In my previous incarnation it was the accepted wisdom that the police, unlike ourselves, made little use of microphones and phone taps. Their misnomered discreet enquiries were confined to pestering neighbours, tradesmen, and bank managers, but stopped short of our private preserve of electronic surveillance. Or so we thought. I decided to take refuge in the distant past.

"So far as I remember, it was the occasion when Larry was taking some kind of public farewell from left-wing socialism and wished his friends to be part of the process," I said.

Still seated before the fire, Luck laid a long hand to his cheek, seeming to nurse a neuralgic pain. "Is this *Russian* socialism we're talking?" he demanded in his surly voice.

"Whatever kind you like. He was deradicalising himself—that was his expression—and he needed his friends to watch him do it."

"Now, when would that have been, exactly, Mr. Cranmer, sir?" asked Bryant from my other side.

"A couple of years ago. More. It was while he was still cleaning up his act before applying for the job at the university."

"November 'ninety-two," said Luck.

"I beg your pardon?"

"If we're talking the Doctor's public renunciation of radical socialism, we're talking his article entitled 'Death of an Experiment,' published *Socialist Review* November 'ninety-two. The Doctor linked his decision to an analysis of what he termed the underground continuum of Russian expansionism whether it was conducted under the tsarist, Communist, or, as of now, federalist flag. He also referred to the West's newfound moral orthodoxy, which he likened to the early phases of Communist social dogma without the fundamental idealism to go with it. One or two of his left-wing academic colleagues considered that article a rather hefty act of betrayal. Did you?"

"I had no opinion of it."

"Did you discuss it with him?"

"No. I congratulated him."

"Why?"

"Because that was what he wanted."

"Do you always tell people what they want?"

"If I'm humouring somebody who is being a bore, Mr. Luck, and I want to get on with something else, yes, I very likely do," I said, and ventured a glance at my French striking clock in its glass dome. But Luck was not so easily confounded.

"And November nineteen ninety-two—when Pettifer *wrote* this famous article—that would have been about the time you were retiring from whatever it was you were doing in London, I take it?"

I didn't like Luck drawing parallels between our two lives, and I detested his assertive tone.

"Probably."

"Did you approve of him renouncing socialism?"

"Are you asking me to tell you what my politics are, Mr. Luck?"

"I was merely thinking it must have been slightly risky for you, knowing him during the Cold War period. You being a civil servant and him, in those days, as you have said this very moment, a revolutionary socialist."

"I never made any secret of my acquaintance with Dr. Pettifer. It was no crime that we were contemporaries at university or went to the same school, though you appear to think otherwise. It was certainly never an issue with my department."

"Ever meet any of his Soviet-bloc friends? Any of the Russians, Poles, Czechs, and so forth that he knocked around with?"

I am sitting in the upper room of our safe house in Shepherd Market, sharing a farewell drink with Counsellor (Economic) Volodya Zorin, in reality head resident of the revamped Russian intelligence service in London. It is the last of these semiofficial exchanges between us. In three weeks I shall take my leave of the secret world and all its works. Zorin is a grizzled Cold War horse with the secret rank of colonel. Saying goodbye to him is like saying goodbye to my own past.

"So what shall you do with the rest of your life, friend Timothy?" he asks.

"I shall limit it," I reply. "I shall do a Rousseau. I shall turn my back on grand concepts, cultivate my grapes, and perform good works in miniature."

"You will build a Berlin Wall around yourself?"

"Unfortunately, Volodya, I already have one. My uncle Bob put his vineyard inside an eighteenth-century walled garden. It's a frost trap and a haven for disease."

"No, Dr. Pettifer never introduced me to anybody of that kind," I replied.

"Did he talk to you about them? Who they were? What he got up to with them? The deals they were hatching together? Mutual services performed, anything of that nature?"

"Deals? Of course not."

"Deals. Mutual services. *Transactions*," Luck added with threatening emphasis.

"I've no idea what you're talking about. No, he didn't discuss anything of the sort with me. No, I don't know what they did together. Talked hot air, most likely. Solved the problems of the world in three easy bottles."

"You don't like Pettifer, do you?"

"I neither like nor dislike him, Mr. Luck. I am not of a judgmental slant, as you appear to be. He's an old acquaintance. Taken in small enough doses, he's an amusement. I have always treated him as such."

"You ever had a serious quarrel with him?"

"Neither a serious quarrel nor a serious friendship."

"Did Pettifer ever offer to cut you in on a piece of the action in exchange for favours of some sort? You being a civil servant. Or an ex one. Some path you could smooth for him, a tip-off, a recommendation you could put his way?"

If Luck was intending to annoy me, he was making a rare job of it. "The suggestion is totally improper," I retorted. "I might as well ask you whether you take bribes."

Once more, with a laboriousness calculated to exasperate me, Bryant lumbered to the rescue. "Forgive him, Mr. Cranmer, sir. Oliver is but young." He put his hands together in mock prayer. "Mr. Cranmer, sir—*please*—if I may, sir."

"Yes, Mr. Bryant?"

"I think we have distracted ourselves once more, sir. We're rather good at that, I notice. We're talking the telephone, and the next thing I know we're talking a piece of history two years ago. What about *today*, sir? When was your most *recent* conversation with Dr. Pettifer on the electric telephone: put it that way. Never mind the subject or topic; just tell me when. That's what I'm after, and I'm beginning to think that for some reason you don't want to give me a straight answer, which is why young Oliver there was getting a bit testy just now. Yes, sir?"

"I'm still thinking."

"Take all the time you require, sir."

"It's like his visits. You just forget them. He always telephones when you're slap in the middle of things." Making love with Emma, for instance, in the days when love was what we made. "Have I seen such and such an article in the newspaper; did I see that jackass So-and-so on television, lying in his teeth about the whatever? That's what happens with undergraduate friendships. What was charming twenty-five years ago becomes a pest. You grow up. Your friends don't. You adjust. They stay the same. They become old kids, then they become bores. That's when you switch off."

I did not like Luck's glower any more than I liked Bryant's moustachio'd leer.

"Now, by *switch off*, sir," said Bryant, "do we mean here literally switch off? Switch off our telephone? Have it disconnected? Because that is what I believe we did on the first of August last, Mr. Cranmer, sir, and did not resume contact with the outside world for three full weeks thereafter. At which point we acquire a new number."

I must have been ready for him, for I struck back quickly, and at both of them.

"Inspector Bryant. Sergeant Luck. I think I've had rather more than enough of this. One minute you're engaged in a missing person enquiry. The next you're asking a lot of extraneous nonsense about unethical contacts while I was a civil servant, my politics, whether I'm a security risk, and why I went ex-directory."

"So why did you?" Luck said.

"I was being intruded upon."

"Who by?"

"Nobody of the smallest consequence to you."

Bryant's turn. "Now, if that was the case, sir, why didn't you get in touch with the police? Not as if you're a wilting violet, is it? We're more than happy to assist with nuisance phone calls, be they threatening or obscene. In collaboration with British Telecom, naturally. No need to cut yourself off from the outside world for three weeks."

"The calls I found objectionable were neither threatening nor obscene."

"Oh? So what were they, sir, if you don't mind?"

"They were not your business. They aren't now." I added a second excuse where one would have served well enough: "Besides, three weeks without the telephone are a rest cure."

Bryant was delving in an inside pocket. He extracted a black note-book, removed the elastic band, and opened it longways on his lap.

"Only you see, sir, me and Oliver here have been making quite a study of the Doctor's phone calls, going back over his entire period of residence in Bath," he explained. "We are highly fortunate in the Doctor having a very Scottish landlady and a shared telephone line. Every outgoing call was timed and noted down. Her late husband the Commander started the practice. Mrs. Macarthur carries it on."

Bryant licked a thumb and turned a page.

"Incoming calls, the Doctor had any number of them, many from far-flung places by the sound of them, and a lot cut off in midstream. Quite often the Doctor was speaking this language she can't place, too. But outgoing, that's different. When we're talking outgoing, you were the Doctor's star telephone partner until August first this year, according to Mrs. Macarthur. Six hours and twenty minutes the Doctor notched up with you in May and June alone."

He paused, but I still didn't interrupt him. I had played an impossible hand and lost. I had wriggled and ducked, I had hoped to satisfy them with half-truths. But against such a well-planned assault I had no defence. Casting round for a scapegoat, I lighted upon the Office. If the fools in the Office were aware of Larry's disappearance, why the devil hadn't they sent me an early warning? They *must* know the police were looking for him. Then why didn't they stop them? And if they couldn't stop them, why leave me dangling in the wind, not knowing who knew what or why?

I AM ATTENDING my last meeting with Jake Merriman, Head of Personnel. He is sitting in his carpeted rooms overlooking Berkeley Square, snapping his Rich Tea biscuit in half while he moans about the Wheel of History. Merriman has played the English bloody fool so long that neither he nor anybody else knows anymore whether he is the genuine article.

"Done your job, Tim, old boy," he complains in his drawled, echoless voice. "Lived the passion of your time. Who can do more?"

I say, Who indeed. But Merriman has no ear for irony except his own.

"It was there, it was evil, you spied the hell out of it, and now it's gone away. I mean we can't say, simply because we won, there was no point in fighting, can we? Much better to say, Hooray, we trounced them, the Commie dog is dead and buried, time to move on to the next party." He manages a little whinny of amusement. "Not Party with a capital *P.* The small kind." And he subdivides one section of his Rich Tea before lowering the point of it into his coffee.

"But I'm not invited to the new party, am I?" I say.

Merriman never gives you the bad news himself. He prefers to drag it out of you.

"Well, I don't think you are, Tim, are you?" he agrees, with a commiserating tilt of his fleshy head. "I mean twenty-five years do rather shape the mind, don't they? I'd have thought you'd be *far* better off agreeing you'd served your stint, and time to find pastures new. After all, you're not a pauper. You've got your nice place in the country, and a little bit of your own. Your dear uncle Robert has had the grace to die, which is more than we can say for some rich uncles. What could be jollier?"

There is a saying in the Office that you have to be careful with Merriman lest you resign by mistake, rather than waiting for him to sack you.

"I don't think I'm too old to take on new targets," I say.

"Cold Warriors of forty-seven don't recycle, Tim. You're all far too nice. You have too many rules of engagement. You'll tell Pettifer, won't you? It's best coming from you."

"Tell him what, exactly?"

"Well, the same as I've just told you, I suppose. You don't think we can direct *him* against the terrorist target, do you? Do you *know* what he's costing me? Just for his retainer? Not to mention his expenses, which are a joke."

"Since it's my section that is responsible for paying him, yes."

"Well, I mean for what anymore? Hang it all, when you're trying to persuade chaps to join the Baghdad Brotherhood for you or whatever, you need every penny you can get. The Pettifers of this world are extinct. Admit it, says I."

Too late, as usual, I start to lose my temper. "That wasn't the Top Floor's ruling when his case last came up for review. It was agreed by all parties that we would wait and see whether Moscow dreamed up a new role for him."

"We waited and we got bored." He slides a cutting from the *Guardian* across the desk at me. "Pettifer needs a context, or he'll be trouble. Talk to the resettlement people. Bath University is looking for a linguist who can double up on something called global security, which sounds to me like the oxymoron of all time. Temporary but could be permanent. Their Big I Am is ex-Office and well disposed, provided Pettifer keeps his nose clean. I didn't know Bath *had* a university," he adds grouchily, as if nobody ever tells him anything. "Must be one of those Techs in drag."

IT IS THE worst moment of our twenty-something operational years together. Life has decreed that we sit in parked cars on hilltops. This time we are in a lay-by on a hilltop outside Bath. Larry sits beside me, his face buried in his hands. Above the trees I can make out the grey outlines of the university that we have just inspected and the two pairs of dirty metal tubular chimneys that are its ominous landmark.

"So what do we believe in now, Timbo? Sherry at the dean's and stripped pine furniture?"

"Call it the peace you fought for," I suggest lamely.

His silence, as always, is worse than his abuse. He reaches up his hands but finds, instead of free air, the roof of the car.

"It's a safe haven," I say. "For half the year you're bored, for the other half you're free to do whatever you want. That's a damned sight better than the world average."

"I'm not tameable, Timbo."

"No one's asking you to be."

"I don't want a safe haven. I never did. To hell with safe havens. To hell with stasis. To hell with dons and index-linked pensions and cleaning my car on Sundays. To hell with you too."

"To hell with history, to hell with the Office, to hell with life, and to hell with growing old," I suggest, enlarging on his thesis for him.

Nevertheless I have a lump in my throat, I can't deny it. I would put my hand on his shoulder, which is trembling and hot with sweat, except that it is not our way to touch each other.

"Listen," I say to him. "Are you listening? You're thirty miles from Honeybrook. You can come every Sunday for lunch and tea and tell me how bloody it all is."

It is the worst invitation I ever extended to anyone in my life.

BRYANT was talking to his notebook, which he held before his face while he taunted me with the record of Larry's phone calls.

"Mr. Cranmer-sir also features on the incomings, I see. It's not *all* your funny foreigners. An educated gentleman, always very polite, more like the BBC than human, is how the landlady describes you. Well, that's exactly how I'd describe you myself, no disrespect." He licked a finger and gaily flipped a page. "Then all of a sudden you turn round and cut off the Doctor without a shilling. Well, well. No more incomings, no more outgoings, for three whole weeks. What you might term a radio silence. Slammed the door in his face, you did, Mr. Cranmer-sir, and me and Oliver here were wondering why you did that to him. We wondered what had gone on *before* you cut him off and what *stopped* going on once you did. Didn't we, Oliver?"

He was still smiling. If I had been taking my last walk to the gallows his smile would not have altered. My anger against Merriman swung gratefully towards Bryant.

"Inspector," I began, gathering heat as I went. "You call yourself a public servant. Yet at ten o'clock on a Sunday night, without a warrant and without an appointment, you have the impertinence to barge your way into my house—two of you—"

Bryant was already on his feet. His facetious manner had fallen from him like a cloak. "You've been very kind, sir, and we've overstayed our welcome. We got carried away by your conversation, I expect." He slapped a card on my coffee table. "Give us a call, sir, won't you? Anything at all. He rings, he writes, he turns up on your doorstep, you hear something from a third party which could be of assistance in locating him . . ." I could have knocked his insinuating smile through his head. "Oh, and in *case* the Doctor surfaces, would you be so kind as to give us your new telephone number? Thank you."

He scribbled to my dictation while Luck looked on.

"Nice piano," Luck said. He was suddenly too close to me, and too tall.

I said nothing.

"You play, do you?"

"It's been known of me."

"Your wife away?"

"I have no wife."

"Same as Pettifer. What branch did you say you were? Of the civil service? I forget."

"I didn't mention a branch."

"So what were you?"

"I was attached to the Treasury."

"As a linguist?"

"Not especially."

"And you didn't find that too negative? The Treasury? Cropping public spending, pegging pay-rounds, no more money for the hospitals? I think that would get me down." Again I disdained a reply. "You should keep a dog, Mr. Cranmer. A place like this. Crying out for one."

The wind had dropped dead. The rain had ceased, leaving a pall of ground mist that made autumn bonfires of the Peugeot's headlights.

2

I AM NOT given to panic, but that night I came as near to it as I had ever come. Which of us were they pursuing—Larry or me? Or both of us? How much did they know of Emma? Why had Checheyev visited Larry in Bath and when, when, when? Those policemen weren't looking for some fringe academic who had gone walkabout for a few days. They were on a trail, smelling blood, hunting someone who appealed to their most aggressive instincts.

Yet who did they think he was—Larry, *my* Larry, *our* Larry? What had he *done?* This talk of money, Russians, deals, Checheyev, me, socialism, me again . . . How could Larry be anything except what *we* had made him: a directionless English middle-class revolutionary, a permanent dissident, a dabbler, a dreamer, a habitual rejecter; a ruthless, shiftless, philandering, wasted, semicreative failure, too clever not to demolish an argument, too mulish to settle for a flawed one?

And who did they think *I* was—this solitary retired civil servant, speaking his foreign languages to himself, making wine, and playing the Good Samaritan in his desirable Somerset vineyard? *You should keep a dog* indeed! Why should they assume, just because I was alone, that I was incomplete? Why pursue *me*, merely because they couldn't get their hands on Larry or Checheyev? And Emma—my fragile, or not so fragile, departed mistress of Honeybrook: how long before she too is in their sights? I went upstairs. No, I didn't. I ran. The telephone was by my bed, but as I lifted the receiver I humbled myself by forgetting the number I meant to dial, a thing that in the tightest operational situations had never happened to me through my entire secret life.

Yet why had I come upstairs at all? There was a perfectly good phone in the drawing room, another in the study. Why had I rushed upstairs? I remembered some gung-ho lecturer at training school boring us on the arts of siege-breaking. When people panic, he said, they panic upward. They make for lifts, escalators, stairs, any way to go up, not down. By the time the boys go in, anyone who is not too petrified to move is in the attic.

I sat on the bed. I dropped my shoulders to relax them. I rolled my head around on the advice of some colour-supplement guru I had read on the subject of do-it-yourself massage. I felt no relief. I crossed the gallery to Emma's side of the house, stood outside her door, and listened—for what, I didn't know. The tap-tap of her type-writer as it promiscuously embraced each Hopeless Cause in turn? Her doting murmurs on the telephone until I cut them off? Her tribal music from remotest Africa—Guinea, Timbuktu? I tried the door handle. It was locked. By me. I listened again but did not enter. Was I afraid of her ghost? Her straight, accusing, over-innocent stare that said: Keep out, I'm dangerous, I've scared myself and now I'm scaring you? About to return to my own side, I paused at the long landing window and gazed at the far outlines of the walled garden glowing in the pale light of the greenhouses.

IT IS a warm, late-summer Sunday at Honeybrook. We have been together six months. First thing this morning we have stood shoulder-to-shoulder in the bottling room, while Cranmer the great vinicul-turalist breathlessly measures the sugar content of our Madeleine Angevine grapes, yet another of Uncle Bob's questionable selections. The Madeleine is as capricious as any other woman, a visiting French expert assured me, with much winking and nodding: ripe and ready one day, over the hill the next. Prudently, I do not relay this sexist analogy to Emma. I am praying for seventeen percent but sixteen percent will promise a harvest. In the fabled *année* of 1976, Uncle Bob touched an amazing twenty percent before the English wasps had their share and the English rain the rest. Emma watches as I ner-vously hold the refractometer to the light. "Pushing eighteen percent," I intone at last, in a voice better suited to a great general on the eve of battle. "We pick in two weeks."

Now we are lounging in the walled garden among our vines, telling ourselves that by our presence we are nurturing them to the last stage of their fruition. Emma has the swing chair and is wearing the Watteau look that I encourage in her: wide hat, long skirt, her blouse unbuttoned to the sun, while she sips Pimm's and reads sheets of music and I watch her, which is all I want to do for the rest of my life. Last night we made love. This morning after our sugar-measuring ceremony we made more love, as I pretend to myself that I can tell by the polish of her skin and the lazy pleasure in her eyes.

"I reckon if we got a sensible crew in, we could clear this lot in one day," I declare boldly.

She turns a page, smiling.

"Uncle Bob made the mistake of inviting friends. Hopeless. Total waste of time. Real villagers will pick you six tons in a day. Five anyway. Not that we've got more than three here, at the outside."

Her head lifts, she smiles but says nothing. I conclude that she is gently mocking me for my yeoman's fantasies.

"So I reckon if we have Ted Lanxon and the two Toller girls, and if Mike Ambry isn't ploughing, and maybe Jack Taplow's two sons from the choir could come after church if they're free—in exchange for our support at Harvest Festival, naturally. . . ."

An expression of distraction passes across her young face, and I fear that I am boring her. Her brow puckers, her hands lift to close her blouse. Then I realise to my relief that it is merely some sound that she has heard and I have not, for her musician's ear hears everything before I do. Then I hear it too: the wheeze and clatter of a frightful car as it pulls up in the sweep. And I know at once whose car it is. I do not have to wait until I recognise the familiar voice, never raised yet never too quiet to hear.

"Timbo. Cranmer, for God's sake. Hell are you hiding, man? Tim?"

After which, because Larry always finds you, the door of the walled garden swings open and he is standing there, slim as a whip in his not very white shirt and baggy black trousers and disgraceful buckskin boots, the Pettifer forelock dangling artistically over his right eye. And I know that, nearly a year late, just when I am beginning to believe I have heard the last of him, he has come to claim the first of my promised Sunday lunches.

"Larry! Fantastic! Good heavens!" I cry. We shake hands, then to my surprise he embraces me, his designer stubble scraping against my freshly shaved cheek. All the time he was my joe, he never once embraced me. "Marvellous. You've made it at last. Emma, this is Larry." I am holding his arm now. Again, the holding is all new to me. "God sent us both to Winchester and then to Oxford, and I haven't been able to get rid of him since. Right, Larry?"

At first he seems unable to focus on her. He is guillotine pale and a little fierce: his Lubyanka glower. To judge by his breath, he is still drunk after an all-night binge, probably with the university porters. But as usual his looks do not reveal this. According to his looks, he is a studious and sensitive duellist, about to die too young. He stands before her, head tipped critically back to examine her. He rubs his knuckles along his jaw. He smiles his scampish, self-deprecating smile. She smiles, scampish also, the shadow of her sun hat making a mystery of her upper face, a thing she knows perfectly well.

"Well, stone the crows," he declares happily. "Turn, beauty, turn. Who is she, Timbo? Hell did you find her?"

"Under a toadstool," I reply proudly, which if unsatisfactory to Larry sounds a great deal better than "in a physiotherapist's waiting room in Hampstead on a wet Friday evening."

Then their two smiles connect and light each other—hers quizzical, and his, perhaps because of her beauty, momentarily less confident of its reception. But a mutual smile of recognition all the same, even if it doesn't quite know what it recognises.

But *I* know.

I am their broker, their intermediary. I have guided Larry's search for more than twenty years. I am guiding Emma's now, protecting her from what in the past she has too often found, and swears she doesn't want to find again. Yet as I observe my two destiny-seekers taking stock of one another, I realise that I have only to step out of the ring to be forgotten.

"She knows nothing," I tell Larry firmly as soon as I can get him alone in the kitchen. "I'm a retired Treasury boffin. You're you. That's absolutely *it*. There's no subtext. Okay?"

"Still living the old lie, eh?"

"Aren't you?"

"Oh sure. All the time. So what's she?"

"What do you mean?"

"What's she doing here? She's half your age."

"She's half yours too. Less three years. She's my girl. What do you think she's doing here?"

He has his face in the fridge, where he is looking for cheese. Larry is always hungry. Sometimes I wonder what he would have eaten all those years if he hadn't been my joe. A local cheddar takes his fancy.

"Where's the bloody bread? Then a beer, if you don't mind. A beer first, then an alcohol."

He scented her, I think, as I rummage for his bloody bread. *His voices have told him I'm living with a girl, and he's come to check her out.*

"Hey, saw Diana the other day," he says, in the deliberately careless voice he uses for referring to my ex-wife. "Looks ten years younger. Sends her love."

"That's new," I say.

"Well, not in as many words. But *implied*, as the great loves always are. The same old creamy look in her eyes whenever your name crops up."

Diana was till now his ultimate secret weapon against me. Having ridiculed her to hell and back while I was married to her, he now professes a brotherly fondness for her and wheels it out whenever he thinks it will discomfit me.

"*Heard* of him?" Emma protests that evening, offended that I should even have to ask. "Darling, I've sat at Lawrence Pettifer's feet since *infancy*. Well, not *literally*. But metaphorically he's a *god*."

So as quite often happens, I learn something new about her. A few years ago—it is Emma's nature, I would almost say her tradecraft, not to be precise—she decided that mere music was not enough for her and that she would therefore educate herself. So instead of doing the Alternative Music Festival in Devon—which honestly, Tim, is all tai chi and pot these days, she explains with a disdainful smile that does not convince me in the least—she plumped for a summer foundation course in politics and philosophy at Cambridge: "And I mean on the radical stuff, which was what I went for, naturally. Pettifer on practically *anything* was absolutely *mandatory*. . . ." She is doing too much with her hands. "I mean his paper on 'Artists in Revolt' . . . *and* 'The Materialist Desert' . . ." She seems suddenly to run out, and since she has the titles right but doesn't go beyond them, I wonder rather unkindly whether she has read him or only heard about him.

After which the subject of Larry is by tacit agreement shelved. The next Sunday we clean The Sulky Hun and prepare him for battle. All the while we do this I am listening for Larry's beastly car, but it doesn't materialise. But the Sunday afterwards, surer than Fate and once more unannounced, Larry appears, arrayed this time in a French peasant blouson and his tattered Winchester straw boater, which we used to call a strat, and a spotted red neckerchief, with its ends flying away like wings.

"All right, fine. Very funny," I warn him with less than my customary grace. "But if you're picking grapes, you bloody well pick them."

And of course he picks his heart out, which is Larry to the life. When you want him to zig, he zags. When you want him to zag, he casts a spell over your girl. Three weeks later fermentation is complete, and we rack the wine off the yeast as a prelude to rough filtering. And by then I am laying three places at table automatically: one for Cranmer, one for Emma, one for the metaphorical god at whose feet she has been sitting since infancy.

I RAN down to the study and dug out my address book. Under Merriman nothing, but then I'm not looking for Merriman. I'm looking for Mary, which is my homophobe code name for him. Emma, I was certain, would never have dreamed of invading my address book. But if she had, she would have found, instead of Merriman, a woman called Mary who lived in Chiswick and had an office in London. Larry, on the other hand, made a point of reading my private correspondence and anybody else's without a qualm. And who should blame him? If you encourage a man to dissemble and steal hearts, you have only yourself to thank when he turns round and robs you of your secrets and whatever else you've got.

"Hullo?" A woman's voice.

"Is that six six nine six?" I asked. "This is Arthur."

It was not her telephone number I was quoting to her but my personal key code. There had been a time when I was impressed by such devices.

"Yes, Arthur, who do you want?" she asked in a minor-royal drawl.

It occurred to me that my key code had revealed me as an ex-member rather than a current one. Hence her unyielding tone, since ex-members are by definition trouble. I imagined her tall, horsy, and thirty-something, with a name like Sheena. There had been a time when I regarded Sheenas as the backbone of England.

"I'd like to speak to Sidney, please," I replied. "Sort of by yesterday, if it's possible."

Sidney for Jake Merriman. Arthur for Tim Cranmer, alias Timbo. Nobody who is anybody uses his own name. What good had it ever done us, this cloak-and-dagger rigmarole? What harm had it done us, this endless wrapping up and hiding of our identities? *Squeak. Ping.* A mysterious resonance as computer speaks to computer, then to God. The sound of water running out of a bath.

"Sidney will call you back in two minutes, Arthur. Wait where you are."

And with a click she vanished.

But where am I? How will Sidney know where to reach me? Then I remembered that all the stuff about tracing calls went out with bustles and the old building. My phone number was probably on her screen before she picked up the phone to me. She even knew which extension I was speaking from: *Cranmer is in his study. . . . Cranmer is scratching his arse. . . . Cranmer is lovesick. . . . Cranmer is an anachronism. . . . Cranmer is thinking that as eternity is reckoned, there's a lifetime in a second, and wondering where he read it. . . . Cranmer is picking up the phone again. . . .*

A vacuum, followed by more electronic matter. I had prepared my speech. I had prepared my tone. Detached. No unseemly emotion, which Merriman deplores. No suggestion that yet another ex-member might be trying to talk himself back into the fold, a thing for which ex-members are notorious. I heard Merriman and started to apologise for ringing late on Sunday night, but he wasn't interested.

"Have you been playing silly buggers with your telephone?"

"No. Why?"

"I've been trying to get hold of you since Friday evening. You've changed your number. Why the devil didn't you tell us?"

"I rather imagined you'd have your ways of finding out."

"At the weekend? You're joking."

I closed my eyes. British Intelligence has to wait till Monday morning to get hold of an unlisted number. Try telling that to the latest useless watchdog committee charged with making us cost-effective, or accountable, or—joke of jokes—open.

Merriman was asking me whether I had had a visit from the police.

"An Inspector Percy Bryant and a Sergeant Oliver Luck," I replied. "They said they came from Bath. I thought they came from Central Casting."

Silence while he consulted his diary, or a colleague, or for all I knew his mother. Was he in the Office? Or his desirable Chiswick gent's res, just a poodle's pee-walk from the Thames? "The earliest I can manage is tomorrow at three," he said, in the voice my dentist uses when he is being asked to fit a worthless pain case into a lucrative schedule: *Well, does it really hurt?* "You know where we are these days, I suppose? You can get here all right?"

"I can always ask a policeman," I said.

He didn't find that funny. "Come to the main door and bring your passport."

"My *what?*"

He had gone. I took a grip on myself: Calm down. That wasn't Zeus talking, that was Jake Merriman, lightest of the Top Floor lightweights. Any lighter he'd blow off the roof, we used to say. Jake's idea of a crisis was a bad olive in his dry martini. Besides, what was so sensational about Larry going missing? It was only because the police had got into the act. What about some of the other times when Larry had gone missing? At Oxford, when he decides to bicycle to Delphi rather than sit his Prelims? In Brighton, on the day he is supposed to make his first clandestine rendezvous with a Russian courier but prefers instead to get drunk with a circle of congenial fellow souls he has picked up in the bar of the Metropole?

IT IS three in the morning. As my agent, Larry is still cutting his milk-teeth. We are parked on another of our remote hilltops, this time on the Sussex Downs. The lights of Brighton are below us. Beyond them lies the sea. Stars and a half-moon make a nursery window of the sky.

"Don't see the *goal*, Timbo, old horse," Larry is protesting as he peers myopically through the windscreen. He is a boy still, in silhouette a Pan child—long eyelashes and full lips. His air of reckless daring and highborn purpose greatly endears him to his Communist suitors. They do not understand—and how should they?—that their newest conquest can turn full circle in an instant if his perpetual craving for action is not answered; that Larry Pettifer would rather see the world hurtling towards catastrophe than standing still. "You've got the wrong man, Timbo. Need a lesser sort of chap. Bigger sort of shit."

Here, eat something, Larry, I say, giving him a piece of pork pie. Here, have another swig of lime juice. For this is the crime I commit each time he starts to weaken: I talk down the resistance in him; I wave the awful flag of duty. I do my head prefect number, the way I used to speak to him at school when Larry was a parson's son in revolt and I was king of Babylon.

"Can you hear me?"

"Hearing you."

"It's called service, remember? You're cleaning the political drains. It's the dirtiest job democracy has on offer. If you want to leave it to someone else, we'll all understand."

Long silence. Larry drunk is never stupid. Sometimes he is a lot more perspicacious drunk than sober. And I have flattered him. I have offered him the high, hard road.

"You don't think, democratically speaking, Timbo, that we might actually be *better off* with dirty drains, do you?" he asks, now playing the custodian of our libertarian democracy.

"No, I don't. But if that's your view, you'd better say so and go home."

Which is perhaps a little heavy of me, but I am still at the greedy stage with Larry: he is my creation and I must have him, whichever strings I have to pull in order to keep him mine. It is only a few weeks since the reigning head resident at the Soviet Embassy in London, a man supposedly named Brod, after an endless fan dance, recruited him as his agent. Now every time Larry is with Brod I worry myself sick. I dare not think what seditious opinions are swaying his moody, impressionable nature, filling the vacuum of his constant boredom. When I send him out into the world, I intend that he should come back to me more mine than when he left me. And if this sounds like some possessioner's fantasy, it is also the way we young puppetmasters have been taught to run our joes: as our wards, as our other family, as the men and women we are there to lead, counsel, service, motivate, nurture, complete, and own.

So Larry listens to me, and I listen to me. And surely I am as persuasive and reassuring as it is possible to be. Which is perhaps why Larry falls asleep for a while, because suddenly his sweating, boy-genius head lurches into the vertical, as if he has just woken up.

"Got a serious problem, Timbo," he announces in a brave, confiding voice. "Top serious, actually. Ultra."

"Tell it to me," I say generously.

But my heart is already in my boots. A woman, I am thinking. Yet another. She's pregnant, she's cut her wrists, left home, her husband is looking for Larry with a horsewhip. A car, I am thinking: yet another. He has smashed one, stolen one, parked one and forgotten where. All of these problems have arisen at least once in our brief operational life together, and in low moments I have begun to ask myself whether Larry is worth the candle, which is what the Top Floor has been asking me almost from the start of our endeavour.

"It's my innocence," he explains.

"Your *what?*"

He reiterates, very precisely. "Our problem, Timbo, is my purblind, incurable, omnivorous innocence. I can't leave life alone. I love it. Its fictions and its facts. I love everybody, all the time. Best of all I love whoever I was speaking to last."

"And the corollary to that?"

"And the corollary to that is that you've got to be jolly careful what you ask of me. Because I'll do it. You're such an eloquent swine. Such a *brick*. Got to be *sparing*, follow me? Ration yourself. Don't take all of me all the time."

Then he turns and lifts his face to me, and I see the alcoholic tears running down it like rainwater, though they don't seem to affect his voice, which as always is self-consciously mellow: "I mean it's all right for *you*, selling your soul. You haven't got one. But what about mine?"

I ignore his appeal. "The Russians are recruiting left, right, and centre," I say in the voice of pure reason that he hates the most. "They're totally unscrupulous and very successful. If the Cold War ever turns hot, they'll have us over a barrel unless we can beat them at their own game."

And my tactic works, for the next day, contrary to everybody's expectation except mine, Larry makes the fallback rendezvous with his contact and, in his role of Secret Protector of the Righteous once more, goes through his paces like an angel. Because in the end—such was my younger man's conviction in those days—in the end, properly led, the parson's son always comes to heel, his purblind innocence notwithstanding.

MY PASSPORT lay in the top right drawer of my desk. A blue-and-gold true British ninety-four-page foreigner-frightener of the old school, in the name of Timothy D'Abell Cranmer, accompanied by no children, profession not given, expires seven years hence, let's hope before its bearer.

Bring your passport, Merriman had said.

Why? Where does he want me to go? Or is he saying, in the spirit of old comradeship: You've got till three tomorrow afternoon to run for it?

My ears were singing. I heard screaming, then sobbing, then the groaning of the wind. A storm was getting up. God's anger. Yesterday a crazy autumn snowfall and tonight a veritable sea storm, slapping the shutters and whistling in the eaves and making the house crack. I stood at the study window, watching the raindrops slash across the glass. I peered into the blackness and saw Larry's pale face grinning at me, and Larry's pretty white hand tap-tapping on the windowpane.

IT IS New Year's Eve, but Emma has her backache and is in no mood to celebrate. She has retired to her royal apartments, where she is stretched out on her bed board. Our sleeping arrangements would be a puzzle to anyone looking for the conventional lovers' bower. There is her side of the house and there is my side, which is how we agreed that it should be from the day she came to me: each would have his sovereignty, his territory, his right to aloneness. She demanded this and I granted it, never quite believing she would hold me to my promise. But she does. Even when I take her tea or broth or whatever I decide will cheer her up, I knock and wait until I hear her telling me I may approach. And tonight, because it is New Year's Eve, our first, I am allowed to lie on the floor beside her, holding her hand while we talk to the ceiling and her stereo plays lute music and the rest of England makes merry.

"He really is the end," she complains—with humour of a sort, it is true, but not enough to conceal her disappointment. "I mean even *Larry* knows when it's Christmas. He could at least have *rung*."

So I explain to her, not for the first time, that Christmas is an abomination to him; how every Christmas since I have known him he has threatened to convert to Islam; and how every Christmas he undertakes some crazy grudge-trip in order to escape the awfulness of English sub-Christian revelry. I paint a facetious picture of him trekking across inhospitable desert with a bunch of Bedouin Arabs. But I have the feeling she is barely listening.

"After all, there's nowhere in the world you can't *ring* from these days," she says severely.

For the fact is that Larry has by now become our worry bead, our errant genius. Almost nothing in our lives takes place without some sort of nod at him. Even our latest *cuvée*, though it will not be drinkable for a year, bears the in-house nickname Château Larry.

"We ring *him* often enough," she complains. "I mean he could at least let us know he's *all right*."

Actually it is she who rings him, though it would be an infringement of her sovereignty to point this out. She rings him to make sure he got home safely; to ask him whether it's really all right to buy South African grapes these days; to remind him that he's pledged to go to dinner with the dean, or present himself sober and correct at a meeting of the Senior Common Room.

"Perhaps he's picked up some beautiful girl," I suggest, more hopefully than she can possibly imagine.

"Then why doesn't he tell us? Bring her, if he must, the bitch. It's not as if we're going to disapprove, is it?"

"Far from it."

"I just hate thinking of him being alone."

"At Christmas."

"Any time. I just get the feeling, whenever he walks out of the door, he'll never come back. He's—I don't know—endangered somehow."

"I think you may find he's a bit less delicate than you suppose," I say, also to the ceiling.

I have noticed recently that we talk better without eye contact. Perhaps it is the only way we can talk at all. "Peaked early, that's Larry's trouble. Brilliant at university, fizzled in the real world.

There were two or three like that in my generation. But they're survivors. Takers is a better word."

Call it cover, call it something shabbier: again and again over the last weeks I have heard myself play the long-suffering Good Samaritan while in my secret heart I am the worst Samaritan on earth.

But tonight God has had enough of my duplicity. For hardly have I spoken than I hear, not the crowing of a cock, but the sound of tapping at a ground-floor window. But so distinctly—so much in time with the rhythm of her lute music—that for a second I wonder whether it's a tap-tapping in my own head, until Emma's hand tears itself free of mine as if I'd stung her, and she rolls onto her side and sits up. And like Larry, she doesn't shout, she speaks. To him. As if Larry, not I, were lying alongside her. "Larry? Is that you? Larry?"

And from below us, after the tap-tapping, I hear the down-soft voice that defies gravity and three-foot-thick stone walls in its ability to find you wherever you are hiding. He hasn't heard her, of course. He can't have done. He has no earthly reason to know where we are or whether we're at home at all. True, a couple of downstairs lights are burning, but I do that anyway to discourage burglars. And my Sunbeam is locked safely in its garage, out of sight.

"Hey, Timbo. Emm. *Darlings.* Let down the drawbridge. I'm home. You remember Larry Pettifer the great educator? Pettifer the Petomane? Happy New Year. Happy, happy what-the-hell."

Emm is his name for her. She does not object to it. To the contrary, I am beginning to think she wears it like his favour.

AND I? Have I no lines in this cabaret? Is it not my role, my duty, to humour him? To rush to my bedroom window, throw up the sash, lean out, yell at him: "Larry, it's you, you made it—are you alone? Listen, Emma's back is playing her up. I'll be down!" To be delighted, welcome him, my oldest friend, alone on New Year's Eve? Timbo, his rock, the one that crushed him, as he likes to say? To rush downstairs, put on the outside lights, and peer at him through the fish-eye as I unbolt the locks, his Byronic frame rocking in the darkness? Fling my arms round him in accordance with our new habit of embracing—round his beloved green Austrian raincoat that he calls his moleskin—though he is soaked to the bone, having driven most of the way from London by car until the blasted thing developed a will of its own and rolled into a ditch, obliging him to hitch a lift from a bunch of drunk spinsters? His designer stubble tonight is not one day old but six, and there is a superior glow about him that is more than drink: some sheen, some sparkle of distant places. I was right, I think: he has been on one of his heroic voyages, and now he's going to boast about it.

"Bad *back?*" he is saying. "Emm? Bollocks. Can't have a bad *back*, not *tonight*, not *Emm!*"

He's right.

Already with Larry's arrival Emma has undergone a magical cure. At midnight she is about to begin her day again, as if she has never had a backache in her life. Chasing round my dressing room as I run Larry's bath—rooting out fresh socks for him, slacks, shirt, a pullover, and a pair of bedroom slippers to replace his dreadful buckskin boots—I listen to her scamper back and forth across her bedroom in joyous indecision. My designer jeans or my long fireside skirt that Tim bought me for my birthday? Her cupboard door shrieks; the skirt has it. My high white blouse or the low black? High white; Tim doesn't like me tarty. And with the high white I can wear the intaglio necklace that Tim insisted on giving me for Christmas.

We dance.

Dancing embarrasses me, but Emma, if she remembers this, chooses to disregard it. Larry is a natural: now a stately Colonial British fox-trotter, now a crazy Cossack or whatever he thinks he is, hands on hips, strutting round her in imperious rings, slapping the polished wood floor with my bedroom slippers. We sing, though I am no singer and in church have long learned to mouth the hymns rather than incant them. First we stand in a tight triangle, listening to the clock strike twelve. Then we link arms, one soft white arm apiece, and belt out "Auld Lang Syne" while Larry camps a Winchester choirboy's descant and the intaglios glint and bob at Emma's throat. And though her eyes and smiles are for me, I do not need to take lessons in the school of love to know that every contour and inlet of her body, from the pitch of her dark head to the chaste arrangement of her skirt, is referred to him. And when at half past three it is our second bedtime of the night, and Larry is flopped in the wing chair, dead bored again and watching us, and I stand behind her and work her shoulders for her, I know it is his hands, not mine, that she is feeling on her body.

"So anyway, you've been on one of your trips," I say to him next morning, finding him in the kitchen ahead of me, making himself tea and baked beans on toast. He has not slept. All through the small hours I have listened to him prowling my study, rummaging among my books, pulling open drawers, stretching out, getting up again. All through the night I have endured the rank stink of his beastly Russian cigarettes: Prima for when he wants to feel like a cloth-cap intellectual; Belomorkanal when he's needing a little soothing lung cancer, he likes to say.

"So anyway, yes, I have," he agrees at last. For he has been untypically reticent about his absence, reviving in me the hope that he has found a woman of his own.

"Middle East?" I suggest.

"Not really."

"Asia?"

"Not really. Strictly European, in fact. Bulwark of European civilisation."

I don't know whether he is trying to shut me up or provoke me into trying harder, but either way I deny him the pleasure. I am not his keeper anymore. Resettled joes—though when did Larry ever settle in the first place?—are the responsibility of Welfare Section, unless other arrangements are made in writing.

"Anyway, it was somewhere nice and pagan," I suggest, about to turn to other subjects.

"Oh, it was nice and pagan, all right. For the full Christmas experience, try tasteful Grozny in December. Pitch dark, stinks of oil, dogs are all drunk, teenagers wear gold and carry Kalashnikovs."

I stare at him. "Grozny in Russia?"

"Chechenia, actually. North Caucasus. It's gone independent. Unilaterally. Moscow's a bit miffed."

"How did you get there?"

"Thumbed a lift. Flew to Ankara. Flew to Baku. Sneaked up the coast a bit. Turned left. Piece of cake."

"What were you doing?"

"Seeing old friends. Friends of friends."

"Chechens?"

"One or two. And some of their neighbours."

"Have you told the Office?"

"Didn't think I'd bother, actually. Christmas trip. Nice mountains. Fresh air. What's it to them? Does Emm do shoog in her tea?"

He is halfway to the kitchen door, a fresh teacup in his hand.

"Here. Give that to me," I say sharply, taking it from him. "I'm
going upstairs anyway."

Grozny? I repeat to myself, over and over. According to recent
press reports from the region, Grozny today is one of the most
inhospitable cities on earth. Not even Larry, I would have wagered,
would risk immolation by bloodthirsty Chechens as an antidote to
English Christmas. So is he lying? Or trying to shock me? What does
he mean by old friends, friends of friends, neighbours? Grozny and
then where? Has the Office re-recruited him without telling me? I
refuse to be drawn. I behave as if the entire conversation never happened. And so does Larry—except for his damned smile and his
superior glow of far away.

"Emm's agreed to do a spot of dogsbodying for me," Larry is saying
as we saunter on the upper terrace one sunlit Sunday evening. "Help
out with a few of my Hopeless Causes. That all right by you?"

It is no longer just Sunday lunch by now. Sometimes the three of
us are so happy together that Larry feels obliged to stay for supper
too. In the eight weeks since he has been coming to us, the tenor of
his visits has changed entirely. Gone the dreary stories of academic
lowlife. Instead we have Larry *redux*, Larry the world-dreamer and
Sunday sermoniser, one moment raging against the shameful Western inertia, the next painting treacly visions of altruistic wars conducted by a United Nations strike force empowered to put on its
Batman uniform and head off tyranny, pestilence, and famine at a
moment's notice. And since I happen to regard such fantasies as dangerous hogwash, it is my luckless role to act the family skeptic.

"So who will she be saving?" I enquire with too much sarcasm. "The
Marsh Arabs? The ozone layer? Or the dear old common whale?"

Larry laughs and claps a hand on my shoulder, which at once puts
me on my guard. "All of 'em, blast you, Timbo, just to spite you.
Single-handed."

But as his hand stays on my shoulder and I return his overbright
smile, I am bothered by something more substantial than his nick-

name for her. What I see on the surface of his smile is the promise of a mischievous but harmless rivalry. But what I read behind it is the warning of an imminent reckoning: "You started me running, Timbo, remember?" he is saying, with his mocking eyes. "That doesn't mean you can switch me off."

But I have a dilemma, and that is provided by my conscience—or, as Larry would have it, my guilt. I am Larry's friend as well as his inventor. And as his friend, I know that the so-called Hopeless Causes with which he beats the fetid air of Bath—Stop the Outrage in Rwanda, Don't Let Bosnia Bleed to Death, Action for Molucca Now—are the only means he has to fill the void the Office left behind when it dumped him and continued on its way.

"Well, I hope she's of some help to you," I say handsomely. "You can always use the stables, you know, if you need more office space."

But when I catch his expression a second time, I like it no better than the first. And when a day or two later I pick my moment to find out what exactly Larry has roped her into, I bump up against, of all things, a wall of secrecy.

"It's sort of Amnesty stuff," she says, without looking up from her typewriter.

"Sounds marvellous. So what does that involve—getting people out of political prison and so forth?"

"It's all of it really." She types something.

"Quite a canvas, then," I suggest awkwardly, for it is a strain to keep the conversation going across the length of her attic studio.

IT IS a lot of Sundays later, but all Sundays have become one. They are Larry day, then they are Larry-and-Emma day, then they are hell, which for all its variations has a suffocating sameness. More accurately it is early Monday morning, and first light is breaking over the Mendips. Larry left us a full half hour ago, yet the clatter of his dreadful car clanking and farting down the drive rings in my ears, and his sweetly modulated "Sleep well, darlings" is an order my head stubbornly refuses to obey—as Emma's does too, apparently, for she is standing at the window of my bedroom, a naked sentry, marking how the black puffs of cloud break and regroup against the fiery sunrise. I never in my life saw anything so unreachable or beautiful as Emma with her long black hair falling down her back, naked, gazing at the dawn.

"That's *exactly* what I want to be," she says in the chatty, over-enthusiastic tone I am beginning to suspect in her. "I want to be broken up and put together again."

"That's what you came here for, darling," I remind her.

But she no longer likes me sharing her dreams.

"What *is* it about you both?" she says.

"Which both?"

She ignores this. She knows, and I know, that there is only one other partner in our lives.

"What *sort* of friends were you?" she asks.

"We weren't boyfriends, if that's what you're thinking."

"Perhaps you should have been."

Sometimes I resent her tolerance. "Why?"

"You'd have got it out of your systems. Most of the public school Englishmen *I* know had boyhood love affairs with other boys. Didn't you even have a crush on him?"

"I'm afraid I didn't. No."

"Perhaps he had a crush on you. His shining older knight. His role model."

"Are you being sarcastic?"

"He says you were a big influence on him. His straight man. Even after school."

Call it tradecraft, call it lover's frenzy: I am ice cold. Operational cold. Has Larry broken *omertà*—Larry, after twenty years before the secret mast, has made a Come-to-Jesus confession to my girl? Using the self-same specious formulations that he once flung in the face of his long-suffering case officer? *Cranmer perverted the humanity in me, Emma, Cranmer seduced me, exploited my purblind innocence, made me a liar and dissembler.*

"What else did he tell you?" I ask with a smile.

"Why? Is there more?" She is still naked, but now her nakedness no longer pleases her, so she takes up a wrap and covers herself before returning to her vigil.

"I just wondered what form my evil influence is supposed to have taken."

"He didn't say evil. You did." Now it was her turn to force a laugh. "I can wonder whether I'm caught between the two of you, can't I? You've probably been to prison together. That would explain why the Treasury chucked you out at forty-seven."

I have to believe for her sake that she means this as a joke; as an escape from a subject that is threatening to get out of hand. She is probably waiting for me to laugh. But suddenly the gap between us is unbridgeable and we are both afraid. We have never been this far apart or stood so consciously before the unsayable.

"Will you go to his lecture?" she asks, in a mistaken effort to change the subject.

"What lecture? I'd have thought a lecture every Sunday was enough."

I know perfectly well what lecture. It's called "The Squandered Victory: Western Foreign Policy since 1988," and it is yet another Pettifer diatribe on the moral bankruptcy of Western foreign policy.

"Larry has invited us to his memorial lecture at the university," she replies, wishing me to know by her voice that she is exercising supernatural patience. "He's given us two tickets and wants to take us on to a curry afterwards."

But I am too threatened, too alert, too angry to be agreeable. "I don't think I'm a curry man these days, thank you, Emma. And as to your being caught between us—"

"Yes?"

I stop myself in time, but only just. Unlike Larry, I detest large talk; all life has taught me to leave dangerous things unsaid. What use to tell her it isn't Emma who is caught between myself and Larry, but Cranmer who is caught between his two creations? I want to shout at her that if she is seeking examples of undue influence, she need look no further than Larry's manipulation of herself; at his remorseless moulding and seduction of her by weekly and now daily appeals to her infinitely approachable conscience; at his unscrupulous recruitment of her as his helpmeet and body servant under the guise of the so-called Hopeless Causes he continues to espouse; and that if deception is her enemy, let her look for it in her newfound friend.

But I say none of it. Unlike Larry, I am not a confrontation man. Not yet.

". . . I only want you to be free," I say. "I don't want you to be trapped by anyone."

But in my head the helpless scream is like a bandsaw: *He's playing you! It's what he does! Why can't you see beyond your nose? He'll raise you higher and higher, and when he's bored with you he'll leave you up there, tottering on the brink without him. He's all the things you wanted to escape, rolled into one by me.*

IT'S MY Dark Age. It's the rest of my life before Emma. I'm listening to Larry at his posturing worst, boasting to me about his conquests. Seventeen years have passed since Cranmer's pep talk to his tearful young agent on the Brighton hilltop. Today Larry is rated the best gun in the Office's arsenal of joes. Where are we? In Paris? Stockholm? In one of our London pubs, never the same twice running? We are in the safe flat in the Tottenham Court Road, before they pulled it down to make way for another chunk of modern nowhere, and Larry is pacing, drinking Scotch, scowling his Great Conductor scowl, and I am watching him.

His waistband at half-mast round his slender hips. The ash of his beastly cigarette spilling over the unbuttoned black waistcoat that he has recently decided is his hallmark. His fine fingers pointed upward as he milks the air to the rhythm of his half-wisdoms. The famous Pettifer forelock, now shot with grey but still swinging across his brow in immature revolt. Tomorrow he leaves for Russia again, officially for a month's academic powwow at Moscow State University, in reality for his annual spell of rest and recreation at the hands of his latest KGB controller, the unlikely assistant cultural attaché Konstantin Abramovich Checheyev.

There is something majestic as well as anachronistic about the way Moscow handles Larry these days: VIP treatment at Sheremetyevo Airport, a Zil with blackened windows to whisk him to his apartment, the best tables, the best tickets, the best girls. And Checheyev flown over from London to play majordomo in the background. Step through the looking glass, you could imagine they were paying him the departing honours due to a long-standing agent of the British secret service.

"Loyalty to women is a load of junk," Larry declares as he pokes out his coated tongue and studies its reflection. "How can I be responsible for a woman's feelings when I'm not responsible for my own?" He flops into an armchair. Why does even his clumsiest movement have such a careless grace? "With women, the only way to find out what's enough is to do too much," he announces, and practically tells me to write that down for posterity.

I try not to think critically of Larry at times like this. My job is to cosy him along, accommodate his moods, talk up his courage, ride his insults, and come up smiling every time.

"Tim?"

"Yes, Emma."

"I need to know."

"Whatever you like," I say generously, and close my book. One of her women's novels, and I am finding it hard going.

We are in the breakfast room, a circular pepper pot stuck onto the southeast corner of the house by Uncle Bob. The morning sun makes it a pleasant place to sit. Emma is standing in the doorway. Ever since she went alone to Larry's lecture, I have scarcely seen her.

"It's a lie, isn't it?" she says.

Drawing her gently into the room, I close the door so that Mrs. Benbow cannot overhear us. "What's a lie?"

"You are. You don't exist. You made me go to bed with someone who wasn't there."

"You mean Larry?"

"I mean *you!* Not Larry. *You!* Why should you think I've been to bed with Larry? *You!*"

Because you have, I think. But by now, in order to hide her face from me, she is embracing me. I look down and am surprised to see my right hand operating on its own initiative, patting her back and bestowing comfort on her because I have misunderstood her cover story. And it occurs to me that when there's nothing useful left for you to do on the whole of God's earth, patting someone's back is as good a way to pass the time as any. She is choking and sobbing against me, she is blurting Larry, Tim, and accusing me in preference to accusing herself, though much of what she is saying is mercifully lost in my shirtfront. I catch the word *façade*, or perhaps it is *charade*. And the word *fiction*, but it could have been *friction*.

Meanwhile I am doing a good deal of thinking about who is ultimately to blame for this scene and others like it. For in the world where Larry and I did our growing up, it would be quite wrong to suppose that merely because the right hand is bestowing consolation, the left is not considering covert action of its own.

AND STILL she can't leave me. Sometimes in the depth of night she creeps into my room like a thief and makes love to me without saying a word. Then creeps away, leaving her tears on my pillow before the daylight finds her out. A week goes by with scarcely a nod passing between us while each inhabits his separate space. The only sound from her side of the house is the tap-tapping of her typewriter: Dear Friend, Dear Supporter, Dear God, get me out of here, but how? She telephones, but I have no idea who she speaks to, though I guess. Occasionally Larry telephones, and if I take the call I am all sweetness and so is he, as befits two spies at war.

"Hi, Timbo. How's tricks?"

There is only one trick I can think of, and he has played it. But who cares when we are such good friends?

"Very chirpy, thanks. Just fine. It's for you, darling. From Mission Control," I say, passing the call through to her on the internal exchange.

Next day I instruct the exchange to disconnect my telephone, but still she neither runs nor stays.

"Just for information, how will I know when you've left me?" I ask her one night when we meet like ghosts on the landing between our two sides.

"I'll have taken my piano stool with me," she replies.

She means the fold-up stool for her back that she brought to the house on the day she moved in with me. A friendly Swedish osteopath made it for her; how friendly I may only guess.

"And I'll give you the jewellery back," she adds severely.

And I see in her face a glance of angry panic, as if she has misspoken and is cursing herself for doing so.

She means the ever growing collection of costly trinkets that I have been buying her from Mr. Appleby of Wells in order to fill gaps in our relationship that can't be filled.

The next day being Sunday, it is required practice that I go to church. When I return, there are the marks of the departed piano stool in the carpet in front of the Bechstein. But she has not left the jewellery behind. And such is the madness of deceived lovers that the absence of her jewellery provides me with a certain forlorn hope—though never enough to weaken the resolve of my left hand.

. . .

I LAY dressed on my bed, my reading light switched on. I lay to my side of it—my pillows, my half. *Try her*, my tempter whispered. But sanity prevailed, and instead of lifting the receiver, I reached down and pulled the jack from the wall, sparing myself the humiliation of being passed yet again from one slack-mouthed cutout to another:

"Emma's not *here*, I'm afraid, Tim, no. . . . Better try Lucy. . . ." "Hang on, Tim, Luce is playing in Paris. Try Sarah. . . ." "Hey, Deb, it's Tim; what's Sarah's number these days?" But Sarah, if she can be found, knows no better than anyone else where Emma is. "Maybe at John-and-Gerry's, Tim, only they've gone to the rave. Or try Pat, *she'll* know." But Pat's phone gives only a high-pitched wail, so perhaps she's gone to the rave as well.

THE VILLAGE clock chimed six. But in my mind's eye I was watching the two policemen's faces floating in the fish-eye lens. And somewhere behind them, Larry's face, drowned and swollen like their own, staring up at me from the moonlit water of Priddy Pool.

3

A SUBVERSIVE afternoon rain made grubby curtains across the Thames as I huddled under my umbrella on the south side of the Embankment and contemplated my former service's new headquarters. I had caught the mid-morning train and lunched at my club, at a single table by the food lift, set aside for the discomfort of country members. Afterwards I had bought a couple of shirts in Jermyn Street and was wearing one of them now. But nothing could console me for the sight of the appalling building that rose before me. Larry, I thought, if Bath University is the Lubyanka, how about this?

I had had fun fighting world Bolshevism from Berkeley Square. To sit at my desk charting the unstoppable progress of the great proletarian revolution and in the evening to step onto the golden pavements of capitalist Mayfair, with their scented ladies of the night, glittering hotels, and whispering Rolls-Royce cars—the irony never failed to put a spring into my tread. But this—this sullen multistorey blockhouse, rooted amid tearing traffic, all-night cafés, and down-at-heel clothing shops: whom did it think it was scaring or protecting with its scowl?

Grasping my umbrella, I set off across the road. Already the first glum lights had appeared in the net-curtained windows: chrome chandeliers and cut-price desk lamps for the upper levels, neon for the unwashed lower down. A breeze-block chicane led to the front door. Unsmiling young acolytes in chauffeurs' suits hovered at a temporary reception desk of plywood. Cranmer, I said, as I handed over my umbrella and the shirtmakers' pretty box inside its carrier bag: I'm expected. But I had to empty my pockets of keys and loose change before the metal detectors would accept me.

"Tim! Fab! Long time no see! How's the world been using you? Pretty *good*, man, judging by what I see, pretty bloody *good!* Hey, listen, have you remembered your passport?"

All this as Andreas Munslow pumped my hand, clapped me on the shoulder, snatched a slip of pink paper from the acolyte, signed for me, and gave it back.

"Hullo, Andy," I said.

Munslow had served as a probationer with my section until I abruptly had him moved elsewhere. And I'd sack you again tomorrow, I told him cheerfully in my mind as we processed down the passage, chatting like old buddies reunited.

The door was marked H/IS. In Berkeley Square, no such post had existed. The anteroom was furnished in plastic rosewood. In Berkeley Square we had rather gone for chintz. A notice said PRESS BELL, AWAIT GREEN. Munslow glanced at his deep-sea-diver's watch and muttered, "Bit early." We sat down without pressing bell.

"I'd have thought Merriman would have wangled himself something on the top deck," I said.

"Yeah, well, you see, Jake thought he'd turn you straight over to the people who handle this stuff, Tim, catch up with you later kind of thing."

"What stuff?"

"Well, you know. Post-Sov. New Era."

I wondered what was new era about an ex-agent disappearing.

"So what does IS stand for? Inquisitors' Section? Imminent Sackings?"

"Best ask Marjorie that one, actually, Tim."

"Marjorie?"

"I'm not totally versed, know what I mean?" He made a show of brightening. "Hey, great to see you. Really super. Not a day older, all that."

"You too, Andy. You haven't changed a bit."

"If I could just have that passport, actually, Tim."

I gave it to him. Time went by.

"So how's life in the Office these days?" I asked.

"Tim, the overall feeling is good. It's a great place to be. Really hopping."

"I'm glad."

"And you're making wine, Tim. Right?"

"I tread a few grapes."

"Great. Fabulous. They say British wine is really up and running."

"Do they indeed? How very nice of them. Unfortunately, there's no such thing. There's English wine. There's Welsh wine. Mine's inferior English, but we're studying to improve."

I remembered that he had a hide like a horse, for he seemed quite unmoved.

"Hey, how's Diana? The queen of vetting, they used to call her, back in the old days. Still do. That's quite a compliment."

"She's well, I hope, thank you, Andy. But we've been divorced these seven years."

"Oh, Christ, sorry about that."

"Well, don't be. I'm not. Neither is Diana."

He pressed bell and sat down again while we awaited green.

"Hey, listen, how's the back?" he asked in another spurt of inspiration.

"Thank you for remembering, Andy. Not a murmur since I left the Service, I'm proud to say."

It was a lie, but Munslow was one of those people with whom you do not want to share the truth, which was why I wouldn't have him in my section.

PEW, SHE said. As in church. Marjorie Pew.

She had a good handshake and a straight gaze, grey-green and slightly visionary. She wore pale face powder of a translucent quality. She was dressed in broad-shouldered navy blue, with the white stock at her throat that I associate with women barristers, and a gold fob-chain round it which I guessed had been her father's. She had a young figure and a very English carriage. Bending from the hip and holding out her hand to me, she lifted her elbow sideways, suggesting country girl and public school. Her brown hair was cropped like a boy's.

"Tim," she said. "Everyone calls you Tim, so I shall too. I'm Marjorie with an i-e. *Nobody* calls me Marge."

Not twice they don't, I thought as I sat down.

No rings on her fingers, I noticed. No framed photographs of hubby ruffling the spaniel's ears. No gap-toothed ten-year-olds on a camping holiday in Tuscany. Would I like tea or coffee? Coffee, please, Marjorie. She lifted a telephone and ordered it. She was used to giving orders. No papers, pens, toys, or tape recorder. Or none visible.

"So shall we take it from the top?" she suggested.

"Why not?" I said, equally hospitably.

She listened to me the way Emma listens to music, motionless, sometimes smiling, sometimes frowning, never quite at the places I expected. She had the judicious superiority of a psychiatrist. She made no notes and waited till I had finished before asking her first question. I was fluent. Part of me had been rehearsing my act all day and probably all night. The arrival of a half-forgotten colleague distracted me not at all. The door opened—a different door from the one I'd come in by—and a well-dressed man set a coffee tray between us, winked at me, and said Jake would be along in a minute, the FO was in a flap. With a start of pleasure, I recognised Barney Waldon, king of the Office's police liaison team. If you were mounting a domestic burglary or planning a small kidnapping or your daughter had been caught, drugged out of her mind, racing her souped-up Mini round the M25 at three in the morning, Barney was the one who made sure the Might of the Law was on your side. I felt a little safer for his presence.

Marjorie had placed her hands primly below her chin. While I spoke she observed me with a saintly concern that put me on my guard. I omitted all mention of Emma, I made light of changing my telephone number—vague talk of misrouted computer calls making one's life utter hell—and I confessed I had rather welcomed the chance of a respite from late-night drunken conversations with Larry. I made a rueful joke of it: something about anyone who shoulders the burden of Larry's friendship becoming an instant expert in the arts of self-protection. It won a watery smile from her. Perhaps I should have been more frank with the police, I said, but I was concerned not to appear close to Larry in case they drew the wrong conclusions—or the right ones.

Then I sat back in my chair in order to show her I had told her the whole truth and nothing but. I exchanged a friendly glance with Barney.

"Tough one," he said.

"A bit uncalled for," I agreed. "But typical Larry."

"You bet."

Then we both looked at Marjorie with an i-e, who had not spoken. She was staring at a spot on her desk as if she had something to read there. But she hadn't. I noticed two doors behind her, one to each side. It occurred to me that this was not her room but an anteroom, and that real life was lived elsewhere. I had a feeling we were being listened to. But in the Office you have that feeling anyway.

"Forgive me, Tim. Didn't it cross your mind to tell the police to come back later, and phone us immediately? Instead of simply opening your doors to them?" she asked, still studying the desk.

"I had a choice—as in any operational situation," I explained, perhaps a trifle patronisingly. "I could have sent them packing and phoned you, which would have sounded their alarm bells. Or I could play it as it lay, normally. Just a normal police enquiry about a normal missing friend. That's how I played it."

She was happy to take my point. "And besides, it probably *was* normal, wasn't it? It may still be. As you say, all Larry has done is disappear."

"Well, there was the reference to Checheyev," I reminded her. "The landlady's description of Larry's foreign visitor fitted him to a T."

At the mention of CC, her grey-green gaze lifted to me inhospitably.

"Did it?" she said, more as a question of herself than of me. "Tell me about him."

"Checheyev?"

"Isn't he a Georgian or something?"

Oh, Larry, I thought, you should be with us now.

"No, I'm afraid he was quite the other thing. He came from the North Caucasus."

"So he was Chechen," she said, with the peculiar dogmatism I was beginning to expect of her.

"Well, nearly but not quite," I said kindly, though I'd half a mind to tell her to go and look at a map. "He's an Ingush. From Ingushetia. Next door to Chechenia but smaller. Chechenia one side, North Ossetia the other. Ingushetia in the middle."

"I see," she said with the same blank stare as before.

"In KGB terms, Checheyev was a one-off. Russians from the old Muslim minorities didn't make the foreign side of the KGB as a rule.

They don't make much at all. There are special laws to control them, they're known as blackarses and kept in the provinces. CC broke the mould."

"I see."

"CC was Larry's name for him."

"I see."

I wished she would stop saying that, since it was so patently untrue.

"Blackarse sounds much worse in Russian than in English. It used to apply only to Central Asian Muslims. In the new spirit of openness it's been extended to include the North Caucasians."

"I see."

"He cut a heroic figure, at least in Larry's eyes. Dashing, cultured, physical, very much the *gorets*, and even something of a wit. After some of the dross Larry had had to put up with over the last sixteen years, Checheyev was a breath of air."

"*Gorets?*"

"Mountain man. Plural *gortsy*. He was a good case officer too."

"Really." She consulted her hands.

"Larry likes to idealise people," I explained. "It's part of his eternal immaturity. When they let him down, nothing's bad enough for them. But with CC that never happened."

I had reminded her of something.

"Didn't Larry have some *position* on the Caucasus?" she asked with disapproval. "I seem to remember we had to call in the Foreign Office so that he could be *heard*."

"He thought we should be taking a greater interest in the region during the dying days of Soviet power."

"Greater interest *how?*"

"He saw the North Caucasus as the next powder keg. The next Afghanistan. A string of Bosnias waiting to happen. He felt that the Russians shouldn't be trusted with the region. He hated them interfering. Dividing and ruling. He hated the demonisation of Islam as a substitute for the anti-Communist crusade."

"And *do?*"

"I'm sorry?"

"Do. What were we in the West supposed to *do*, in Pettifer's lexicon, to redress our sins?"

I shrugged, perhaps a little rudely. "Stop siding with the old Russian dinosaurs . . . insist on a proper respect for small nations . . . renounce our love of large political groupings and give more thought to individual minorities . . ." I was quoting Larry word for word—the Pettifer Sunday sermons. Like Larry, I could have gone on all day. "Care about the detail. The humanity, which was what we fought the Cold War for in the first place."

"Did we?"

"He did."

"And Checheyev influenced him in this, obviously."

"Obviously."

Her eyes had scarcely left mine all this time. Now they flashed accusingly. "And did you share this view—you personally?"

"Checheyev's view?"

"This perception of our Western duty."

No, I bloody well didn't, I thought. It was Larry at his worst, stirring up a storm because he was bored. But I didn't say that. "I was a professional, Marjorie. I didn't have the time to share views or reject them. I believed whatever was necessary to the job at the time."

But I had the feeling, as she continued watching me, that she was listening less to my words than to things I hadn't said.

"Anyway, we heard him," she said, as if that absolved us of blame.

"Oh, we heard him, all right. Our analysts heard him. The Foreign Office's expert on Southern Russia heard him. But it wasn't a success."

"Why not?"

"They told him there was no British interest in the area. We'd told him much the same ourselves, but when he heard it from the horse's mouth he lost his temper. He quoted a Mingrelian proverb at them. 'Why do you want light if you're blind?' "

"Did you know Checheyev retired from his service with full honours two years ago?"

"Of course."

"Why of course?"

"It was happening by the time we stood Larry down. Checheyev's departure was a contributing factor to the Top Floor's decision to wrap up the Pettifer operation."

"Had Checheyev been offered another posting?"

"According to him, no. He was resigning."

"Where was he going? According to him."

"Home. He wanted his mountain back. He was tired of being an intellectual and wanted to go back to his tribal roots."

"Or that was his story."

"It's what he told Larry, which is slightly different."

"Why?"

"They liked to think they had a relationship of trust. Checheyev never lied to him. Or so he said, and Larry believed him."

"Did you?"

"Lie to Larry?"

"Believe Checheyev."

"We never caught him out."

Marjorie Pew placed the thumb and forefinger of her right hand to the bridge of her nose, as if adjusting its position.

"But of course Checheyev wasn't head resident here, was he?" she said, leading me for the benefit of the jury.

Not for the first time, I wondered how much she knew and how much she was depending on my answers. I decided that her technique was a blend of ignorance and cunning; that she was rehearsing me in things she already knew and concealing what she didn't.

"No, he wasn't. The head resident was a man named Zorin. A blackarse could never have made top man in a major Western post. Not even Checheyev."

"Didn't you have dealings with Zorin?"

"You know I did."

"Tell us about them."

"They occurred under the strict orders of the Top Floor. We met every couple of months or so in a safe house."

"Which one?"

"Trafalgar. In Shepherd Market."

"Over what period?"

"Altogether I suppose we had a dozen meetings. They were recorded, naturally."

"Did you have meetings with Zorin that were not recorded?"

"No, and he brought his own tape recorder along for good measure."

"And the purpose of these meetings?"

I gave her the whole mouthful, exactly as it had read in my brief: "Informal exchanges between our two services on matters of potential mutual interest, to be conducted in the new spirit of cooperation."

"And precisely?"

"Shared headaches. Drugs traffic. Maverick arms pedlars. Bomb-slinging extremists. Cases of major international fraud involving Russian interests. When it began, we were keeping our voices low and not quite telling the Americans. By the time I left, the collaboration was pretty well official."

"Did you form a bond with him?"

"Zorin? Of course. It was my job."

"Has it endured?"

"You mean, are we still in love? If I had had any further dealings with Zorin, I would have reported them to the Office."

"What was your last word of him?"

"He quitted London soon after I did. He said he was taking a dreary desk job in Moscow. I didn't believe him. He didn't expect me to. We had a last drink, and he presented me with his KGB hip flask. I was duly touched. He probably had twenty of them."

She didn't like my being duly touched. "Did you ever discuss Checheyev with him?"

I had given up expressing shock to her. "Of course not. Checheyev was officially cultural and under deep cover, whereas Zorin was declared to us as the diplomat with intelligence responsibility. The last thing I wanted to do was suggest to Zorin that we had rumbled Checheyev. I could have compromised Larry."

"What *sort* of international fraud did you discuss?"

"Particular cases? None. It was a matter of establishing future links between our investigators and theirs. Bringing honest men together, we called it. Zorin was old school. He looked like something out of the October Parade."

"I see."

I waited. So did she. But she waited longer. I am back with Zorin for our farewell drink in Shepherd Market. Till now it was always the Office's whisky that we drank. Today it is Zorin's vodka. Before us on the table stands the shining silver hip flask embellished with the red insignia of his service.

"I am not sure what future we may drink to now, Friend Timothy," he confesses with an uncharacteristic show of humility. "Perhaps you will propose an appropriate toast for us."

So I propose the Russian word for order, knowing that order, not progress, was what the old Communist soldier loved the best. So order is what we drink to, at our net-curtained second-floor window, while the shoppers come and go below us, and the tarts eye their customers from doorways, and the music shop blasts out its mayhem.

"The questions put to you by the police about Larry's business dealings," Marjorie Pew was saying.

"Yes, Marjorie."

"They didn't jog your memory at all?"

"I assumed the police had got the wrong man as usual. Larry is an infant about business. My section was forever sorting out his tax returns, expenses, overdrafts, and unpaid electricity bills."

"You don't think that might have been cover."

"Covering what?"

I didn't like her shrug. "Covering hidden money he had acquired and didn't want anyone to know about," she said. "Covering a good business head."

"Absolutely not."

"Is it your theory that Checheyev is in some way linked to Larry's disappearance?"

"It's not my theory; it was what the police seemed to be suggesting."

"So you don't think Checheyev's presence in Bath is of any significance?"

"I don't have an opinion in this, Marjorie; how can I have? Larry and Checheyev were close. I know that. They had a mutual admiration society going. I know that. Whether they still have is quite another question." I saw my chance and took it. "I don't even know when Checheyev's visits to Bath are supposed to have taken place."

But she refused to take the bait. "You don't think it possible Larry and Checheyev have entered into a business arrangement, for instance? Of any kind? Never mind what?"

Wanting someone to share my irritation, I again glanced at Barney, but he was playing possum.

"No. Absolutely not," I said. "As I told the police, several times." And I added, "Out of the question."

"Why?"

I did not like being made to repeat myself. "Because Larry never gave a hoot about money and had absolutely no head for business. He called his Office pay his Judas money. He felt bad taking it. He felt—"

"And Checheyev?"

I was getting sick of her interrupting me, too. "Checheyev *what?*"

"Did he have a business head?"

"Absolutely not. He rejected it. Capitalism . . . profit . . . money as motive—he hated all of it."

"You mean he was above it?"

"Below it. Whatever."

"Too truthful? Too honest? You accept the Larry view of him?"

"It's the pride of the *gortsy* that money buys nothing in the mountains. Greed makes a man stupid, they say." I was quoting Larry again. "Manhood and honour are all that count. It's probably romantic nonsense, but that was the line he pushed with Larry, and Larry was duly impressed by it." I'd had enough. "I'm not a feature in this, Marjorie. Larry's retired, so's Checheyev, so am I. I thought you should know that Checheyev had visited Larry in Bath and that Larry had disappeared. If you didn't know already. Why is anybody's guess."

"But you're not anybody, are you? You're the expert on the Larry-Checheyev relationship—whether you're retired or not."

"The only experts on that relationship are Larry and Checheyev."

"But didn't you invent it? Control it? Isn't that what you've been doing all these years?"

"Twenty-odd years ago I engineered a relationship between Larry and the KGB head resident of the day. Under my guidance Larry trailed his coat at him, played hard to get, finally said yes, I'll spy for Moscow."

"Go on."

I was going on anyway. I didn't know why she was goading me, and I wasn't sure she knew. But if she wanted a lecture on Larry's case history, she could have it. "First came Brod. After Brod we had Miklov, then Kransky, then Sherpov, then Mislanski, finally Checheyev, with Zorin as boss but Checheyev as Larry's handler. Larry found his own way to each of them. Double agents are chameleons. Good doubles don't *act* their parts, they live them. They *are* them. When Larry was with Tim, he was with Tim. When he was with his Soviet controller, he was with his Soviet controller whether

I liked it or not. My job was to make sure we were getting the best end of the deal."

"And you were confident that we were."

"In Larry's case, yes, I was."

"And you still are."

"In my retirement, recalling events in tranquility, yes, I still am. With doubles you assume a certain wastage of loyalty. The opposition is always more attractive to them than the home side. That's their nature. They're constant rebels. Larry was a rebel too. But he was *our* rebel."

"So Larry and his Russian case officers could have got up to anything they liked and you wouldn't have been the wiser."

"Not so."

"Why not?"

"We had collateral."

"From?"

"Other live sources. Audio surveillance. The flat of an intermediary. A restaurant we'd bugged. A car we'd nobbled. Whenever we got microphone coverage, it tallied stitch by stitch with Larry's version. We couldn't fault him. All this stuff's on file, you know."

She gave me a flinty smile and resumed her study of her hands. The momentum seemed to have gone out of her. It occurred to me that she was tired and that it was unfair of me to imagine she could read twenty years' worth of files in one weekend of crisis. She took a breath.

"You refer in one of your last reports to Larry's 'remarkable affinity' with Checheyev. Would that include areas you might not know about?"

"If I didn't know about them, how can I answer your question?"

"What did it include?"

"I've told you already. Larry appointed Checheyev his university of the North Caucasus. Larry does that. He eats people whole. When Checheyev arrived here, Larry knew as little about the region as anyone else. He had a decent general knowledge of Russia, but the people of the Caucasus are a subject apart. After a few months, he could hold forth on the Chechen, the Ossetians, the Dagestanis, the Ingush, the Circassians, the Abkhazians, the you-name-them. Checheyev handled him really well. He had an instinct for him. He could crack the whip, and he could charm him out of the trees. He was droll. He had a gallows humour. And he kept Larry's conscience ticking. Larry always had to have a ticking conscience—"

Again she interrupted me. "Are you saying that your own affinity with Larry was *more* remarkable?"

No, Marjorie dear, I am not saying anything of the kind. I'm saying that Larry was a love thief on a seesaw, and as soon as he'd finished enchanting Checheyev he had to race back to me and make it right, because he was not only a spy but a clergyman's son with a diminished sense of responsibility, who needed everybody's absolution for betraying everybody else. I'm saying that for all his breast-beating and moralising and supposed intellectual breadth, he took to spying like an addict. I'm saying that he was also a bastard; that he was sly and vengeful and would steal your woman as soon as look at you; that he was a natural for tradecraft and the black arts and that my sin was to promote the cheat in him above the dreamer, which is why he sometimes hated me a little more than I deserved.

"Larry loves archetypes, Marjorie," I replied, adopting a weary tone. "If they don't exist, he appoints them. He's an action freak, to use the modern parlance. He likes scale. Checheyev delivered it."

"Did you?"

I gave an indulgent laugh. What on earth was she getting at—apart from me? "I was the home side, Marjorie. I was his England, warts and all. Checheyev was exotica. He was a closet Muslim the way Larry is a closet Christian. When Larry was with CC, he was on holiday. When he was with me, he was at school."

"And it lasted," she said. And left me dangling a moment. "Thanks to you." She consulted her hands again. "Long after our other Cold War agents had been laid off, Larry continued to enjoy a full operational life. Checheyev's tour in London was actually extended by Moscow so that he could go on handling Larry. Isn't that rather odd, looking back?"

"Why should it be?"

"With other Cold War agents being run down?"

"Larry's relationship with Moscow was unique. We had every reason to believe it could survive the Communist era. So did his Russian controllers."

"That was certainly the view you encouraged."

"Of course I did!" I had forgotten the force of my convictions in those days. "All right, there was a sea change. There was no Communist experiment left for Larry to admire, but then Larry was never that kind of agent anyway, not in their eyes, not in his. He was a scourge of Western materialism, a champion of Russia good or bad. What powered him—in the fiction and the reality—was his romanticism, his love of the underdog, his gut contempt for the British Establishment and its crawling adherence to America. Larry's hatreds didn't change when Communism collapsed. Neither did his loves. His dreams of a better, fairer world didn't change—his love of the individual over the collective—his love of differentness and eccentricity. Neither did our pigs-in-clover society. After the Cold War it got worse. On both sides of the Atlantic. More corrupt, inward, conformist, intolerant, isolationist, smug. Less equitable. I'm talking Larry talk, Marjorie. I'm talking the renegade humanist who wants to save the world. The Britain that Larry was sabotaging in his imagination all those years is alive and well today. The worst government, the greyest leadership, the saddest, most deceived electorate we've ever had . . . Why *shouldn't* Larry continue to betray us?"

Descending from my soapbox, I was pleased to see her blush. I imagined uncles in the cabinet and blue-rinsed aunts who were the backbone of the Tory right. "Leave Larry out there. That was my argument. Wait and see what the new Russian intelligence service does with him. They're only the same crowd in different hats. They're not going to sit back and let one corrupt superpower run the earth. Wait for the next act, instead of ditching him and then trying to catch up when it's too late, which is what we usually do."

"However, your eloquence failed to carry the day," she pointed out while she thoughtfully fingered her fob-chain.

"Unfortunately, yes. Anyone who had an ounce of history in him should have known it would be business as usual in a year or two. But that didn't include the Top Floor. It wasn't the Russians who dumped Larry. It was us."

Her hands let go the fob-chain, joined, and prayed beneath her chin again. There was premonition in her stillness. On the other side of the room, Barney Waldon gazed into the middle air. Then I realized they had heard something that they were attuned to and I was not—some electronic beep or buzz or tinkle from another room—

and it reminded me of Emma in the orchard, hearing Larry's car before I did, on the day he made his first appearance.

Without explanation, Marjorie Pew got up and stepped as if commanded towards one of the inner doors. Like a ghost she passed through it, leaving it as securely closed as before.

"Barney, what the bloody hell's going on?" I whispered as soon as we were alone. We were both straining our ears, but the acoustics were immaculate, and I for one heard nothing.

"Lot of clever women in the shop these days, Tim," he replied, still listening. I couldn't tell whether this was a boast or a lament. "Suits them, mind, the nit-picking. Right up their alley."

"But what does she *want* from me?" I pressed. "I mean, Christ, Barney, I'm in retirement. I'm a has-been. Why's she giving me the hairy eyeball?"

Marjorie Pew returned, sparing him a reply. Her face was stony and even paler than before. She sat down and put her fingertips together. I saw that they were trembling. You've been getting the slow handclap, I thought. Whoever's listening has told you to get hostile or get out. I felt a quickening of my pulses. I wished I could stand up and walk around. I've been too bloody glib, I thought, and now I'm going to pay for it.

4

"Tim."

"Marjorie."

"Am I right in suggesting that Larry was at odds with us by the time he left?" A harder, clotted voice. A faster glance.

"He was always at odds with us, Marjorie."

"But by the end quite specifically, I gather."

"He thought we weren't worthy of the luck that history had dealt us."

"Luck *how?*"

"As the winners in the Cold War. He regretted the unreality of it all."

"Of *what* all?" Acidly.

"Of the Cold War. Of two discredited ideologies fighting for a peace neither wanted, with weapons that didn't work. That's another Larry quote."

"Did you agree with him?"

"To a point."

"Do you think he felt we owed him something? We the Office. Something he was entitled to help himself to, for example?"

"He wanted his life back. That was rather more than we could do for him."

"Do you think he felt the Russians owed him something?"

"Quite the reverse. He owed them. He does a pretty good line in guilt too."

She gave an impatient toss of her head, as if guilt were not her responsibility. "And you are saying that throughout the last four years of his operational life for us, Larry had no financial dealings with Konstantin Abramovich Checheyev? Or none that you reported?"

"I am saying that if he had them I wasn't aware of them and therefore I didn't report any."

"What about you?"

"I'm sorry?"

"Did *you* have any financial dealings with Checheyev you did not report?"

"No, Marjorie, I have not had any financial dealings with Checheyev or any other member of Russian intelligence past or present."

"Not with Volodya Zorin."

"Not with Zorin."

"And not with Pettifer either."

"Apart from keeping him out of bankruptcy, no."

"But you do have private means, of course."

"I have been fortunate, Marjorie. My parents died when I was young, so I had money instead of love."

"Will you please give me some idea of your personal expenditure over the last twelve months?"

Did I say Merriman had joined us? Perhaps not, for I am not sure at what point he did so, though his entry must have followed quite soon upon Marjorie's return. He was a big man, a floater, very light on his feet, the way large men often are, and I suppose the door he came in by must have been ajar, left that way by Marjorie. Yet it puzzled me that I had not noticed this, for like many people in my trade, I have a thing about unclosed doors. I could only suppose that in the internal mayhem brought on by Marjorie Pew's assault, I had failed to observe the displacement of air and light as Merriman soundlessly lowered his ample rump onto the convenient arm of Barney's sofa. I had turned in indignation to Barney, protesting the enormity of her question. Instead I found myself looking at Merriman. He was wearing a stiff white collar, a silver tie, and a red carnation. Merriman was always dressed for someone's wedding.

"Tim. How nice."

"Hullo, Jake. You're just in time. I'm being asked to say how much money I've spent this year."

"Yes, how much have you? There's the Bechstein for a start. That cost a bomb. Then there's your little pilgrimages to Mr. Appleby's nice jeweller's shop in Wells, never cheap—you've dropped thirty grand *there*—not to mention all the frillies and smart frocks you've bought her. Must be quite a gal. Lucky she disapproves of motorcars, or I can see a Bentley with mink-lined seats. I know you inherited early from your parents, I know your uncle Bob left you *Schloss* and contents, but what about the rest? Or is it all from naughty Aunt Cecily, who died so conveniently in Portugal a few years back? For a fellow who never cared about money, you certainly know how to pick a relative."

"If you don't believe me, check with my solicitors."

"My dear boy, they bear you out entirely. Half a million quids' worth of the best, added to what you've already got, paid in two instalments from a nice Channel Islands trust fund. The solicitors never *met* the aunt, mind. They were instructed by a firm in Lisbon. The firm in Lisbon never met her either. They were instructed by her business manager, a lawyer in Paris. I mean really, Tim, I've seen *money* laundered before, but never *lawyers*." He turned to Marjorie Pew and spoke as if I weren't in the room. "We're still checking, so he needn't think he's in the clear. If Aunt Cecily turns up in a pauper's grave, Cranmer's for the high jump."

"Tim?"

It was Marjorie again. She would like to go back to the logic of my behaviour last night, she said. She wondered whether she might run it by me one more time to make sure she had it straight, Tim.

"Be my guest," I said, using a phrase I had never used in my life.

"Tim, why did you telephone us from your house? You said it was in your mind that the police might have been running illegal taps and that they'd made up the story about Larry's vigilant Scottish landlady as cover. Mightn't they have been tapping your phone too? I'd have thought that with your training and experience, you'd have driven to the village and used the public box."

"I used the established procedure."

"I'm not certain you did. Rule One is to make sure it's safe."

I glanced at Merriman, but he had adopted the posture of a hostile audience, eyeing me as he might a prisoner in the dock.

"The police could have put a tap on the village box as well," I said. "Not that they'd have got much joy of it. It's usually bust."

"I see," she said, implying once again that she didn't.

"It would have looked pretty damned odd, at eleven at night, if I had driven a mile into the village to make a call. Particularly if the police were watching my house."

She looked at the tips of her groomed fingers, then at me again, as she began counting off the points that were troubling her. Merriman had decided he preferred the ceiling. Waldon the floor.

"You cut yourself off from Pettifer. You think his disappearance may be perfectly normal. But it worries you so much you can't wait to tell us about it. You know Checheyev has retired. You know Pettifer has. But you suspect they're up to something, though you don't know what or why. You think the police may be tapping your phone. But you use it to ring us. You spend twenty minutes staring at this building before you pluck up the courage to enter it. One could therefore be forgiven for assuming that ever since the police called on you last night, you have been in a state of stress quite disproportionate to Pettifer's disappearance. One might even suppose that you had something very weighty on your mind. So weighty that even a person as overcontrolled as yourself makes a string of tradecraft errors at odds with his training."

My apprehensions had given way to outright rejoicing. I forgave her everything: her courtroom pomposity, her shrouded savagery, her description of me as overcontrolled. Angel choirs were singing in my ears, and as far as I was concerned, Marjorie Pew as in church was one of the angels. I had told her nothing. Never mind that she couldn't or wouldn't tell me the date of Checheyev's last visit. She had told me something even more important: *They didn't know about Emma and Larry.*

They knew about Emma and me, because under Office rules I had been obliged to tell them. But they hadn't drawn the third line of the triangle. And that, as we used to say, was three-star intelligence: worth the whole journey.

I selected a sentimental, wounded tone. "Larry was more than my *agent*, Marjorie," I said. "He was my friend for quarter of a century.

On top of that, he was the best live source we had. He was one of those joes who make their own luck. In the beginning, the KGB recruited him on spec. He wasn't big enough to be an agent of influence; he didn't have access worth a hoot. They gave him a small salary and let him loose on the international conference circuit, armed with a bunch of briefs written by Moscow Centre, and they hoped that in time he would amount to somebody. He did. He became their man, talent-spotting left-wing students, earmarking tomorrow's friendlies for the Kremlin, and flying kites at world conferences. After a few years, thanks to Larry, this office had put together its own cast of tame Communist agents, some Brit, some foreign, but all wholly owned by this service, who between them fed Moscow some of the most sophisticated disinformation of the Cold War, and the KGB never rumbled it. He attracted subverts like fly-paper. He worked the Third World fence-sitters till he had blisters on his backside. He had a memory that most of us would kill for. He knew every bought MP in Westminster, every suborned British journalist, lobbyist, and agent of influence on Moscow Centre's London payroll. There were people in the KGB and people in the Office who owed him their living and their promotion. I was one of them. So yes, I was concerned. I still am."

IN THE respectful silence that followed this peroration, I realised that I knew what H/IS stood for. If Jake Merriman was Head of Personnel and Barney Waldon was Office liaison at Scotland Yard, Marjorie Pew was that hated jackal of the Service, formerly known to the lower orders as the Polit-Commissar and now dignified by the title Head of Internal Security. Her job involved everything from unemptied wastepaper baskets to thinking dirty about the love lives of past and present employees and reporting her suspicions to Jake Merriman. Why else would Merriman and Waldon defer to her like this? Why else would she now be asking me to describe—*in my own words*, as if I were about to use someone else's—how I had succeeded in acquiring Larry for the Office in the first place? Marjorie Pew wanted to test some cockeyed conspiracy theory that Larry and I had been in cahoots from the beginning; that I had not recruited Larry but Larry had recruited himself; or, better, that Larry and Checheyev between them had recruited me in some crooked and self-serving enterprise.

I trod cautiously all the same. In our trade, theories like hers had wrecked good men's lives on both sides of the Atlantic before being laid sheepishly to rest. I answered her with care and accuracy, even if, to demonstrate my ease of mind, I allowed myself occasional flights of flippancy.

"When I first met him he was a total gypsy," I said.

"That was at Oxford?"

"No, at Winchester. Larry was a new boy the same term I became a prefect. He was an exhibitioner of some sort. The school paid half his fees, the Church of England provided him with a bursary for being impoverished and picked up the rest. The school was still in the dark ages. Fagging, flogging, bullying galore, the whole Arnoldian package. Larry didn't fit, and he didn't want to. He was sloppy and clever, he refused to learn his Notions but couldn't keep his mouth shut, which made him unpopular in some quarters and a bit of a hero in others. He got beaten blue. I tried to protect him."

She smiled tolerantly, acknowledging the homosexual undertone but too shrewd to articulate it. "Protect him *how*, exactly, Tim?"

"Help him curb his tongue. Stop him making himself so damned unpopular. It worked for a few halves, then he got caught smoking, then he got caught drinking. Then he got caught at St. Swithin's girls' school doing the other thing, which excited the envy of less brave souls—"

"Such as yourself?"

"—and cut him off from the homosexual mainstream," I went on, with a nice smile for Merriman. "When flogging didn't have the desired effect, the school expelled him. His father, who was canon of some big cathedral, washed his hands of him; his mother was dead. A distant relative stumped up the money to send him to school in Switzerland, but after one term the Swiss said no thanks and sent him back to England. How he got his scholarship to Oxford is a mystery, but he did, and Oxford duly fell in love with him. He was very good-looking; the girls rolled over for him in droves. He was a beautiful, lawless"—I felt suddenly embarrassed—"extrovert," I said, using a word I thought would please her.

Jake Merriman chimed in. "And he was a Marxist, bless him."

"And a Trotskyist and an atheist and a pacifist and an anarchist and anything else so long as it scared the rich," I retorted. "For a while he favoured a conjunction of Marx and Christ, but it fell apart for him when he decided he couldn't believe in Christ. And he was a voluptuary." I threw this out carelessly and was pleased to observe a tautening of Marjorie Pew's undecorated lips. "By the end of his second year the university had to decide whether to send him down or give him a fellowship to All Souls. They sent him down."

"For what, *precisely?*" Pew said, in an effort to limit my effusion.

"Being too much. Too much drink, too much politics, too little work, too many women. He was too free. He was excessive. He must go. The next time I saw him was in Venice."

"By which time you were married, of course," she said, contriving to insinuate that my marriage was somehow a betrayal of my friendship with Larry. And I saw Merriman's head go back once more and his eyes resume their watch on the ceiling.

"Yes, and in the Office," I agreed. "Diana was in the Office too. We were on our honeymoon. And suddenly there Larry was, in St. Mark's Square, dressed in a Union Jack and holding up his Winchester straw hat on the point of a rolled umbrella." No smiles anywhere, except from me. "He was playing tour guide to a group of American matrons, and as usual every one of them in love with him. And so they should have been. He knew everything there was to know about Venice, he was inexhaustibly enthusiastic, he had good Italian and talked English like a lord, and he couldn't make up his mind whether to convert to Catholicism or light a bomb under the Vatican. I yelled, 'Larry!' He saw me, flung his hat and brolly in the air, and embraced me. Then I introduced him to Diana."

I said this, but my mind was on the subtext: the aching monotony and unhappy lovemaking of our honeymoon, by then in its second week, the sheer relief—to Diana too, as she later told me—of having a third person in our lives, one as wild as Larry into the bargain, even if he made fun of her conventional ways. I saw Larry in his red-white-and-blue T-shirt kneeling dramatically at Diana's feet, one hand clutched to his heart, the other holding out his hat, *the* hat, his Wykehamist strat, the same miraculous survivor that he had worn for our grape harvest at Honeybrook just a year ago. Its lid taped down, varnished, and enamelled, then, as now, its basket life long over. And around its crown, tattered but victorious, our sacred House hatband. I heard his mellow voice with its bogus Italian accent ripping theatrically through the Venice sunlight as he yells his crazy salutation: *It's a-Timbo! The Boy-a Bishop himself! And you're his a-lovely bride-a!*

"We took him to restaurants, visited his awful digs—he was living with a Pomeranian countess, naturally—and one morning I woke up and had this inspiration: He's exactly what we're looking for, the one we've been talking about at the Friday seminars. We'll sign him up and take him all the way through."

"And it didn't bother you that he was your friend?" she suggested.

At the word *friend*, a different pain swept over me. Friend? I never came near him, I thought. Familiar maybe, but friend never. He was the risk I would never take.

"It would have bothered me a lot more if he had been my enemy, Marjorie," I heard myself replying silkily. "We're talking the depths of the Cold War. We were fighting for our survival. We believed in what we were doing." I could not resist the gibe: "I imagine these days that comes a little harder."

And then, in case the New Era had blurred her memory of the old one, I explained what it meant to take someone all the way through: how the agent-running section was constantly under pressure to find a young man—in those days it had to be a man—to trail his coat at the busy-bee Russian recruiters who were working the Oxbridge circuit from the Soviet Embassy in Kensington Palace Gardens. And how Larry fitted in almost every possible way the profile we had drawn of the man we dreamed of finding, or they did—we could even send him back to Oxford to do a third year and sit his Finals.

"Blast the fellow, he landed an outright First against my rather shaky Second," I said with a sporting laugh, which no one shared: not Merriman, who was continuing his examination of the ceiling, or Waldon, who had set his jaw in such a grim lock that you could have wondered whether he would ever speak again.

And how we would give the Russian recruiters precisely what they were looking for and had found for themselves in the past to such effect, I went on: a classy Englishman on the slide, an intellectual explorer, a Golden Boy Going Wrong, a God-seeker sympathetic to the Party but not compromised by formally belonging to it, unanchored, immature, unstable, politically omnivorous, crafty in a vague way, and, when he needed to be, larcenous—

"So you propositioned him," Marjorie Pew interrupted, managing to make it sound as if I had picked Larry up in a public lavatory.

I laughed. My laughter was annoying her, so I was doing quite a lot of it.

"Oh my goodness, not for months, Marjorie. We had to fight it through the system first. A lot of people on the Top Floor said he'd never accept the discipline. His school reports were awful, university reports worse. Everyone said he was brilliant, but for what? Can I make a point here?"

"Please do."

"The recruitment of Larry was a group operation. When he agreed to take the veil, my section head decided I should have the handling of him. But only on the understanding that I report to him before and after every meeting with Larry."

"So *why* did he take the veil, as you call it?" she asked.

Her question filled me with a deep tiredness. If you don't know now, you never will, I wanted to tell her. Because he was footloose. Because he was a soldier. Because God told him to and he didn't believe in God. Because he had a hangover. Or hadn't. Because the dark side of him liked an airing too. Because he was Larry and I was Tim and it was there.

"He relished the challenge of it, I suppose," I said. "To be what you are, but more so. He liked the idea of being a free servant. It answered his sense of duty."

"A *what?*"

"It was a bit of German he had in his head. *Frei sein ist Knecht.* To be free is to be a vassal."

"Is that all?"

"All what?"

"Is that the full range of his motivation or were there more practical considerations?"

"He was lured by the glamour. We told him there wasn't any, but that only whetted his appetite. He saw himself as some sort of heretic Templar knight, paying his tribute to orthodoxy. He liked having two fathers, even if he never said so—the KGB and us. If you asked me to write it all down, you'd have a string of contradictions. That's Larry. That's joes. Motive doesn't exist in the abstract. It's not who people are. It's what they do."

"Thank you."

"Not at all."

"And the money?

"I'm sorry?"

"The money that we paid him. The substantial tax-free income. What part did the money play in his calculations, do you suppose?"

"Oh, for God's sake, Marjorie, nobody worked for money in those days, and Larry never worked for money in his life. I told you. He called his pay Judas money. He's money-illiterate. A financial Neanderthal."

"Nevertheless he got through an awful lot of it."

"He was feckless. Whatever he had he spent. He was a touch for everyone with a sob story. He had one or two expensive upper-class habits, which we encouraged because Russians are snobs, but in most ways he was totally unmaterialistic."

"Like what?"

"Like buying his wine from Berry's. Like having his shoes made."

"I don't call that unmaterialistic. I call it extravagant."

"That's just words," I flung back.

For a while no one spoke, which I took as a good omen. Marjorie was making yet another tour of her unvarnished fingernails. Barney was looking as if he would prefer to be safely back among his policemen. Finally Jake Merriman, emerging from his unnatural trance, straightened himself, smoothed his hands over his waistcoat, then ran a finger round the inside of his stiff white collar to free it from the folds of flesh that threatened to engulf it.

"Your Konstantin Abramovich Checheyev has milked the Russian government of thirty-seven million quid and rising," he said. "They're still counting. Friday last, the Russian ambassador here sought parley with the foreign secretary and presented him with a file of evidence. Why he chose a Friday, when the secretary was just leaving for his dacha, God alone knows. But he did, and Larry's hoofprints are all over the file. Daylight, premeditated banditry, Tim Cranmer, by your ex-agent and his former KGB controller. Odds are, Checheyev got word that the balloon was about to go up and hightailed it to Bath to advise Larry to do a runner before the ambassador made his démarche. Are you trying to say something? Don't."

I had shown no sign of this that I knew of, so shook my head, but he was already talking again.

"It's a simple enough racket they were working, but don't let's knock it for that. Very few Russian banks are empowered to transfer money abroad. Those that are tend to have close links with the former KGB. A U.K.-based accomplice sets up a bogus U.K. company—import, export, you name it—and bangs in bogus bills to his mates in Moscow. The bills are authenticated by crooked officials, mafia linked. Then they're paid. There's a gloss I like particularly. It seems the Russian legal code hasn't yet got round to addressing such modern eccentricities as bank fraud, so nobody gets hammered and everyone who might make a stink gets a cut instead. Russian banks are still in the ice age, profits are an abstraction nobody takes seriously, so in the immortal words of Noel Coward, whistle up the caviar and say, 'Thank God.' "

Another hiatus while Merriman raised his eyebrows at me in invitation, but I remained silent.

"Having landed the cash, Checheyev did what we'd all do. He buried it in a string of no-see-um accounts in Britain and abroad. In most of these enterprises your old friend Larry functioned as his intermediary, bagman, and red-toothed accomplice: registering the companies, opening the accounts, presenting the bills, stashing the loot. In a minute you're going to tell me it's all in Checheyev's weaselly imagination; he forged Larry's signature. You'll be wrong. Larry's in it up to his nasty neck, and for all we know, so are you. Are you?"

"No."

He turned to Barney. "How far down the line are the rozzers?"

"Commander, Special Branch, is reporting to the cabinet secretary at five this evening," Barney said, having first cleared his throat.

"Is that where Bryant and Luck come from?" I asked.

Barney Waldon was about to confirm this when Merriman cut rudely in: "That's for us to know and him to guess, Barney."

But I had my answer: yes.

"Rumour has it that their investigations are getting nowhere fast, but that may be bluff," Barney went on. "The last thing I can do is show undue interest. I've told Special Branch it's not our problem; I've put my hand on my heart to say it's not. I've told the Met, I've told the Somerset Constabulary. I've sold them the Lie Direct." It seemed to bother him.

Merriman again: "So don't you go spoiling our game, Tim Cranmer, do you hear? If they catch Larry and he claims he worked for us, we'll deny it and go on denying it right up to the trial and out the other end. If he says he worked for you, then Mr. Timothy Cranmer, ex-Treasury, gets dropped down a very deep hole. And in the new spirit of openness, dear boy: If you so much as open your mouth, God help you."

"Is their ambassador presenting Checheyev as a bona fide diplomat?"

"Ex-diplomat. Yes, he is. And since we never raised a finger of complaint against Checheyev in the four years he was in London, for the obvious reason that we wanted to keep the intelligence flowing, we're taking the same position. If anyone breathes the word *spook*, the Foreign Office will have the vapours."

"What about Checheyev's relationship with Larry?"

"What about it? It was legit. Checheyev was a cultural attaché, active, popular, and effective. Larry was a pinko intellectual has-been who accepted regular freebies to Mother Russia, Cuba, and other unsavoury corners of the globe. Now he's a quietly flowing don in Bath. Their relationship was natural and proper, and if it wasn't, no one's saying so." Merriman had not taken his eyes off me. "If the Russians ever get the idea that Larry Pettifer worked for this service—had been, for the last twenty and more years, as you have repeatedly reminded us, our most obedient servant—there will be an earthquake, do you follow me? They've already given your nice friend Zorin the summary heave-ho—alcoholism, passive conspiracy, having his head up his arse—he's under house arrest and by all accounts stands a good chance of being shot at dawn. It's extremely nice of us not to have done the same to you. If they ever take it into their tiny minds—the police, the Russians, either or both: it's the same thing in this situation, since the police are flying blind and we propose to keep them that way—that this service, in cahoots with one or other of the Russian mafias, elected at a time when the Russian economy is dying of the common cold to con it out of thirty-seven million quids' worth of the best . . ." He gave up. "You can finish the sentence for yourself. Yes, what is it?"

It was the eternal refrain in me. Even in my turmoil, I could not hold it back: "When was Larry last seen?" I said.

"Ask the police, except don't."

"When did Checheyev last visit Britain?"

"No Checheyev entered Britain in the last six months. But since it was received wisdom that Checheyev was never his name in the first place, it would be fairly surprising if he came back as somebody he'd never been."

"Have you tried his aliases?"

"May I remind you that you're retired?" He had had enough of small talk. "You're to do nothing, young Tim Cranmer, d'you hear? You're to sit in your castle, perform your good works, churn out your vintage pipi, act natural, and look innocent. You're not to leave the country without Mummy's permission, and we've got your passport, though these days that's not the guarantee it used to be, alas. You're not to make the smallest move towards Larry by word, deed, gesture, or telephone. Not you, not your agents or instruments, not your delicious Emma. You're not to discuss Larry or his disappearance or any part of this conversation with anyone at all, and that includes colleagues and connections. Does Larry still flirt with Diana?"

"He never did. He just kept up with her to annoy me. And because they decided they hated the Office."

"Absolutely nothing has happened. Nobody is missing. You're an ex–Treasury boffin who lives with a neurotic child composer, or whatever she is, and grows bloody awful wine. Over and out. If you call us, make it a full-blown clandestine call from a safe phone. The number we're giving you has a rotating final digit for each day. Sunday's one, Monday's two. Do you think you can handle that?"

"Seeing that I invented the system, yes."

Marjorie Pew handed me a slip of paper with an 071 number typed on it. Merriman kept talking.

"If the rozzers want to talk to you again, you're to continue lying in your teeth. They're trying to find out what research you were doing at the Treasury, but Treasury is being as anally retentive as Treasury usually is, and the rozzers will get nowhere. As far as we're concerned, you don't exist. You were never here. Cranmer? Cranmer? Never heard of him."

WE WERE alone, Merriman and Cranmer, blood brothers as always. Merriman had taken my arm. He always took your arm to say goodbye.

"After all we've done for him," he said. "A pension, a fresh start, a good job after practically every university in England had turned him down, status. Now this."

"It's too bad," I agreed. There seemed nothing else worth saying.

Merriman smiled roguishly. "You haven't executive-actioned him, have you, Tim?"

"Why should I have done?"

For the first time that day, I came within an ace of losing the last of what Marjorie Pew had called my overcontrol.

"But why *shouldn't* you have done?" Merriman countered archly. "Isn't that rather what crooks do to each other, in preference to dividing up the loot?" A mirthless giggle. "And is it simply *marvellous* with Emma? Are you *deliriously* in love?"

"Yes, but she's away at the moment."

"I can't bear it. Where?"

"Attending a couple of performances of her stuff in the Midlands."

"Shouldn't you be there to chaperone her?"

"She prefers to do those things alone."

"Of course. Her independent streak. And she's not too young for you?"

"When she is, I've no doubt she'll tell me."

"Bully for you, Tim. Stout boy. Never withdraw your cavalry from the battle, I always say. The Emmas of this world require our constant attention. Look at her record."

"No, thank you."

But with Merriman you never score. "No, thank you? You haven't peeked?"

"No, and I don't intend to."

"But, my dear boy, you must! So full, so varied, *quel courage!* Change the names, you could write a blockbuster in your old age. Far more lucrative than Uncle Bobby's weasel's piss. Tim?"

"What is it?"

His fingers tightened round my biceps. "This long, long connection you had with dear Larry. Winchester, Oxford, the Office . . . So fruitful at the time. So appropriate. But today, dear boy, a no-no."

"What on earth are you talking about?"

"The image, dearie. The noble past, the old era. In the hands of Grub Street, dynamite. They'll be crying university spy rings and the love that dare not speak its name before you can say Kim Philby. And you weren't, were you?"

"Weren't what?" I replied, fighting off the memory of Emma standing naked at my bedroom window, asking me the same question.

"Well, you know. You and Larry. Any of that. Were you?"

"If you're enquiring whether we were homosexuals and traitors, we were neither. Larry was that public school rarity the Compleat Heterosexual."

He gave my arm another lingering squeeze. "Poor you. What a disappointment for a healthy lad. Ah well, that's the way of it, isn't it? Punished for the crimes we never committed, while we get away with grand larceny somewhere else. So important that we're all terribly, terribly careful. The worst is scandal. Lie as much as you like, but spare me scandal. Very hard for the Office to find its niche these days. Lot of flies round the honey pot. Always here, dear boy. Anytime."

Munslow was hovering in the anteroom. Seeing me emerge, he fell in beside me. His hands dangled uncomfortably at his sides. Neither of them carried my passport.

5

I HAD two hours to kill before the last train left for Castle Cary, and probably I walked. Somewhere I must have bought an evening newspaper, though I loathe them. It was in my raincoat pocket the next morning, folded into a grimy wad of illiterate newsprint, with the crossword completed in spiky capitals quite unlike my own. And I must have had a couple of Scotches along the way, for I remember little of the journey beyond the reflection riding along beside me in the black window, and sometimes the face was Larry's, sometimes mine, and sometimes Emma's with her hair up, wearing the eighteenth-century pearl collar I had given her the day she brought her piano stool to Honeybrook. So much was in my head that nothing was. Larry has stolen thirty-seven million; Checheyev is his accomplice; I am supposed to be another. He has fled with the loot; Emma has gone after him. Larry, whom I taught to steal, rifle desks, pick locks, photograph papers, memorise, bide his time, and, if he ever had to, run and hide. Colonel Volodya Zorin, once the pride of Moscow's England section, is under house arrest. Crossing the footbridge at Castle Cary station, I was confused by the clatter of young shoes in the Victorian ironwork and fancied I smelled steam and burning coals. I was a boy again, lugging my school suitcase down the stone steps for another solitary holiday with Uncle Bob.

My splendid old Sunbeam stood in the station car park, where I had left it. Had they tampered with it, fitted it with bugs and tracking devices, sprayed it with the latest magic paint? The modern technology was beyond me. It always had been. Driving, I was irritated by a pair of car lights close on my tail, but on that winding lane only fools and drunks attempt to overtake. I cleared the ridge and passed through the village. On some nights the church was floodlit. Not tonight. In cottage windows the last television screens flickered like dying embers. The headlights came racing up behind me, flashing from dip to full beam and back again. I heard the honking of a horn. Pulling over to let whoever it was pass, I saw Celia Hodgson waving hilariously at me from her Land-Rover. I waved hilariously back. Celia was one of my local conquests from the days before Emma, when I was the absentee landlord of Honeybrook and the most eligible weekend divorcé in the parish. She lived in penury on a large estate near Sparkford, rode to hounds, and masterminded our country holiday scheme for urban children. Inviting her to lunch with me one Sunday, I was surprised to find myself in bed with her before the avocado. I still chaired her committee, we still chatted in the grocer's shop. I never slept with her again, and she didn't seem to grudge me Emma. Sometimes I wondered whether she remembered the episode at all.

The stone gateposts of Honeybrook rose before me. Slowing to a crawl, I switched on my brass foglight and willed myself to study the tyre marks in the drive. First John Guppy's postal van. Any other driver swings left when he wants to avoid the three big potholes in the dip, but John, despite my best entreaties, prefers to swing right because that's what he's been doing these forty years, churning the grass verge and trampling the daffodil bulbs.

Beside John Guppy ran the brave thin line of Ted Lanxon's bicycle tyres. Ted was my grower, bequeathed to me by Uncle Bob with orders to keep him till he dropped, which he resolutely refused to do, preferring to perpetuate my uncle's many errors. And bouncing through the middle of everything came the Toller sisters in their jungle-painted Subaru, as much off the ground as on it. The Tollers were our part-time helpers and Ted's bane, but also his delight. And straddling the Tollers ran the alien imprint of a heavy lorry. Something must have been delivered. But what? The fertiliser we ordered? Came on Friday. The new bottles? Came last month.

In the gravel sweep before the house I saw nothing untoward, until the nothing began to bother me. Why were there no tyre tracks in the gravel? Had the Toller girls not roared through here on their way to the walled garden? Had not John Guppy parked here when he delivered my mail? And what about my mystery lorry, which had come all this way only to make a vertical takeoff?

Leaving my lights burning, I got out of the car and patrolled the sweep, scouring it for the marks of feet or car tyres. Somebody had raked the gravel. I switched off the lights and mounted the steps to the house. On the train journey, my back had acted up. But as I let myself into the porch, the pain left me. A dozen envelopes lay on the doormat, most of them brown. Nothing from Emma, nothing from Larry. I studied the postmarks. They were all a day late. I studied the gummed joins. They were too well sealed. When would the Office ever learn? Setting the envelopes on the marble-topped side table, I climbed the six steps to the Great Hall without putting on the light and stood still.

And listened. And sniffed. And caught a waft of warm body on the still air. Sweat? Deodorant? Men's hair oil? If I couldn't define it, I could recognise it. I eased my way down the passage towards my study. Halfway along, I caught it again: the same deodorant, the faintest whiff of stale cigarette smoke. Not smoked on the premises—that would be insanity. Smoked in a pub or car perhaps—not necessarily by the person whose clothes had borne the stale fumes—but alien cigarette smoke all the same.

I had laid no clever traps before I set out for London this morning, no hairs in locks, no bits of cotton thread stretched across the hinges, had taken no Polaroid pictures. I hadn't needed to. I had my dust. Monday is Mrs. Benbow's day off. Her friend Mrs. Cooke will come only when Mrs. Benbow comes, which is her way of disapproving of Emma. Between Friday night and Tuesday morning, therefore, nobody dusts the house unless I do. And usually I do. I enjoy a little housework, and on Mondays I like to polish my collection of eighteenth-century barometers and one or two oddments that receive less than their fair share of Mrs. Benbow's rather strict ministrations: my Chinese Chippendale footstools and the campaign table in my dressing room.

This morning, though, I had risen early, and with the tradecraft that seemed to have been laid on me since childhood, I had let the dust lie where it was. With a log fire in the Great Hall and another in the drawing room, I get a fine crop by Monday morning but an even better one by Monday night. And I saw as soon as I entered my study that there was no dust on my walnut desk. On its entire surface not one speck of honest dust. The brass handles pristine. I could smell the polish.

So they came, I thought without emotion. It's a given: they came. Merriman summons me to London, and while I am safely under his eye he sends his ferrets in a furniture van, or an electricity van, or whatever vans they use these days, to break into my house and search it, knowing that Monday is a good day. Knowing that Lanxon and the Toller girls work five hundred yards away from the main house, inside a brick-walled garden cut off from everything except the sky. And while he is about it, Merriman slaps a mail check on me for good measure and by now, no doubt, a telephone check as well.

I went upstairs. Smoke again. Mrs. Benbow does not smoke. Her husband doesn't. I don't, and I detest the habit and the smell. If I have returned from somewhere and have smoke in my clothing, I require a complete change, a bath, and a hairwash. When Larry has been visiting, I have to fling open all the doors and windows that the weather permits. But on the landing I again smelled stale cigarette smoke. In my dressing room and bedroom, more stale smoke. I crossed the gallery to Emma's side of the house: her side, my side, and the gallery a sword between us. Larry's sword.

Key in hand, I stood before her door, as I had done last night, again uncertain whether I should enter. It was oak and studded, a front door that had somehow made it up the stairs. I turned the key and stepped inside. Then quickly closed and locked the door behind me, against whom I didn't know. I hadn't trespassed here since the day I tidied up after her departure. I breathed in slowly, mouth and nose together. A whiff of scented talc mingled with the musk of disuse. So they sent in a woman, I thought. A powdered woman. Or two. Or six. But women certainly: some asinine piece of Office decorum insists on it. Married men cannot be allowed to rootle among young women's clothing. I stood in her bedroom. To my left, the bathroom. Ahead, her studio. On her bedside table, no dust. I lifted her pillow. Beneath it lay the exquisite silk nightdress from the White House in Bond Street that I had put into her Christmas stocking but never seen her wear. On the day she left me, I had found it still wrapped in its tissue paper, pushed to the back of a drawer. In my role of Operational Man I had unfolded it, shaken it out, and placed it under her pillow for cover. *Miss Emma has gone up north to listen to her music being played, Mrs. Benbow. . . . Miss Emma will be back in a few*

days, Mrs. Benbow. . . . Miss Emma's mother is desperately ill, Mrs. Ben-
bow. . . . Miss Emma is still in bloody limbo, Mrs. Benbow. . . .

I pulled open her wardrobe. All the clothes I had ever bought for
her hung neatly from their gibbets, exactly as I had found them on
the day of her disappearance: long silk jersey dresses, tailored suits, a
sable cape she resolutely refused even to try on, shoes by someone
grand, belts and handbags by someone grander. Staring at them, I
wondered who I had been when I bought them, and what woman I
had thought I was dressing.

It was a dream, I thought. Yet why should any man need to dream
who has Emma for his reality? I heard her voice in the darkness: *I'm
not* bad, *Tim. I don't need changing and disguising all the time. I'm fine as
I am. Honest.* I heard Larry's voice jeering at me from the darkness of
the Mendip night. *You don't love people, Timbo. You invent them. That's
God's job, not yours.* I heard Emma again: *It's not me who needs to change,
Tim, it's you. Ever since Larry walked into our walled garden, you've been
behaving like someone on the run.* I heard Larry again: *You stole my life.
I stole your woman.*

I closed the cupboard, stepped into her studio, switched on the
lights, and managed a skimming glance of the kind that is ready to
take evasive action the moment something unseeable presents itself.
But my eyes detected nothing they needed to avoid. Everything was
as I had left it when I had re-created the seeming after her departure.
The Queen Anne kneehole desk I had given her for her birthday was,
thanks to my labours, a model of organisation. Its drawers, all tidied,
were stocked with fresh stationery. The grate, now sparkling bright,
was laid with newspaper and kindling. Emma loved a fire. Like a cat,
she would stretch herself before it, one hip raised, one crooked arm
cradling her head.

My investigations allowed me a momentary easing of my burden.
If the entire break-in team had crowded in here with cameras, rubber
gloves, and headsets, what would they have seen apart from what
they were supposed to see? *Cranmer's woman is of no operational significance. She plays the piano, wears long silk dresses, and writes of country
matters at a lady's kneehole desk.*

Of her files of correspondence, of her rekindled determination to
cure the entire world of its maladies, of the tap-tapping and wheez-
ing of her electric typewriter at all hours of the day and night, they
knew nothing.

. . .

I was suddenly ravenous. Raiding the fridge, Larry style, I polished off the rest of a pheasant left over from an excruciating dinner party I had given for a bunch of village worthies. There was half a bottle of Pauillac waiting to be finished too, but I had work to do. I forced myself to switch on the television news, but of missing professors and female composers on the run not one dangling participle or split infinitive. At midnight I went back upstairs, turned on the light in my dressing room, and, behind drawn curtains, slipped on a dark zip-up pullover, grey flannels, and black plimsolls. I switched on the bathroom light so that it would be visible from outside and after ten minutes turned it off again. I did the same in my bedroom, then stole downstairs and, still in darkness, put on a country cap and wound a black scarf round my face before tiptoeing down the servants' staircase to the kitchens, where by the glow of the pilot light from the gas burner I removed an ancient ten-inch key from its hook in the butler's pantry and dropped it into my trousers pocket.

I opened the back door, closed it behind me, and stood motionless in the freezing night, waiting for my eyes to grow accustomed to the dark. At first it seemed they never would, for the night was pitch black, without a star. The cold hung like a cloak of ice around my shivering body. I heard bird cries and the whimpering of a small animal.

Gradually I made out the stone path. It went by way of four flights of sandstone steps down the terraces to the brook that gives the house its name. Across the brook ran a footbridge, and beyond it stood a wicket gate leading to a treeless hillock on which by degrees I discerned the familiar silhouette of a small and sturdy church, so solid against the sky that it was like an imprint embossed on the darkness.

I crept forward. I was going to church. But not to pray.

I am not a God man, though I believe society is the better for Him than without Him. I do not reject Him, as Larry does, and then go scurrying after Him to apologise. But I do not accept Him either.

If deep down I believe in some central meaning, some *Urgeist*, as Larry would call it, my route to it is more likely to be the aesthetic one—the autumnal beauty of the Mendips, say, or Emma playing Liszt for me—than the path of prayer.

Yet destiny had decreed that I become a keeper of the faith, for when I inherited Honeybrook from blessed Uncle Bob and decided to appoint it my Cold Warrior's rest, I acquired also the title of squire, and with it the advowson to the benefice of the Church of St. James the Less, an early-Gothic cathedral in miniature, perched at the eastern boundary of my land, complete with antechapel, wagon roof, miniature hexagonal bell tower, and a superb pair of giant ravens—but because of its remoteness and the decline in religious interest, fallen into disuse.

Fresh from London, and flushed with dutiful enthusiasm for my new bucolic life, I had determined, with the full consent of the diocesan authority, to revive my church as a working place of worship, not realising, any more than did the bishop, that by doing this I would be imperilling the already diminished congregation of the parish church a mile away. At my own expense I repaired the roof and saved the timbers in the splendid little porch. With the personal encouragement of the bishop's wife, I had the altar cloth repaired, organised a cleaning rota of willing spirits and, when all was ready, obtained the services of a pallid curate from Wells, who, for informal reward, gave bread and wine to a mixed bag of farmers, weekenders, and us retired types, all doing our best to look pious for him.

But after a month of this, both the diocese and I were forced to recognise that my efforts were misplaced. First, my willing spirits ceased to be so willing, ostensibly on account of Emma. They did not take kindly, they said, to arriving in their Land-Rovers with their mops and pails, only to find her perched in the organ loft, playing Peter Maxwell-Davies to a congregation of one. They implied ungraciously that if the cradle-snatching Londoner and his fancy girl wanted to use the church as their private concert hall, they could do their cleaning for themselves. Next, an unprepossessing man in a blazer and a pair of Larry's buckskin boots presented himself, claiming to speak for some unheard-of ecclesiastical body and requiring information of me: the numbers of our congregation, for instance, the sums and destination of our offertories, and the names of our visiting preachers. In another life I would have suspected his credentials, for he also asked me whether I was a Freemason, but by the time he left I had decided that my days as the saviour of St. James the Less were over. The bishop gladly agreed.

But I did not desert my charge. There is a natural butler in me somewhere, and in no time I discovered the soothing satisfactions of mopping down flagstones, dusting pews, and buffing brass candlesticks in the stillness of my seven-hundred-year-old private church. But by then I had other reasons to persist: in addition to spiritual solace, St. James was providing me with the best safe house I could ever hope to find.

I am not speaking of the lady chapel, with its worm-eaten panelling so adrift you could stuff a complete archive behind it and it wouldn't show; or of the capacious vaults where the crumbling tombstones of the abbot-farmers offer any number of natural dead-letter boxes. I am speaking of the tower itself: of a secret, windowless hexagonal priesthole reached by way of a cope cupboard in the vestry, and thence by a tiny curling staircase to a second door, and, as I truly believe, not entered for centuries by a living soul until I happened on it by accident after puzzling over the discrepancy between the tower's external and internal measurements.

I say windowless, but whatever genius designed my secret chamber—whether for refuge or for venery—had had the further ingenuity to provide one slender horizontal arrow slit high in the wall at each point where the main joists support the wooden canopy that skirts the outside of the tower. So that by standing my full height and moving from one arrow slit to another, I commanded a perfect all-round view of the enemy's approach.

As to light, I had made the test a dozen times. Having rigged up a crude electric lighting system, I had undertaken elaborate tours of the church, now at a distance, now close to. It was only when I pressed myself against the wall of the tower and craned my head upward that I detected the palest glow, reflected on the inside of the wood canopy.

I have described my priesthole in detail because of its importance to my inner life. Nobody who has not lived in secrecy can appreciate its addictive powers. Nobody who has renounced the secret world, or been renounced by it, recovers from his deprivation. His longing for the inner life is at times unendurable, whether of the religious or clandestine kind. At any hour he will dream of the secret hush reclaiming him in its embrace.

And so it was for me each time I entered the priesthole and revisited my little treasure hoard of keepsakes: the diaries I should not have kept but, having done so, kept still; old encounter sheets, unsanitised operational logs, jottings dashed off in the cool of conspiracy, uncensored debriefing tapes, and here and there whole files ordered for destruction by the Top Floor and so certified—only to be spirited into my private archive, partly for the enlightenment of posterity, but partly as a piece of personal insurance against the rainy day I had always feared might come and now had: when some misperception on the part of my employers, or some foolish act of my own, would cast a crooked backward light on things that I had said and done in honour.

And finally, as well as my papers, I had my personal escape kit for the event that nothing, not even the record, could protect me: my reserve identity in the name of Bairstow, comprising passport, credit card, and driving licence, all legitimately acquired for some aborted operation, then kept back and artificially extended by myself, to be tested and retested until I was confident that the Office quartermaster had ceased to be aware they still existed. And serviceable, you understand. We are talking of the Office functioning on home soil, not some cheapjack forger taking a one-time risk. Each of them fed into the right computers, credit rated and proofed against outside enquiry, so that, provided a man had his tradecraft about him, and I had—and his money, and I had that too—he could live a whole other life more safely than he could live his own.

A SINUOUS cloud of freezing mist curled at me out of the brook as I crossed the footbridge. Reaching the wicket gate, I disengaged the latch and lowered it to its housing. Then I rammed the gate back as fast as I could, causing an indignant shriek to add itself briefly to the night sounds. I stole up the path and through the old cemetery that was Uncle Bob's last resting place, to the porch, where I groped for the keyhole. In total blackness I guided the key into the lock, gave it a sharp twist, shoved the door, and stepped inside.

Church air is like no other. It is the air the dead breathe, humid, old, and frightening. It echoes even when there is no sound. Feeling my way to the vestry as quickly as I dared, I located the cope cupboard, opened it, and, with my palms flat on the ancient stones, wriggled up the spiral staircase to my sanctuary and put on the light.

I was safe. I could think the unthinkable at last. A whole internal life that I dared not acknowledge, let alone explore, until I was secure inside the confines of my priesthole, was once more open to my scrutiny.

Mr. Timothy D'Abell Cranmer. How do you say? Did you or did you not, on or about the night of September 18, at Priddy Pool in the County of Somerset, murder by battery and drowning one Lawrence Pettifer, formerly your friend and secret agent?

WE ARE fighting, as only brothers can. All my gentling and cosseting of him, all the careless insults I have swallowed whole—beginning with his sneering asides about Diana, my first wife; continuing for twenty more years with gibes about my emotional inadequacy, about what he calls my rent-a-drool smile, and my good manners that do duty for a heart; and culminating in his wanton theft of Emma—all my cancer-giving forbearance, has turned outward in a pent-up, furious revolt.

I am showering blows on him and probably he is hitting me back, but I feel nothing. Whatever is hitting me is merely an obstruction on the path to him, because I am going to kill him. The intention I have come with is about to be fulfilled. I am hitting him as we hit when we are boys, wild, heaving, artless blows, everything we are taught not to do at combat camp. I would tear him apart with my teeth if my fingers weren't strong enough for the job. *All right!* I am shouting. *You* called *me an espiopath, now you've got a bloody espiopath!* And between whiles, without the least hope of getting an answer, I am shouting the questions at him that have been burning my soul ever since Emma left me: *What have you done with her? What lies have you told her about us?* I meant what truths. *What have you promised her that she can't get from me?*

A full moon is shining. The long sour grass beneath our feet has grown into great tufts under the lashing Mendip winds. Advancing on him, swinging blows at him, I feel the mounds thumping at my knees. I must be falling, because the moon swings away from me and then comes back, and I see a vertical skyline with the jagged rims made by the opencast mining. But I am still hitting him with my gloved hands, still shouting questions like the worst interrogator in the world. His face is wet and hot, and I think he must be bleeding all over it, but in the shadowy light of the moon nothing is to be trusted: a film of sweat and mud can look like an obliterated face. So I trust nothing and keep hitting him and screaming at him: *Where is she? Give her back to me! Leave her alone!* His taunting has given way to self-pitying sobs as I strike home. I have defeated him at last, Larry, the true version of me, as he calls himself, the Timbo Unbound whose life I never dared to lead until I led it vicariously through him. *Then die*, I yell at him as I hit him—with my elbow now; I am tired and am remembering a few tricks. In a minute I'll be giving him a chop to the windpipe, or thrusting his lusting eyes back into their sockets with the leading fingers of my gloved hand. *Die, and then there'll be only one of us to live my life. Because two of us living it, Larry, old boy, is actually a crowd.*

It has been a long conversation, you understand, all this talk of breaking *omertà* and whose life is whose, whose girl is whose, where she is hiding and why. It has reached into our far, dark past. All the same, talk is only talk, and I have come to kill him. I have the .38 in my waistband, and in the fullness of time I intend to shoot him with it. It's an unattributable gun, unnumbered, unsourced. Neither the British police nor the Office has ever heard of it. I have arrived here in a car that is nothing to do with me, wearing clothes I shall never wear again. It is clear to me by now that I have been planning Larry's murder for years without being aware that I was doing so, perhaps from the day we embraced each other in St. Mark's Square. Perhaps already at Oxford, where he took such pleasure in publicly humiliating me: *Timbo, who can't wait to be middle-aged; Timbo, our college virgin, our bourgeois striver, our boy bishop.* Perhaps even at Winchester, where for all the caring I invested in him, he was never sufficiently in awe of my exalted status.

I have been crafty too. Everything covert, like the old days. This is no Sunday lunch cooked by Timbo, dialogue courtesy of Larry, and a romantic stroll with Emma thrown in afterwards. I have invited him for a clandestine meeting up here on the Mendip Hills, on this moonscape plateau nearer to the sky than to the earth, where the trees throw dead men's shadows on the whited lane and no cars pass. I have suggested an urgent but unspecified operational context to allay his suspicions. And Larry has presented himself early, because for all his bohemian posturing, after twenty years of my patient manipulation he is Operational Man to his fingertips.

And I? Do I shout? No, no, I don't think so. "It's actually about Emma, Larry," I explain by way of introduction as we face each other under the moon. I probably give him my rent-a-drool smile. Timbo Unbound is still waiting to spring free. "About our relationship."

Our relationship? *Whose* relationship? Emma's and mine? Larry's and mine? *Theirs* and mine? *You pushed me at him,* Emma is saying through her tears. *You set me up for him without even knowing it.*

But he sees my face—distorted, I am sure, by the moonlight and already wild enough to raise a warning in him. And instead of taking fright he produces a reply so insolent, so perfectly in keeping with all I have learned to hate about him over thirty years, that unknowingly he signs his death warrant. It is a reply that has rung in my head ever since. It hovers before me in the dark like a lamp I must track down and put out. Even in broad daylight it echoes brazenly in my ear.

"*Hell's your problem, actually, Timbo? You stole my life. I stole your woman. Simple as that.*"

I realise he has been drinking. I smell Scotch as well as autumn on the Mendip wind. I hear that arrogant extra note that gets into him when he's about to deliver one of his word-perfect monologues, complete with subordinate and relative clauses and, practically, the semicolons. The notion that he is not clear-minded fills me with indignation. I want him sober and accountable.

"She's a fully paid-up woman, you idiot!" he chokes at me. "Not some late developer's bed toy!"

Maddened, I draw the .38—across the body, from the waistband, the way both of us were taught—and I point it, from about a foot away, at the bridge of his nose.

"Ever seen one of these, Larry?" I ask him.

But pointing it at him only seems to make him stupid. He squints at it, then raises his eyebrows at me in an admiring smile.

"Well, you *have* got a big one," he says.

At this I lose my temper and, using both hands, smash the butt into the side of his face.

Or I think I do.

And perhaps that was when I killed him.

Or perhaps I am remembering the seeming, not the being.

Perhaps the rest of my blows, if I ever struck them at all, were wasted on a dead or dying body. Neither in my dreams nor waking did I any longer know. The days and nights between have brought me no enlightenment, only terrible variations of the same scene. I drag him to the Pool, I bump and roll him into it, he scarcely makes a splash, just a kind of sucking noise, as if he has been drawn right down. I can't tell whether it is panic or remorse that has the upper hand as I perform this final act. Perhaps self-preservation has it, for even as I cart him feet first over the tufts of grass, as I watch his nodding, moon-white head grin up at me and then go under—I seriously debate whether to put a bullet through him or drive him at breakneck speed to Bristol Infirmary.

But I don't do either of these things. Not in the seeming and not in the being. He slides into the water headfirst, and his best friend drives home alone, stopping only to change cars and clothes along the way. Am I exhilarated? Am I in despair? I am both, one minute lighter of heart than I have been for years, the next in murderer's remorse.

But have I murdered him?

I have fired no bullet. None is missing from the revolver.

There is no blood on the butt of my revolver.

He was breathing. I saw bubbles. And dead men, unless they are Larry and drunk, don't breathe even if they grin.

So perhaps I only killed myself.

Larry is my shadow, I think in some far outstation of my mind, as I drive in dream-like detachment between the sandstone gateposts of Honeybrook. The only way to catch him is to fall on him. Then I remember something he once said to me, a quotation from one of his literary icons: "To kill without being killed is an illusion."

Safely back in my study, hands shaking at last, I pour myself a huge whisky and gulp it down; then another and another and another. I have not drunk like this since one Guy Fawkes night at Oxford, when Larry and I poisoned each other nearly to death by drinking glass for glass in competition. It's the black light, I am thinking as I shove aside the empty bottle and, stubbornly sober, embark upon a second: the black light that the boxer sees as he goes down for the count; the black light that lures decent folk across the moor with revolvers in their belts to murder their best friends; the black light that will shine from this night on, inside my head, over everything that did or didn't happen at Priddy Pool.

.   .   .

I woke myself. I was sitting head in hands at the trestle table in my priesthole, my files and keepsakes heaped around me.

But Larry a *thief* as well as my dead nemesis? I asked myself. An embezzler, a conspirator, a lover of secret wealth as well as women?

Everything I knew about myself and Larry revolted against the idea. *He had no use for money:* How many times did I have to scream this at the empty air before someone believed me? *Greed makes you stupid.*

Never once, on all the occasions we had prodded him towards this or that step in his agent's career, had he asked me: How much will you pay me?

Never once had he demanded an increase in his Judas money, complained about our niggardly approach to his expenses, threatened to fling down his cloak and dagger unless he was promised more.

Never once, when he received from his Soviet case officer the monthly briefcase stuffed with cash to pay the salaries of his notional subagents—we are talking here of tens of thousands of pounds—had he raised any objection when Office rules obliged him to hand the whole lot over to me.

And now a thief, suddenly? Checheyev's bagman and accomplice? Thirty-seven million pounds and rising, squirrelled away in foreign bank accounts, by *Larry?* And *Checheyev?* With the connivance of *Zorin?* All three common swindlers together?

"Hey, Timbo!"

It is evening in Twickenham, where neither of us lives, which is why we have come here. We are sitting in the saloon bar of a pub called The Cabbage Patch, or perhaps it is The Moon Under Water. Larry selects his pubs solely for their names.

"Hey, Timbo. You know what Checheyev told me? They steal. The gortsy do. Stealing's honourable as long as they're stealing from Cossacks. You go off with your rifle, shoot a Cossack, pinch his horse, and come home to a hero's welcome. In the old days they used to bring back their victims' heads as well, for the kids to play with. Cheers."

"Cheers," I say, steeling myself for Larry at his most impressionable.

"No law against killing, either. If you're caught up in a blood feud, *noblesse* obliges you to top everyone in sight. Oh, and the

Ingush like to start Ramadan earlier than scheduled so that they can shove it up their neighbours and demonstrate how pious they are."

"So which are you going to do?" I ask tolerantly. "Steal for him, kill for him, or pray for him?"

He laughs but does not directly answer me. Instead I must be treated to a discourse on Sufism as practised among the gortsy, and the powerful influence of the tariqats in preserving ethnic unity; I must be reminded that the Caucasus is the true crucible of the earth, the great barrier to Asia, the last redoubt of small nations and ethnic individuality—forty languages in an area the size of Scotland, Timbo! I must be told to reread Lermontov and Tolstoy's *Cossacks*, and dismiss Alexandre Dumas as a romantic slob.

And at one level, if Larry is happy, I am. Before Checheyev's arrival in London, I wouldn't have given twopence for the future of our operation. Instead all three of us are enjoying a renewal. Come to think of it, so, in clouded secrecy, is Checheyev's poker-backed boss, the venerable Volodya Zorin. But at another level I distrust Larry's relationship with Checheyev more than any he has conducted with his previous Russian controllers.

Why?

Because Checheyev is touching Larry where his predecessors have not. And neither have I.

LARRY TOO bloody word perfect, I was reading in an irritable footnote in my own hand on the encounter sheet. *Convinced he and CC are cooking something up. . . .* Yes, but cooking up *what?* I demanded impatiently of this useless insight. Robbing lowlanders for sport? It was too absurd. Larry under a stronger man's influence could get up to a lot of things. But falsify receipts, open foreign bank accounts? Take part in sustained, sophisticated fraud to the tune of thirty-seven *million* pounds? This Larry was nobody I knew. But then which Larry did I know?

CC PERSONAL, I read, in Cranmer's stern capitals, across the cover of a fat blue folder that contained my private papers on Checheyev, starting on the day of his arrival in London and ending with Larry's last officially recorded visit to Russia.

"CC's a star, Timbo—half noble, half savage, all Mensch, and bloody funny. . . ." Larry is rhapsodising. "He used to hate all things Russian because of what Stalin did to his people, but when Khrushchev came along he became a Twentieth Party Conference man. That's what he keeps saying when he gets drunk: 'I believe in the Twentieth Party Conference,' like a creed. . . .

" 'CC, how did you get into the spook business,' I ask him. It was while he was studying in Grozny, he says. He had fought his way into the university against heavy bureaucratic odds. Apparently Ingush returnees are not welcome at neighbouring Chechenia's only university. A bunch of hotheads tried to persuade him to come and blow up Party headquarters as a protest against the way the Ingush were being kicked around. CC told them they were crazy, but they wouldn't listen. He told them he was a Twentieth Party Conference man, but they still wouldn't listen. So he beat the daylights out of them, waited till they'd bolted to the hills, then peached to the KGB. . . .

"The KGB were so impressed that when he'd finished his studies they scooped him up and sent him to school outside Moscow for three years of English, Arabic, and spying. Hey, and get this—he acted Lord Goring in *An Ideal Husband*. He says he was an absolute wow. An Ingush acting Lord Goring! I love him!"

Confirmed by microphone intercepts, prosaic Cranmer had duly noted, in his bank clerk's hand.

GROZNY IN *Russia?* I hear myself ask.

Chechenia, actually. North Caucasus. It's gone independent.

How did you get there?

Thumbed a lift. Flew to Ankara. Flew to Baku. Sneaked up the coast a bit. Turned left. Piece of cake.

TIME, I thought, staring blindly at the stone wall before me.

Cling to time.

Time the great healer of the dead. I had been clinging to it for five weeks, but now I was clinging to it for dear life.

On August 1 I cut off my telephone.

Several Sundays later—Sunday being our day of destiny—Emma removes her piano stool and antique jewellery and departs without leaving a forwarding address.

On September 18, I do or do not kill Larry Pettifer at Priddy Pool. Until Emma left, I knew only that in the best civil service tradition, steps would have to be taken. Time becomes blank space lit by black light.

Time becomes time again when, on October 10, the first day of Larry's appointed lecture course at Bath University and twenty-two days after Priddy, Dr. Lawrence Pettifer goes officially missing.

Question: *How long had Larry been missing before he went officially missing?*

Question: *Where was Emma when I was or wasn't killing Larry?*

Question: *Where is Emma now?*

And the biggest question of all, which nobody will answer for me even if anybody knows: *When did Checheyev visit Larry?* For if CC's last visit to Bath occurred after September 18, Larry's resurrection was complete. If before, I must continue wandering in the black light, a murderer to myself if not to Larry.

After time, matter: *Where is Larry's body?*

There were two pools at Priddy, the Mineries and Waldegrave. It was the Mineries that we locals called Priddy Pool, and in summer children scrambled on its banks all day. At weekends, middle-class families picnicked on the tufted moorlands and parked their Volvos in the lay-by. So how could a corpse as large as Larry's—how could *any* corpse—stink and rot and float there undetected for thirty-six days and nights?

First theory of matter: *The police have found Larry's body and are lying.*

Second theory of matter: *The police are playing me along, waiting for me to provide the proof they lack.*

Third theory of matter: *I am ascribing too much wit to the police.*

And the Office, what are they doing? *Oh, my dear, what we always did! Riding all the horses in the race at once, and coming nowhere.*

Fourth theory of matter: *Black light becomes white light, and Larry's body isn't dead.*

How MANY times had I gone back to Priddy to take a look? Nearly. Got out the car, put on an old sports coat, turned out of the drive, only to invent some other purpose—pop down to Castle Cary, do some shopping, look in on Appleby of Wells instead?

Dead women float upward, I had read somewhere. Dead men keep their faces in the water. Or was it the other way round? Was it Larry's grin that was going to accuse me—still there, still staring up at me in the moonlight? Or the back of his broken head as he peered forever into the muddy waters of the hereafter?

I HAD turned up a pencilled record of Checheyev's postings, composed from his formal biography and Larry's embellishments:

1970   Iran, under the name of Grubaev. Made his repu-
        tation by contacting local (forbidden) Communist
        Party. Named and praised by Central Committee,
        of which KGB head of personnel is ex-officio
        member. Promoted.

1974   South Yemen, under the name of Klimov, as
        deputy head of residentura. Derring-do, desert
        skirmishes, throat-cutting. [Larry's indelicate
        description: he was a Russian Lawrence, living off
        camel's piss and roast sand.]

1980–82 Crash posting to Stockholm as Checheyev to
        replace local second man expelled for activities
        incompatible, etc. Bored stiff. Hated Scandinavia,
        except for the aquavit and the women. [Larry: he
        was ticking over at about three a week. Women
        and bottles.]

1982–86 Moscow Centre England Section, eating his heart
        out and getting reprimanded for cheek.

1986–90 In London as Checheyev, second man in the resi-
        dentura under Zorin [because as I had told dear
        Marjorie, no blackarse will ever make top man in a
        major Western residency].

From an envelope pinned to the inside cover of the file I extracted a bunch of snapshots mostly taken by Larry: CC outside the Soviet Embassy dacha in Hastings, where Larry was sometimes invited to spend weekends; CC at the Edinburgh Festival, living his cultural cover in front of posters proclaiming "A Caucasian Entertainment of Dance & Music."

I looked again at Checheyev's face, as I had looked at it so often in the past: honed but pleasant-featured, an air of wry humour and resourcefulness. Thirty-seven million pounds' worth of calm eyes.

AND WENT on looking at it. Took up Uncle Bob's old magnifying glass to look deeper into it than ever before. Great generals, I had read, carried photographs of their adversaries around with them, hung them in their tents, mooned over them before saying their prayers to the beastly God of Battles. But my feelings towards Checheyev contained nothing of hostility. I had wondered, as I always did of Larry's other parent, how on earth Larry managed to fool him. But that was the way with doubles the world over. If you were on the right side, the wrong side looked absurd. And if you were on the wrong side, you fought like hell to convince people you were on the right side until it was too late. And surely I had puzzled how anybody whose people had been hounded by Russian colonial rule for three hundred years could talk himself into serving his oppressors.

"He's a Caucasian werewolf, Timbo," Larry is saying excitedly. "Rational spy by day, gorets by night. By six in the evening you can see his fangs appear. . . ."

I waited for his enthusiasm to fade. For once it didn't. So that gradually, with Larry as our go-between, I began quite to like Checheyev too. I came to rely on his professionalism. I marvelled aloud at his ability to hold Larry's respect. And if I didn't understand what Larry called the wolf in him, I was able, even at one remove, to sense the pull of his revolt against the dreary system that he served.

I AM IN the surveillance house in Lambeth, seated beside Jack Andover, our chief watcher, while he runs video film of Checheyev in Kew Gardens, emptying a dead-letter box that Larry has filled an hour earlier. First he strolls past the warning signal, which denotes that the letter box is filled, and the camera shows us the child's chalk mark that Larry has scrawled on the brick wall. Checheyev registers it with the corner of his eye and strolls on. His walk is buoyant, almost insolent, as if he knows he's being filmed. He advances casually on a rose bed. He stoops and affects to read the botanist's description of the stems. As he does so, his upper body makes one swift lunge while his hand whisks a package from its hiding place and secretes it in his clothing: but so deftly, so imperceptibly, that I am reminded of a military tattoo that Uncle Bob once took me to, with Cossack horsemen who slid beneath the bellies of their bareback mounts at full gallop, to reemerge at the salute.

"Your bloke got any Welsh blood in him at all?" Jack asks me, as Checheyev resumes his innocent inspection of the rose beds.

Jack is right. Checheyev has the miner's neatness and the miner's roll.

"My boys and girls have taken a real shine to him," Jack assures me as I leave. "Slippery isn't the word. They say it's a privilege to follow him, Mr. Cranmer." And shyly: "Any word of Diana at all, by any chance, Mr. Cranmer?"

"Fine, thank you. She's happily remarried and we're good friends."

My former wife, Diana, had worked in Jack's section before she saw the light.

MONEY again.

After time, matter, and Konstantin Checheyev, consider money. Not my annual expenditure, or how much I inherited from Uncle Bob or Aunt Cecily, or how I afforded Emma's Bechstein that she didn't want. But real money, thirty-seven millions of it, milked from the Russian government, planned white-collar banditry, Larry's hoofprints all over the file.

Rising from the table, I began a tour of my priesthole, peering from each arrow slit in turn. I was reaching for memories that danced away from me as soon as I went after them.

Money.

Call up occasions when Larry mentioned money in any context except tax, debts, forgotten bills, pigs-in-clover materialism of the West, and the cheques he hadn't got round to paying in.

Returning to my table, I started to sift once more among the files, till I came on the entry I was looking for without quite knowing what it was: one sheet of yellow legal pad, scored with prim annotations in my blue rollerball. And along the top, couched in the self-conscious terms I use when I am talking to myself aloud, the question: *Why did Larry lie to me about his rich friend in Hull?*

I ADVANCE on the question slowly, just as Larry does. I am an intelligence officer. Nothing exists without a context.

Larry is just back from Moscow. We are entering his last year in harness. Our safe flat this time is not in the Tottenham Court Road but in Vienna's Hohe Warte, in a sprawling green-tiled mansion scheduled for demolition, the furniture Ministry of Works Biedermeier. Dawn has broken, but we haven't gone to bed. Larry flew in late last night and as usual we launched straight into the debriefing. In a few hours he will be delivering a keynote speech to a conference of International Journalists Concerned, whom Larry has predictably rechristened "Jerkers." He sprawls on the sofa, one slender hand dropped low like a Sickert drawing and the other balancing a mahogany whisky on his belly. A coven of middle-aged *Russian analysts*—the term "Moscow-watcher" is already out of date—has left him at odds with the approaching daylight. He is talking about the world: our part of it. Even approaching the subject of money, Larry must first talk about the world.

"West's compassioned out, Timbo," he announces to the ceiling, not bothering to stifle a huge yawn. "Running on empty. Fuck us."

You're still in Moscow, I'm thinking as I watch him. With age the switching back and forth between camps is getting harder for you and you take longer to come home. When you stare at the ceiling I know you are staring at the Moscow skyline. When you stare at me you're comparing my nourished contours with the deprived faces you've left behind. And when you curse like this I know you're washed out.

"Vote for the new Russian democracy," he resumes vaguely. "Anti-Semitic, anti-Islam, anti-Western, and corruption to die for. Hey, Timbers . . ."

But even on the brink of talking about money, Larry must first eat. Eggs, bacon, and fried bread, his favourite. Nothing makes him fat. The eggs free range and turned, the way he likes them. Fortnum & Mason's English Breakfast Tea, flown in with the coven. Full-fat milk and caster sugar. The bread whole meal. Lots of salted butter. Mrs. Bathhurst, our resident safe-housekeeper, knows all Mr. Larry's little ways, and so do I. The food has mollified him. It always does. In the long brown moth-eaten dressing gown that he takes with him everywhere, he has become my friend again.

"What is it?" I reply.

"Who do we know who does money?" he asks with his mouth full. We have arrived at his goal. Not knowing this, of course, I am uncharacteristically short with him. Perhaps with the end of the Cold War he tires me more than I am prepared to admit.

"All right, Larry, what kind of hash are you in this time? It's only a couple of weeks since we bailed you out."

He breaks out laughing, too heartily for my blood. "Come off it, you ass. This isn't for *me*. It's for a chum of mine. I need a red-toothed fascist banker. Who do we know?"

So away we go. About money. This chum of mine at Hull University, he explains genially as he spreads his marmalade. Chum you wouldn't know, he adds, before I can ask his name. Poor sod's come into a pot of cash, he says. A mega pot. Totally out of the blue. Rather like you did, Timbo, when your aunt whosit kicked the bucket. Needs his hand held. Needs accountants, solicitors, trusts, all that junk. Someone big league, offshore, sophisticated—who do we know? Come on, Timbo, you know everyone.

So I ponder for him, though mostly I am studying to understand why he has chosen this particular moment to discuss something as irrelevant as the financial anxieties of his chum in Hull.

And it so happens that only two days earlier I have been sitting shoulder-to-shoulder with just such a banker, in my capacity as honorary trustee of a private charity called the Charles Lavender Urban and Rural Trust for Wales.

"Well, there's always the great and good Jamie Pringle," I suggest cautiously. "Nobody could call him sophisticated, but he's certainly big league, as he's the first to tell you."

Pringle was our contemporary at Oxford, a rugger-playing scion of Larry's Unbearable Classes.

"Jamie's an oaf," Larry declares, swilling his English Breakfast Tea. "Where's he hang out anyway? In case this chum's interested?"

But Larry is lying.

How do I know? I know. It doesn't take the soured perceptions of post–Cold War depression to see through his wiles. If you have run a man for twenty years, if you have schooled him in deception, immersed him in it, coaxed out the guile in him and made it work; if you have sent him away to sleep with the enemy and chewed your nails waiting for him to come back; if you have nursed him through his loves and hates, his fits of despair and wanton malice and ever-present boredom, and struggled with all your heart to distinguish between his histrionics and the real thing, then either you know his face or you know nothing, and I knew Larry's like the map of my own soul. I could have drawn it for you, if I had only been an artist: every emphasis of his features, every lift and fall of every telltale line, and the places where nothing happens and a saintly stillness settles when he lies. About women, about himself. Or about money.

CRANMER's tight-lipped note to self, undated: *Ask Jamie Pringle what on earth LP was up to.*

But with Merriman's axe poised above us, and LP grating quite unusually on my nerves, Cranmer must have had other things to do.

So IT IS not till a couple of months back, when we are two free men and Emma, enjoying our umpteenth Sunday lunch at Honeybrook, and I have directed the rather stilted conversation away from the anguish of Bosnia, and the ethnic cleansing of the Abkhazians, and the decimation of the Moluccans, and I forget what other raging issues of the day that consume them both, that Jamie Pringle's name accidentally crops up. Or perhaps some demon in me gives it a nudge, for I am starting to get a little reckless now.

"Yes—my gosh—however did *that* go, by the way, with Jamie?" I ask Larry, with the extra carelessness we spy-men use when removing a topic from its secret wrapping in the presence of an ordinary mortal. "Did he deliver the goods for your chum in Hull? Was he helpful? What happened?"

Larry glances at Emma, then at me, but I have ceased to wonder why he looks at Emma first, because everything that passes among the three of us is by now a matter of tacit consultation between the two of them.

"Pringle's an arsehole," Larry replies curtly. "Was. Is now. And ever shall be. Amen."

Then, while Emma stares demurely at her plate, he launches himself into a diatribe against what he calls the useless mouths of our

Oxford generation, thus converting the subject of Jamie Pringle into another diatribe against the compassion fatigue of the West.

He's turned her, I'm thinking, in the jargon of our trade. She's gone. Defected. Crossed over. And doesn't even know it.

THROUGH the arrow slits, grey streaks of morning were appearing behind the hills. An ungainly young barn owl flopped at grasstop height over the frosted hillside in search of breakfast. So many shared dawns, I thought: so much life lavished on one man. Larry is dead for me whether I killed him or not, and I am dead for him. The only question is: Who is dead for Emma?

I returned to my table, buried myself once more in my papers, and when I touched my face I felt to my surprise a thirty-six-hour stubble. I blinked round my secret sanctuary and counted the coffee cups. I consulted my watch and refused to believe it was three in the afternoon. But my watch was right, and the sun was entering the southwestern arrow slit. I was not living some vicarious daylit night in Helsinki or pacing my hotel room, praying for Larry's safe return from Moscow or Havana or even Grozny. I was here in my priesthole, and I had pulled out strands but not yet made a thread of them.

Peering round, my eye fell upon a corner of my kingdom that was barred to me by my own decree. It was an alcove, screened by a makeshift blackout curtain that I had found in the attic and nailed across the entrance. I called it Emma's archive.

"YOUR LOVELY Emma's quite a gal," Merriman announces with relish, two weeks after I have been obliged to submit her name to him as my intended companion. "No risk to anyone, you'll be pleased to hear, except possibly to you. Would you like to take a tiny deniable peek at her biog before you plunge? I've made up a little doggy bag for you to take home."

"No."

"Her appalling parentage?"

"No."

The doggy bag, as he calls it, lies already between us on the desk, an anonymous buff A4 folder with half a dozen pages of anonymous white paper peeping out.

"Her missing years? Her exotic foreign ramblings? Her disgraceful love life, her absurd causes, her barefoot marches, picketings, her ever bleeding heart? Some of these young musicians these days, you wonder they have time to learn their scales."

"No."

How could he ever understand that Emma is my self-imposed security risk, my new openness, my one-girl glasnost? I wish for no stolen knowledge of her, nothing she does not tell me of her own accord. Nevertheless, to my shame, I take the file as he knows I will and jam it angrily beneath my arm. The pull of my old profession is simply too strong for me. Knowledge never kills, I have preached for twenty years to anybody who would listen to me: but ignorance can.

SETTING everything in order for my next visit, I fed my weary body down the winding staircase to the cope cupboard. In the vestry I helped myself to overalls, a broom, a duster, and a floor polisher. Thus equipped, I proceeded to the main aisle, where I paused and faced the altar and, in the shifty manner of us agnostics, offered some clumsy acknowledgement or obeisance to the Maker I could not bring myself to believe in. This done, I went about my cleaning duties, for I was never a man to neglect my cover.

First I dusted the mediaeval pew ends, then I mopped the tiled floor and ran over it with the polisher, to the vexation of a family of bats. Half an hour later, still in my cleaner's overalls and bearing the broom as additional testimony to my labours, I ventured into the daylight. The sun had disappeared behind a blue-black cloud stack. Shadowy bands of rain pressed down on the bare hilltops. My heart stopped dead. I was staring at the hill we call the Beacon. It is the highest of the six. Its outline is pitted with shaped stones and hummocks said to be the remnants of an ancient burial ground. Among these stones, cut black against the seething skyline, stood the silhouette of a man in a long coat or raincoat that seemed to have no buttons down the front, for it flapped and billowed in the gusting wind, though his hands were plunged into its pockets.

His head was turned away from me, as if I had just hit him with a .38 revolver butt. His left foot was pointed outward in the quaintly Napoleonic pose that Larry liked to strike. He wore a flat cap, and though I did not remember ever seeing Larry in a cap, this meant nothing, for he was forever leaving his hats at people's houses and helping himself to others he preferred. I tried to call out, but no sound escaped me. I opened my mouth, wanting to shout "Larry!" but for once my tongue couldn't make the L. Come back, I mutely begged him, come down. Let's begin again; let's be friends, not rivals.

I took a step forward, then another. I think I was intending to charge at him as I had at Priddy, vaulting the stone walls, ignoring the gradient, yelling, "Larry, Larry! Larry, are you all right?" But as Larry was always telling me, I am not much good at spontaneity. So instead I set down my broom and cupped my hands to my mouth and shouted something shy, like "Hullo there, who is that, is it you?"

Or perhaps by then I had realised that for the second time in as many days I was addressing the unlovely person of Andreas Munslow, sometime member of my section and full-time keeper of my passport.

"What the devil do you think you're doing here?" I shouted at him. "How dare you come here snooping on me? Go away. Get out of here."

He was loping down the hill at me, glissading in spidery strides. I had not realised till now what an agile creature he must be.

"Afternoon to you, Tim," he said, with none of the previous day's deference. "Been cleaning up for God?" he asked, eyeing my broom, then me. "Don't you shave these days?"

"What are you doing here?"

"I'm keeping watch over you, Tim. For your safety and comfort. Orders of the Top Floor."

"I don't need keeping watch over. I can keep watch over myself. Get out."

"Jake Merriman thinks you do. He thinks you're messing him around. He's ordered me to tag you. Put a bell up your arse was how he put it. I'm at the Crown, day or night." He shoved a piece of paper at me. "That's my cell phone. Daniel Moore, room three." He stabbed his index finger into my chest. "And screw you, actually, Cranmer. Totally screw you. You gave me one and I owe you one. That's a warning."

EMMA's ghost was waiting for me in the drawing room. She was seated at the Bechstein on her special stool, thinking her notes aloud with that strict posture she has that nips the waist and spreads the hips. She was wearing all her antique jewellery to please me.

"Have you been flirting with Larry again?" she asked above her music.

But I was in no mood to be laughed at, least of all by her.

EVENING fell, but I had already entered the black light of my own soul. Broad daylight would not have saved me. I wandered the house, touching things, opening books and closing them. I cooked myself food and left it uneaten. I put on music and didn't listen to it. I slept and woke dreaming the same dream that had destroyed my sleep. I returned to the priesthole. What trail was I pursuing, what clues? I was picking through the rubble of my past, looking for the fragments of the bomb that had destroyed it. More than once I rose in despair from my trestle table and placed myself before the old rag of wartime curtain, and my hand braced itself to rip aside the self-imposed barrier to Emma's forbidden territory. But each time I restrained myself.

6

"Our usual, was it, Mr. Cranmer?"

"If you please, Tom."

"Expect you're looking forward to your Senior Citizen's any day now."

"Thank you, Tom, I have a few years to wait, and I'm glad to do it."

Laughter in which I share, for this is our standing bad joke every other Friday when I buy my ticket to Paddington and take my place on the platform among the London suits. And if today had been an ordinary Friday, I am sure I would have fantasised a little, imagining I was still in harness. And Emma in the good days would have playfully straightened my tie for me, and smoothed the lapels of my jacket, and wished me a nice day at the office, darling, before treating me to a last, delicious, disgracefully suggestive kiss. And in the bad days, she would have watched my departure from the shadows of her upper window, unaware apparently that I was watching her also, in the wing mirror of my Sunbeam, knowing that I was leaving her alone all day to her typewriter and telephone, and Larry thirty miles down the road.

But this morning I was feeling, in place of Emma's amateurish eye, the prickle of professional surveillance on my back. Bartering trivia with a forlorn baronet known locally as poor Percy, who, having inherited a thriving engineering business and run it into the ground, now sold life insurance on commission, I had glimpsed Tom the ticket clerk's silhouette ease across the window of his office to the telephone and speak into it with his back to me. And as the train pulled out of the station I spotted a man in a country cap and raincoat standing in the car park, zealously waving at a woman a few seats behind me, who paid him not the least attention. He was the same man who had followed me in his Bedford van from the crossroads at the end of my lane.

Arbitrarily I awarded Tom to the police, and the cap and raincoat to Munslow. Good luck to them, I thought. Let all pursuing parties note that on this duty Friday, Tim Cranmer is once more going about his customary business.

I was wearing my blue pinstripe. I dress up to people; I can't help it. If I am calling on the vicar, I don a tweed suit; watching a cricket match, a blazer and a sporting tie. And if, after four days' nightmarish incarceration inside my own head, I am attending the bimonthly trustees' meeting of the Charles Lavender Urban and Rural Trust for Wales under the stewardship of Pringle Brothers PLC of Threadneedle Street, I cannot help but look a little like a banker myself as I board the train, study the financial pages of my newspaper, step into the chauffeur-driven car that awaits me among Brunel's splendid arches, give Pringle's uniformed doorman good morning, and see reflected in the glass-and-mahogany door the same unoccupied cab with its light off that had followed me all the way from Praed Street.

"MR. CRANMER, hellao, reelly grite to see you," Jamie's supine secretary, Pandora, whined in her Roedean Cockney as I entered the leathery Edwardian antechamber of which she was the mistress.

"Hell's teeth, Tim!" cried Jamie Pringle, all sixteen stone of him, in his striped shirt and mulberry braces, as he forced me into touch with a crushing handshake. "Don't tell me it's Friday week already, what, what?"

Pringle's an arsehole, I heard Larry saying in my inner ear. *Was. Is now. And ever shall be. Amen.*

Monty drifted in like his own shadow. He wore a hollowed black waistcoat and stank of the cigarettes he wasn't allowed to smoke on the partners' floor. Monty kept the books and paid our quarterly expenses with cheques that Jamie signed.

After him came Paul Lavender, still shaking from the hazardous voyage by Rolls-Royce from his house in Mount Street. Paul was

feline and fair and seventy, and very slow-moving in patent moc-
casins with languid tassels. His father, our benefactor, had started life
as a schoolmaster in Llandudno, before founding a hotel chain and
selling it for a hundred million pounds.

After Paul came Dolly and Eunice, his two spinster sisters. Dolly
wore a diamond racehorse. Years ago Dolly had won the Derby, or so
she claimed, though Eunice swore Dolly had never owned anything
larger than an overfed chihuahua.

And after them again came Henry, the Lavenders' family solicitor.
It was thanks to Henry that we met so often. And at four hundred
pounds an hour, who could blame him?

"Plonk still holding up?" he asked doubtfully as we shook hands.

"Oh, I think so, thank you. Rather well."

"Cheap Frog stuff not pricing you out of the market at all? I must
have been reading the wrong newspapers."

"I'm afraid you must, Henry," I said.

WE WERE seated round the famous Pringle boardroom table. Each of
us had before him one copy of the minutes of the last meeting, one
statement of the accounts, and one Wedgwood bone china teacup
with a sugared shortbread biscuit on the saucer. Pandora poured.
Paul rested his head on one bloodless hand and closed his eyes.

Jamie, our chairman, was about to speak. The fists that thirty
years ago had clawed muddy rugger balls out of seething scrums con-
verged upon a tiny pair of gold-framed half-lenses and pulled them
on ear by ear. The market, Jamie said, was depressed. He held the
foreigners to blame:

"What with your Germans refusing to cut their interest rates,
your yen going through the roof, and your High Street takings going
through the floor—" He peered about him in bemusement, as if he
had forgotten where he was. "I'm afraid that U.K. gilts are weather-
ing something of a *trough*." Then he gave a nod at Henry, who with
a frightful *clack* opened the two levers of a fibreglass document case
and read us an interminable report:

Discussion with the local authorities regarding the provision of
sports facilities in the inner cities is proceeding at the pace one has to
expect of local civil servants, Jamie. . . .

The trust's offer of an extra children's ward at the Lavender Hospital for Mothers cannot be taken further until additional trust monies are set aside for staffing. None are presently available for such a purpose, Jamie. . . .

Our proposal to supply a mobile library to meet the needs of children in illiterate areas has run up against political objections from the local council—one side arguing that the days of free libraries are dead and buried, another that the selection of books should be determined by the county's education authorities, Jamie. . . .

"*Bloody bollocks!*"

Eunice had exploded. At about this stage in the proceedings, she usually did.

"Our dad would be turning in his grave," she roared in her smothered Welsh accent. "Free books for the ignorant? That's daylight bloody *Communism!*"

Equally furiously, Dolly disagreed. She usually did.

"That's a living lie, Eunice Lavender. Dad would be standing up and clapping his hands off. Children's what he prayed for with his last breath. He loved us. Didn't he, Paulie?"

But Paul was in some far Wales of his own. His eyes were still closed, and he wore a misty smile.

Jamie Pringle deftly passed the ball to me. "Tim. Very quiet today. Got a view?"

For once my diplomatic skills eluded me. On any other day I could have dredged up a distracting topic for him: pressed Henry to move faster in his dealings with the city authorities, raised an eyebrow at the Pringle administration costs, which were the only item in the accounts to show an increase. But this morning I had too much of Larry in my head. Wherever I looked round the table, I kept seeing him lounging in one of the empty thrones, dressed in my grey suit that he'd never given back, spinning us some story about this chum in Hull.

"Monty. Your shout," Jamie ordered.

So Monty dutifully cleared his throat, seized a piece of paper from a pile before him, and treated us to a report on our distributable income. But alas, after deduction of charges, costs, and sundry disbursements, there was for the tenth meeting running no income to distribute. Not even the House of Pringle had yet come up with a formula for distributing percentages of nothing to the Poor and Needy Gentlefolk of Wales as defined by the Borders Act of whenever it was.

WE LUNCHED. That much I know. In the panelled sanctum where we always lunched. We were served by Mrs. Peters in white gloves, and we polished off a couple of magnums of the 1955 Cheval Blanc, which the trust had thoughtfully laid down twenty years ago for the resuscitation of its hard-pressed officers. But I forget, thank God, almost everything of our dreadful conversation. Dolly hated niggers: I remember that. Eunice thought them lovely. Monty thought they were all right in Africa. Paul preserved his mandarin smile. A splendid ship's clock, which by tradition determined House of Pringle time, kept noisy record of our progress. By two-thirty, Dolly and Eunice had stormed out in a red-faced huff. By three, Paul had remembered something he had to do, or was it somewhere he had to go, or someone to meet? Must be his barber, he decided. Henry and Monty left with him, Henry murmuring outstanding matters in his ear at four hundred pounds an hour, and Monty desperate for the first of a large number of cigarettes to get him back to par.

JAMIE and I sat pensively over our decanter of partners' port.

"Jolly good, then," he said profoundly. "Yes. Well, then. Cheers. Here's to us."

In a moment, if I did nothing to stop him, he was going to launch himself upon the great issues of our time: the cockiness of women, the mystery of where North Sea oil profits had gone—he gravely feared to the unemployed—or how decent banking had been ruined by the computer. And in thirty minutes exactly, Pandora would pop her stupid pedigree face round the door and remind Mr. Jamie that he had another meeting before close of play: which was Pringle Brothers code for "The chauffeur is waiting to drive you to the airport for your golf at St. Andrew's" or "You promised to take me to Deauville for the weekend."

I asked after Henrietta, Jamie's wife. I always did, and dared not vary the ritual.

"Henrietta is bloody marvellous, thank you," Jamie replied defensively. "Hunt's imploring her to stay on, but old Hen isn't sure she wants to. Getting a bit tired, frankly, of the Antis buggering everything up."

I asked after his children.

"Kids are doing splendidly, Tim, thank you. Marcus is captain o' Fives, Penny's coming out next spring. Not *real* coming out, not the way the girls did it in *our* day. But a lot better than nothing," he added, and gazed wistfully past me at the illustrious names of Pringle's Fallen of Two Wars.

I asked whether he'd seen any of the mob recently, meaning our crowd at Oxford. Not since the Oriel bash at Boodle's, he replied. I asked who had been there. It took me two more moves before, seemingly off his own bat, he was talking about Larry. And really it was no great work of art on my part, because in our year if you talked old buddies, sooner or later you talked Larry.

"Extraordinary chap," Jamie pronounced with the absolute certainty of his kind. "Gifted, vast talents, charm. Decent Christian background, father in the Church, all that. But no stability. In life, if you haven't got stability, got nothing. Pinko one week, chucking it all in next. Chucked it in for good this time. Coms are all capitalists now. Worse than the bloody Yanks." And then, almost too easily, as if my guardian angel were whispering in his ear: "Came to see me not long ago. Bit *seedy*, I thought. Bit *hangdog*. Certain awareness of having backed the wrong side there, I rather think. Natural enough when you look at it."

I let out a delighted laugh. "Jamie! You're not telling me Larry's become a capitalist entrepreneur, are you? I think that's too ripe."

But Jamie, though he could laugh like a maniac without warning—and usually without humour—only helped himself to more port and waxed more sonorous. "Don't know *what* he's become, to be frank. Not my business. More than a mere entrepreneur, that's for sure. Something bit more *eloquent of the moment*, if you ask me," he added darkly, ramming the decanter at me as if he never wanted to see it again. "Not a lot of due respect there either, to be frank."

"Oh dear," I said.

"Rather exaggerated idea of himself." A resentful swallow of port. "Bit of overcompensation going on. Lot of crap about our duty to help the newly freed nations find their feet, right old wrongs, establish norms of social justice. Asked me whether I intended to pass by on the other side. 'Steady on, old boy,' I said. 'Hang about. Weren't you one of the chaps who gave the Sovs a bit of a leg up? You've got me a bit foxed, if you don't mind my saying. Bit stumped. Confused.' "

I leaned forward, showing him that I was all attention. I composed my face into an expression of fascinated, sycophantic incredulity. I strove with all my body language to will his damned story out of the fogged thickets of his lonely little mind: "Go on, Jamie. This is riveting. More."

"Only duty *I've* got is to this house, I told him. Wouldn't listen. I thought he was an intellectual sort of chap. How can you be an intellectual, not listen? Talked straight through me. Called me an ostrich. I'm not an ostrich. I'm a family man. Pathetic."

"But what on earth did he want you to *do*, Jamie? Turn over Pringle Brothers to Oxfam?" It flitted through my mind as I said this that it wouldn't be at all a bad idea. But my face, if it was doing its job, revealed only my sincere sympathy that Jamie should have been the target of such bad form.

A half minute's silence while he rounded up his intellectual resources. "Soviet Communist Party was going private. Right?"

"Right."

"That was the story. Selling off Party property. Buildings. Rest homes, offices, transport, sports palaces, schools, hospitals, foreign embassies, land galore, priceless paintings, Fabergé, Christ knows what. Billions of dollars of the stuff. Make sense?"

"Indeed it does. Russia Limited. It began in secret with Gorbachev, then it ran riot."

"How Larry got in on the act, anybody's bloody guess. Pringle Brothers doesn't have his connections, pleased to say." Yet another huge swallow of port. "Wouldn't want 'em. Wouldn't touch 'em with a barge pole, thank you. No way, José."

"But, Jamie—" I dared not sound as if I cared, though my time was running out. "But, Jimminy"—his Oxford nickname—"*sport*, what was he asking you to *do?* Buy the Kremlin? I'm fascinated."

Jamie's reddened gaze fixed itself once more on his company's Roll of Honour. "You still working for whoever you used to be working for?"

I hesitated. Jamie had once applied to join us, but without success. Since then he had tossed me the odd snippet from time to time, usually after we had had the same information better and earlier from other sources. Did he relish our mystique or resent it? Would he tell me more if I answered yes? I chose the middle path.

"Just the odd bit of this and that, Jamie. Nothing onerous. Listen, you're killing me with curiosity. What on earth was Larry up to?"

A delay for more port and grimacing.

"I'm sorry?"

"Two cracks of the whip. Phoned me a couple of years ago, talked a lot of crap about wanting to put a nice piece of business in my way, was I game, matter of several millions, old-pals act, come and see me next time he was in town, bugger all happened. Went off the air."

"And the second bout? When was that?"

I scarcely knew which to press harder: the what or the when. But Jamie took the decision for me.

"Larry Pettifer was up to the following," he announced in an alarming boom. "Larry Pettifer claimed that he had been authorised, by a certain ex-Soviet state agency, name not supplied—correction, by persons in that agency, *their* names also not supplied—to conduct a dialogue with this house, concerning the possibility of opening an account with this house—series of accounts: offshore, naturally—whereby this house would receive substantial sums of hard currency from sources not accurately defined—would in effect hold said monies on a no-name basis—and make certain disbursements in accordance with such instructions as would from time to time be received by this house from persons entrusted with a certain code word or letter reference, which would be matched by a similar code word or letter reference held by this house. The disbursements would be substantial, but they would never exceed assets, and we would never be asked for credit."

Jamie's monologue had slowed to fifteen revolutions per minute, and there were only nine minutes left to go by the ship's clock.

"Were they big sums? I mean, *banking* big? How much money was Larry talking about?"

Jamie again consulted the board behind my head. "If you were to think of a figure in the order of the figure that certain trustees and their advisors were deliberating this morning—I would not think you far wrong."

"Thirty million sterling? What on earth would they be buying? Where did they get it from? I mean that's money, isn't it? Even for you? It certainly is for *me!* Whatever was he up to? I'm absolutely entranced."

"Laundering, what it came down to. Acting under instructions, my feeling, and hadn't got the hang of 'em. Had some associate or partner we'd be dealing with up north. He'd be some sort of co-signatory up to certain sums. Stank."

My time was running out. So was Jamie.

"Did he say *where* up north?"

"What's that?"

"You said he had some pal up north."

"Macclesfield. An associate in Macclesfield. Could have been Manchester. No, it wasn't. It was Macclesfield. Used to screw a girl there. Cindy. Worked in the silk trade. Silky Cindy."

"But where in God's name does Larry Pettifer get thirty million pounds from? All right, they're not his—but they must be *some-body's!*"

Wait. Count. Pray. Smile.

"*Mafias,*" Jamie growled. "Isn't that what they call 'em over there? Competing *mafias?* Papers are full of 'em." He shook his head and muttered something like *His* business.

"So what did you do?" I asked, trying desperately to preserve a tone of amused mystification. "Call in your partners? Send him packing?"

The ship's clock was ticking like a bomb, but to my despair Jamie still said nothing. Until suddenly he gave a violent start of impatience, as if it were *I* who had kept *him* waiting.

"One doesn't send people packing in these situations, thank you. One gives 'em lunch. One talks old times. Says one will think about it, discuss it with the board. I did tell 'em there were a couple of problems, some practical, some ethical. I suggested it would be nice if they told me who their client actually *was*, what he was proposing to trade *in*, and what the *tax* status would be. A little authentication would *help*. I suggested they organise an approach through the Foreign Office—at a high level, of course. They did have some *letter* with them from the embassy in London. Signed by some *official*. Not the ambassador. Could have been forged. Could have been kosher. One simply doesn't know."

He was examining the assay marks on the back of his coffee spoon, comparing them with the spoon from the empty place next to him. "Broken set," he muttered. "Extraordinary thing." He was crestfallen. "Hell did that happen? Ask Ma Peters. *Bloody* careless."

"You said *they*, Jamie," I said.

"What's that, old boy?"

I put a hand on his sleeve. "I'm sorry, Jamie—I may have misheard. I thought you said *they*. Do you mean Larry didn't come alone? I don't think I quite got that bit."

" 'They' is correct." He was still studying the spoons.

My head was racing. Checheyev? The associate in Macclesfield? Or Larry's chum from Hull University?

"So who came too?" I asked.

To my surprise, Jamie gave a superior and very salacious smile. "Pettifer brought an *assistant*. Dolly girl is what I would have called her. Assistant was going to be his intermediary, he said. Do the brainwork. Mathematics not up Larry's street, but this girl—mustard. Brighter than Larry by a mile, when it came to numbers."

I was greatly amused. I must have been, for I gave a jolly laugh, though the inside of me was frozen in alarm. "All right, Jamie. Don't hold out on me. She was Russian. She had snow on her boots."

His superior smile would not let go of him. He put down the offending spoons. "Wrong. Decent English girl, far as you could tell. Decently dressed. Spoke the Queen's English well as you and me. Wouldn't be surprised if she was the moving force. Given her a job here any day."

"Pretty?"

"No. Not pretty. She was *beautiful*. Word I use very seldom, matter o' fact. Hell she was doing mixed up with a shit like Pettifer, God knows." He had entered the territory he loved best. "Figure to kill for. Lovely little bottom. Legs all the way up. Sat right there in front of me, swingin' 'em at me." He struck a philosophical note. "One of the most extraordinary things in life, Tim, and I've observed it over and over. Pretty girl, have anyone she wants, who does she go for? A shit. Pound to a penny Pettifer beats her up. She probably likes it. Masochist. Same as m' sister-in-law, Angie. Money to burn, looks to kill, Angie goes from one shit to another. Lucky to have any teeth left, way they treat her."

"Did she have a name?" I asked.

"Sally. Sally someone." One side of his mouth slipped down in a terrible smirk. "Jet-black hair, all pinned up on the top of her head, waiting for you to let it down. Absolute fatal weakness of mine. Love a black bush. Whole of womanhood there. Gorgeous."

I was hearing nothing, seeing nothing, feeling nothing. I was behaving and collecting and recording. That was all I was doing in the world, while Jamie looked sad and old and nodded at me and slurped his port.

"Have you heard from him since?"

"Not a peep. Neither of 'em. Rather think they got the message. Not the first time we've shown a con man the door. Or his moll."

I had five minutes left by the ship's clock.

"Did you pass him on to someone? Suggest where he might go?"

A frightful grimace, a last charge. "We're not very clued up on that type of business at Pringle Brothers, thank you. Used to be a little outfit up the road called B.C.C.I. that handled stuff like that once upon a time. One gathers they're under a bit of a cloud."

I had a penultimate question. I sent my rent-a-drool smile with it, and a lot of good fellowship and grateful savouring of the port.

"And you didn't think, Jamie, when he'd gone—or they had—to pick up the phone to whoever it was I used to work for and tip them the wink about Larry? Now that I'm no longer at that desk? Larry and his girl?"

Jamie Pringle fixed me in a bull-like glare of outrage.

"Rat on Larry? Hell are you talking about? I'm a banker. If he'd strangled his dear mother and bunged her in a bucket of acid, I suppose it's just conceivable I'd pick up the phone to somebody. But when a fellow Oriel man comes in here to discuss a banking proposition with me—which, all right, I happen to think stinks to high heaven—I am *sworn* to absolute and *total* secrecy. *You* want to tell 'em, that's *your* business. Help yourself."

It was achieved. Only the terrible hurdle remained. Perhaps it was the self-torturer in me who had decreed that, after forcing the question too hard upon the police and Pew-Merriman, I should this time hold it back until the very end. Or perhaps it was simply the field man, telling me to gather in everything else first, before going for the crown jewels.

"So when, Jamie?"

"'S'at, old boy?"

He was half asleep.

"When? When did they descend on you? Larry and his girl? They came by appointment, presumably, or you wouldn't have given them lunch," I suggested, hoping by this means to encourage him to look in his diary or pick up the house phone to Pandora.

"Grouse," he announced loudly, and at first I thought he was telling me that he or Larry—or even Emma—had lodged some sort of complaint.

"Gave 'em grouse," he continued. "Ma Peters did. Oriel man. Old times. Hadn't seen him for twenty-five years. Put out the red carpet. Duty. Last week of September, last grouse o' the season, far as this house was concerned. Bloody Arabs overshot 'em. Worse than Eyeties. Come mid-September, hardly a bird left. Self-discipline essential. Family hold back, whatever the foreigners do. Can't say wogs these days. Not PC."

My mouth was numb. I had had a dental injection. My upper gums were frozen, and my tongue had disappeared down my throat.

"So the *end* of September," I managed, as if addressing the very old or deaf. "Right? Right, Jamie? They came to you in the last week of September? Jolly generous of you to give them grouse. I hope they were duly grateful. Considering you might just as well have shown them the door. I mean *I* would have been grateful. So would you. End of September. Yes?"

I fumbled on, but I don't know that Jamie ever answered me: not beyond a show of shrugging and grimacing and backbench burbling of sounds like "Naa" and "Quarright." I know the clock struck. I remember the bun face of Pandora appearing round the door, announcing Cinderella's coach. I remember thinking, as the thousand-voiced choir of angels struck up inside my head, that if you're celebrating your emergence from the black light, a bottle of '55 Cheval Blanc and a large dose of Graham's '27 port make an appropriately celestial accompaniment.

Jamie Pringle had risen heavily to his feet and was displaying a passion I had not seen in him outside the rugby field.

"Pandora. Just the girl. Look here. Bloody outrage. Get on to Mrs. Peters *now*, will you, darling? Broken set of teaspoons. Could ruin the whole service. Find out *why* and find out *where* and find out *who*."

But I had found out when.

. . .

MY EUPHORIA, if it survived in certain areas of my head, was short-lived in the rest of them. The white light to which I had been restored enabled me to see more clearly than ever the monstrosity of their shared betrayal. All right, I had taken a gun. I had conspired, plotted, hired a car, and driven into the night determined to slaughter my friend and agent of a lifetime. But he had deserved it! And so had she!

I WALKED.

Emma.

I was drunk. Not wine drunk. Or not consciously. After twenty years in the Office, I have a head like an ox. But drunk all the same: blind, humiliated drunk.

Emma.

Who are you being or seeming, with your hair up, swinging your legs at Jamie Pringle? What other lies have you been living while you laughed at me behind my back, the two of you—at Timbo, stuffy old Timbo, the late developer with his rent-a-drool smile?

Playing the angel. Toiling at your Hopeless Causes till late into the night. Telephoning, tap-tapping, looking grave, looking high-minded, preoccupied, aloof, borrowing the Sunbeam to slip down to the post, to the railway station, to Bristol. For the oppressed of the earth. For Larry.

I WALKED. I fumed. I rejoiced. I fumed again.

Yet furious as I was, I still noticed how the nondescript couple across the street abandoned their study of a shop window and set off along the far pavement at the same speed and in the same direction as myself. And I knew there would be a team of three pedestrians behind me, and a tame car or van or taxicab to service them. And therefore I knew, for all my anger and relief and new purpose and altered status as a creature of the common daylight, that I must attend to the seeming. I must make no gesture that suggested I was anything but a well-lunched trustee and former spy going about his legitimate pursuits. And I was grateful, to Larry, to Emma, and to my watchers, for imposing this responsibility on me. Because the seeming had always been an activity with rules, a discipline to keep the anarchy at bay, and the anarchy inside me was at this moment in full cry:

Emma! How in God's name did he spirit you this far down the road?

Larry! You manipulative, vengeful, thieving bastard.

Both of you! What the hell are you up to, and why?

Cranmer! You're not a murderer! You can walk tall! You're clean!

I WAS a fool.

A raging, furious, overcontrolled fool, even if I was a fool set free. I had imagined myself terribly in love, and admitted a viper to my life.

Adopted, spoiled, served, anointed her, doted on her idiosyncrasies. Lavished jewels and freedom on her, made her my clotheshorse and my love object, my woman to end all women, icon, goddess, daughter, and, as Larry would say, slave. Loved her for her love of me, for her spells of gravitas and laughter; for her frailty and promiscuity and for the trust she placed in my protection. And all this on the strength of *what?* On what impulse, beyond the dewy longings of a late developer?

In my new, unfettered fury, a veritable windstorm of unreason took possession of me: she was a trap, a honey trap, foisted on me by a conspiracy of my enemies! I, Cranmer, evader, closet romantic, veteran of a raft of futile love affairs, had fallen cloak-over-dagger for the oldest trick in the book!

She was a setup from the first day! By Larry. By Checheyev. By Zorin. By the two of them, the three of them together, the four of them!

But *why?* To what end? To use me as cover? Honeybrook as cover? It was too absurd.

Ashamed of falling prey to such wayward, unprofessional imaginings, I drew back from them and looked for other ways to stoke my burgeoning paranoia.

What did I know of her? On my own insistence, nothing, except what she had cared to tell me or, on Sundays, tell Larry in my hearing. Merriman's doggy bag still lay behind its curtain in my priesthole, unread, gathering dust, a symbol of my lover's integrity.

An Italian name.

A dead father.

An Irish mother.

A drifting, dilettante childhood.

An English boarding school.

Studied music in Vienna.

Gone east, gone mystic, espoused every softheaded cause known to the hippie trail, gone to the devil.

Come home, drifted again, studied more music, composed it, arranged it; cofounded something called the Alternative Chamber Group, introducing the traditional instruments of the new world to the classical music of the old—or was it the other way round?

Got bored, attended a summer course at Cambridge, read or didn't read the comfortable words of Lawrence Pettifer on the degeneracy of the West. Returned to London, gave herself to anyone who asked nicely. Scared herself, met Cranmer, appointed him her willing, doting, blinded protector.

Met Larry. Vanished. Reappeared with hair up, calling herself Sally and swinging her legs at Jamie Pringle.

My Emma. My false dawn.

WE ARE naked, playing. She is arranging her black hair round my shoulders.

"Shall I call you Timbo?"

"No."

"Because Larry does?"

"Yes."

"I love you, you see. So naturally I'll call you anything you want. I'll call you Hey You, if you want. I'm completely flexible."

"Tim will do nicely. Just Tim. And yes, you are completely flexible."

WE ARE lying in front of the fire in her bedroom. She has hidden her head in my neck.

"You're a spy, aren't you?"

"Of course. How did you guess?"

"This morning. Watching you read your mail."

"You mean you *saw* the secret ink?"

"You don't put things in wastepaper baskets. Anything to be thrown away gets put in a plastic bag and taken to the incinerator. By you."

"I'm a very young wine grower. I was born six months ago when I met you."

But a germ of suspicion has been planted. Why was she watching me? Why was she thinking about me that way? What has Larry put into her head that causes her to put her protector under close surveillance?

I HAD reached my club. In the hall, old men were reading stock prices. Someone greeted me, Gordon someone: Gordon, marvellous, how's Prunella? Settling into a leather armchair in the smoking room, I stared into an unreadable newspaper while I listened to the murmurs of men who thought their murmurs mattered. The seasonal fog lapped at the long sash windows. Charlie, the Nigerian porter, came round to switch on the reading lamps. Outside in Pall Mall my gallant band of watchers were stamping their feet in doorways and envying the Friday commuters going home for the weekend. I could see them clearly in my other mind. I sat in the smoking room till dusk, not reading but seeming. The grandfather clock chimed six. Not a retired admiral stirred.

"LARRY really believes, doesn't he?" she is saying.

A Sunday evening. We are in the drawing room. Larry left ten minutes ago. I have poured myself a large Scotch and am slumped in my armchair like a boxer between rounds.

"What in?" I ask.

Ignored.

"I never met an Englishman who believes before. Most of them just say 'on the one hand and on the other hand' and don't do anything. It's as if the middle bits of his engine had been taken out."

"I still don't get it. *What* does he believe?"

I have annoyed her.

"Never mind. You obviously weren't listening."

I take another pull of Scotch. "Perhaps we hear different things," I say.

What did I mean by that? I wondered as I gazed through the lace-curtained windows of the smoking room at the smouldering pink night. What did I hear that Emma didn't, when Larry did his material for her, sang his political arias, excited her, drew her out, shamed her and forgave her, drew her out a little more? I was listening to Larry the great seducer, I decided, replying to my own question. I was thinking that my prejudices were leading me astray, that Larry was far smarter than I had ever been at stealing hearts. And that for twenty years I had harboured a very one-sided delusion about who, in the great Cranmer-Pettifer standoff, was running whom.

After that, while the coal fire in the smoking room burned lazily in the grate, I fell to wondering whether Larry, by some occult means I had yet to understand, had almost engineered his murder. And whether, if I had succeeded in delivering the fatal blow instead of pulling back from it, I would have been doing him a favour.

THE PINK fog that I had observed through the windows of my club thickened as my cab began its ascent of Haverstock Hill. We were entering Emma's badland. It began, so far as I had ever been able to establish, around Belsize Village and extended to Whitestone Pond in the north, Kentish Town to the east, and Finchley Road to the west. Whatever lay between was enemy territory.

What Hampstead was supposed to have done to her she never told me, and I, out of respect for the sovereignty that mattered so deeply to us both, never asked. From things she let slip, I had a picture of her being passed from hand to hand by intellectual princelings older and less ethereal than herself. Quality journalists loomed large in her bestiary. Shrinks of whatever sex were the pits. There was a time when I had imagined my poor beauty wading repeatedly out of her depth and too often nearly drowning as she lashed back to shore.

The surgery was a former Baptist church. A brass plate on the gatepost celebrated Arthur Medawi Dass and his many learned qualifications. A notice board in the waiting room offered aromatherapy, Zen, and vegetarian bed-and-breakfast. The receptionist had gone home. A fraught-faced woman in green sat in Emma's chair. I suppose I kept looking at her, because she blushed. But what I saw was not a woman in green but Emma in her guise of tragic heroine on the evening we first met.

DRESSED to snare. Not *decently* dressed, as for Pringle's bank. Not swinging her legs at me, though I do recognise that, even hunched in pain, she is a tall girl, and a very pretty one, and that her legs are remarkably good. A demure skullcap pulls her black hair free of her forehead. Her eyes are stoically averted. Her clothes part Salvation Army, part Edith Piaf on the stomp. A long jute skirt, black, a waif's black boots. A tabby woollen waistcoat vaguely of the outback. And to protect her pianist's hands, fingerless knitted gloves, black and slightly frayed.

My back is really acting up. Hot snakes from head to toe. Yet as I covertly examine her, her plight matters more to me than my own. Her pain is too old for her, too ugly. It makes her too much the governess and not enough the rascal. I want to find the best doctors for her, the warmest beds. I catch her eyes again. Her pain makes her faster to relate, I realise: more attaching than a beautiful young woman would normally permit herself to be. The old tactician in me urgently considers his options. Offer sympathy? It is already implicit, since we are fellow sufferers. Play the veteran—ask her whether this is her first time here? Better not to patronise her. With girls being what they are these days, she may be more of a veteran at twenty-something than you are at forty-seven. I plump for droll humour.

"You look really awful," I say.

The eyes still far away. The gloved hands linked in mutual consolation.

But oh, glory, suddenly she is smiling!

A raffish, twenty-two-carat smile is shining full-beam at me across the room, triumphing over vinyl seats, white striplights, and two bad backs. And I notice that her eyes are smoky blue, like pewter.

"Well, thanks a lot," she says in the fashionably discoloured English of the modern young. "That's just what I wanted someone to tell me."

And we have not exchanged a dozen more lines before it is clear to me that hers is the most gallant smile in London. For imagine: this very night, while she waits to be released from her agony, she is missing the first professional engagement of her musical career! If it weren't for her back, she would even now be seated in a concert hall in Wimbledon, listening to her own arrangement of folk and tribal music from around the world!

"Is it a recurrent thing," I ask, "or have you just ricked it or sprained it or something? It can't be *my* sort of thing at *your* age."

"The police did it."

"Which police? Good Lord."

"Some mates of mine were going to be evicted from a squat. A bunch of us went round to picket the building. A great big copper tried to pick me up and put me in a van, and my back just *went*."

My customary respect for authority evaporated. "But that's awful. You should sue him."

"Well, he should sue me really. I bit him."

And I fall right in, eyes wide shut. I swallow every beguiling word. I cast her as one of the world's rare untarnished souls. I do everything that is expected of a five-star sucker. Right down to promising her the best dinner in London as soon as she is mended, in trivial recompense for her misfortune.

"Do we get seconds?" she asks.

"As many as you like."

To my amazement she is not even a vegetarian.

OURS IS scarcely a whirlwind romance—why should it be? From my very first sighting of her, I know that she is of neither the age nor the category from which my usual conquests are selected: the compliant female colleague or senior secretary; the sporting adulteress of the English country round. She is young. She is intelligent. She is uncharted waters. She is risk. And it is years, if ever, since Cranmer has stepped outside the limits of his self-confinement, played the brave game, waited impatiently for evening, lain awake till dawn.

Does she have a stable of us? I wonder: older men who collect her from her flat, drive her to some makeshift concert hall in London's outer reaches—one night a disused theatre in Finchley, next week a gymnasium in Ruislip or someone's private drawing room in Ladbroke Grove—then perch in the back row, listening to her peculiar music in loyal rapture before taking her to dinner? And over dinner talk her up if she is low, and down if she is high, finally to leave her on her doorstep with no more than a brotherly peck on the cheek and a promise to do the same next week?

"I'm such a *tart*, Tim," she confides to me over our splendid dinner at Wilton's. "I walk into a crowded room, people look at me, and I start flirting with the entire field. The next thing is, I'm stuck with someone who looked okay in the window but is an absolute *pill* when you get him home!"

Is she deliberately provoking me? Is she romancing? Is she urging me to try my luck? Surely I can't be a worse bet than some wet-jawed Hampstead banker of thirty with a Porsche? Yet how do I know it's not a bluff—and if I declare myself and she rejects me, what will become of our relationship? Is she mad? Certainly her erratic path through life has a flavour of madness, even if it's one I envy: a wild dash from London to Khartoum on the off chance of bumping into this amazingly dishy Italian she spoke to once for thirty seconds in Camden Lock; submerging herself for six months in some ashram in Central India; walking across the Darien Gap from Panama to Colombia in her search for the music of the Somebodies; biting an officer of the law—unless of course the bitten policeman is another instance of her romancing. As to her heedless espousal of causes, it's a caricature of every Sunday columnist who arrogates to himself the conscience of the chattering classes. Yet why *should* I mock her for refusing to eat Turkish figs because look what they're doing to the Kurds? Or Japanese fish because look what they're doing to the whales? What was so risible—so un-English—about conducting your life according to principles, even if, in my jaded judgment, such principles were ineffectual?

Meanwhile I stalk her, imagine her, try to second-guess her, and I wait: for her encouragement, for the spark that never quite flies, unless you count the moments when, in the midst of one of our brother-sister evenings, she reaches out her hand and lays it along my cheek, or rubs her knuckles up and down my fellow sufferer's back. Only once does she ask me what I do for a living. And when I say Treasury:

"Whose side are you on, then?" she enquires, her dimpled jaw stuck forward in challenge.

"None. I'm a civil servant."

This won't do for her at all.

"You can't be *no* side, Tim. That's like not existing. We have to have an object of faith. Otherwise we're not defined."

One day she asks me about Diana: what went wrong?

"Nothing. It was wrong before we married and it stayed wrong afterwards."

"So why did you get married?"

I suppress my irritation. Past mistakes in love, I want to tell her, can no more be explained than rectified. But she is young and still believes, I suppose, that everything has an explanation if you look hard enough for it.

"I was just bloody stupid," I reply with what I hope is disarming frankness. "Come on, Emma. Don't tell me *you* haven't made a fool of yourself a few times. You keep *telling* me you have."

To which in a rather lofty way she smiles, and I, in a fit of secret anger, find myself comparing her with Larry. You beautiful people are exempt from life's difficult tests, aren't you? I want to tell her. You don't have to try so hard, do you? You can sit there and judge life instead of being judged by it.

But my bitterness, or whatever it is, has got through to her. She takes my hand in both of hers and presses it thoughtfully to her lips while she studies me. Is she wise? Is she plain dumb? Emma defies these categories. Her beauty, like Larry's, is its own morality.

And the next week we are the same old friends again, which is how things continue until the day Merriman calls me to his office and tells me that Cold Warriors cannot be recycled and that I may with immediate effect put myself out to pasture in Honeybrook. But instead of the conventional despondency that should overcome me on hearing my sentence, I am conscious only of a heedless vigour. Merriman, you've got it right for once! Cranmer is free! Cranmer has paid his dues! From today and for the rest of his life, Cranmer, against all previous principle, will follow Larry's advice. He will leap before he looks. Instead of giving he will take.

7

But Cranmer will do more than take. He will go small, go country, go free. He will remove himself from the complexities of the big world, now that the Cold War is won and over. Having helped secure the victory, he will with dignity leave the field to the new generation that Merriman speaks of so warmly. He will literally harvest the peace to which he has himself contributed: in the fields, in the soil, in rustic simplicity. In decent, structured, overt human relationships he will finally savour the freedoms he has defended these twenty-something years. Not selfishly, not by any means. To the contrary, he will engage in many socially beneficial acts: but for the microcosm, the small community, and no longer for the so-called national interest, which these days is a mystery even to those best placed to cherish it.

And this amazing prospect, granted me from such an improbable quarter, goads me into an act of magnificent irresponsibility. I choose the Grill Room at the Connaught, my shrine for great occasions. If I had acted with more forethought I would have opted for somewhere humbler, for I recognise too late that I have overtaxed her wardrobe. Never mind. Enough of forethought. If she ever comes to me, I shall dress her from top to toe in gold!

She listens to me carefully, though carefully is not how I speak—except that on the matter of my secret past, naturally my lips are sealed.

I tell her that I love her and fear for her night and day. For her talent, her wit, her courage, but particularly her fragility and what I might even call—since she has alluded to it herself—her perilous availability.

The truth speaks out of me as never before. Perhaps more than the truth, perhaps a dream of it, as I am carried away by the joy of being untactical after a lifetime of subterfuge. I am free to feel at last. All thanks to her. I wish to be everything to her a man can be, I tell her: first to protect and shelter her, not least from herself; then to advance her art, to be her friend, companion, lover, and disciple; and to provide the roof under which the disparate parts of her may be reconciled in harmony. To which end I am proposing that here and now she join me in my yeoman's life: in the emptiest quarter of Somerset, at Honeybrook, to walk the hills, grow wine, make music and love, and cultivate a Rousseau-like world in microcosm, but jollier; to read the books we always meant to read.

Amazed by my recklessness, not to mention eloquence—excepting of course in the delicate matter of how I have spent the last twenty-five years of my life—I listen to myself firing off my complete arsenal in one huge salvo. My love life, I say, has till tonight been a comedy of misalliances, the clear consequence of never allowing my heart to leave its box.

Am I quoting Larry again? Sometimes to my dismay I discover too late that he has fed me my best lines.

But tonight, I say, my heart is out and running, and I look back with shame at the too many wrong turnings I have taken. And surely—unless I misunderstand her—this could even be something which, despite the gap in our ages, we have in common: for is she not constantly confessing to me that she too is sick to death of small loves, small talk, small minds? As to her career, she will continue to have London at her doorstep. She will have her friends, she need give up nothing she cares about, she will be a free soul, never my prisoner in the tower. And with reservations, I believe myself, every word, every effusion. For what is cover for, if not to enable us to shed one life and grow another?

For a long while she seems unable to speak. Perhaps I have subjected her to a more impetuous onslaught than was to be decently expected of a staid bureaucrat selecting a mate for his retirement. Indeed, as I wait for her reaction, I begin to wonder whether I have spoken at all or merely been listening to the freed Sirens of my years of clandestine incarceration.

She is looking at me. Observing is a better word. She is reading my lips, my expressions of fear, adoration, earnestness, desire—whatever is in my face as I unbare myself to her. The pewter eyes are steadfast but aroused. They are like the sea waiting for thunder. Finally she commands my silence, though I am no longer speaking. She does this by laying a finger on my lips and leaving it there.

"It's all right, Tim," she says. "You're a good man. Better than you know. All you have to do now is give me a kiss."

In the Connaught? She must have seen my astonishment in my face, for at once she bursts out laughing, stands up, comes round the table, and without the smallest sign of embarrassment plants a long, explicit kiss on my lips, to the approval of an elderly wine waiter whose eye I inadvertently catch as she releases me from the clinch.

"On one condition," she adds sternly, sitting down.

"Name it."

"My piano."

"What about your piano?"

"Can I bring it? I can't arrange without a piano. That's how I do my tiddely-pom."

"I know how you do your tiddely-pom. Listen, bring six. Bring a fleet. Bring all the pianos in the world."

The same night we are lovers. The next morning, on winged feet, I race ahead to Honeybrook to call in the decorators. Do I once look back—do I pause to consider whether I have done the right thing? Whether I have paid too high a price for something that could have been more easily obtained? I do not. All my life I have ducked and weaved and peered round corners. From now on, with Emma as my precious ward, I intend to make my thoughts and actions one—in earnest of which, that very day I put through an urgent call to Mr. Appleby of Wells, purveyor of fine antique jewellery and furniture. And I commission him on the spot, expense no object, to comb the land for the sweetest, prettiest baby grand piano that was ever built of man: something of real age and quality, Mr. Appleby, and in a fine wood: I am thinking of satinwood; and while we're about it, do you still have that superb three-string pearl collar with the cameo clasp that I happened to spot in your window not a month ago?

MR. DASS was too shy to ask you to undress. If you were a man you faced him standing in your stockinged feet, stripped to the waist and clutching at your trousers while your braces dangled round your

thighs. Even when he had you lying on your stomach and was working the base of your spine, he exposed only the smallest margin of
flesh necessary to his purpose.

And Mr. Dass talked. In his caressing Oriental lilt. To inspire confidence and forestall intimacy. And sometimes, to stop you dozing
off, he asked you questions, though today, in the alertness of my new
condition, I would have wished to ask them for myself: Have you
seen them? Has she been here? Did he bring her? When?

"Have you been doing your exercises, Timothy?"

"Religiously," I lied in a drowsy voice.

"And how is the lady in Somerset?"

I was quick inside my seeming somnolence. He was speaking, as I
well knew, of a professional colleague of his in Frome, whom he had
recommended when I moved to Honeybrook. But I preferred a different interpretation.

"Oh, she's fine, thanks. Working too hard. Touring a lot. But fine.
You've probably seen her more recently than I have. When did she
last come to you?"

He was already laughing, explaining the misunderstanding. I
laughed with him. My affair with Emma was no secret from Mr. Dass
or anyone else. It had been my pleasure, in the early months of my
new life, to declare her to whoever would listen to me: Emma, my
live-in girl, my grand passion, my ward, nothing underhand.

"She's nowhere near as good as you are, Mr. Dass, I can you tell
that," I said, belatedly answering his question—and promptly threw
him into a flurry of embarrassment.

"Now, Timothy, that is not necessarily the case at all," he insisted
as he flattened his scalding palms on my shoulders. "Do you go to her
regularly? One session here and there and forget it for six months,
that's no good at all."

"Try telling that to Emma," I said. "She promised me she'd come
to you last week. I'll bet she never did."

But Mr. Dass for all my probing maintained an elliptical silence. I
kept drawing him out, I expect clumsily, for I was too much on edge.
Was she here yesterday? Today? Was he dodging my questions
because he was embarrassed to tell me she had come with Larry?
Whatever the cause, he would not be drawn. Perhaps he heard the
tension in my voice, or felt it in my body. Since Mr. Dass was blind,

there was no knowing what telltale messages might not come to him by way of his extrasensory ear or gently probing fingers.

"Next time I think you will give me more concentration, Timothy," he said sternly as I handed him my twenty pounds.

He unlocked his cash box, and my eye fell on the receptionist's appointments book lying beside the telephone. Steal it, I thought. Grab it and walk out. Then you can see for yourself whether she was here, who with, and when. But I could not have robbed blind Mr. Dass in order to spy on Emma if it had meant solving the mysteries of the cosmos.

STANDING on the pavement outside the surgery, I breathed heavily, feeling the thick fog sting my eyes and nostrils. Ten yards away, a parked car lurked in the short arc of a street lamp. My watchers? I strode to the car, slammed my hands on the roof, and yelled, "Anyone there?" The echo of my voice sped away into the fog. I marched twenty paces and swung round. Not a shadow dared approach me. Not one close sound came back at me from the fog's grey wall.

My quarry has changed, I remembered. I am no longer searching fearfully for signs of Larry's life or death. I am looking for both of them alive. For their conspiracy. For the reason why.

I hastened in and out of light cones, down side streets, under spiky overhanging trees. The muffled shapes of refugees flitted past me. I pulled on my raincoat. I found a flat cap in the pocket and pulled that on too. I have changed my profile. I am invisible. Three dogs were padding round each other in a melancholy changing of the guard. I stopped again, listening to nothing. I walked back a distance. My watchers have departed.

AFTER ten years, the house still scared me. Though I had escaped from it, I haunted it. Behind its grey walls, clad in the mauve half-mourning of wisteria, lay the remains of my dreams of lifelong happiness. When I had first removed myself to a humble flat further out of town, I would take detours on my journey to the Office rather than go past its door. And if necessity led me in its direction, I would fantasise about being hauled back inside to serve another sentence.

But after a time my revulsion gave way to a furtive curiosity, and the house attracted me despite myself. I would leave the tube a stop early and scurry across the Heath just to peer into its lighted windows. How do they live? What do they talk about, apart from me? Who was I when I lived there? That Diana had left the Office I knew only too well, for she had written Merriman one of her letters.

"Your darling ex has decided we're the Gestapo," he announces, seething with outrage. "And she's been bloody rude with it. Unconstitutional, incompetent, and unaccountable, that's us. Did you *know* you were nursing a viper to your breast?"

"That's just Diana. She lets fly."

"Well, what's she going to do about it? Wash her conscience in public, I suppose. Splash us all over the *Guardian*. Do you have *any* influence over her?"

"Do you?"

She's studying to become a psychotherapist, I hear on the grapevine. She's a marriage counsellor. She's lost weight. She attends yoga classes in Kentish Town. Edgar's an academic publisher.

I rang the bell. She opened the door at once.

"I thought you were Sebastian," she said.

It was on the tip of my tongue to apologise for being the wrong person.

WE PERCHED in the drawing room. I had forgotten how low the ceilings were. Perhaps Honeybrook had spoiled me. She was wearing jeans and a Cornish fisherman's top from our holidays at Padstow. It was faded blue and suited her. Her face was lighter than I remembered it and wider. Her complexion creamier. Her eyes less shaded. Edgar's books went from floor to ceiling. Most were on subjects I'd never heard of.

"He's on a seminar in Ravenna," she said.

"Oh, right. Great. Jolly nice." I had no natural voice in which to speak to her. No ease. I never had. "Ravenna," I repeated.

"I've got a patient coming in about half a minute, and I don't keep patients waiting," she said. "What do you want?"

"Larry's disappeared. They're looking for him."

"Who is?"

"Everyone. The Office, the police. Separately. The police can't be told of the Office connection."

Her face hardened, and I feared she was about to give me one of her diatribes on the need for us all to tell each other everything straight out, and how secrecy was not a symptom but a disease.

"Why?" she said.

"You mean why can't they be told or why's he disappeared?"

"Both."

Where did she get this power over me? Why do I stammer and placate her? Because she knows me too well—or never knew me at all?

"He's supposed to have stolen money," I said. "Scads of it. The police suspect me of being his accomplice. So does the Office."

"But you're not."

"Of course I'm not."

"So why've you come to me?"

She was sitting on the arm of a chair, back straight, hands folded on her lap. She had the professional listener's mirthless smile. There was drink on the sideboard, but she didn't offer me any.

"Because he's fond of you. You're one of the few women he admires and hasn't been to bed with."

"You know that, do you?"

"No. I assume it. It also happens to be the way he describes you."

She gave a superior smile. "Does it really? And you're prepared to take his word for it, are you? You're very trusting, Tim. Don't say you're getting soft in your old age."

I nearly flew at her. I was proposing to tell her I had always been soft, and she was the only one who hadn't noticed it; and I'd half a mind to add that I didn't give a brass farthing whether she slept with Larry or a two-toed sloth; and that the only reason Larry had taken the remotest interest in her was in order to get at me. Fortunately she came in ahead of me with another barb of her own:

"Who sent you, Tim?"

"No one. I'm flying solo."

"How did you come here?"

"Walked. Alone."

"I just have this picture of Jake Merriman waiting for you in a car down the road, you see."

"He isn't. If he knew I was here, he'd set the dogs on me. I'm practically on the run myself." The doorbell was ringing. "Diana. If you know anything about him—if he's been in touch—phoned, written, dropped by—if you know how to get hold of him—please tell me. I'm desperate."

"It's Sebastian," she said, and went to the hall.

I heard voices, and the sound of young feet going down the basement stairs. I realised in a fit of anachronistic indignation that she must have commandeered my old study and put her consulting room in it. She returned to her chair and sat on the arm exactly as before. I thought she was going to tell me to leave, for her face was firmly set. Then I realised she had reached one of her decisions and was about to communicate it.

"He's found what he was looking for. That's all I know."

"So what's he looking for?"

"He didn't say. And if he had said, I probably wouldn't tell you. Don't interrogate me, Tim; I won't have it. You dragged me into the Office for seven years, and that was bad enough. I don't subscribe to the ethic, and I don't accept the imperatives."

"I'm not interrogating you, Diana. I am asking you a question: What is he looking for?"

"His perfect note. That was his dream always, he said. To play one perfect note. He was always graphic; that's his nature. He telephoned. He'd found it. The note."

"When?"

"A month ago. I had the impression he was leaving for somewhere and saying his goodbyes."

"Did he say where?"

"No."

"Did he *suggest* where?"

"No."

"Was it abroad? Was it Russia? Was it somewhere exciting? New?"

"He gave absolutely no clue. He was emotional."

"You mean drunk?"

"I mean emotional, Tim. Just because you brought out the worst in Larry doesn't mean you have rights of ownership to him. He was emotional, it was late at night, and Edgar was here. 'Diana, I love you, I've found it. I've found the perfect note.' Everything was in place for him. He was together. He wished me to know that. I congratulated him."

"Did he tell you her name?"

"No, Tim, he wasn't talking about a woman. Larry's too mature to suppose we're the answer to everything. He was talking about self-discovery and being who he is. It's time you learned to live without him."

I had not expected to shout at her, and I had gone to some lengths till now to avoid doing so. But since she had appointed herself the high priestess of self-expression, there seemed no reason to restrain myself. "I'd *adore* to live without him, Diana! I'd give my entire bloody fortune to be rid of Larry and his works for the rest of my natural life. Unfortunately, we are inextricably involved with each other, and I have to find him for my own salvation and probably for his."

She had turned her smile to the floor, which I suspected was what she did when patients ranted at her. Her voice took on an extra sweetness.

"And how's Emma?" she enquired. "As young and beautiful as ever?"

"Thank you, she is well. Why do you ask? Did he talk about her too?"

"No. But you didn't either. I wondered why not."

I WAS climbing. In Hampstead if you are climbing you are exploring, and if you are descending you are going back to hell. Thinner air, thicker fog, pieces of brick mansion and Georgian façade. I entered a pub and drank a large Scotch and then another, then several more, remembering the night I returned to Honeybrook with the black light glowing in my head. If there were people in the pub I didn't see them. I walked again, feeling no different.

I entered an alley. To one side, a high brick wall. To the other, iron railings like spears. And at the further end a white wood church, its spire severed at the neck by fog.

I began cursing.

I cursed the goad of Englishness that had held me back and spurred me forward all my life.

I cursed Diana for stealing my childhood, and despising me while she did it.

I remembered all my agonising lurches for connection, the mismatches, and the return, time and again, to burning alone.

And after I had cursed the England that had made me, I cursed the Office for being its secret seminary, and Emma for luring me from my comfortable captivity.

And then I cursed Larry for shining a lamp into the cavernous emptiness of what he called my dull rectangular mind and dragging me beyond the limits of my precious self-mastery.

Above all I cursed myself.

I was suddenly desperate to sleep. The weight of my head was too great for me to carry. My legs were giving up on me. I thought of lying down on the pavement, but by good fortune a cab appeared, so instead I returned to my club, where Charlie the porter handed me a telephone message. It was from Detective Inspector Bryant, asking me to be so good as to call the following number at my earliest convenience.

No ONE sleeps in clubs. You smell the male sweat and cabbage, you listen to the snuffles of fellow inmates, and you remember school.

It is the night after Sixes Match, the annual festival of Winchester Football, a game so arcane that even experienced players may not know all the rules. The House has won. To be immodest, I have won, for it is Cranmer, the team captain and hero of the match, who has led the extraordinarily savage charge. Now, by tradition, the victorious six are feasting themselves in House Library while the New Boys stand on the table and regale them with songs and entertainment. Some New Boys sing badly and must have books buzzed at them to improve their voices. Others sing too well and must be cut down to size with gibes and flying bread. And one New Boy refuses to sing at all and must in the fullness of time be beaten; and that is Pettifer.

"Why didn't you sing?" I ask him later that night as he bends over the same table.

"It's against my religion. I'm a Jew."

"No you're not. Your father's in the Church."

"I've converted."

"I'll give you one chance," I say expansively. "What is the Notion for Winchester football?" It is the easiest test I can think of in the entire school vernacular, a gift.

"Jew baiting," he replies.

So I have no alternative but to beat him, when all he needed to say was Our Game.

8

THE WINDOW was too small to jump from, and too high to see from unless you had a yen for orange cranetips and banks of rain-soaked Bristol cloud. There were three chairs, and like the table they were bolted to the floor. A mirror was screwed to the wall. I assumed a one-way glass. The air was old, foul, and beery. A curled notice warning me of my rights trembled to the traffic five floors down.

Bryant sat one end of the table, I sat the other, Luck between us in his shirtsleeves. I wondered where his jacket was. On the floor to Luck's right lay an open briefcase in fake brown leather. In its partitions I spotted four rectangular packages of different sizes, each wrapped in black plastic and labelled. On the labels were references written with a red felt-tipped pen, such as *LP Exb* 27, which I took to mean Exhibit 27 in the case of Lawrence Pettifer. It was somehow natural to my attenuated state of mind that I found myself worrying less about Exhibit 27 than about the other twenty-six. And if twenty-seven, why only four of them in the briefcase?

There was no preamble. Nobody apologised for hauling me over to Bristol on a Saturday afternoon. Bryant had one elbow on the table and was resting his chin in his clenched fist like a man holding his beard. Luck fished a chipped black cassette recorder from the briefcase and dumped it on the table.

"Mind if we do this?"

Not waiting to hear whether I minded or not, he pressed the start switch, snapped his fingers three times, stopped the tape, and wound it back. So we listened to Luck's fingers snapping three times. He had acquired a shaving rash since I had last seen him, and bags under his little eyes.

"Does your friend Dr. Pettifer possess a *car*, Mr. Cranmer?" he demanded morosely. And beckoned at the recorder with his long head: speak to that thing, not to me.

"In London, Pettifer had a stable of cars," I replied. "They tended to be other people's."

"Whose?"

"I never asked. I was not familiar with his acquaintance."

"How about in Bath?"

"In Bath I have no idea what arrangements he made for his transport."

I was being dull and literal. I was much older than I had been a week ago.

"When did you last see him in a car?" said Luck.

"I would be pressed to remember."

Bryant had acquired a new smile. It had something of victory in it. "Oh, we'll *press* you if that's what you want, Mr. Cranmer, sir. Won't we, Oliver?"

"I understood that you had called me here to identify some property," I said.

"We did," Bryant agreed.

"Well, if it's his car you're talking about, I'm afraid it's most unlikely I can help you."

"Ever see him in a green or black Toyota, model circa 1990?" Luck asked.

"I am no expert in Japanese cars."

"Mr. Cranmer-sir is no expert in anything," Bryant explained to Luck. "He don't know nuffink, Officer. You can tell by all those big foreign books he's got in his mansion."

From the briefcase Luck handed me a thumbed police manual of line drawings of cars. As I turned its pages I saw the outlines of a 1989 blue Toyota Carina with the black flashing just like the one Larry had used for his positively last Sunday appearance at Honeybrook. Luck had seen it too.

"How about this one?" he was demanding, holding down the page with his bony finger.

"I'm afraid it doesn't ring a bell."

"Meaning no?"

"Meaning I do not recall him driving such a car."

"Then why does Mr. Guppy, your local postman, *recall* seeing a black or green Toyota driven by someone answering to Pettifer's description entering your drive just as he was coming out of the village *church* on a very hot Sunday, he thinks in July?"

I was sickened that they should have questioned John Guppy. "I have no idea why he should recall or not recall any such thing. And since the entrance to my drive is not visible from the church, I am inclined to doubt whether he did."

"The Toyota passed the church heading in *your* direction," Luck retorted. "It disappeared out of sight below the churchyard wall and did *not* come out the other end. The only turning it could have taken was into *your* drive."

"The car could have emerged without Mr. Guppy's noticing," I replied. "It could have stopped on the verge."

While Bryant looked on, Luck again foraged in his briefcase, extracted one of the packages and from it a plastic-covered bankbook from Larry's bank in London. It was such an old friend to me I almost smiled. I must have been through hundreds of them in my time, always trying to puzzle out what had happened to Larry's money, who he had given it to, which cheques he had forgotten to pay in.

"Did Pettifer ever make you a present of any *cash*, by any chance?" Luck asked.

"No, Mr. Luck, Dr. Pettifer never gave me any money."

"How about you giving him some?"

"I lent him small sums from time to time."

"How small?"

"Twenty here. Fifty there."

"You call that small, do you?"

"I'm sure it would feed a lot of starving children. It didn't keep Larry going long."

"Do you wish to change, in any shape or form, your story to the effect that you and Pettifer were never once involved in any type of business transaction?"

"It's the truth. Therefore I do not wish to change it."

"Page eight," he said, and tossed the bankbook at me.

I turned to page eight. It was the statement covering September 1993, which was the month when the Office paid Larry his hard-earned gratuity: £150,000, drawn on the account of Mills & Highborn, Trustees, of St. Helier, Jersey, wiping out an overdraft of £3,728.

"Do you have any idea *at all*," Luck demanded, "where, how, or why Dr. Pettifer got hold of one hundred and fifty thousand pounds sterling in September 1993?"

"None. Why not ask the people who made the payment?"

My suggestion annoyed him. "Mills and Highborn, thank you, is one of your old-fashioned, blue-chip, father-to-son Channel Islands law firms. Partners do *not* like talking to policemen and are *not* disposed to hand out customer information without a court order effective in the Islands. *However—*"

Upstaging him, Bryant placed his forearms on the table, squaring himself for combat.

"*However*," Luck repeated, "my researches *do* reveal that the same firm of trustees has also been paying Pettifer an annual *salary*, apparently on the instructions of certain foreign *publishing* and *film* companies registered in funny places like Switzerland. Does that surprise you at all?"

"I don't know why it should."

"Because the so-called salary payments were bogus, that's why. Pettifer never did the work. Foreign book royalties for books he didn't even *write*. Retainer money that didn't *retain* him. The entire structure was a figment from start to finish, and not a very competent one either, if you want my opinion. You haven't any *theories* to offer, I don't suppose, at all, have you, Mr. Cranmer, as to who might be going to all this trouble on the Doctor's behalf?"

I had none and was quick to say so. And I was appalled to confirm that the Top Floor's vaunted arrangements for paying Larry his Judas money could, as I had always suspected, be cracked open in a couple of days by one fanatical policeman with a desktop computer.

"There's a very funny thing about this firm Mills and Highborn which I might be permitted to share with you," Luck resumed with dinning sarcasm. "One of its *fringe* activities, so far as we can establish from certain sources, is channelling unofficial payments on behalf of Her Majesty's government." My world rocked. "By which I mean receiving large cash sums from Her Majesty's *Treasury* and turning them into other forms of disbursement"—sticking out his jaw at me on the word *Treasury*—"such as bribes for foreign potentates, such as slush funds for defence contracts and other so-called grey areas of government spending. You wouldn't know anything about that side of things, would you? Mr. Bryant and myself were somewhat enchanted by the coincidence, you see, of you being in Treasury and British government funds being siphoned off to Pettifer's Channel Islands benefactors."

In my wildest nightmares it had not occurred to me that Pay & Allowances Section could be so crass as to use the Larry laundromat for other, unrelated clandestine operations, thus multiplying to infinity the risk of compromising Larry and anybody else on the payroll.

"I'm afraid all this is far beyond me," I said.

"Maybe you'll tell us what *isn't* beyond you, then," Bryant suggested coarsely. "You being a high-ranking Treasury gentleman, which is about all we're allowed to know about you."

"I've no idea what you are trying to imply."

"Imply? Me? Oh, nothing, nothing, Mr. Cranmer-sir. That would be above my station. Very heady stuff, Treasury slush money, they tell me. Well, I can understand that. After all, if you're slipping a few million to some Arab shyster for helping you flog off your clapped-out fighter planes, why not slip yourself a few bob for being an English gentleman? Or slip it to your accomplice, better still?"

"That's a scandalous and totally untrue allegation."

"Page thirteen," Luck said.

"NOTICE anything?" Luck asked.

It was hard not to. Page thirteen of Larry's bankbook covered the month of July 1994. Until the twenty-first of that month Larry's current account stood at upwards of £140,000. On the twenty-second Larry had withdrawn £138,000, leaving £2,176 to his credit.

"What do you make of it?"

"Nothing. He probably bought a house."

"Wrong."

"He invested it. What do I care?"

"On the twenty-second of July, *having* advised the manager of his intention by telephone two days before, Dr. Pettifer drew the *entire* sum of one hundred and thirty-eight thousand pounds in cash across the counter of his *bank*, in brown envelopes of twenty-pound notes. He refused to accept fifties. He had failed to bring a *container*, so the cashier had a whip round among the girls till one of them produced a Safeways carrier *bag*, into which the envelopes were stashed. The next day he paid one thousand pounds cash to his landlady and settled four outstanding bills, including his wine bill. The destination of the remainder of the cash—totalling one hundred and thirty thousand pounds precisely—is as of now *unknown*."

Why? I was thinking stupidly. What logic is at work here, when a man who is swindling the Russian Embassy of thirty-seven millions has to empty his own bank account for a hundred and thirty thousand? For whom? For what?

"Unless he gave it to *you*, of course, Mr. Cranmer," Bryant proposed from the head of the table.

"Or unless it was yours in the first place," Luck suggested.

"Not legally, of course," said Bryant. "But we're not talking legal, are we? More the thieves' code. You fiddled it. The Doc banked it. He was your winger. Your accomplice. Right?"

I disdained to reply, so he continued in his tone of laboured knowingness.

"You're a money bug, aren't you, Mr. Cranmer, sir? Magpie is what I like to call them. You've got a lot, but you want more. Way of the world, isn't it? You sit there in the Treasury all day, or you did. You see these big piles of money going here, there, and everywhere, and a lot of them doing no good, I dare say. And you say to yourself: 'Now, Timothy, wouldn't a little of that be better in my pocket than in theirs?' So you fiddle a bit. And no one notices. So you fiddle another bit. A bigger bit. And still no one notices. So as a good businessman you expand. Well, we can't stand still, can we, not in this day and age. No one can. Not human nature, is it? Not after Mrs. Thatcher. And one day an opportunity arises, let us say, for you to break into a certain foreign market. A market where you speak the lingo and have the expertise. Like Russia, for instance. So you pull the big one. You and the Doctor and a certain foreign gentleman of his acquaintance who calls himself Professor. Experts in your ways, all of you. But Mr. Cranmer-sir is the mastermind. The Mister Big. He has the class. The cool. The rank. Am I getting warm at all, sir? You can tell us. We're little people, aren't we, Oliver?"

When you are accused of monstrous things, nothing sounds so feeble as the truth. I had devoted my working life to protecting my country from its predators. Now I was being cast as a predator myself. I had never misappropriated a single penny entrusted to me. Now I was being accused of squirrelling large sums in the Channel Islands and paying them to myself by way of my former agent. Yet as I heard myself protest my innocence, I sounded like any other guilty man. My voice slipped and became strident, my fluency deserted me, I became as unconvincing to myself as to my accusers. *Well, that's the way of it*, I heard Merriman say: *punished for the crimes we never committed while we get away with grand larceny somewhere else.*

"We're only thinking *aloud*, Mr. Cranmer, sir," Bryant explained with elephantine sweetness, when they had heard me out. "No *charges* are being preferred, not at this stage. It's collaboration we're after, not warm bodies. *You* tell us where to find what *we're* looking for, *we* put it back where it came from, everybody goes home and has a nice glass of Honeybrook wine. Know what I mean?"

"No."

A disjointed interlude followed while Luck produced earlier bankbooks, which differed only in degree from the first. The pattern was clear. Whenever Larry had any substantial money in his account, he drew it in cash. What he did with it remained a mystery. There was a monthly season ticket, still current, for the journey between Bath and Bristol, cost £71. They claimed to have found it in a drawer of the desk in his lecture room. No, I said, I had no idea why Larry should wish to be so much in Bristol. Perhaps for the theatres or the libraries or the women. For a happy moment Luck appeared becalmed. He sat as if winded, mouth open, shoulders rising and falling inside his sweaty shirtsleeves.

"Did Dr. Pettifer ever *steal* from you at all?" he asked, with that adamant sourness that made him such an unpleasant conversation partner.

"Of course not."

"Odd, that is. You don't have a very high opinion of him in other respects. Why are you so sure he wouldn't steal from you?"

The question was a trick, a prelude to some new onslaught. But not knowing what sort of trick, I had no option but to provide him with a straight answer.

"Dr. Pettifer may be many things, but I do not regard him as a thief," I said, and had scarcely spoken before Bryant was yelling at me. I thought at first it was a tactic to wake me from my absorption. Then I saw him waving a padded envelope in the air above his head.

"What do you regard this lot as, then, Mr. Cranmer, sir?"

I heard it before I saw it: Emma's antique jewellery, rattling and skidding down the table at me, every piece I had bought for her since my first timid offering of a pair of Victorian jet earrings, graduating by way of the three-string pearl collar to the intaglio necklace, the emerald ring, the garnet pendant, and the gold-backed cameo that could have been of Emma herself—all slewed down the table at me like so much dross by the inexpert hand of Detective Inspector Bryant.

I was standing. The jewels lay along the table like a trail, and the trail ended with me. I must have got up quickly, because Luck was standing also, blocking my path to the door. I picked up the intaglio necklace and ran it fearfully through my fingers as if to confirm it was unharmed, though in my mind it was Emma I was touching. I turned her cameo over, then her brooch, her pendant, finally the ring. A babble of Office buzzwords went through my head: linkage . . . spillage . . . interconsciousness. *Keep her separate from Larry*, I was telling myself. *Whatever they do or threaten: Emma stays separate from Larry.*

I sat down.

"Recognise any of these items at all by any chance, do we, Mr.-Cranmer-sir?" Bryant was asking benignly, like a conjuror who had performed a clever trick.

"Of course I do. I bought them."

"Who from, sir?"

"Appleby of Wells. How did you come by them?"

"On what precise *date* did you purchase them, if you don't mind, from Messrs. Appleby of Wells? We do know you're a trifle weak on dates overall, but—"

He got no further. I had driven my fist onto the table so hard that the jewellery danced and the tape recorder rose in the air and turned belly-up as it landed.

"Those jewels are Emma's. Tell me where you got them from. Stop taunting me!"

It is a rare thing when emotion and operational necessity coincide, but they had done so now. Bryant had shed his smile and was studying me with calculation. Perhaps he thought I was about to offer him my confession in exchange for her. Luck sat upright, craning his long head at me.

"*Emma?*" Bryant repeated thoughtfully. "I don't think we know an *Emma*, do we, Oliver? Who would Emma be, sir? Perhaps you could enlighten us."

"You know very well who she is. The whole village knows. Emma Manzini is my companion. She's a musician. The jewels are hers. I bought them for her and gave them to her."

"When?"

"What does it matter when? Over the last year. On special occasions."

"Foreign, is she?"

"She had an Italian father, who is dead. She is British by birth and was brought up in England. Where did you find them?" I resorted to a wistful fiction. "I'm her common-law husband, Inspector! Tell me what's going on."

Bryant had put on horn-rimmed spectacles. I don't know why they should have shocked me, but they did. They seemed to drain his eyes of the last dregs of human kindliness. His moth-eaten moustache had turned downward in an angry sneer.

"And is Miss Manzini in any way friendly with our Dr. Pettifer at all, Mr. Cranmer, sir?"

"They've met. What does it matter? Just tell me where you got her jewellery from!"

"Prepare yourself for a shock, Mr. Cranmer, sir. We obtained your Emma's jewels from Mr. Edward Appleby of the Market Place in Wells, the selfsame gentleman as sold you the said treasures in the first place. He tried to contact you, but your phone had gone funny. So, fearing the matter might be urgent, he reported it to the Bath police, who, being somewhat short-handed at the time, took no further action." He had awarded himself the role of storyteller. "Mr. Appleby is doing his rounds of Hatton Garden, you see, calling on his jeweller friends, which is his way. All of a sudden one of them turns round and, knowing that Mr. Appleby deals in the antique variety of jewellery, offers him your Miss Manzini's necklace—the Roman number, what do they call it? By your left hand there."

"Intaglio."

"Thank you. And after offering Mr. Appleby the entirely-o, he offers him the whole works. Everything you see before you. Is that everything you bought for Miss Manzini, sir—the full collection?"

"Yes."

"And since all dealers know each other, Mr. Appleby asks him where he got the stuff from. The answer is a Dr. Pettifer of Bath. Twenty-two thousand pounds the Doctor obtained for his jewels. Family heirlooms they were, according to him. Inherited from his old mother, now alas passed on. That's a fair price for this lot, is it—twenty-two thousand pounds?"

"It was a trade price," I heard myself say. "They were insured for thirty-five."

"By you?"

"The jewels are recorded as being in Miss Manzini's possession. I pay the premiums."

"Has any claim been made at all to an insurance company for the loss of these jewels?"

"Nobody knew they were missing."

"You mean *you* didn't. Could the Doctor or Miss Manzini have made a claim on your behalf?"

"I don't see how. Ask the insurance company."

"Thank you, sir, I will," said Bryant, and wrote down the name and address from my diary. "The Doctor wanted cash for his old mother's legacy, but the shop in Hatton Garden couldn't do that for him," he resumed in his false-friendly voice. "Regulations, you see, sir. The best they could manage was a cheque made out to cash because he said he hadn't got a bank account. The Doctor then pops up the road and presents it at the jeweller's bank, collects his loot, and is seen by the jeweller no more. Left his full name behind, though; he had to. Verified by his driving licence, which is rather amusing, considering how many points it's got against it. Address Bath University. The jeweller rang the registrar's office for verification: yes, we have a Mr. Pettifer."

"When did all this happen?" I said.

How he loved to torture me with his knowing smiles. "That really bothers you, doesn't it," he said. "When. You can't remember dates, but you're always asking when." He made a show of relenting. "The Doctor flogged your lady's jewellery on July twenty-ninth, a Friday."

Which was roughly when she stopped wearing it, I thought. After Larry's public lecture, and the curry for two that did or didn't follow it.

"Where *is* Miss Manzini, by the way?" Bryant asked.

I had my answer prepared and delivered it with authority. "When last heard of, somewhere between London and Newcastle on a concert tour. She likes to travel with the group that plays her music. She's their guiding spirit. Where she is at this precise moment, I don't know. It's not our way to be in constant touch. I'm sure she will telephone me very soon."

Now it was Luck's turn to have his fun with me. He had opened another package, but it seemed to contain nothing but inky notes he had written to himself. I wondered whether he was married and where he lived—if he lived anywhere outside the shiny, disinfected corridors of his trade.

"Did Emma happen to *inform* you that her jewellery was missing at all?"

"No, Mr. Luck, Miss Manzini did not."

"Why not? Are you trying to tell us your Emma's been shy of thirty-five thousand quid's worth of jewellery for a couple of months and hasn't even bothered to *mention* it?"

"I'm saying Miss Manzini may not have noticed that the jewels were missing."

"And she's been *around*, has she, these last months? I mean around *you*. It's not that she's been touring all that time."

"Miss Manzini has been at Honeybrook throughout the entire summer."

"Nevertheless you did not have the smallest inkling that one day Emma *had* her jewellery, and the next day Emma was *without* it."

"None whatever."

"You didn't notice that she wasn't *wearing* the stuff, for instance? That might have been a clue, mightn't it?"

"Not in her case."

"Why not?"

"Miss Manzini is capricious, like most artists. One day she will appear in her finery, then whole weeks can go by when the notion of wearing something valuable is anathema to her. The reasons can be many. Her work—something has depressed her—she is in pain from her back."

My reference to Emma's back had produced a pregnant silence.

"Injured, was it, her back?" Bryant enquired solicitously.

"I'm afraid it was."

"Oh dear. How did that happen, then?"

"I understand she was manhandled while taking part in a peaceful demonstration."

"There could be two views about that, though, couldn't there?"

"I'm sure there could."

"Bitten any more policemen recently, has she?"

I refused to answer.

Luck resumed. "And you don't ask her: Emma, why aren't you wearing your ring? *Or* your necklace? *Or* your brooch? *Or* your ear-rings . . . for instance?"

"No, I don't, Mr. Luck. Miss Manzini and I don't speak to each other that way."

I was being pompous and knew it. Luck had that effect on me.

"All right. So you don't talk to each other," he blurted. "Same as you don't know where she is." He appeared to be losing his temper. "All right. In your highly personal, highly privileged Treasury opin-ion, how does your friend Dr. Lawrence Pettifer, in July this year, come to be flogging off your Emma's jewellery at two-thirds what *you* gave for it, to a *dealer* in Hatton Garden, claiming the jewels came from his mother, when in fact they came from *you*, via *Emma?*"

"The jewellery was Miss Manzini's to dispose of as she wished. If she had given it to the milkman I could not have raised a finger." I saw a means to strike at him and seized it gratefully. "But surely your Mr. Guppy has already provided you with your solution, Mr. Luck?"

"What's that supposed to mean?"

"Wasn't it July when Guppy claims he saw Pettifer approach my house? A Sunday? There's your burglar for you. Pettifer approaches the house and finds it empty. On Sundays there are no staff around. Miss Manzini and I have gone out for lunch. He forces the window, enters the house, goes to her apartment, and helps himself to the jewellery."

He must have guessed that I was teasing him, for he had coloured. "I thought you said Pettifer didn't steal," he objected suspiciously.

"Let's say you have given me reason to revise that opinion," I replied suavely as the tape recorder gave a choke and stopped rotating.

"Leave it like that a minute, will you, please, Oliver," Bryant ordered sweetly.

Luck had already reached out to change the tape. Now, somewhat ominously, I thought, he removed his hand and laid it beside its companion on his lap.

"Mr. Cranmer, sir."

Bryant was standing close beside me. He had cupped his hand on my shoulder in the traditional gesture of arrest. He was stooping, and his lips were not an inch from my ear. I had forgotten physical fear till now, but Bryant was reminding me of it.

"Do you know what this means, sir?" he asked me, very quietly, as he gave my shoulder a painful squeeze.

"Of course I know. Take your hand off me."

But his hand didn't budge. The pressure of it increased as he continued speaking.

"Because this is what I'm going to be doing to you, Mr. Cranmer, sir, unless I have a lot more of the collaboration I spoke about than I am getting from you at the present time. If you don't play ball with me very soon, I'm going to fake any pretext, bend any evidence, as the old song goes, and I'm going to make it my personal business to see you spend the remaining best years of your life looking at a very boring wall instead of at Miss Manzini. Did you hear that, sir? I didn't."

"I can hear you perfectly well," I said, trying in vain to shake off his hand. "Let go of me." But he held me all the more firmly.

"Where's the money?"

"What money?"

"Don't 'what money' me, Mr. Cranmer, sir. Where's the money you and Pettifer have been salting away in foreign bank accounts? Millions of it, the property of a certain foreign embassy in London."

"I've no idea what you're talking about. I have stolen nothing, and I am not in league with Pettifer or anybody else."

"Who's AM?"

"Who?"

"AM who's all over Pettifer's diary in his lodgings. Phone AM Brief AM Visit AM"

"I have absolutely no idea. Perhaps it means morning. And PM means afternoon."

I think in a different place he would have hit me, for he lifted his eyes to the mirror as if appealing for permission.

"Where's your pal Checheyev, then?"

"Who?"

"Don't give me bloody who again. Konstantin Checheyev is a Russian cultural gentleman, formerly of the Soviet, then Russian, embassy in London."

"I've never heard the name in my life."

"Of course you haven't. Because what you are doing to *me*, Mr. Cranmer, sir, is lying in your nasty upper-class teeth, whereas you should be assisting me in my *enquiries*." He squeezed my shoulder and pressed down on it at the same time, sending lines of pain shooting through my back. "Do you know what I think you are, Mr. Cranmer, sir? Do you?"

"I don't give a damn what you think."

"I think you're a very greedy gentleman with a lot of arrogant appetites to feed. I think you have a little friend called Larry. And a little friend called Konstantin. And a little gold digger called Emma, who you spoil rotten, who thinks the law's an ass and policemen are there to be bitten. And I think you play Mr. Respectable, and Larry plays your little lamb, and Konstantin sings along with some very naughty angels in the Moscow choir, and Emma plays your piano. What was that I heard you say?"

"I didn't speak. Get off me."

"I distinctly heard you insulting me. Mr. Luck, did you hear this gentleman using insulting language to a police officer?"

"Yes," said Luck.

He shook me hard and shouted in my ear. *"Where is he?"*

"I don't know!"

The pressure of his fist did not relent. His voice dropped and became confiding. I could feel his hot breath in my ear.

"You are at a crossroads in your life, Mr. Cranmer, sir. You can play ball with Detective Inspector Bryant, in which case we shall turn a blind eye to many of your misdeeds, I'm not saying all. Or you can go on leading us up the garden path, in which case we shall not exclude from our enquiries any person who is precious to you, be she never so young and musical. Were you shouting filth at me again, Mr. Cranmer, sir?"

"I said nothing at all."

"Good. Because your lady shouts it, according to our records. And her and me are going to be chatting quite a lot in the near future, and I won't have bad manners, will I, Oliver?"

"No," said Luck.

With a final squeeze, Bryant released me.

"Thank you for coming to Bristol, Mr. Cranmer. Expenses downstairs if you wish to claim, sir. Cash."

Luck was holding the door open for me. I think he would have preferred to smash it into my face, but his English sense of fair play restrained him.

WITH THE humiliating imprint of Bryant's fist burning my shoulder, I stepped into the grey evening drizzle and struck a vigorous course up the hill for Clifton. I had booked rooms in two hotels. The first was the Eden, four stars and a nice view down the Gorge. There I was Mr. Timothy Cranmer and heir to Uncle Bob's old Sunbeam, pride of the car park. The second was a seedy motel called the Starcrest on the other side of town. There I was a Mr. Colin Bairstow travelling representative and pedestrian.

Seated now in my elegant room at the Eden overlooking the Gorge, I ordered a minute steak and a half bottle of Burgundy and asked the switchboard to put through no calls till morning. I dropped the steak into the shrubbery below my window, poured the wine down the sink—all but a small glass, which I drank—placed the tray and a spare pair of shoes outside my door, hung up the Do Not Disturb notice, and slipped down the fire stairs and out of the side entrance and walked.

From a call box I dialled the Office emergency number, using 7 as the final digit because it was a Saturday. I heard the sugared voice of Marjorie Pew.

"Yes, Arthur. How can we help you?"

"The police questioned me again this afternoon."

"Oh yes."

And oh yes to you, I thought.

"They've rumbled the payments to ABSOLOM through our friends in the Channel Islands," I said, using one of Larry's battery of code names. I imagined her typing up ABSOLOM on her screen. "They've unearthed a Treasury connection, and they think I've been siphoning off government funds and paying them to ABSOLOM as my accomplice. They've convinced themselves that this is the same trail that will lead them to the Russian gold."

"Is that all?"

"No. Some fool in Pay and Allowances has been crossing the wires. They've been using the ABSOLOM pipeline to pay other friends apart from ABSOLOM."

Either she was giving me one of her trenchant silences or she couldn't think of anything to say.

"I'm staying in Bristol tonight," I said. "The police may want to have another go at me tomorrow morning."

I rang off, mission accomplished. I had warned her that other sources might be at risk. I had fed her my excuse for not returning to Honeybrook. The one thing she would not be doing was rushing to the police to check my story.

COLIN BAIRSTOW's bed at the motel was a lumpy divan with a glittering orange counterpane. Stretched on it full length, with the telephone at my side, I stared at the grimy cream ceiling and considered my next step. From the moment I had received Bryant's telephone message at my club, I had placed myself on operational alert. From Castle Cary station I had driven to Honeybrook, where I collected my Bairstow escape pack: credit cards, driving licence, cash, and passport, all crammed into a scuffed attaché case with old labels testifying to the salesman's wandering life. Arriving in Bristol, I had deposited Cranmer's Sunbeam at the Eden and Bairstow's briefcase in the manager's safe here at the motel.

From the same briefcase I now extracted a ring-backed address book with a speckled fawn gazing from the cover. How much had Office routine changed with the move to the Embankment? I wondered. Merriman hadn't changed. Barney Waldon hadn't. And if I knew the police, any procedure that had worked for twenty-five years was likely to be working for the next hundred.

Heart in mouth, I dialled the Office's automated switchboard and, guided by the numbers in the address book, keyed myself into the Whitehall internal network. Five more digits gave me Scotland Yard's intelligence liaison room. A plummy male voice answered. I said I was North House, which used to be the code name for my section. The plummy voice manifested no surprise. I said the reference was Bunbury, which used to be the code name of the section chief. The plummy voice said, "Who do you wish to speak to, Bunbury?" I asked for Mr. Hatt's department. Nobody had ever met Mr. Hatt, but if he existed, he had charge of vehicle information. I heard rock music in the background, then a breezy girl's voice.

"It's Bunbury from North House with a boring one for Mr. Hatt," I said.

"That's all right, Bunbury. Mr. Hatt likes being bored. This is Alice. What can we be doing you for?"

For two decades I had kept track of Larry's cars. I could have recited the number of every wreck he had ever shown up in, plus colour, age, decrepitude, and luckless owner. I gave Alice the number of the blue Toyota. I had barely spoken the final letter before she was reading the computer printout.

"Anderson, Sally, 9A Cambridge Street, off Bellevue Road, Bristol," she announced. "Want the dirt?"

"Yes, please."

She gave it to me: insurance, owner's phone number, car's visible characteristics, first registered, expiry date, no other cars registered in this name.

At the motel desk, a spotty boy in a red dinner jacket gave me a thumbed street map of Bristol City.

9

I TOOK a cab to Bristol Temple Meads railway station and walked from there. I was in an industrial desert made sumptuous by the night. Heavy lorries tore past me, spewing oily mud and plucking at my raincoat. Yet a tender haze hung over the city valley, moist stars filled the sky, and a languid full moon drew me up the hill. As I walked, lane upon lane of orange-lit railway line opened below me, and I remembered Larry and his season ticket, Bath to Bristol, £71 a month. I tried to imagine him as a commuter. Where was business? Where was home? Anderson, Sally, at 9A Cambridge Street. The lorries had deafened me. I couldn't hear my footsteps.

The road, which had begun as a viaduct, joined itself to the hillside. The summit moved to my right. Directly above me stood a terrace of flat-fronted cottages. A red-brick wall made a battlement round them. *Up there*, I thought, remembering my map. *Up there*, I thought, remembering Larry's affection for abandoned places. I came to a roundabout, pressed the pedestrians' button, and waited for the motorised cavalry of England to come squealing and clanking to a halt. Gaining the other pavement, I entered a side street festooned with overhead cables. A serious black boy of about six was sitting on the doorstep of the Ocean Fish Bar Chinese Takeaway.

"Is this Cambridge Street? Bellevue Road?"

I smiled, but he didn't smile back. A bearded Druid in a baggy Irish cap stepped a little too carefully out of Robbins Off Licence. He carried a brown paper bag.

"Watch your feet, man," he advised me.

"Why?"

"You want Cambridge Street?"

"Yes."

"You're bloody near standin' on it, man."

Following his instructions, I walked fifty yards and turned right. The cottages were on one side only. On the other lay a platform of grass. Round the grass, in crinkle-crankle pattern, ran the brick parapet with red coping that I had seen from below. Playing the accidental tourist, I placed myself before it. From the station, the discontinued high roads of empire streamed into the darkness.

I turned and surveyed the cottages. Each had two windows upstairs, a flat roof, a chimney stack and television aerial. Each was painted a different pastel shade. Front doors to the left, bay windows to the right. In most, as my eye ran along the line of them, the bay window was lit, or a bedroom was lit, or a television flickered, or a phosphorescent doorbell glistened, and you felt a life behind the curtains. Only the last house stood in darkness, and it was 9A. Had the occupants fled? Had two lovers taken off their wristwatches and fallen asleep in one another's arms?

Deliberately, a person with no secrets, I linked my hands behind my back and, colonial style, prepared to inspect the ranks. I am an architect, a surveyor, a potential purchaser. I am a wine-growing Englishman of a certain class. Parked cars blocked the pavement. I took the centre of the road. No blue Toyota. No Toyota of any kind. I walked slowly, making a show of reading the house numbers. Shall I buy this one, or this one? Or all of them?

Sweat was running down my ribs. I'm not prepared, I thought. Not able, not trained, not armed, not brave. I've been too deskbound too long. After fear came a storm of guilt. He's here. Dead. He staggered back and died here. The murderer is about to discover the body. A guilty man has come to take his medicine. Then I remembered that Larry was alive again, and had been alive since Jamie Pringle had remembered the last grouse of the season, and my guilt crept back into its lair.

I had reached the end of the row. Number 9A was a corner house, as every safe house should be. The drawn curtains in the upper windows were orange and unlined. Pale light from the street lamp shone on their poor fabric. There was no light from inside.

Continuing my reconnaissance, I turned into the side street. Another upstairs window, unlit. A plastered wall. A side door. Crossing to the opposite pavement, I took a proprietary look up and down the street. A yellow cat stared back at me from behind a net curtain. Among the dozen cars parked each side of the street, one had a plastic cover to protect it from the weather.

Another controlled glance at the doorways, pavements, and parked cars. The shadows were not easy to read, but I could make out no human shape. With the toe of my right shoe I raised the plastic cover and saw the buckled rear bumper and familiar registration number of Larry's blue Toyota. It was one of the little tricks we taught on training courses, for the joes to forget the moment they returned to the real world: if you're worried about your car, put a cover over it.

The side door of the house had neither a handle nor a keyhole. Passing it on my way back, I gave it a furtive push, but it was locked or bolted from inside. A smear of chalk in the shape of an L ran across the centre panels. The lower stroke of the L tailed downward. I touched the chalk mark. It was wax based and resistant to rain. I turned the corner back into Cambridge Street, marched confidently up to the front door, and pressed the bell. Nothing happened. Electricity's cut off. Larry's way with bills. I gave the knocker a diffident tap-tap. It's Honeybrook on New Year's Eve, I thought as the din echoed inside the house: my turn to knock the happy lovers out of bed. I was acting boldly, nothing up my sleeve. But I was thinking seriously of the chalk mark.

I lifted the flap of the letter box and let it slap shut. I rapped on the bay window. I called, "Hey, it's me!"—more for the seeming than the being, for there were people going past me on the pavement. I wrenched at the sash window, trying to move it up and down, but it was locked. I was wearing leather gloves, and they reminded me of Priddy. Still at the bay, I put my face against the glass and by the light from the street lamp squinted inside. There was no entrance hall. The front door opened straight into the living room. I made out the ghostly shape of a portable typewriter on a desk and, below me to my left, a heap of mail, mostly bills and printed matter: Larry could step over them for weeks without a thought. I looked again and saw what I had half seen the first time: Emma's piano stool set in front of the typewriter. Finally, assuming I had by now attracted the interest of the neighbours, I did what legitimate people do in such cases: I took out my diary, wrote in it, tore the page out, and dropped it through the letter box. Then I walked off down the road to give their memories a rest.

I took a brisk walk round the block, keeping at the centre of the road because I didn't like the shadows, till I had reentered the street from the opposite end. I passed the side door a second time, looking not at the chalk mark but in the direction indicated by the tail of the L. L for Larry. L for Larry's tradecraft in the days when he and Checheyev exchanged their secret materials by way of dead-letter boxes and safety signals. In parks. In pub lavatories. In parking lots. In Kew Gardens. L for "I have filled the dead-letter box," signed Larry. The L converted to a C for "I have emptied it," signed CC. Back and forth, not once but more like fifty times in the four years of their collaboration: microfilm for you; money and orders for me; money and orders for you; microfilm for me.

The tail pointed downward, and it was strongly drawn. A defined tail. It ran diagonally towards my right foot, and at the toe of my right foot ran the skirting of the door, and underneath the skirting a flattened cigarette end protruded, and I suppose a very curious person might just have wondered quite how a cigarette end came to be flattened and wedged beneath the skirting of a door unless someone had deliberately stood on it and kicked it there; and the same person might also have remarked that the beam of the corner street light shone brightly onto the lower part of the door, so that once you were aware of the conjunction of the chalk mark and the cigarette end, you marvelled that there wasn't a great crowd of people round you, staring at the same thing.

I did not, however, possess Checheyev's physical dexterity; I could not achieve the lightning swing of the upper body that had put Jack Andover, our chief watcher, in mind of Welsh miners. So I did what middle-aged spies do the world over: I stooped and made a show of fastening my shoelace, while with one hand I pinched hold of the cigarette end, and of the string that was inside it, and I tugged: to be rewarded, after a further length of string, with the flat brass Yale door key that was attached to it. Then, with the key concealed in my hand, I stood up and walked confidently round the corner to the front door.

"They're on holiday, darling," a bass voice called from beside me.

I turned quickly, my rent-a-drool smile hoisted in readiness. A large blond-headed woman, backlit by the light of her own hall, was standing in the neighbouring doorway, dressed in what seemed to be a white nightgown and clutching a glass of something strong.

"I know," I said.

"*Feebs* is what he calls me. I'm Phoebe really. You were here before, weren't you?"

"That's right. I forgot to collect the key and had to go back and get it. I'll forget my own name next. Still, a holiday was what they needed, wasn't it?"

"*He* did," she said darkly.

My brain must have been working overtime, for I divined her meaning immediately. "Of course! Poor man," I cried. "I mean how was he looking? Better? On the mend? Or was he still all colours of the rainbow?"

But some sense of need-to-know held her back from further confidence. "What do you want, then?" she asked sullenly.

"It's what *they* want, I'm afraid. Sally's typewriter. More clothes. Practically anything I can carry."

"You're not a debt collector, are you?"

"Good Lord, no." I laughed and took a couple of paces towards her so that she could see what a trustworthy fellow I was. "I'm his brother. Richard. Dick. The respectable one. They phoned me. Would I put together some stuff for them? Take it up to London. He'd had this accident. Fallen downstairs, he said. Poor love, if it's not one thing, it's another. Did they manage to leave together? I gather it was all rather rushed."

"There's no accidents round here, darling. Everything's deliberate." She giggled at her own wit. So did I, elaborately. "He went first, she followed him, I don't know why." She took a sip from her glass, but kept her eyes on me. "I don't think I like you going in, you see. Not while they're in France. I think I'm worried."

Stepping back into her house, she slammed the front door. A moment later a wet crack like a training grenade split the air as an upper window of the house was flung open and a broad-headed hairy man in an undershirt leaned out.

"You! Come 'ere! You're Terry's brother, are you?"

"Yes."

"Dick, right?"

"Dick is correct."

"Know all about him, do you?"

"Pretty much."

"What's his favourite football team, then, Dick?"

"Moscow Dynamo," I replied, before I had given myself time to think, for soccer was one of Larry's many incongruous obsessions. "And Lev Yashin was the greatest goalkeeper of all time. And the greatest goal ever scored was by Ponedelnik for Russia against Yugoslavia in 1960."

"Bloody hell."

He disappeared, and a delay followed, presumably while he conferred with Phoebe. Then he was back and smiling.

"I'm Arsenal myself. Not that he minded. Here. How'd he get his black eye, then? I've seen some shiners, but he was classic. 'What happened?' I says to him. 'She close her legs too soon?' Walked into a door, he says. Then Sally turns round and says it was a car smash. You don't know who to believe these days, do you? Want a hand at all?"

"Maybe later. I'll give you a shout, if I may."

"I'm Wilf. He's a mad bugger, but I like him."

The window slammed shut.

I CLOSED the front door behind me and stepped round the heap of mail on the floor. In a spurt of futile optimism I flipped the light switch, but no light came. Fool that I was, I had brought no hand torch with me. I stood in the half dark, not daring to breathe. The silence scared me. Bristol has been evacuated. Hurry or you'll be killed. The sweat again, this time oily cold. I breathed out, then slowly in again, and smelled an old house going into her dotage. I peered round me, trying to let more light into my eyes. The only source was the street lamp. But its glow fell across the bay window, not into it. To see into the interior, my eyes had to scavenge light from the bay and hurry with it across the room, like carrying water in cupped hands.

Her piano stool, unscathed. I ran my hand over it: the light alloy tubes, like an angled reading lamp that reached out and then returned, pressing the padded support against the small of her back. Her portable electric typewriter. It stood on a table, but I could hardly see the table for the papers on it, and I could hardly see the papers for the dust. Then I saw a second table, except that it wasn't a table but a tea trolley, and on the tea trolley a digital telephone with an answering machine attached to it, with a typical Pettifer lash-up of wires and aerials and the judicious use of Scotch tape. But no light burned on the answering machine, because there was no electricity in the socket.

The room grew smaller, and the walls came towards me. My eyes were seeing more. I could follow the typewriter wire all the way to the wall. I began to distinguish signs of hasty departure: desk drawers pulled out and half emptied, documents spilled across the floor, the grate stuffed with charred paper, the wastebasket lying on its side. I recognised more bits of Larryana: piles of fringe magazines stacked against the wall, with tags of paper marking the places; an ancient poster of Josef Stalin at his most benign, cutting roses in a garden. Larry had drawn an imperial crown on his head and scribbled the words WE NEVER CLOSED across his chest. Scrawled messages on rectangles of sticky paper, posted on an etching of Notre Dame hanging over the grate. With my gloved hand I pulled off a couple of them and took them to the bay, but I couldn't read them, except to see that the first was written by Emma and the second by Larry. Peeling off the rest in order, I stuck one on top of the other before dropping them into my pocket in a wad.

I returned to the front door and gathered a handful of letters from the heap on the floor. Miss Sally Anderson, I read crookedly, Free Prometheus Ltd., 9A Cambridge Street. Postmark not Macclesfield but Zurich. Terry Altman, Esq., I read, Free Prometheus Ltd.— Terry Altman, who had been one of Larry's work names, and Prometheus, who for his trickery had been chained to a mountain in the high Caucasus until Larry and Emma had set him free. Pamphlets, lurid brochures, Russian quality. Printed matter from the BBC Monitoring Service at Caversham, headed "Southern Russia (West)." To the Manager, Free Prometheus Ltd. To Sally, Free Prometheus Ltd. Bank statements. A folder full of letters, incoming to Emma and handwritten by Larry, for whom a letter could be anything from a beer mat to a paper napkin to the title page of a radical paperback published by some fly-by-night anarchist in Islington. Addressed to Darling, Darling Emm and continuing Oh Christ I forgot to tell you. A newsletter headed "Media Manipulated" and subtitled "How the Western Press Plays Moscow's Game." Stay calm, I told myself as I dropped everything back on the pile. Method, Cranmer. You're a field man, veteran of innumerable Office break-ins, some of them with Larry as your inside man. Pace yourself. One job at a time. A red-and-white pamphlet in Russian called "Genocide in the Caucasus" in blazing capitals, school of Soviet agitprop, vintage 1950, except that it was dated February 1993 and referred to "The Holocaust of Last October." I opened it at random and saw the stabbed and bloated bodies of small children. *Caucasian Review* II (Munich '56), see pages 134–156. *Caucasian Review* V (Munich '56), see pages 41–46. Side-lined passages. Angry marginal scrawls, illegible in the ailing light.

There was an interior door, and geography dictated that it led to the part of the house that gave onto the side street. I turned the handle. Nothing happened. I pushed hard and the door gave, shrieking on the linoleum. I smelled rancid butter, dust, and Lifebuoy soap. I was in a scullery. Through a window above the sink more street light streamed onto the flagstones. A line of plates stood drying in a rack. They had been drying so long they were filthy again. In the shelves, a selection of Larry's undemocratic self-indulgences: pepper sardines from a grand grocer in Jermyn Street, Oxford marmalade, and Fortnum's English Breakfast Tea. In the fridge, rancid yoghurt, sour milk. Beside it a wooden door with bolts top and bottom, and a latch with a chain and pin. It was the side door I had inspected from the pavement. As I returned to the living room I looked at my watch. Three minutes was how long eternity had so far lasted.

The stairs were in pitch darkness, rickety and uncarpeted. I counted fourteen from ground level. I reached a landing, groped, felt a door, then a door handle. I pushed and stepped inside. I was in a lavatory. I stepped out again, closed the door, and, with my back against it, groped either side of me until I found another door, opened it, and entered Emma's bedroom in broad daylight, because the halogen light from the street lamp poured straight in the window, passing through the threadbare curtains as if they didn't exist. I gave her everything, I thought, surveying the bare floorboards and cracked washbasin, the dead flowers in a paste pot, the wonky reading lamp, the brown-flowered wallpaper peeling in strips; and she wanted none of it. This is what I saved her from. And she preferred it.

On the floor lay a futon, and it was prepared the way she liked to prepare our bed when we were going to make love: sideways to the fire, lots of pillows, a white duvet. Across the duvet, the severe little Marks & Spencer nightdress she had brought with her when she came to live with me, its long sleeves stretched out for the embrace. I saw her naked on her stomach with her chin in her hands, turning to look at me over her shoulder as she hears me enter. And the light of the log fire drawing finger shadows on her flanks. And her unpinned hair falling like black flames over her shoulders.

Two books, one his side, one hers. For Larry, a red-cloth nineteen-twentyish volume by one W. E. D. Allen, with the unlikely title *Béled-es-Siba*. I opened it at random and came on a memorial tribute to the poet Aubrey Herbert and, underlined, the words: *he lacked the caddishness of genius*. I had a vague memory that Herbert had fought to save Albania from the self-styled Liberators of the Balkans, and that he was one of Larry's heroes. For Emma, Fitzroy Maclean's *To Caucasus*, subtitled *The End of All the Earth*.

A sepia poster. Not of Josef Stalin this time, not of anyone I recognised. But a bearded, strong-jawed, dark-eyed modern prophet in what I took to be the traditional garb of a Caucasian hillsman: fur hat, skin waistcoat with loops for ammunition. Looking closer, I made out the name Bashir Haji in sharp Cyrillic script across the lower corner and, with difficulty, the words "to my friend Misha the great warrior." It seemed a strange sort of trophy to hang in a love nest. Tugging it from its fastenings, I laid it on the bed next to Emma's nightdress. Clothes, I thought: I need more clothes. Nobody who leaves in a hurry takes all his clothes. A curtain hung across a recess beside the chimney breast, reminding me of Uncle Bob's blackout curtain across the alcove in my priesthole. I pulled it aside and took a sharp step backward.

I am on Priddy, grappling with him. I have seized him by the lapels of his green Austrian raincoat that he calls his moleskin. It is a flowing, long-skirted, olive-coloured affair, silky to the touch. Its softness is offensive to me. As I haul him towards me, I hear a rent and I laugh. As we fight, I have an image of it turning to shreds. As I drag him feetfirst and mud-caked towards the pool, I see its tatters in the moonlight, trailing after him like a beggar's shroud.

And I saw it now, dry-cleaned and none the worse for wear, hanging from a wire coat hanger with the cleaner's tag still stapled to the inside lining. I checked the buttons. All there. Did I pull the buttons off? I had no memory of doing so. The rip, where was the rip? I had distinctly heard cloth ripping. I could find not one tear, not a mend, whether in the lining, the hem, or round the buttonholes. Nor round the lapels where I had seized him.

I examined the belt. He had worn it knotted. It had a perfectly good buckle, if you have to wear a belt with your raincoat, but the buckle wasn't good enough for Larry. He had to knot his belt like a gigolo, which is why I had taken such pleasure in seeing my gloved fists clutching it as I dragged him along the ground, with his head going bumpety-bump and his grin switching on and off in the moonlight.

It's a different coat, I thought. Then I thought: When did Larry ever have two of anything except women?

BENEATH the kitchen sink I had found a roll of black plastic bin bags. Tearing one free, I stuffed the mail into it, making no distinction between printed and personal letters. As I did so I saw the bayonetted children again, and remembered Diana and his perfect note. What was perfect, I wondered, about the screams of dying children? On my knees before the fireplace, I scraped together the charred paper in the grate and with huge care laid it in a second bag. I filled a third and fourth with files and papers strewn around the desk. I tossed in an Esso diary, and a singed account book that somebody had attempted to burn but failed, and a forties pop-up Bakelite address book I associated with neither Larry nor Emma which seemed to be some foundling in their lives, until I realised it was Russian. I extracted the tape from the typewriter, pulled the plug out of the socket, and set the typewriter on the kitchen table on its way to the side door. And that was for the seeming, because I had told Phoebe I needed to collect Sally's typewriter. I put the tape in the third bin bag.

I returned to the drawing room and made to unplug the answering machine, but on second thoughts picked it up, base and receiver both, and by the glow of the street lamp identified the redial button on the telephone, lifted the receiver, and pressed redial. A number rang out. I heard a man's voice, soft, foreign, and well-spoken like Mr. Dass: "Thank you for calling the offices of Hardwear Carpets International. If you wish to leave a message or place an order, kindly speak after the tone. . . ." I listened to the message twice, unplugged the machine, and set it on the kitchen table beside the typewriter. My eye caught sight of a set of car keys hanging from a nail. The Toyota. I put them in my pocket, grateful that I wasn't going to have to jump the wires in a dark side street late on a Saturday night. I rushed upstairs. There was no hard reason for this excessive haste, but perhaps if I hadn't run I wouldn't have found the courage to walk.

I stood at the bedroom window. Cambridge Street was deserted. Waiting for my head to clear, I stared out over the grass platform at the rivers of railway line. The night was darker. Bristol was putting itself to sleep. This is where Emma stood when she was waiting for him to arrive, I thought. Naked, as she used to wait for me when she had decided we would make love. I stood at the futon. The pillows were stacked to one side, for a single head. What was she thinking as she lay here alone? *He went first, she followed him,* Phoebe had said. And this was where she lay, all on her own, before she went. I bent down, intending to pick up the signed poster of the hillsman. Imagined or real, the scent of her body rose at me from the bedclothes. I folded the poster until it would fit my pocket. I removed Larry's green raincoat from its hanger and slung it over my arm. I returned slowly downstairs and walked to the kitchen. Slowly. I slid back the bolts of the side door, cocked the latch, and poked the pin in place to hold it open. Slowly. It was very important to me that I should do nothing hasty.

Leaving the door ajar, I walked down the pavement to the car, pulled off the cover, and saw Larry's buckskin boots lying on the back seat. I determined to make nothing dramatic of the boots. They were Larry's boots, and Larry was alive. What was so remarkable about his damned boots, made to measure by Lobb of St. James's and paid for to screams of pain from the Top Floor, all because Larry had decided that it was time he put our love for him to the test?

I noted the caked mud on them, as one notes mud on anything: take a wire brush to them, do it later. The hatred in me was aflame again. I wished I could call a rematch, go back to Priddy and finish him off.

I walked to the kitchen, collected the typewriter and answering machine, and walked back to the car with them, agonising about whether it was intending to start. I made some fanciful calculations about how long it would take to push the car to the top of the hill so that I could roll it down to the station and, if it still didn't start, transfer my new possessions to a cab.

My courage almost exhausted, I returned to the house for the remainder of my load: Larry's moleskin raincoat, which I seemed to need as proof positive of his survival, and my four bin bags, which I carried by their necks and packed around the typewriter, all but the bag containing the burned paper, which out of respect for its delicacy I laid on the passenger seat. And now all I wanted in the world was to get into the car and drive myself and my treasures to a safe place. But I was worried about Phoebe and Wilf. During the break-in they had become major characters in my imagination. I had been grateful for their acceptance of me, but I needed to know that I had done everything possible to preserve their good opinion, particularly Phoebe's, because she doubted me. I didn't want them phoning the police. I wanted them easy in their minds.

So I went back to the house, bolted the side door top and bottom from the inside, slipped the locking pin into its housing, then walked through the living room again, passing Emma's piano stool on my way. I let myself out of the front door, double-locking it because that was how I had found it. Then I stood on the crown of the road and called to the upper window.

"Thanks, Wilf. Mission accomplished. All done."

No answer. I don't think I remember a longer twenty yards in my life than the distance from the front door of 9A to the blue Toyota, and I was halfway when I realised I was being followed. I thought at first it might be Larry behind me, or Munslow, because my follower was so quiet that my awareness of him was communicated less by hearing than by my other professional senses: the prickle on your back; the reflection in the air before you, made by someone just behind you; the sense of presence each time you check a shop window and see nothing.

I stooped to open the car door. I cast about but still saw nothing. I rose and swung round with my forearm in the strike position, and found myself standing face-to-face with the small black boy from the Ocean Fish Bar, who had been too serious to speak to me.

"Why aren't you in bed?" I asked him.

He shook his head.

"Not tired?"

He shook his head again. Not tired or no bed.

I climbed into the driver's seat and turned the ignition key while he watched me. The engine fired first time. He put his thumbs up, and before I could stop myself I had dragged Colin Bairstow's wallet from the sweat-sodden recesses of my jacket and given him a ten-pound note. Then I drove off down the road calling myself every kind of fool, because in my imagination I was hearing Inspector Bryant enquiring in his most blandishing voice what the nice white middle-aged gentleman in the blue Toyota thought he was buying for himself when he handed you that tenner through the window, son.

THERE is a hilltop on the Bristol side of the Mendips that gives one of the longest and most beautiful views in England, steeply downward over small fields and unspoiled villages and outward between two great hills towards the city. It was one of the places where I had driven Emma on sunny evenings, when we liked to hop in the car and go somewhere for the joy of it. In spring and summer there is quite a traffic of young lovers up there. Fathers kick footballs with their children in the nearby fields. But by late October, between one and seven in the morning, you may be pretty confident of privacy.

I sat with my arms on the wheel of the Toyota, and my chin in my arms, and stared into the shifting night. Stars and moon hung above me. Smells of dew and bonfire filled the car.

By the courtesy light I read the lovers' exchange of messages, one square of yellow paper after another stuck along the dashboard of the car in the order in which I had removed them from the picture frame.

EMMA: AM expects your call 5.30 today.

Who's AM? I heard Bryant say. *AM who's all over Pettifer's diary?*

LARRY: Do you love me?
EMMA: CC rang. Didn't say where from. Still no carpets.
LARRY: Where's the bloody Bovril, woman?

Larry hated coffee but was an addict. Bovril was what he called his methadone.

LARRY: I am NOT obsessed by you. It's just that I can't get you out of my stupid head. Why won't you make love to me?
EMMA: AM rang. Carpets arrived. All present as promised. Because I'm off games. Wait till Thursday.
LARRY: Can't.

The hours crawled by like all the useless hours I had wasted waiting for spies to come and go—in cars, on street corners, in railway stations and lousy cafés. I had two beds in two hotels and couldn't sleep in either of them. I owned a comfortable, leather-upholstered Sunbeam with a brand-new heater but was obliged to freeze in a clapped-out Toyota. Gathering Larry's moleskin over my shoulders like a cape, I tried repeatedly to go to sleep, in vain. By seven I was pacing the gravel, fretting about the fog. I'm stranded! I'll never get down the hill! By eight-thirty, in perfect visibility, I arrived at the entrance to the covered car park of a new shopping centre, only to learn that on Sundays it didn't open till nine. I drove to a cemetery and mindlessly studied headstones for half an hour, returned to the shopping centre, and embarked on the next leg of my spy's odyssey. I parked in the car park, bought shaving cream and razor blades for the seeming, caught a cab to Clifton, collected my Sunbeam from the Eden, and drove it back to the shopping centre. I parked the Sunbeam as close to the Toyota as I could, freed a reluctant trolley from its string of partners, placed it alongside the Toyota, dumped the four bin bags into it, boots, typewriter, answering machine, and green raincoat, and transferred the whole lot to the Sunbeam.

All this without shame or circumspection, because when God invented the supermarket, we used to say in the Office, he provided us spies with something we had till then only dreamed of: a place where any fool could transfer anything in the world from one car to another without any other fool noticing.

Then, because I had no wish to draw attention to Miss Sally Anderson of Cambridge Street—or for that matter Free Prometheus Ltd., or Terry Altman, Esq.—I drove the Toyota to a filthy industrial estate beyond the city's parking zone, pulled the plastic cover over it, and wished it an unfond farewell.

Then back to the supermarket car park and so by Sunbeam to the Hotel Eden, where I parked, paid my bill with a Cranmer credit card, and took a cab to the Starcrest motel, where I paid a second bill with Bairstow's credit card.

Thence to the Eden to collect my car, and so to Honeybrook to sleep, perchance to dream.

·   ·   ·

OR NOT, as Larry would say.

On the verge opposite the main gates, two cyclists were busy doing nothing. In the hall, a painfully written note from Mrs. Benbow regretted that "what with my husband's heart and the questions going on by police," she would not be obliging me in the future. The rest of my mail was scarcely more cheerful: two demands from the Bristol Constabulary for payment of parking fines I had not incurred; a letter from the office of the Value Added Tax inspector advising me that, acting on information received, he proposed to launch a full investigation of my assets, income, outgoings, and receipts over the last two years. And a premature bill from Mr. Rose, my carrier, who had never been known to send a bill to anyone unless someone went round to his home and threatened him with the collectors. Only my friend the excise officer seemed to have escaped enlistment:

Dear Tim,

I propose to make one of my surprise visits to you next Wednesday around midday. Any chance of a bite of lunch?

Best,

David

David Beringer, ex-Office. Never happier than when he was resettled.

A last envelope remained. Brown. Poor quality. Typed on an old portable. Postmark Helsinki. The flap tightly sealed. Or, as I suspected, resealed. One sheet of paper inside, ruled. Inky handwriting. Male. Blotched. Headed Moscow and dated six days ago.

Timothy, my friend,

They have let loose an unjust hell on me. I am a prisoner in my own house, disgraced for nothing. If you have cause to come to Moscow, or if you are in touch with your former employers, please assist me by making my oppressors see reason. You can contact Sergei, who is arranging to post this letter for me. Phone him *in English only* at the number you know, and mention only the name of your old friend and sparring partner:

Peter

I continued staring at the letter. Peter for Volodya Zorin. Peter for talking on the telephone and arranging to meet him in Shepherd Market. Peter for deniable initiatives of friendship. Peter the victim of an unjust hell, under house arrest and waiting to be shot at dawn, welcome to the club.

It was a Sunday, and on Sundays, even without Larry to cook for, there was a lot of seeming to attend to. Eleven o'clock found me in the village church, kneeling on Uncle Bob's embroidered hassock in my lovat suit and mouthing the middle notes of Sung Eucharist, which I heartily dislike. Mr. Guppy took the collection, and the poor old man couldn't bring himself to raise his eyes as he passed me the bag. After church it was the turn of the Misses Bethel in the Dower House to give us bad sherry and alarm us with the latest rumours of the bypass. But today they weren't interested in the bypass, so we talked about nothing while they shot sideways glances at me whenever they thought I wasn't looking. But by the time I crept down to my priesthole under cover of darkness, my booty loaded onto Ted Lanxon's handcart, I was beginning to feel less the master of my house than the burglar who was breaking into it.

I STOOD before the strip of old blackout curtain that I had tacked across the alcove. Even tonight, Emma's privacy was as dear to me as it had ever been to her. To spy on her was to sin against the convictions I had never held until I met her. If she had received a phone call and I happened to take it, I passed it to her without comment or enquiry. If a letter, it lay *intacta* on the hall table till she chose to notice it. I would make nothing of the postmark, the gender of the hand-writing, the quality of the stationery. If the temptation became unbearable—I had recognised Larry's handwriting, or another male pen was becoming too familiar to me—then I would stomp cheerily upstairs, flapping the envelope at my side, yelling "Letter for Emma! Letter for Emma! Emma, letter for you!" and with pious relief ease it under the door of her studio, and goodbye to it.

Until now.

Until, with the very reverse of triumph, I tugged aside the curtain and peered down at the eight wine boxes I had blindly filled with the contents of her kneehole desk that Sunday when she left me; and at the anonymous buff folder that Merriman had gaily dubbed my doggy bag, lying askew across the top of them.

I opened it quickly, the way I had always imagined I might swallow poison. Five unheaded A4 pages, compiled by his Sheenas. Without even granting myself time to sit, I read them at one gulp, then again more slowly, waiting for the epiphany that would have me clutching at my throat and crying, "Cranmer, Cranmer, how could you have been so blind?"

None came.

For instead of some cheap textbook solution to Emma's mystery, I found only the affecting confirmation of things that I had assumed or known already: transient lovers, the repeated involvements and escapes, the quest for absolutes in a world of botch and falsehood. I recognised her readiness to be unprincipled in pursuit of principle; and the ease with which she shrugged off her responsibilities when they conflicted with what she perceived as her life's quest. Her parentage, though not as lurid as she would have me think, was quite as ill-starred. Brought up by her mother to believe she was the love child of a great musician, she had visited his home town in Sardinia, to discover that he had been a bricklayer. It was from her mother, if anyone, that her musical talent was derived. But Emma had hated her, and so, as I read the file, did I.

Setting the folder gently aside, I found time to wonder what Merriman had imagined he was achieving by pressing it upon me. All it had done was rekindle the anguish that I felt for her and my determination to save her from the consequences of whatever madness Larry had drawn her into.

I seized the nearest box, overturned it, and seized the next, till all eight of them were empty. The four bin bags from Cambridge Street, their throats bound with ligatures of paper wire, stared at me like masked inquisitors. I ripped off their nooses and shook their contents to the floor. Only the bag of charred paper remained. Gingerly I tipped it out and with my fingertips stroked the unburned fragments into separate piles. On my hands and knees before the detritus of Emma's unscripted disappearance, I launched myself upon the task of entering the secret world of my mistress and her lover.

10

I was reading as I had never read before. What my eye missed, my hands found and my head construed. I was flattening sheets of paper, piecing together others carelessly torn up, setting them in piles, and filing them in my memory at the same time. I was doing in hours what once I would have done in weeks, because hours, unless I was mistaken, were all I had. If there was blind logic to my frenzy, there was also the dawning of a mad relief. Here is the explanation! Here at least is how, and why, and when, and where—if only I can decode them! Here amid these papers—and not in some paranoid corner of Cranmer's overactive fantasy—are buried answers to questions that have been haunting me night and day for weeks on end: Was I framed, set up, the target of a devilish conspiracy? Or am I merely the fool of love and of my own menopausal imaginings?

How much I was behind Larry and Emma, how much ahead of them, is something I couldn't measure. I knew, I half knew. Then I knew nothing again. Or I had divined their actions but was mystified by their purpose. Or I knew their purpose but refused to countenance their motive: it was too mad, too far, too alien, too wantonly obscure, to be believed. Or suddenly I would discover myself sitting back in my chair and, against all reason, grinning beatifically at the ceiling: I was not the target, I was not the object of their deception; they were after bigger game than me; Cranmer was just a not very innocent bystander.

Sheets of figures, business letters, letters from banks, and copies of letters back to them. Literature from something called the Survival for Tribal People Association; literature from Munich; a brochure called "God as Detail" from somebody called P. Wook in Islington. The Esso diary, a marked calendar, the pop-up Russian address book, Larry's crazy scrawls. Bills for telephone, electricity, water, rent, groceries, and Larry's whisky. Bills decently kept, paid, receipted. Emma's kind of bill, not Larry's, addressed variously to S. Anderson or T. Altman or Free Prometheus Ltd., Cambridge Street. A child's exercise book, but the child was Emma. It was sandwiched inside a bunch of files and came loose when I started to sort through them. I opened it, then closed it again in a spontaneous act of self-censorship before opening it more cautiously. Amid household notes and musical jottings, I had stumbled on random messages to her former lover, Cranmer:

Tim, I try to understand what's happened to us so that I can explain to you, but then I think: why should I explain anything to you? and the next minute I think I'll just say it straight out anyway, which is what I've decided to do. . . .

But this fine resolve was not matched by performance, for the signal ended. Damp batteries in the transmitter? Secret police banging on the door? I turned a couple of pages.

Emma to Emma: *Everything in my life has prepared me for this. . . . Every wrong lover, wrong step, my bad side and my good side, all my sides, are marching in the same direction for as long as I march with Larry. . . . When Larry says he doesn't believe words, I don't believe them either. Larry is action. Action is character. In music, in love, in life . . .*

But Emma to Emma only sounded like a parody of Larry.

Emma to Tim: *. . . what you left in me was a huge yawning gap where I had kept my love for you until I realised you weren't there. How much I guessed about you and how much you told me, or Larry did, doesn't matter, except that Larry never betrayed you in the way you think, and never in the way you . . .*

Oh sure, I thought savagely; well, he wouldn't, would he? I mean stealing his best friend's girl isn't betrayal, any more than stealing thirty-seven million pounds and making you his accomplice is. That's altruism. That's nobility. That's sacrifice!

Six pages of Larry-inspired self-absorption went by before she braced herself to address me again, this time in patronising terms:

You see, Tim, Larry is life continued. He will never let me down. He is life made real again, and just to be with him is to be travelling and taking part, because where Tim avoids, Larry engages. And where Tim . . .

Signal ends again. Where Tim *what?* What was left of me to destroy that she hadn't destroyed already? And if Larry was life continued, what was Tim in the gospel according to St. Larry, passed down to us by the disciple Emma? Life discontinued, I supposed. Better known as death. And death, when she found herself living with it, became a bit infectious, presumably—which is why she plucked up the courage to bolt that Sunday morning while I was at church.

But I am not guilty, I thought. *I am the deceived, not the deceiver.*

"Make me one person, Tim," she implores me on our first night in Honeybrook. "I've been too many people for too long, Tim. Be my one-man convent, Tim, my Salvation Army. Never let me down."

Larry will never let you down, you simpleton! Larry's going to dump you in the deepest pit you ever saw! That's what he does! Don't preach to *me* about your love for him! Larry as *life?* Your sacred feelings? How many times can you be true to your feelings and have any feelings left to be true to? How many times can you consign yourself to the sweet blue sky of eternity, only to come slinking home in the small hours of the morning with your dress torn and two teeth missing?

Yet the protector in me was on full alert, even as the bonds of guilt and ignorance fell away. Every page and every word I read injected me with fresh urgency, spurring me forward in my desire to free her from her latest, greatest folly.

Emma as artist. Emma as mistress of the Freudian doodle. Emma as the echo of Larry's eternal outcry against a world he can neither join nor destroy. "*For us*," she has written. A lighthouse is the most charitable description of it. It rises proudly up the centre of the page. It has four slender, tapering walls with windows not unlike my arrow slits. It has a conical tip like a helmet and like other conical tips. On the ground floor she has drawn a soulful cow, on the first floor Larry and Emma are eating out of bowls, on the second they are embracing. And on the top floor, naked as in Paradise, they are keeping watch from opposite windows.

But for when? For what? Now it was Cranmer, her saviour, who scrambled after her, calling *Stop!* and *Wait!* and *Come back!*

AN INDIGNANT Larry dissertation, all for Emma, on the origin of the word *ingush*, which turns out to be a Russian notion, imposed by the invader. *Ingush*, it seems, is simply the Ingush word for people, as *chechen* is the Chechen word for people (cf. the Boer colonialists' use of *bantu* for the black people of Africa). The Ingush word for the people of Ingushetia is evidently *Galgai*. Larry is incensed by such insensitivity on the part of the Russians, and naturally wishes Emma to share his anger . . .

I WAS reading burned paper.

Sometimes I had to hold it to the light. Sometimes I was obliged to use a magnifying glass or complete a garbled sentence for myself. Paper burns badly, as every spy knows. Print survives, if only white on black. But Emma was no spy, and whatever security precautions she had imagined she was taking, they were not those recommended by the likes of Marjorie Pew. I was reading letters and numbers. Her italic handwriting was clear despite the flames.

$$25 \times MKZ22 \ldots\ldots\ldots\ldots 200 \text{ appro}$$
$$500 \times ML7 \ldots\ldots\ldots\ldots 900$$
$$1 \times MQ18 \ldots\ldots\ldots\ldots 50$$

Against each entry, a tick or cross. And along the bottom of the page the words: *Order confirmed by AM, Sept 14, 10.30 a.m., his phone call.*

I heard Jamie Pringle: *Mathematics not up Larry's street . . . Brighter than Larry by a mile, when it came to numbers.* I had a vision of her sitting at the desk in Cambridge Street, her black hair tucked sternly behind her ears and into the collar of her high-necked blouse, while she works out the arithmetic that her musician's brain is good at, and waits for Larry to hurry up the hill from Bristol Temple Meads station after another tiring day at the Lubyanka, darling.

Grand total 4½ approx, I read at the foot of the following page. Her numbers were italic too.

Four and a half *whats*, damn you? I asked, angry with her at long last. Thousands? Millions? A few of the thirty-seven and rising? Then why did Larry have to sell your jewellery for you? Why did he have to give away his Office gratuity?

I heard Diana again and felt my hackles rise: *one perfect note*.

The image was forming. Perhaps it had already formed. Perhaps the *what* was there, and only the *why* remained. But Cranmer in this mood was a desk officer. And deductions, if he made them at all, came after, not before and not during, his researches.

I WAS listening.

I had an urge to laugh, to wave, to answer back, "Emma! It's me. I love you. Actually, I still do! Incredibly, irrationally, I adore you, whether I'm life or death or just boring old Tim Cranmer!"

Outside my arrow slits the world was going to the devil. The chapel tower grumbled, shutters banged, lead downpipes hurled themselves against stone walls as the thunder struck. Gutters overflowed and gargoyles could not spew out the rushing water fast enough. The rain stopped and the uneasy truce of a country night returned. But all I was thinking was: "Emma, it's you," and all I was hearing was Emma speaking on the answering machine from Cambridge Street in a voice so lovely that I wanted to hold the machine against my face: a warm and patient voice as well as a musical one, made a little lazy by lovemaking, perhaps, and addressed to people who might not speak much English or be conversant with such Western mysteries as the answering machine.

"This is Free Prometheus of Bristol, and this is Sally speaking," she was saying. "Hullo, and thanks for calling. I'm afraid we can't talk to you just now, because we have had to go out. If you wish to leave a message, wait until you hear a short whistle, then begin speaking immediately. Are you ready . . . ?"

After Emma, the same message again, read to us by Larry in Russian. And Larry when he spoke Russian slipped into another skin, because the Russian language had been his refuge from tyranny. It was where he had locked himself away from the father who had lectured him, and the school that had urged conformity on him, and the prefects who had flogged him to give the message force.

After he had spoken Russian he spoke again, in a language that I arbitrarily placed in the Caucasus—since I didn't understand a syllable. But I couldn't mistake the air of drama, the pulse of conspiracy, that he managed to squeeze into such a formal little message. I listened to him again in Russian. Then again in the unfamiliar language. So charged, so heroic, so full of moment. What did he remind me of? The book beside his bed in Cambridge Street? Memories of his hero Aubrey Herbert, who had fought to save Albania?

I had it—the Canning!

We are back at Oxford; it's nighttime and it's snowing. We are sitting in someone's rooms in Trinity; there are a dozen of us, and we are drinking mulled claret, and it's Larry's turn to read us a paper on whatever pretentious subject has caught his fancy. The Canning is just another self-regarding Oxford discussion group, except that it's a bit older than most and has some decent silver. Larry has chosen Byron and intends to shock us. Which he duly does, insisting that Byron's greatest loves were men, not women, and dwelling upon the poet's devotion while at Cambridge to a choirboy, and while in Greece to his page, Loukas.

But what I hear in my memory's ear as I recall the evening is not Larry's predictable relish for Byron's sexual exploits but his zeal for Byron the saviour of the Greeks, *sending his own money* to help prepare the Greek ships for battle, *raising soldiers and paying them* so that he himself can lead the attack on the Turks at Lepanto.

And what I see is Larry seated before the gas fire, clutching his goblet of hot wine to his breast, a Byron of his own imagining; the forelock, the flushed cheeks, the fervent eyes alight with wine and rhetoric. Did Byron sell his beloved's antique jewellery to fund the hopeless cause? Turn over his gratuity in cash?

And what I remember is Larry again, during yet another of his Honeybrook lectures, telling us that Byron is a Caucasus freak, on the grounds that he wrote a grammar on the Armenian language.

I switched to the incoming messages. I became a secondary addict, sharing the pipe dream and inhaling the fumes, bathing in the dangerous glow.

"SALLY?" A guttural foreign voice, male, thick and urgent, speaking English. "Here is Issa. Our Chief Leader will visit to Nazran tomorrow. He will speak secretly to council. Tell this to Misha, please."

Click.

Misha, I thought. One of Checheyev's cover names for Larry. Nazran, temporary capital of Ingushetia, in the North Caucasus barrier.

A different voice, male and dead tired, speaking unguttural Russian in a drenched murmur. "Misha, I have news. The carpets have arrived on the mountain. The boys are happy. Greetings from Our Chief Leader."

Click.

A man is speaking breezy English with a slight Oriental accent: Mr. Dass's sound-alike from the redial call I had made in Cambridge Street.

"Hullo, Sally, this is Hardwear, calling from the *car*," it announced proudly, as if the telephone or the car were a brand-new acquisition. "Message just in from our suppliers saying stand by for next week. Time for some more money talk, I think. [Giggle] Cheers."

Click.

And after him again, Checheyev's voice, as I had heard him countless times in telephone and microphone intercepts. He is speaking English, but as I go on listening, his voice has the unnatural courtesy of a man under fire.

"Sally, good morning, this is CC. I need to get a message to Misha quickly, please. He must not go north. If he has started his journey, he should please discontinue it. This is an order from Our Chief Leader. Please, Sally."

Click.

Checheyev again, the calm if anything more pronounced, the pace slower:

"CC for Misha. Misha, take heed, please. The forest is watching us. Do you hear me, Misha? We are betrayed. The forest is on its way to the north, and in Moscow everything is known. Don't go north, Misha. Don't be foolhardy. The important thing is to get to safety and fight another day. Come to us and we shall take care of you. Sally, please tell this to Misha urgently. Tell him to use the preparations we have already agreed."

Click. End of message. End of all messages. The forest is northward bound and Birnam Wood has come to Dunsinane, and Larry has or hasn't got the message. And Emma? I wonder. What has she got?

· · ·

I WAS counting money: bills, letters, cheque stubs. I was reading burned letters from banks.

"Dear Miss Stoner"—the top right corner of the page charred, writer's address incomplete, except for the letters SBANK and the words *des Pays, Genève*. Miss Stoner's address 9A Cambridge Street, Bristol. "We note from the . . . losed state . . . tha . . . have substan . . . quid . . . ts in . . . ur . . . urrent acc . . . Should you . . . no immedi . . . call upon . . . may wish to . . . ferring them to . . ."

Left side and lower half of letter destroyed, Miss Stoner's response unknown. But Miss Stoner is by now no stranger to me. Or to Emma.

"Dear Miss Roylott."

Quite right: Miss Roylott is Miss Stoner's natural companion. It's Christmas evening before the big fire in the drawing room at Honeybrook. Emma wears her intaglio necklace and a long skirt and sits in the Queen Anne wing chair while I read aloud Conan Doyle's "Speckled Band," in which Sherlock Holmes rescues the beautiful Miss Stoner from the murderous designs of Dr. Grimesby Roylott. Drunk with happiness, I affect to continue reading from the text, while I ingeniously depart from it:

"And if I may be permitted, madam," I intone, in my most Holmesian voice, "to confess a humble interest in your immaculate person, then permit me also to propose that in a few moments we repair upstairs and put to the test those desires and appetites which, with the impetuosity of my sex, I am scarcely able to contain—"

But by now Emma's fingertips close my lips, so that she may kiss them with her own. . . .

"Dear Miss Watson."

The writer is in Edinburgh and signs himself "Overseas Portfolio Exe . . ." And Watson should have been braving the wild beasts of Dr. Grimesby Roylott's private zoo with an Eley's N° 2 revolver in his pocket, not masquerading as a woman named Sally with an address in Cambridge Street, Bristol.

"We take pleasure in . . . osing . . . short-term . . . combi . . . high yie . . . wit . . . condi . . . withdraw . . . fshore."

I'll bet you take pleasure, I thought. With thirty-seven million to play with, who wouldn't?

"Dear Miss Holmes."

And more of the same unction from the banker's greasy bottle.

I WAS collecting carpets.

Kilims, Hamadans, Balouchis, Kolyais, and Azerbaijans, Gebbehs, Bakhtiaris, Basmackis, and Dosemealtis. Notes about carpets, scribbled memos about carpets, phone messages, letters typed on spotty grey paper posted by our good friend So-and-so who is travelling to Stockholm: Have the Kilims arrived? Are they on their way? Last week you said next week. Our Chief Leader is distraught, so much anxious talk of carpets. Issa is also distraught, because Magomed has no carpets to sit on.

CC rang. Hopes to be here next month. Didn't say where from. Still no carpets. . . .

CC rang. OCL ecstatic. Carpets being unpacked this moment. Excellent storage found at high altitude, everything intact. When can he expect more?

Carpets from AM. To Our Chief Leader or, as the Winchester *Notion* has it, OCL.

"Dear Prometheus." Badly burned letter on plain white paper, electronic type. "We are . . . posi . . . to arra . . . ear . . . livery of 300 Qashqais as discussed, an . . . shall be happy to take mat . . . to next agreed stage on receipt you . . ." The signature a jagged hieroglyph resembling three pyramids side by side, sender's address The Hardwear Company, Box (number illegible) . . . sfield.

Petersfield?

Maresfield?

Some other English field?

It was Macclesfield, I hear Jamie Pringle say in port-fed tones. *Used to screw a girl there.*

And below the signature an internal office memo, Larry to Emma in his impatient scrawl:

Emm! Vital! Can we scrape this together while we wait for CC to lay his egg? L.

Exit her jewellery, I thought. Exit his gratuity. And at long last a precious date, scribbled in Larry's restless hand: 18/7—July 18, just a few days before Larry drew his Judas money.

And yes, they scraped it together—witness the uncharred, perfectly preserved half page of carpet purchases in Emma's precise italic:

Kilims. *60,000*
Dosemealtis. *10,000*
Hamadans. *1,500*
Kolyais . . . . *10 × 1,000*

And at the bottom of the page, also in her handwriting:

*Total payment to Macclesfield
so far*. . . . . £*14,976,000*

Lubyanka
Between parades

Emm, listen up!

Last night I put my head on your tummy and distinctly heard the sea. Had I been drinking? Had you? Answer: no, just dreaming on my solitary pallet. You cannot imagine the soothing effect of a friendly navel in one's ear, and the sound of distant water at the same time. Do you *know*—have you the wit to *imagine*—what it is like to be alert in every whisker for sheer unadulterated, frustrated love of Emm? Probably not. Too thick. But work on it and I'll be back tonight, which come to think of it is twelve hours before this letter will arrive, but that's just another symptom of my *ludicrous, divine, insane* love for you.

Please make an *extra*
effort to love and worship
your

Larry

and accept no substitutes.

PS. Seminar in half an hour. Marcia will weep if I insult her and weep if I don't. Talbot—who on earth christens these wretched children?—will mount his infant throne and I shall vomit.

PPS. *Post boring-'em tristis.* I very nearly strangled Talbot. Sometimes I think it's the entire middle English mind-set of Thatcher's children that I'm at war with.
PPPPPPPS. Marcia brought me a *ccccake!*

The letter, being Larry's, is undated.

Emm! Concerning Timbo.

Timbo is the box I came in. Timbo is reinsurance made perfect. He's the only man I know who can go forwards and backwards at the same time and make it look like progress or retrenchment, depending where your fancy lies.

Timbo is also fireproof, since the man who believes in nothing, and therefore has space for everything, has a terrible advantage over us. What passes for a kindly tolerance in him is in reality a craven acceptance of the world's worst crimes. He's an immobilist, an apathist, and a militant passivist with a big V. And of course he's a dear sweet man. Unfortunately, it's dear sweet men who screw up the earth. Timbo's a spectator. We're doers. And *wow* do we do!

L.

PS. I am deep inside you and propose to remain there until we meet—when I shall be deep inside you. . . .

Emm,

Nietzsche said something frightfully stern about humour being an escape from serious thought, so I'll bow to N and give you serious thought. I love you. The heart, the laughs, the shoulder-to-shoulder, the pluck, the silences, every dimple and inlet, tuft, mole, freckle, nipple, and peerless plane. I love you until it comes out of my eyes. In the trees, the sky, the grass, and in Vladikavkaz on the river Terek, where the Caucasus takes us into its sanctuary and shields us from Moscow and the Christian maw. Or should do, if the bloody Ossetians weren't sitting in it.

One day you'll taste it, then you'll understand. I have Negley Farson on my knee as I write. Listen to his comfortable words. "Strange as it may seem for they are among the wildest mountains on earth, the one thing you feel about the lonely places of the Caucasus is a deep personal tenderness, a brotherhood: and the aching wish, vain as you know it to be, that you could guard their rare beauty. They possess you. Once you have felt the spell of the Caucasus you will never get over it." Confirmed and reconfirmed by my trip last Christmas. God, I love you. The Arts Subcommittee meets in one hour. How typical of the Lubyanka that even the Arts Committee should be sub. You are my Caucasus. *Ich bin ein Ingush.*

Yours in Allah,

L.

Emm,

Question from Thatcherchild Talbot, who has decided to grow a beard: Please, Larry, why did the West fall for Shevardnadze?

Answer, dear Talbot, because Shevers has a sad, bungey face and looks like everybody's daddy, when actually he's a KGB dinosaur with a background of deals with the CIA and a disgraceful record of repressing dissidents.

Question from Thatcherchild Marcia: Why did the West refuse recognition to Gamsakhurdia after he was fairly elected? Then, as soon as Shevardnadze was put in as Moscow's puppet, not only recognise the little twerp but turn a blind eye to his genocide of the Abkhaz, the Mingrelians, the you-name-them?

Answer, dear Thatcherchild Marcia, thank you for your ccccake and please come to bbbbed with me, it's the Good Old Boys getting together on both sides of the Atlantic and agreeing that minority rights can seriously threaten world health. . . .

I love you to despair and back. When you hear me coming up the hill, please be lying pensively on one elbow, naked and dreaming of the hills.

L.

. . .

My FINGERS had gone black.

Snakes were tickling my ankles.

I was standing arms outstretched in crucifixion, drawing the typewriter tape from its cassette, passing it across the light and letting it pile up round my feet. At first I could understand nothing. Then I realised I had broken in upon Larry the letter writer again, this time in his more familiar guise of academic terrorist:

> Your article entitled "Forcing Reason on the Caucasus" is an abomination. Its greatest offence is its attempt to justify the prolonged persecution of proud and fiercely independent peoples. For three hundred years Imperial and Soviet Russians have pillaged, murdered, and dispersed the mountaineers of N. Caucasus in an effort to destroy their culture, religion, and way of life. Where confiscation, slavery, enforced conversion, and the creation of deliberately divisive land borders failed to do the trick, the Russian oppressors resorted to wholesale deportation, torture, and genocide. Had the West taken the smallest interest in understanding the Caucasus during the dying days of Soviet power, instead of listening openmouthed to those with vested interests—of whom your writer is a flagrant example—the awful conflicts that have recently disfigured the region would have been avoided. So might those that are shortly to engulf us.
>
> L. Pettifer

A broadside directed against yet another of Larry's enemies was incomplete:

> . . . which is why the Ossetians today are Moscow's dependable henchmen as they were under the Communists and before them the Tsars. In the south, it is true, the Ossetians have lost out to those other ethnic cleansers, the Georgians. But in the north, in their war of attrition against the Ingush, in which they have been shamelessly assisted by regular units of highly equipped Russian troops, they emerge the absolute winners. . . .

Typed by Emma three days before I nearly killed the author. For which his unnamed enemy was no doubt duly grateful.

"My darling."

Larry in his steady hand: the one he used for writing his State of the Universe letters to me. I already loathed his sonorous, elder-brother tone of structured egocentricity.

There is something I have to say to you as we get deeper into this, so see this as my *ur*-letter at the crossroads, offering you a last chance to turn back.

It happens to be the Ingush, and I needn't tell you that I incline to people who have no voice in the world and not a prayer about how to operate in the media marketplace. . . . The Ingush right to survive is *my* right and *your* right and the right of any good, free soul not to conform with the vile forces of uniformisation: whether imposed by Coms, Market Pigs, or the emetic Partyspeak of Political Correctitude.

It happens to be the Ingush because I love their love of freedom, because they never had a feudal system or an aristocracy, no serfs, no slaves, no social superiors or inferiors; because they love forests and climb mountains and do a lot of things with their lives that the rest of us should do in preference to study-ing Global Security and listening to Pettifer talk platitudes.

It happens to be the Ingush because the sins committed against the Ingush and the Chechens are so incontestably awful that there's no earthly point in casting round for a bigger injustice committed against someone else. That would just be another way of turning your back on the little bugger bleeding on the floor. . . .

Now I was terrified. But for Emma, not myself. My stomach churned; the hand that held the letter was damp with sweat.

It happens to be the Ingush (and not the Marsh Arabs or the Common Whale, as Tim kindly suggested) because I've seen them, in their little valley towns and in their mountains, and like Negley Farson I saw a kind of Paradise and must take it in my care. In life, as we both know, it's the luck of the draw, who you meet and when and how much you have left to give, and the point at which you say, To hell with everything, this is where I go the distance, this is where I stick. You know those photos of old fellows in their great big mountain capes, their *bourkas?* Well, in an uneven fight, when a North Caucasus warrior is surrounded by enemies, he will throw his *bourka* to the ground and stand on it to show he will not retreat one step from the surface covered by his *bourka*. Me, I throw down my *bourka* somewhere on the road to Vladikavkaz, on a perfect winter's day, when the whole of creation is sitting up ahead of you, inviting you to come in, whatever the risk and whatever the cost.

Outside the tower, bats squeaked, owls hooted. But the sounds I was listening to were within my head: the drumbeat of revolt, the cry to arms.

It happens to be the Ingush because they exemplify everything most shabby about our post–Cold War world. All through the Cold War it was our Western boast that we defended the underdog against the bully. The boast was a bloody lie. Again and again during the Cold War and after it the West made common cause with the bully in favour of what we call stability, to the despair of the very people we claimed to be protecting. That's what we're up to now.

How many times had I been forced to listen to these turgid expositions? And closed my ears to them; my mind as well? So many, I supposed, that I had forgotten their effect upon ears as wide open as Emma's.

The Ingush refuse to be rationalised out of existence, they refuse to be ignored, devalued, or dismissed. And what they are fighting against, whether they know it or not, is a whorehouse alliance between a rotten Russian Empire marching to its old tunes and a Western leadership that in its dealings with the rest of the world has proclaimed moral indifference to be its decent Christian right.

That's what I'll be fighting against too.

Dozing off in my tutorial this afternoon, I woke with a jerk three hundred years later. Helmut Kohl was Chancellor of all the Russias, Brezhnev was marching the Bosnian Serbs into Berlin, and Margaret Thatcher was at the checkout counter, taking the cash.

Which is all to say, I love you, but look out for me, because where I'm heading, there isn't a lot of turning back. Amen and out.

L.

Standing, I positioned myself in front of Larry's green raincoat, which I had hung from a wooden hook in the wall. The mud-caked boots lay beneath it on the floor. In my mind's eye he was smiling his Byronic smile.

"You mad bloody Pied Piper," I whispered. "Where in God's name have you taken her?"

I have locked her in a hollow mountain in the Caucasus, he replied. I have seduced her in accordance with my blood feud against the infidel Tim Cranmer. I have swept her away on the white stallion of my sophistry.

I WAS remembering. Staring at the green raincoat and remembering.

"Hey, Timbo!"

Just the appellation grates on my nerves.

"Yes, Larry."

It's a Bloody Sunday and, as I realise now, our last one. Larry has driven Emma down from London. He just happened to be in town, he just happened to have a car. So instead of driving himself to Bath he has driven Emma to me. How he found her out in London I have no idea. Neither do I know how long they have been together.

"Great news," Larry announces.

"Really? Oh, good."

"I've appointed Emma our Ambassador to the Court of St. James. Her parish will include the Americas, Europe, Africa, and most of Asia. Won't it, Emm?"

"Oh, great," I say.

"I've found her a duplicator. All we need now is some headed notepaper, and we can join the United Nations. Right, Emm?"

"Oh, marvellous," I say.

But that is all I say, because that is how Cranmer's part is written for him. To look down kindly. To be tolerant and unpossessive. To leave the children with their idealism and remain on my side of the house. It is not an easy part to play with dignity. And perhaps Larry sees something of this in my face and is moved, if not to guilt, at least to pity, for he flings an arm around my shoulder and squeezes me against him.

"Pair of old queens, aren't we, Timbers?"

"Talk of the town," I agree, as Emma takes her turn to smile on our friendship.

"Here. Read all about it," says Larry, delving in his scuffed Gladstone bag. And he hands me a white booklet called "A People's Calvary." Which people is not clear to me. Our Sunday seminars have addressed so many insoluble conflicts over the last months that the Calvary could have occurred anywhere between East Timor and Alaska.

"Well, thank you both very much," I say. "It shall be my bedtime reading this very night."

But once back in my study I stuff the document deep in the file-and-forget compartment of my bookshelf, to take its place among other unreadable pamphlets Larry has pressed on me over the years.

I WAS picture gazing.

I was standing before the poster I had removed from Emma's love nest and impaled on a bent nail in my celibate retreat.

Who the hell are you, Bashir Haji?

You are OCL, Our Chief Leader.

You are Bashir Haji because that is how you have signed your name: *from Bashir Haji to my friend Misha the great warrior.*

"Larry, you crazy bastard," I said aloud. "You *really* crazy bastard."

I WAS running. I was dodging through rain and darkness to the house. The urgency in me was something I could not control. I was bent double, knees striking at my chin, leaping down the slope and across the footbridge in the darkness, sliding, falling, barking knees and elbows, while blackened cloud stacks raced across the sky like fleeing armies and the driven rain dashed at me in gusts. Gaining the kitchen entrance, I glanced quickly round before letting myself in, but I could make out little against the density of the trees. With squelching feet I hastened across the Great Hall, down the flagstone corridor to my study, and found what I was looking for in the shelves behind my desk: the shiny, white-bound, desk-printed booklet like a university thesis, called "A People's Calvary." A quick glance inside, my first: three Russian writers were credited. Their names were Mutaliev, Fargiev, and Pliev. Translated by no less a hand than Larry's. Stuffing it under my pullover, I squelched back to the kitchen and let myself once more into the night. The storm had dropped. Palls of steam rose resentfully from the brook. Did I see the shadow of a man against the hillside—one tall man running left to right, fleeing as if observed? Regaining the priesthole, I made an anxious tour of my arrow slits before putting on the light, but I saw nothing I dared call a living man. Back at my trestle table, I opened the white booklet and spread it flat. These dons, so ponderous, so circuitous, no sense of time. In a minute they'll be talking about the meaning of meaning. I turned the pages impatiently. All right, another insoluble human tragedy; the world is full of them. The margins defaced by Larry's childish annotations, I suspected for my benefit: "Cf. the Palestinians"; "Moscow lying in its teeth as usual"; "The lunatic Zhironovsky says all Russian Muslims should be disfranchised."

Belatedly I identified the typeface. Emma's electric portable. She must have typed it for him while they were in London. Then when they came back, they thoughtfully presented me with my complimentary copy. Jolly nice of them.

ONCE AGAIN I cannot tell you how much I knew, or to what extent my disbelieving spirit still demanded proof of what it knew but refused point-blank to acknowledge. But I know that as I uncovered one clue after the other, my guilt, so recently shuffled off, returned, and I began to see myself as the creator of their folly; as its provoker and negative instigator; as the essential bigot who by his intolerance brings about the circumstance he most deplores.

WE ARE arguing, Cranmer versus the Rest of England. The argument began last night, but I managed to put it to bed. At breakfast, however, the smouldering ash again bursts into flames, and this time no sweet words of mine can put them out. This time it is Cranmer's temper that snaps, not Larry's.

He has been goading me about my indifference to the world's agonies. He has gone as far as is courteous, and then a little further, towards suggesting that I epitomise the shortcomings of the morally torpid West. Emma, though she has said little, is on his side. She sits demurely with her hands in front of her, palms uppermost, as if to demonstrate there is nothing in them. Now, with clenched precision, I have responded to Larry's attack. They have cast me as an archetype of middle-class complacency. Very well, then, that is what I shall be for them. In which perversity, I have spoken a mouthful:

I have said that I never considered myself responsible for the world's ills, not for causing them, not for curing them. The world was in my view a jungle overrun with savages, just as it had always been. Most of its problems were insoluble.

I have said I regard any quiet corner of it, such as Honeybrook, to be a haven wrested from the jaws of hell. I therefore found it discourteous in a guest when he brought to it such a catalogue of miseries.

I have said that I have always been, and would continue to be, prepared to make sacrifices for my neighbours, compatriots, and friends. But when it came to saving barbarians from one another in countries no bigger than a letter on the map, I failed to see why I should throw myself into a burning house to rescue a dog I had never cared for in the first place.

I have said all this with brio, but my heart is in none of it, though I refuse to let this show. Perhaps it pleases me to be stuck out on a limb. Suddenly, to our shared surprise, Larry declares he is delighted with me.

"Bang on the nose, Timbo. Spoken from the gut. Congrats. Right, Emm?"

Emma is anything but right.

"You were appalling," she says in a low, vicious voice, straight into my face. "You were actually terminal." She means that to her great relief I have behaved badly enough to justify her transgressions.

And the same night, as she sets off up the great staircase to resume her typing: "You don't understand the first *thing* about involvement."

. . .

I HAD returned to "A People's Calvary." I was reading history and reading it too fast, and history was not my mood, even if the past explained the present. Academic arguments about the founding of the city of Vladikavkaz: did it rise on Ingush or Ossetian territory? References to the "distorted historical facts" being offered by apologists from the Ossetian camp. Talk of the bravery of the plains-dwelling Ingush of the eighteenth and nineteenth centuries, when they were forced to take up arms to defend their villages. Talk of the contested Prigorod region, the sacred *Prigorodnyi raion*, now the great bone of contention between Ossetians and Ingush. Talk of places that might indeed be only the size of a letter on the map, yet when their inhabitants rose up, the power of the entire Russian Empire was held to ransom. Talk of the hopes raised by the coming of Soviet Communism and how these hopes were dashed when the red tsars turned out to be just as terrible as their white predecessors. . . .

Suddenly out of my temporary frustration came a burst of light, and I leapt once more excitedly to my feet.

CRAMMED against the stone wall stood the old school trunk I used as a filing box for my CC archive. From it I extracted a bunch of folders. One contained surveillance reports, a second, character notes, a third, microphone intercepts. Armed with the intercepts, I sped back to the trestle table and resumed my reading: except that this time the Calvary is CC's own, and in my memory I am listening to his modulated Russian voice—one might almost say civilised—as he and Larry sit in their bugged hotel room at Heathrow, drinking malt whisky out of tooth mugs.

There is always something a little magical to me about these meetings between Larry and CC. If Larry feels a kinship with CC, so do I. Do we not have Larry in common? Are we not both alternately delighted and alarmed by him, raised up, brought down, infuriated and enchanted? Are we not, both of us, dependent on him for our good standing with our masters? And am I not justified, as I read the transcripts or listen to the tapes, in taking a certain pride in my controlling interest?

Heathrow is one of Checheyev's favourite places. He can take rooms there by the half day, he can rotate hotels and fancy himself anonymous—though thanks to Larry the listeners are usually ahead of him. At this particular meeting, according to Larry's later account of it, CC has pulled a bunch of faded photographs from his wallet:

"This is my family, Larry, this is my *aul* [translator's gratuitous note: village] as it was in my father's day, this is our house, which is still occupied by Ossetians, this is their washing, hanging on the clothesline that was put up by my father, here are my brothers and sisters, and here is the railroad that deported my people to Kazakhstan. . . . So many died on the journey that the Russians had to keep stopping the train to bury them in mass graves. . . . And here is the place where my father was shot."

After the photographs Checheyev takes his diplomatic pass from his pocket and waves it in Larry's face. The transcribers' English, as leaden as ever:

"You think I was born in 1946. That is not so. Nineteen forty-six is for my cover here, my other person. I was born in 1944, on Red Army Day, which is February twenty-third. That's a big national holiday in Russia. And I was born not in Tbilisi but in a freezing cattle truck headed for the frozen steppes of Kazakhstan.

". . . Do you know what happened on 23 February 1944, when I was being born and everybody was having a nice national holiday, and Russian soldiers were dancing to order in our villages and making festive? I'll tell you. The entire Ingush and Chechen nations were declared criminal by edict of Josef Stalin and carted thousands of miles from their fertile Caucasian plains to be resettled in wastelands north of the Aral Sea. . . ."

I skipped a page or two and read greedily on: "In October '43 the Stalinists had already deported the Karachays. In March '44 they took the Balkars. And in February they came for the Chechen and the Ingush . . . personally, you understand? Beria and his deputies, in the flesh, came down to mastermind our resettlement. Like you take a man from California and resettle him in Antarctica—that kind of resettle . . ."

I flipped a half page. CC's dry humour was beginning to assert itself, despite the banality of the transcribers. "The old ones and the sick were spared the journey. They were herded into a nice building, which was set on fire to keep them warm. Then the building was sprayed with machine gun bullets. My father was a bit luckier. Stalin's soldiers shot him in the back of the neck for not wanting his pregnant wife to be forced onto the train. . . . When my mother saw my father's corpse, she decided she was lonely, so she produced me. The widow woman's son was born on the cattle truck that carried him to exile. . . ."

Here the transcribers in their prissy way indicated a natural break, while CC withdraws to the bathroom and Larry tops up their glasses.

". . . Those who survived the journey were put to work in a gulag, planting the frozen steppes, mining gold sixteen hours a day, which is why the Ingush to this day deal in gold. . . . They were classed as slave labourers on account of their alleged collaboration with the Germans, but the Ingush fought well against the Germans; they just hated Stalin and the Russians more."

"And they hated the Ossetians," Larry says keenly, like a schoolboy wanting to be top.

He has touched a nerve, perhaps deliberately, for CC unlooses a tirade.

"Why should we not hate the Ossetians? They are not of our land! They are not of our blood! They are Persians who claim to be Christians and worship heathen gods in secret. They are the lackeys of Moscow. They have stolen our fields and houses. Why? Do you know why?" Larry affects not to. "Do you know *why* Stalin deported us and said we were criminals and enemies of the Soviet people? Because Stalin was an Ossetian! Not a Georgian, not an Abkhazian, not an Armenian, not an Azerbaijani, not a Chechen, and not an Ingushi—God knows, not an Ingushi—but a foreigner, an Ossetian. Do you love the poet Osip Mandelstam?"

Carried away by the passion of CC's outburst, Larry avows his love of Mandelstam.

"You know why Stalin had the poet Mandelstam shot? For writing in one of his poems that Josef Stalin was an Ossetian! That is why Mandelstam was shot by Stalin!"

I doubted whether this was the reason Mandelstam was shot. I held the better-attested view that he died in a psychiatric hospital. And I doubted whether Stalin was really an Ossetian. And perhaps Larry did too, but in the face of such fervour, his only recorded response is a grunt, followed by a long silence while the two men drink. Eventually CC resumes his narrative. In 1953 Stalin died. Three years later Khrushchev denounced him, and shortly afterwards the Chechen-Ingush autonomous republic resumed its rightful place on the maps:

". . . We come home from Kazakhstan. That's a long walk, but we make it, even if some of us arrive a bit late. My mother dies on the way, and I swear to her that I shall bury her in her homeland. But when we arrive, the doors of our houses are locked against us and Ossetian faces look out of our windows. We are beggars, sleeping in our streets, poaching in our fields. Never mind that the law says the Ossetians have got to go. They don't like the law. They don't recognise the law. They recognise guns. And Moscow has given the Ossetians many guns and taken away ours."

There had been much debate on the Top Floor, I remembered, about whether on the strength of this meeting we should make a pass at Checheyev and try to obtain him as our source. After all, he had broken half the rules in the KGB book. He had blown his own cover, vented anti-Soviet sentiments, and beaten the forbidden ethnic drum. But in the end my impassioned reasoning prevailed, and the barons reluctantly agreed that our most important asset was Larry and we should contemplate no move that might endanger him.

I was standing at the centre of my priesthole again, beneath the overhead light, studying the remnants of a folder of printed pamphlets issued by the BBC monitoring service. Key words, those that had survived, were highlighted with green marker pen. The idiosyncratic spelling of the transcribers had been left untouched.

North Osetia rela . . . calm on fi . . . versary of conflict.
ITAR-TASS news agency (World Se . . . Mosc . . . in Russian 1106 gmt 31 Oct 93
Text of rep . . .
Vladikavkaz, 31 October: The sad anni . . . of the tragedy of 31 October 1992, whe . . . armed confrontation began *in the zon . . . t . . . Oset . . . Ingush conflict . . .* be softened by a. . . .
The tragic tally [for . . . conflict]: *1,300 killed* . . . sides, more than *400* . . . houses destroyed and . . . homeless.

I turned a couple of blackened pages. The highlighting continued: Emma's or Larry's, it made no difference, since I knew now that they shared the same madness:

> . . . *mass disorder and inte* . . . *conflicts accompanied* by the use of *force, weaponry,* and *combat vehicles* . . . the refugee situation . . . catastrophic, with more *than 60,000* . . . situation is a tragedy which has befallen *a people needed by no one* . . . *Russian troops* operating in the state of emergency area on the territory of North Osetia and Ingushetia have been ordered *to eliminate bandit gangs* which fa . . . authorities, said General . . . the interim administration in the Osetian-Ingush conflict zone.

But in the left-hand margin, in angry capitals, Larry had written the following words:

FOR BANDIT READ PATRIOT

FOR GANG READ ARMY

FOR ELIMINATE READ KILL, TORTURE, MAIM, BURN ALIVE.

I WAS in spasm.

In spasm, but overcontrolled.

I was standing, and my back was screaming murder at me and I was screaming murder in reply, but I had found the file I was looking for. LP: LAST DEBRIEFINGS, I had written on the cover, in capitals in my bureaucratic hand. Yet for all my eagerness, I had to punt myself along the wall like a wounded crow in order to carry it to the trestle table.

I was squatting in a chair and leaning low over the table, taking as much weight off my spine as I could. My left elbow was pressed onto a cushion, as Mr. Dass had taught me. But the pains in my back were nothing compared with the shame and anguish in my soul as I stared at the accumulating evidence of my culpable blindness:

> Asked LP whether he could decently duck the Caucasus trip that CC is so keen on. I didn't say so, but customer interest in region v. low and already oversupplied by satellite, humint, sigint, and a flood of reports from US oil companies operating or prospecting in the region. LP not receptive.

LP: *I owe it to him, Timbo. I've promised him for years and never gone. They're what he cares about. They're who he is.*

Licking my fingertips, I clawed painfully through the pages till I came to my account of the debriefing three weeks later:

LP has violently overreacted to Caucasus trip—predictably, in his present menopausal mood. Nothing in scale for him, everything a first and last. *Saddest, most exciting, most moving, tragic experience of my career, etc., masses to report, seething unrest, balloon will go up again any minute, ethnic, tribal, and religious tension everywhere, Russian occupiers total oafs, plight of Ingush archetypal for plight of all small oppressed Muslim nations in region, etc. . . .*

Footnote to source report: H/Evaluation Ex-Sov target told me off the record she was unlikely to file.

BUT CRANMER had filed.

Cranmer had filed and forgotten.

Cranmer in his criminally negligent myopia had consigned the cause of the Ingush people to the dustbin of history, and LP with it, then buried his stupid head in the sweet earth of Somerset—even though he knew that nothing, absolutely nothing in Larry's life, or Cranmer's own pathetic imitation of it, ever went away:

. . . because I've seen them, in their little valley towns and in their mountains. . . . In life, as we both know, it's the luck of the draw, who you meet and when and how much you have left to give, and the point at which you say, To hell with everything, this is where I go the distance, this is where I stick.

A PICTURE postcard. Torn once vertically. Addressed to Sally Anderson in Cambridge Street and showing a dressed couple lying in a field. Postmark: Macclesfield. The artist: one David Macfarlane. The description: "Silent Noon 1, 1979, mixed media 18″ × 24″." Provenance: Emma's wastepaper basket.

Emm. Crucial. AM needs 50,000 in his account by Friday noon. Miss your beautiful eyes. L. PS. Henceforth he's Nutty as in f'cake, nuts-in-whenever, tough Nutty to crack.

I made a brief mental pause, as other old memories began to wake inside my head. AM who is Nutty, who is tough to crack. Nuts in May; who speaks like Mr. Dass and has a new telephone in his car. The memories stirred, ordered themselves, and were set aside to wait their turn.

I took up a sheet of yellow legal pad, crumpled by Emma and unfolded by myself. Provenance: her kneehole desk at Honeybrook.

Emm. Vital. I'm seeing Nutty at 10 tomorrow in Bath. CC has sent the shopping list by bearded friend, and it's awaiting my collection IN LONDON, at the Royal Automobile Club in Pall Mall. Call the Club. Tell them you're my secy. and they must mail the letter EXPRESS to me here, for tomorrow. These are the best days of my life. Thank you for the days, thank you for life. Nutty says we have to calculate around twenty percent in bribes. Auden says we must love one another or die.

L.

A fresh folder of reports from the BBC monitoring service, this time intact, and the marked extracts like the crematorium music of every border war across the globe:

Combat operations in *Prigorodnyi raion* continued 1 November. . . . The fire points of the Ingush irregulars are being suppressed. . . . Many casualties, both killed and wounded, have been registered in many villages. . . . Exchanges of fire continue in conflict zone. . . . Airborne regiments meeting stiff resistance. . . . Rocket artillery used against Ingush villages. . . . Russian premier rules out review of existing borders. . . . Russian armoured column moves into Ingushetia. . . . Ingush refugees take to mountains. . . . Onset of winter fails to temper conflict. . . .

Tim Cranmer, you prize, prizer, prizest fool, I thought. How about *your* purblind innocence—you who used to pride yourself on never missing a trick?

PERHAPS it was this anger with myself that made me lift my head in such a hurry. I lifted my head and listened, and what I heard I don't know, but I heard it. Clutching the wall, I embarked on another laborious cripple's tour of my six arrow slit windows. The thunderclouds had fled. A half-moon draped with cloud cast a grey glow over the surrounding hills. Gradually I made out the shapes of three men placed at intervals around the chapel. They were fifty yards apart and eighty yards away from me. Each stood like a sentry halfway down his own hill. As I watched, the man at the centre took a stride forward and was imitated by his comrades either side of him.

I looked at my house. By the porch light I saw a fourth man standing by my car. This time I didn't panic. No rushing upstairs or forgetting telephone numbers. Panic, like the pain in my back, was a thing of the past. I glanced at the turmoil of papers on the floor, at my trestle table, at my makeshift archive in disarray, my school tuckbox spilling over with files. Resisting a ridiculous impulse to tidy them, I made a swift collection of essential documents.

Bairstow's escape briefcase stood open beside the door. I stuffed the documents into it, together with some spare ammunition, then slipped the .38 into my waistband. As I did so, an instinct reminded me of Zorin's letter nestling in my pocket. Returning to the tuckbox, I delved until I came upon a folder marked PETER. I removed Zorin's personal particulars sheet and added it to the essential documents in the briefcase. I switched off my light and took a last look outside. The men were converging on the chapel. Briefcase in hand, I groped my way down the spiral staircase to the vestry. Closing the cope cupboard behind me, I grabbed a box of matches and stepped into the church.

I was ahead of them. With the moonlight to help me, I unlocked the south door, then made swiftly for the pulpit, which is Norman and finely carved. I climbed the four creaking wooden steps and set the briefcase out of sight against the front panels, where a preacher's feet would be if one were standing there. I went to the altar and lit the candles. Calmly. No shake. Choosing a pew on the north side, I knelt down, put my face in my hands, and, for want of a closer definition of what was going on inside my head, prayed for my deliverance, if only so that I could deliver Emma and Larry from their insanity.

In good time I heard the throaty *clunk* of the south door as it was opened from outside; then the screech of the hinges that I had always been careful not to oil since they provided such an excellent early warning system for anybody working in the priesthole. And after the screech I heard one pair of feet—wet boots, rubber soles—advance a couple of steps and pause, then splash towards me down the aisle.

THERE is a protocol about praying in such circumstances, and I must have thought about that too. You don't, simply because somebody has barged into your private church at two o'clock in the morning, ask him what the devil he thinks he's doing here. But neither do you behave as if worship has rendered you stone deaf. My best course, I decided, was to fidget my reborn back, draw up my shoulders, and bury my face more deeply in my hands to show that I was striving for greater piety in the teeth of boorish behaviour.

But such fineness was wasted on my intruder, for the next thing I knew was a heavy weight descending unceremoniously onto the kneeling board at my left side and a pair of raincoated elbows thumping onto the ledge next to my own, and Munslow's truculent face glowering at me from just a couple of inches away.

"All right, Cranmer. What's this God bit suddenly?"

I sat back. I allowed a sigh to escape me. I passed a hand across my eyes as if the intensity of my meditations were still upon me.

"For pity's sake," I whispered, but this only annoyed him further.

"Don't give *me* that crap. I've checked. There's not a whiff of God on your file. What are you cooking up? Got someone tucked away here, have you? Pettifer? Comrade Checheyev? Your little lady friend Emma that nobody can find? Six hours you've done down here so far tonight. The bloody Pope doesn't do that much."

I preserved my weary, inward tone. "I've got things on my mind, Andy. Leave me alone. I won't be interrogated about my faith. By you or anyone."

"Oh, yes you will. Your old employers would like very much to interrogate you about your faith and a few other things that are troubling them. Starting tomorrow eleven a.m. and continuing for as long as it takes. Meanwhile you've got yourself a few houseguests in case you take it into your head to do a runner. Orders."

He stood up. His knees were close to my face, and I had a ridiculous urge to break them, though I am sure I had forgotten how. There was some hold they had taught us at training camp, a kind of rugger tackle that bent legs the wrong way. But I didn't break his legs or try to. If I had done, he would probably have broken mine. Instead I dropped my head, passed my hand across my brow again, and closed my eyes.

"I need to talk to you, Andy. Time to get it off my chest. How many are you?"

"Four. What's that got to do with it?" But there was greed in his voice, and excitement. At his feet he saw the kneeling penitent who was about to make his reputation for him.

"I'd rather talk to you here," I said. "Tell them to go back to the house and wait for us."

Still on my knees, I listened to him bark graceless commands over his intercom. I waited till I heard an acknowledgement before I drew my gun and thrust the barrel into his groin. I stood up until our faces were very little distance apart. He was wearing a communications harness. Reaching inside his jacket, I switched the microphone to "off." I gave my instructions singly.

"Give me your jacket."

He did so and I laid it on the pew. With the gun still at his groin, I pulled the communications harness from his chest and put it with the jacket.

"Put your hands on your head. Take one step back."

He again did as I asked.

"Turn round and walk towards the door."

He did that, too, and watched me while, with my spare hand, I locked the south door from the inside and removed the key. Then I walked him to the vestry and locked him into it. It's a fine door to the vestry. The key is as splendid as any to the church, but unlike most vestries this one has no door to the outside, and no window.

"If you yell, I'll shoot you through the door," I told him. And I suppose the fool believed me, because he kept quiet.

Hastening to the pulpit, I drew the briefcase from its hiding place and, leaving the altar candles burning, let myself out of the north door, which I locked from the outside as a further precaution. The pale brush strokes of a new dawn lit my way. A bridle path ran out of sight along the vineyard wall to the home farm, where our casking and bottling were done. I followed it at a trot. The air smelled of mushrooms. With a key from my chain, I unlocked the double doors to the tithe barn. Inside stood a Volkswagen van, property of Honeybrook Estates and my occasional runabout. Since my tryst with Larry, I had kept the petrol tank full and a spare jerry can in the back, together with a suitcase of sensible spare clothes, for there is nothing worse, when you are on the run, than being short of decent clothes.

I drove without lights to the lane and still without lights for another mile to the crossroads. I took the old Mendip road, passed Priddy Pool without a glance, and kept driving till I came to Bristol airport, where I left the van in the long-term car park and bought myself a seat on the first flight of the day to Belfast, in the name of Cranmer. I took a shuttle coach to Bristol Temple Meads, and it was packed with exhausted Welsh football fans, singing quiet hymns in harmony. From the station forecourt, I allowed myself a last incredulous stare up the hill at Cambridge Street before boarding an early train to Paddington. I rode with it as far as Reading, where, as Bairstow, I booked myself into a garish commercial travellers' hotel. I tried to sleep, but the terror pulsed in me like another heart, and it was terror of the worst kind, the terror of a guilt-obsessed spectator to a catastrophe he cannot prevent from overtaking people he cannot call to, and the people were my own. It was I who had consigned Larry to a life of fiction, who had taught him the arts of subterfuge and set loose in him the mechanism that had now run so disastrously amok. It was I who had thrown a noose around Emma, never guessing that when I appointed her the perfect mate she would turn out to be the perfect mate for Larry.

In my dismal hotel room I put on all the lights and made myself foul tea with a tea bag and artificial milk, then set myself to revisiting the bundles of paper I had stuffed into the briefcase on my departure from the priesthole. I wrote my bank a long letter of instruction, providing, among other things, for Mrs. Benbow, Ted Lanxon, and the Toller girls. I sealed the envelope, addressed it, and posted it in the centre of the town. I did some telephoning from a public call box, then spent the afternoon in a cinema, though I remember nothing of the film. At five o'clock, in a red Ford hired in the name of Bairstow, I left Reading on the evening tide. Each golden field in its brown hedge was like another shard of my fragmented world.

"It's the sounds and smells of youth coming back to you," Larry had written to Emma. "It's the sky you used to look at when you were a child. You understand ideas again. Money has no power."

I wished I could share his lyricism.

11

"OH, *MARVELLOUS*, Tim," Clare Dugdale had cried in her voice of late-Thatcherite thrill when I telephoned her from a call box, saying I just happened to be in the area. "Simon will be *over the moon*. He hasn't had *any* buddy-buddy talk for *weeks*. Come *nice* and early and we can have a *drink* and you can help me put the children to *bed*, just like the *old* days. You won't *believe* Petronella. She's *enormous*. Do you mind fish? Simon's got a new thing about his *heart*. Shall you be *alone*, Tim, or are you *with*?"

I crossed a bridge and saw below me our white hotel, now turned grey by the recession. The riverside lawns were overgrown. The bar where I had waited for her had DISCO scrawled in chalk across the door. Pinball machines winked in the once stately dining room, where we had eaten *flambé* steak while she probed my crotch with her stockinged foot and we waited till it was all right to go to bed—which we did as soon as decent, because by four in the morning she was perched in front of the mirror, repairing her makeup to go home.

"Mustn't let the children miss me, must I, darling?" she says. "And poor Simon might *easily* decide to give me a wake-up call from Washington. He never *can* sleep on *short* trips."

"Does he suspect?" I ask, more it now seemed to me out of human curiosity than any particular sense of guilt.

Pause while she completes a line of lipstick. "Shouldn't think so. Si's a Berkeleyan. He denies the existence of *everything* he can't per-

ceive." Clare took a Cambridge degree in philosophy before shoul-
dering the intellectual burdens of a Foreign Office wife. "And since
we don't exist, we can do whatever we *jolly* well want, can't we? And
we *still* won't have done it, *will* we?"

In Maidenhead I parked at the railway station and, armed with
Bairstow's briefcase, took a taxi to the hideous fifties barracks where
they lived. A disintegrating climbing frame adorned the overgrown
front garden. Clare's bashed Renault stood abandoned at a dramatic
angle in the weed-infested drive. A faded notice by the bell said
CHIEN MÉCHANT. I presumed it was a relic of Simon's visits to Brus-
sels as a NATO Moscow-watcher. The door opened, and the *au pair*
eyed me with slothful curiosity.

"Anna Greta. Still here, my goodness. How splendid."

I stepped round her into the hall, picking my way between per-
ambulators, children's bicycles, and a wigwam. As I did so Clare came
charging down the stairs and flung her arms around me. She was
wearing the amber brooch I had given her. Simon believed she had
inherited it from a distant cousin. Or so she said.

"Anna Greta, darling, will you *please* go and dish up the vegetables
and put them on the hotplate?" she ordered, taking my hand and
leading me upstairs. "You're still *terribly* yummy, Tim. And Si says
you've found an absolutely super, *frightfully* young girl. I think that's
awfully clever of you. Petronella, look who's here!" She carried my
hand round to my backside and pinched me. "It isn't fish; it's duck. I
decided Si's heart could lump it for once. Let me *look* at you again."

Petronella emerged scowling from the bathroom, dressed in a
towel and a mackintosh hat. She was now an ungrateful child of ten,
with wire round her teeth and her father's hovering smile.

"Why are you kissing my mother?"

"Because we're *very* old friends, Pet, darling," Clare replied with
hoots of laughter. "Don't be so silly. *You'd* like a hug from somebody
as dishy as Tim, *I'll* bet."

"No, I wouldn't."

The twin boys wanted *Rupert Bear.* A visiting girl called Hubbie
wanted *Black Beauty.* The conciliator in me chose *Peter Rabbit,* and I
was coming to the bit about Peter's father having an accident in Mr.
McGregor's garden when I heard Simon's footsteps ascending the
stairs.

"Hullo, Tim, nice to see you," he said, all on one note, as he offered me a lifeless hand. "Hullo, Pet. Hullo, Clive. Hullo, Mark. Hullo, Hubbie."

"Hullo," they said.

"Hullo, Clare."

"Hullo," said Clare.

I went on reading, while Simon listened from the doorway. In my weightless state of mind I had hoped he might like me better now that I was a fellow cuckold. But he didn't seem to, so perhaps it didn't show.

THE DUCK must have been frozen, because parts of it still were. As we hacked our way through the bleeding limbs, I remembered that this was how we had always eaten, when we ate our frightful meals together: potatoes boiled to a sludge and school cabbage floating in a green lake. Did their Catholic souls derive solace from such abstinence? Did they feel closer to God and further from the herd?

"Why are you here?" Simon asked in his dry, nasal voice.

"Visiting a spinster aunt, actually," I replied.

"Not another filthy rich one, Tim?" said Clare.

"Where is she?" said Simon.

"No, this one's indigent," I told Clare. "Marlow," I told Simon.

"Which nursing home?" said Simon.

"Sunnymeades," I said, giving him a name I had plucked from the yellow pages and hoping it was still in business.

"Is she an aunt on your father's side?" Simon asked.

"Actually she's a cousin of my mother's," I said, forestalling the likelihood that Simon would telephone Sunnymeades nursing home and establish that she didn't exist.

"Are you growing many grapes, please?" sang Anna Greta, who had been elevated to guest for the evening.

"Well, not a *bumper* harvest, Anna Greta," I replied. "But fair. And first tastings *extremely* promising."

"Oh," Anna Greta exclaimed, as if astonished.

"I inherited a bit of a problem, quite honestly. My uncle Bob, who founded the business for love, put a lot of trust in his Maker and rather less in science."

Clare gave a hoot of laughter, but Anna Greta's jaw sagged in mystification. For some inexplicable reason, I forged on.

"He planted the *wrong* grapes in the *wrong* place, then he prayed for sun and got frost. Unfortunately, the life expectancy of a vine is twenty-five years. Which means we must either commit genocide or keep on fighting nature for another ten years."

I couldn't stop. Having derided my own efforts, I exulted in the success of my English and Welsh competitors and deplored the tax burdens imposed on them by an uncaring government. I painted a fulsome picture of England as one of the ancient wine-growing countries of the world, while Anna Greta gawped at me with her mouth open.

"Poor you," said Simon.

"So let's hear about this underaged girl you've shacked up with," Clare cut in recklessly; after two glasses of Romanian claret, she was capable of saying absolutely anything. "You're such an old *dog*, Tim. Simon's absolutely *green* with envy. Aren't you, Si?"

"Not in the least," said Simon.

"She's beautiful, she's musical, she can't cook, and I adore her," I proclaimed gaily, grateful to have an opportunity to extol Emma's virtues. "She's also warmhearted and brilliantly clever. What else do you want to know?"

The door opened, and Petronella stormed in, her blond hair brushed over her dressing gown, her blue gaze fixed on her mother in an expression of ethereal agony.

"You're making so much noise I can't *sleep!*" she protested, stamping her foot. "You're doing it *on purpose.*"

Clare led Petronella back to bed. Anna Greta moodily cleared away the plates.

"Simon, I've got a bit of office shop I need to try out on you," I said. "Could we possibly have quarter of an hour alone?"

Simon washed while I dried. He wore a blue butcher's apron. There was no machine. We seemed to be washing up several meals at once.

"What do you want?" said Simon.

We had had these conversations before, in his joyless eyrie at the Foreign Office, with jaded Whitehall pigeons eyeing us through the filthy window.

"I've been approached by someone who wants to be paid a lot of money for some information," I said.

"I thought you'd retired."

"I have. It's an old case come alive."

"You don't have to bother with those; they'll dry by themselves," Simon said. "What's he trying to sell you?"

"A forthcoming armed uprising in the North Caucasus."

"Who's rising against who? Thanks," he said as I handed him a dirty saucepan. "They're rising all the time. It's what they do."

"The Ingush against the Russians and Ossetians. With a little help from the Chechen."

"Tried it in '92 and were trounced. No arms. Only what they'd pinched or bought at the back door. Whereas, thanks to Moscow, the Ossetians were armed to the teeth. Still are."

"What if the Ingush equipped themselves with a decent armoury?"

"They can't. They're scattered and dispirited, and whatever they get hold of, the Ossies will get more of. Weapons are the Ossies' thing. We had a story in last week that they've been buying up Red Army surplus in Estonia and running it down to the Serbs in Bosnia with the help of Russian intelligence."

"My source insists that this time the Ingush are going for broke."

"Well, he would, wouldn't he?"

"He says there's no stopping them. They've got a new leader. A man called Bashir Haji."

"Bashir's yesterday's hero," said Simon, vehemently scouring a very pitted saucepan. "Brave as a lion, great on a horse. Black-belt Sufist. But when it comes to fighting Russian rocketry and helicopter cavalry, he can't lead a brass band."

We had had conversations like this before. In Simon Dugdale, the art of debunking secret intelligence had found its master. "If we believe my man, Bashir is promising to provide high-tech state-of-the-art Western weaponry and send the Russians and Ossetians back where they came from."

"Listen!"

Slamming down his saucepan, Simon splayed a wet hand in my face but managed to stop it a couple of inches short.

"In '92 the Ingush popped their garters and made an armed march on the *Prigorodnyi raion*. They had some tanks, a few APCs, a bit of artillery—Russian stuff, bought or plundered, not a lot. Drawn against them"—he grabbed his thumb with his spare hand—"they had North Ossetian Interior Forces"—he grabbed his index finger—

"OMON Russian special forces; Republican guards; local Terek Cos-sacks"—he had reached his little finger—"and so-called volunteers from South Ossetia flown up by the Russians to cut throats for them and squat the *Prigorodnyi raion.* The only support the Ingush got was from the Chechen, who lent them so-called volunteers and a bit of weaponry. The Chechen are pals with the Ingush, but the Chechen have got their own agenda, which the Russians are aware of. So the Russians are using the Ingush to drive a wedge into the Chechen. If your man is seriously telling you that Bashir or anyone else is plan-ning a full-scale organised attack on the enemies of Ingushetia, either he's making it up or Bashir's gone potty."

His outburst over, he plunged his arms back into the suds.

I tried another tack. Perhaps I wanted to draw something out of him that I knew was there. Something I needed to hear again as an affirmation of Larry's emotional logic.

"So what about the justice of it?" I suggested.

"The *what?*"

I was making him angry. "Of the Ingush cause. Have they got right on their side?"

He slapped a colander facedown on the draining board. "*Right?*" he repeated indignantly. "You mean in absolute terms, as in right and wrong—how has history treated the Ingush?"

"Yes."

He seized a roasting tray and attacked it with a scourer. Simon Dugdale had never been able to resist the lecturer's temptation.

"Three hundred years of having the living shit beaten out of them by the tsars. Frequently returned the compliment. Enter the Coms. False interlude of serendipity, then business as usual. Deported by Stalin in '44 and declared a nation of criminals. Thirteen years in the wilderness. Rehabilitated by decree of Supreme Soviet and allowed to empty the dustbins. Tried peaceful protest. Didn't work. Rioted. Moscow sits on its arse." Pressing down on the roasting tray, he gave it a vengeful scrub. "Coms go down the tube; enter Yeltsin. Sweet-talks them. Russian Parliament passes fuzzy resolution restoring dis-possessed peoples." He kept scrubbing. "Ingush buy it. Supreme Soviet adopts law favouring an Ingush republic within Russian Fed-eration. Hooray. Five minutes later Yeltsin puts the knockers on it with a presidential decree forbidding border changes in the Cauca-sus. Not so hooray. Moscow's latest plan is to force the Ossetians to accept the Ingush back in agreed numbers and on terms. Some bloody hope. Morally, whatever that's supposed to mean, the Ingush case is unassailable, but in the world of conflicting compromises which it's my misfortune to inhabit, that means approximately bugger all. Legally, for whoever gives a toss about post-Sov legality, it's no contest. The Ossies are in breach of the law, the Ingush are blameless. When did that alter the price of fish?"

"So where are the Americans on this?"

"The *what?*" he said—implying that while he might be an expert on the North Caucasus, the United States of America were an unfamiliar concept to him.

"Uncle Sam," I said.

"My dear man—" He had never in his life till now used an endearment towards me. "Listen *up*, do you mind?" He assumed an American accent. It fell somewhere between a Deep South plantation owner and an East End costermonger. "What the fuck's the *Ingush*, man? Some kind o' *Injun*, man? *Ameringush?*"

I pulled a dutiful smile, and to my relief Simon returned to his normal drab voice.

"If America *has* a post-Sov policy down there, it's not to have a policy. Which is consistent with her post-Sov policy everywhere else, I may add. Planned apathy is the kindest description I can think of: act natural and look the other way while the ethnic cleansers do their hoovering and restore what politicians call normality. Which means that whatever Moscow does is okay by Washington, provided nobody frightens the horses. End of policy."

"So what can the Ingush hope for?" I asked.

"Absolutely sweet Fanny Adams," Simon Dugdale replied with relish. "There are bloody great oil fields in Chechenia, even if they've been screwed up by lousy exploitation. Minerals, timber, all the goodies. There's the Georgian Military Highway, and Moscow intends to keep it open whatever the Chechen and the Ingush think. And the Russian army isn't about to march into Chechenia and leave Ingushetia next door as a joker in the pack. Piss."

He had spilled something on his apron, and it had permeated his trousers. He seized another apron and, though it was even dirtier than the first, wrapped it round his midriff. "Anyway," he said accusingly, "who would *you* favour if *you* were the Kremlin? A bunch of bloodthirsty Muslim highlanders, or the Sovietised,

Christianised, arse-licking Ossetians, who pray every day for Stalin to come back?"

"So what would you do if you were Bashir?"

"I'm not. Hypothetical codswallop."

Suddenly, to my surprise, he sounded like Larry dilating on the subject of fashionable and unfashionable wars. "First, I'd buy myself one of those smirking Washington lobbyists with plastic hair. That's a million bucks down the tube. Second, I'd get hold of a dead Ingush baby, preferably female, and put her on prime time television in the arms of a snivelling newscaster, preferably male, also with plastic hair. I'd have questions asked in Congress and the United Nations. And when absolutely sod all has happened as usual, I'd say to hell with it, and if I had any money left, I'd take my family to the south of France and blow the lot. No, I wouldn't. I'd go alone."

"Or go to war," I suggested.

He was crouching, packing saucepans into a pitch-dark cupboard at floor level.

"There's a warning out about you," he said. "Thought I'd better tell you. Anyone who sights you is supposed to tell Personnel Department."

"And will you?" I asked.

"Shouldn't think so. You're Clare's friend, not mine."

I thought he had finished, but there was evidently too much left in him.

"I rather dislike you, to be frank. And your bloody Office. I never believed one word you and your people told me unless I'd happened to have read it in the newspapers first. I don't know what you're looking for, but I'd be grateful if you didn't look for it here."

"Just tell me whether it's true."

"What?"

"Are the Ingush planning something serious? Could they do that? If they had the guns?"

Too late in the day, I wondered whether he was drunk. He seemed to have lost his orientation. I was wrong. He was warming to his subject.

"It's quite an interesting one, that, actually," he conceded, with the boyish enthusiasm he brought to all forms of catastrophe. "From stuff we're getting in, Bashir seems to be raising a pretty good head of steam despite himself. You may be onto something."

I took Emma's part and played the innocent. "Can't *anyone* stop it happening?" I asked.

"Oh sure. The Russians can. Do what they did last time. Turn the Ossies loose on them. Rocket their villages. Gouge their eyes out. Drag 'em down to the valleys, bang 'em up in ghettos. Deport them."

"I meant us. NATO without the Americans. After all, it is Europe. It is our patch."

"Do a Bosnia, you mean?" he proposed in the same triumphant note that in Simon Dugdale celebrated every impasse. "On Russian soil? Brilliant idea. And let's have a few Russian shock troops to sort out our British football hooligans while we're about it." The anger I had been provoking in him had caught light. "The *presumption*," he resumed on a higher note, "that this country—*any* civilised country—has a *duty* to interpose itself between any two groups of knuckle-draggers who happen to be determined to butcher each other . . ." He's talking like me, I thought. ". . . to patrol the globe, mediating between hell-bent heathen savages nobody's ever heard of . . . Do you mind going now?"

"What's the forest?"

"Are you mad?"

"Why would an Ingush warn somebody about the forest?"

Once more his face cleared. "Ossetian Ku Klux Klan. Shadowy mob, fed and watered by the KGB or its derivatives. If you wake up tomorrow morning with your balls in your mouth, which *wouldn't* be the worst thing in the world, in my view, it will like as not be the work of The Forest. After you."

Clare was in the drawing room with a magazine on her lap, watching a black-and-white television set over the top of her reading glasses.

"Oh, Tim, darling, *do* let me run you to the station. We've hardly talked at *all*."

"I'm ordering a cab for him," said Simon, at the telephone.

The cab came and she took my arm and led me to it, while Simon the Berkeleyan stayed indoors, denying the existence of everything he couldn't perceive. I remembered the occasions when I had performed a similar courtesy for Emma, fuming inside the house and grimacing at my reflection while she said goodbye to Larry in the drive.

"I always think of you as a man who *does* things," Clare whispered in my ear, while she chewed it half to pieces. "Poor Si's so *academic*."

I felt nothing for her. Some other Cranmer had slept with her.

. . .

I DROVE, with Larry beside me in the passenger seat.

"You're mad," I told him, taking a leaf from Simon Dugdale's book. "Dangerously, cogently mad."

He affected to weigh this, which was what he always did before he struck back.

"My definition of a madman, Timbo, is someone who is in possession of all the facts."

It was midnight. I was approaching Chiswick. Pulling off the main road, I wove through a chicane and entered a private estate. The house was an overdecorated Edwardian gem. Beyond it lay the black Thames, its surface feathered by the city's glow. I parked, fished the .38 from my briefcase, and jammed it in my waistband. The briefcase in my left hand, I stepped round a broken stile and stood on the towpath. The river air smelled brown and greasy. Two lovers were embracing on a bench, the girl astride. I walked slowly, picking my way round puddles, setting up water rats and birds. On the other side of the hedge, guests were taking leave of their hosts:

"Simply *marvellous* party, darlings, *literally*."

I was reminded of Larry, doing one of his voices. I had reached the house again, this time from the back. Lights burned over the back door and on the garage. Selecting a point where the hedge was lowest, I pushed down the wire, dropped the briefcase the other side of it, and nearly castrated myself. I toppled into a garden of mown lawn and rose beds. Two naked children stared at me, their arms outstretched, but as I advanced on them they became a pair of porcelain cupids. The garage stood to my left. I hastened to its shadow, tiptoed to a window, and peered inside. No car. He's out to dinner. He's been summoned to a war party. Help, help, Cranmer's flown the coop.

I propped myself against the wall, my eyes trained on the front gate. I could wait for hours like this. A cat rubbed itself against my leg. I smelled the liquid stench of fox. I heard a car, I saw its headlights bounce towards me down the unmade road. I pressed myself more tightly yet against the garage wall. The car drove on, to stop fifty yards up the road. A second car appeared, a better one: white lights, two sets, a quieter engine. Be alone, Jake, I warned him. Don't make it hard for me. Don't bring me some Significant Other. Just bring me your Insignificant Self.

Merriman's overpolished Rover car bucked through the front gate and up the little ramp to his garage. It had Jake Merriman at the wheel, and no one else aboard, no Other at all, not of either sex. He drove into the garage, he dowsed the headlights of his car. There followed one of those pauses that I associate with single people of a certain age, while he stayed sitting in the driver's seat and by the interior light fidgeted with things I couldn't see.

"Just don't be alarmed, Jake," I said.

I had opened his door for him and was holding the gun a few inches from his head.

"I won't be," he said.

"Switch the interior light to full time. Give me the car key. Put your hands on the steering wheel. Don't take your hands off the steering wheel. How do the garage doors close?"

He held up a magic box.

"Close them," I said.

The doors closed.

I sat behind him. Holding the gun to the nape of his neck, I put my left forearm across his throat and gently drew his head to me until we were cheek-to-cheek.

"Munslow tells me you've been looking for Emma," I said.

"Then he's a bloody little fool."

"Where is she?"

"Nowhere. We're looking for Pettifer too, in case you haven't noticed. We haven't found him either. We'll be looking for you as well after tonight."

"Jake, I will *do* this. You know that, don't you? I will actually shoot you if I have to."

"I don't need convincing. I'll collaborate. I'm a coward."

"Do you know what I did yesterday, Jake? I wrote a frank letter to the chief constable of Somerset, copy to the *Guardian* newspaper. I described how a few of us in the Office had decided to rip off the Russian Embassy with a little help from Checheyev. I took the liberty of mentioning your name."

"Then you're a stupid little sod."

"Not as a ringleader but as someone who could be counted on to turn a blind eye at the right moments. A passive conspirator like Zorin. The letters will be posted at nine tomorrow morning unless I say the magic word. I shan't say the word unless you tell me what you know about Emma."

"I've told you everything we know about Emma. I've given you a bloody file on Emma. She's a tart. What more do you want to know?"

The sweat was rolling off him in great drops. There was sweat on the barrel of the .38.

"I want an update. And please don't call her a tart, Jake. Call her the nice lady or something. Just not tart."

"She was in Paris. Phoning from a public box in the Gare du Nord. You trained her well."

Larry did, I thought. "When?"

"October."

"We're in October now. When in October?"

"Mid. The twelfth. What on earth do you think you're up to? Relent. Make a confession. Come home."

"How do you know it was the twelfth?"

"The Americans picked her up on a random sweep."

"The *Americans?* How the hell did the Americans get in on the act?"

"Computerland, darling. We gave them a sample of her voice-print. They backtracked through their intercepts. Out popped your precious Emma, speaking with a phony Scottish accent."

"Who was she calling?"

"Philip somebody."

I didn't remember a Philip. "What did she say?"

"She was well, she was in Stockholm. That was a lie. She was in Paris. She wished all the boys and girls to know that she was happy and was proposing to make a new beginning. With thirty-seven million quid to play with, one imagines she very well might."

"Did you listen to her yourself?"

"You don't think I'd leave her to some spotty CIA college boy, do you?"

"Give me her words."

" 'I'm going back to where I came from. I'm making a new start.' To which our Philip says, 'Right, right,' which is what the lower classes say these days. Right, right, and cheers instead of thank you. She's waiting for you, you'll be pleased to hear. She's totally devoted to you. I was proud of you."

"Her words," I said.

" 'I'll wait for him for as long as it takes,' spoken with the most *marvellous* conviction. 'I'll do a Penelope for him, even if it's years. I'll weave by day and I'll unpick by night until he comes for me.' "

With the gun in my hand and the briefcase flying out behind me, I pelted to my car. I drove south till I came to the outskirts of Bournemouth, where I checked into a bungalow motel with crematorium music in the corridors and mauve night-lights marking the fire exits. I'm coming for you, I told her. Hang on. For pity's sake, hang on.

SHE IS dead of cold, except that she is shivering. It's as if I have rescued her from a freezing sea. Her clammy skin sticks as she clutches me. Her face is pressed so hard against mine that I am unable to resist.

"Tim, Tim, wake up."

She has rushed into my room, naked. She has yanked back my duvet and wound her freezing body round me, whispering, "Tim, Tim," when all she means is "Larry, Larry." She is shaking and writhing uselessly against me, but I'm not her lover, just the body she hangs on to while she nearly drowns, the nearest she can get to Larry.

"You love him too," she says. "You must."

She slinks back to her room.

PARIS, Merriman had said. *Phoning from a public box in the Gare du Nord. You trained her well.*

Paris, I thought. For her new beginning.

Dee's place, she is saying. *Where I was made alive again.*

Who's Dee? I ask.

Dee's a saint. Dee saved me when I was flat on the deck.

I'm making a new start, Merriman is saying in his perfumed voice, quoting Emma. *I'm going back to where I came from.*

A GREY morning with no sun. A long drive lifting to the house, gulls and peacocks squawking at my arrival. I spoke my name, the iron gates parted as if I had said "Open Sesame," the mock-Tudor mansion rose before me amid misted lawns, and the tennis court where no one ever played and the pool where no one swam. A flaccid Union Jack dangled from a tall white mast. Behind the house, golf links and dunes. In the distance, a ghostly old battleship stuck halfway up the sky. It had been there ever since I first ventured up the same hill fifteen years ago and timidly suggested to Ockie Hedges that he might consider putting a little back by assisting us in certain matters not unrelated to the arms trade.

"Assist in what *way*, son?" Ockie demands from behind his napoleonic desk. For while officially he trades from the Isle of Wight, his preference in later life is to do business from his Bournemouth hilltop.

"Well, sir," I say awkwardly, "we know you talk to the Ministry of Defence, but we thought you might talk to us as well."

"What about, son?" More irritably yet. "Tell it to us straight. What's the bottom line?"

"The Russians are using Western dealers to supply their covert arms for them," I say.

"Course they are."

"Some of the dealers are business acquaintances of yours," I say, refraining from adding that they are also his partners. "We'd like you to be our listening post, accept questions, talk to us on a regular basis."

A long silence follows.

"*Well?*" he says.

"Well what?"

"What are you *offering*, son? What's the sweetener?"

"There isn't one. It's for your country."

"I'll be damned," says Ockie Hedges devoutly.

Nevertheless, after we have taken several walks round the prinked garden, Ockie Hedges, widower, bereaved father, and one of the biggest crooks in the illegal-arms business, decides it is after all time he joined the armies of the righteous.

A TALL young man in a blazer marched me across the hall. He had broad shoulders and short hair, which was what Ockie liked his tall young men to have. Two bronze warriors with bows and arrows guarded the double doors to Ockie's panelled study.

"Jason, bring us a nice tray of tea, please," Ockie said, grasping my hand and upper arm at the same time. "And if there's a fatted calf, kill it. Mr. Cranmer gets nothing but the best. How are you, son? You'll stay for lunch, I've told them."

He was stocky and powerful and seventy, a pint-sized dictator in a tailor-made brown suit, with a gold watch chain across the flat stomach of his double-breasted waistcoat. When he greeted you he filled his little chest with pride, appointing you his soldier. When he seized your hand, his prizefighter's fist cupped it like a claw. A picture window looked down the gardens to the sea. Around the room lay the polished trophies Ockie valued most: from the cricket club of which he was chairman, and the police club of which he was president for life.

"I've never been more glad to see anyone than what I am you, Tim," Ockie said. He spoke like a British airline steward, oscillating between social classes as if they were wavelengths. "I can't tell you the number of times I nearly picked up that phone there and said, 'Tim. Get yourself up here and let's have some sense.' That young fellow you introduced me to is as much use as a wet weekend. He needs a good barber for a start."

"Oh, come on, Ockie," I said with a laugh. "He's not *that* bad."

"What do you mean, come on? He's worse than bad. He's a fairy."

We sat down, and I listened dutifully to a recitation of my luckless successor's failings.

"You opened doors for me, Tim, and I did some favours for you. You may not be a Mason, but you behaved like one. And down the corridor of the years a mutuality developed which was beautiful. My only regret was you never met Doris. But this new boy you've landed on me, it's all by the book. It's where did you get this from, and who told who that, and why they said whatever they said, and let's have it down in duplicate. The world's not like that, Tim. The world's fluid. You know it, I know it. So why doesn't he? No *time*, that's his trouble. Everything's got to be by yesterday. I don't suppose you're going to tell me you're back in harness, are you?"

"Not in the *long* term," I said cautiously.

"Pity. All right, what's your angle? You never came here without a need that I remember, and I never sent you empty away."

I glanced at the door and lowered my voice. "It's Office but it's not Office, if you follow me."

"No, I don't."

"It's right off the record. Ultradelicate. They want it you and me and no one else. If that's going to bother you, you'd better say so now."

"Bother me? You're joking." He had taken on my tone. "They should check that boy out, if you want my advice. He's a pacifist. Look at those flared trousers he wears."

"I need an update on somebody we used to have an interest in, back in the bad old days."

"Who?"

"He's half a Brit and half a Turk," I said, playing to Ockie's appalling views on race.

"All men are equal, Tim. All religions are paths to the same gate. What's his name?"

"He was cosy with certain people in Dublin and cosier still with certain Russian diplomats in London. He had an interest in a shipment of arms and explosives by trawler out of Cyprus bound for the Irish Sea. You took a piece of it, remember?"

Ockie was already smiling a rather cruel smile. "Via Bergen," he said. "A greasy little carpet seller, name of Aitken Mustafa May."

Payment to AM, Macclesfield, I was thinking as I dutifully congratulated Ockie on his prodigious memory.

"We need your ear to the tracks," I was saying. "His private addresses, trade addresses, the name of his Siamese cat if he's got one."

THERE was a well-trodden ritual about Ockie putting his ear to the tracks. Each time he did it, I had a vision of a terrible inner England that we poor spies can only guess at, with insiders' signals being flashed over secret computer lines, and secret covenants being called in. First he summoned Miss Pullen, a stone-faced woman in a grey twin set, who took dictation standing up. Her other concern was the autobiography with which Ockie was planning to instruct a waiting world.

"Oh, and take a discreet sampling on a firm called Hardwear up north somewhere, will you, a Mr. May, Aitken M. May?" he said, in a lugubriously throwaway voice, after he had given her a list of other commissions to conceal his purpose. "We had a side deal with them way back, but they're not the same people anymore. I'll want credit rating, company accounts, stockholders, current trading interests, principals listed, private addresses, home phone numbers, the usual."

Ten minutes later Miss Pullen returned with a typed sheet, and Ockie retired to a side room and closed the door and made telephone calls that I could only faintly hear.

"Your Mr. May is on a shopping spree," he announced when he returned.

"Who for?"

"The mafia."

I played my part for him: "The *Italian* mafia?" I cried. "But, Ockie, they've got all the guns in the world!"

"You're being stupid deliberately. The Russian mafia. Don't you read the newspapers?"

"But Russia's awash with guns and everything else. The military's been selling them off to all comers for years."

"There's mafias and mafias over there. Maybe there's mafias that want something special and don't want the neighbours looking over their shoulders while they buy it. Maybe there's mafias with hard currency who'd like to pay for a little superiority." He studied Miss Pullen's fact sheet, then his notes. "He's a middleman, your Mr. May. A shyster. If he owns more than one demonstration model of anything, I'd be surprised."

"But *which* mafia, Ockie? There are dozens."

"That's all I know. Mafias. Officially his client is a major nation that wishes to remain below the skyline, so his nominal end-user is Jordan. Unofficially it's mafia, and he's in over his head."

"Why?"

"Because what he's buying is too big for his boots, that's why. He's a scrap dealer is what he is, a greasy scrap dealer. Now all of a sudden he's out there with Stingers, heavy machine guns, antitank, heavy mortars, ammunition like there's no tomorrow, night vision. Where he ships it all to is another story. One says northern Turkey, another Georgia. He's cocky. Dined a friend of mine at Claridges the other night, if you can believe it. I'm surprised they let him in. Here you are. Never trust a man with a lot of addresses."

He shoved a sheaf of papers at me, and I stored them in my briefcase. Ushered by Jason to the dining room, we lunched at a twenty-foot oak table and drank barley water while Ockie Hedges successively dismissed intellectuals, Jews, blacks, the Yellow Peril, and homosexuals with a benign and universal hatred. And Tim Cranmer, he just smiled his rent-a-drool smile and munched his fish, because that was what he had been doing for Ockie Hedges these fifteen years: stroking his little man's vanity, riding out his insults, turning a deaf ear to his bigotries, and paying court to his disgusting calling, in the service of a safer, wiser England.

"Flawed from birth is my view. Subhuman. I'm surprised you boys don't have them shot."

"There'd be no one left, that's the trouble, Ockie."

"Yes, there would. There'd be us. And that's all that's needed."

And after lunch there was the garden to admire, not a petal out of place. There were the latest additions to his collection of antique weaponry, which was kept, like fine wine, in a temperature-controlled cellar reached by a lift designed as a portcullis. So it was after four o'clock by the time he stood on his porch with his arms folded, just another childless old tyrant on a hilltop, glowering after me as I climbed into my humble Ford, with the Union Jack behind him sulking on its flagpole.

"That the best your country can do for you, is it?" he demanded, poking his chin at me.

"It's the New Era, Ockie. No big expense accounts, no nice shiny cars."

"Come more often, I might buy you one myself," he said.

I DROVE again, and for a while the movement dulled my fears. Sometimes a roadhouse offered, but the thought of more stale cigarette smoke and another candlewick coverlet discouraged me, and I kept driving until I was all in. Rain came on, a dark sky lay ahead of me. Suddenly, like Emma, I needed comfort, if only in the form of a decent dinner. The first village provided me with what I was looking for: an old coaching inn with a framed menu and a cobbled yard. The receptionist was a fresh-faced country girl. I smelled roasting beef and wood smoke. I was blessed.

"On the quiet side of the house, if possible, please," I told her while she examined her list of bookings.

And that was when my eye fell on the sheet of printed numbers that lay upside down at her bare elbow. I have little memory for figures as a rule, but I have a nose for danger. There were no names, just groups like groups on a code pad, each group four digits and each line four groups. The heading on the page read WATCHLIST, the source was the credit card company of which Colin Bairstow was a long-standing member.

Not any longer, however. The number of my Bairstow credit card was printed in the bottom right-hand column of the sheet, beneath the word CURRENT in capitals.

"How would you be wishing to pay your bill, sir?" the receptionist asked.

"Cash," I said, and with a fairly steady hand invented a new name for her book of registered guests: Henry Porter, 3 The Maltings, Shoreham, Kent.

I SAT in my room. The car, I thought. Ditch the car. Take off the number plates. I willed myself to calm down. If the Ford was hot, then the Ford was a liability. But how hot was it? How hot was I? How hot could Pew-Merriman allow me to be without blowing their interest to the police? Sometimes, I used to tell my joes, you have to take a deep breath, close your eyes, and jump.

I bathed and shaved and put on a clean shirt. I went down to the dining room and ordered a bottle of the best claret. I lay in bed listening to the sibyl voices: *Don't go north, Misha. . . . Misha, take heed, please. . . . If he has started his journey, he should please discontinue it.*

But the journey was not of my choosing. I was being conveyed, never mind whether The Forest, or the whole valley of the shadow, was watching me pass through.

THE HILL was steep, and the house a stern old lady with her feet firmly planted amid elderly friends. She had a Sunday school face and a stained-glass porch that glowed like heaven in the morning sun. She had pious lace curtains and a hint of grief, and boxed hedges and a bird table and a chestnut tree that was shedding gold leaves. The hill's gorse summit rose behind her like the green hill in the hymn, and behind the hill lay several different heavens: blue for sunshine, black for judgment, and the clear white sky of the north.

I pressed the doorbell and heard the drumming of strong young feet on the stairs. The time was 9.25. The door flew open, and I stood face-to-face with a pretty young woman in jeans, bare feet, and a checked shirt. She was smiling, but her smile faded when she realised I wasn't whoever she'd hoped I was.

"Oh, sorry," she said awkwardly. "We thought you were my friend, giving us a nice surprise. Didn't we, Ali? We thought it was Daddy." Her voice was antipodean but soft. I guessed New Zealand. A barefoot half-Asian boy peered from behind her waist.

"Mrs. May?" I said.

Her smile returned. "Well, near enough."

"Sorry to be a bit early. I've got a date with Aitken."

"With Aitken? Here at the house?"

"My name's Pete Bradbury. I'm a buyer. Aitken and I deal a lot together. We have an appointment here at nine-thirty." My tone still brisk but kindly: just two people chatting on a doorstep on a sunny autumn morning.

"But he *never* has buyers to the house," she objected, as her smile became supplicatory, and slightly disbelieving. "*Everyone* goes to the store. Don't they, Ali? That's the rule. Daddy never brings his business home, does he, pet?" The boy took her hand and swung from it, trying to draw her back into the house.

"Well, I'm a pretty substantial customer of his, actually. We've been trading some while. I know he likes to be private as a rule, but he said he had something a bit special for me to look at."

She was impressed. "Are you the big, *big* buyer? The one that's going to make us all mountainously rich?"

"Well, I hope so. I hope he'll make *me* rich too."

Her confusion increased.

"He can't have *forgotten*," she said. "Not Aitken. He thinks about your deal day and night. He must be on his way." Her doubts returned. "And you really, *really* don't think you've made a mistake and you should be at the store? I mean he could easily have driven straight there from the airport. He keeps *weird* times."

"I've never been to the store. We've always met in London. I wouldn't even know where to find the store."

"Me neither. Ali, stop it. I mean he just never, never does this. He's abroad, you see. Well, he's on his way back, obviously. I mean he could be *here*."

I waited while she talked herself round.

"Look. All right. Why don't you come indoors and have a cup of tea till he shows up? He'll be *terribly* angry. If people stand *him* up, he goes totally spare. He's not a bit Oriental in *that* way. I'm Julie, actually."

I stepped after her into the house, took off my shoes, and put them with the family's in the rack beside the door.

THE LIVING room was a kitchen, playroom, and living room all at once. It had an old doll's house and cane furniture and pleasantly disordered bookshelves with books jammed upward and sideways in English, Turkish, and Arabic. It had a silver-gilt samovar and Koranic texts and silk embroideries. I recognised a Coptic cross and Ottoman carnations. A magic eye in gold and green hung above the door to ward off devils. In a carved wall cabinet, a mother-cult goddess rode sidesaddle on a very obvious stallion. And on the television set stood a studio photograph in colour of Julie and a bearded man seated among pink roses. The television was showing a children's animated film. She turned the sound down, but Ali grizzled so she turned it up again. She made a pot of tea and set shortbread biscuits on a plate. She had long legs and a long waist and a model's studiously casual walk.

"If you knew how unusual this was, it's so stupid, it's so untypical of him," she said. "You didn't come all the way from London just for—well—*this*, did you?"

"It's not a tragedy. How long's he been away?"

"A week. What's your specialty?"

"I'm sorry?"

"What do you deal in?"

"Oh, you name it. Hamadan. Balouchi. Kilims. The best of everything when I can afford it. Are you in the trade yourself?"

"Not really." She smiled, mostly at the window because she was keeping watch. "I teach at Ali's school. Don't I, Al?"

She went to the next room, and the boy went after her. I heard her telephoning. I snatched a closer look at the portrait of the happy couple. The photographer had been wise to pose them sitting, for straightened out, Mr. Aitken Mustafa May would have been a bearded head shorter than his lady, even allowing for the raised heels of his high-gloss, buckled shoes. But his smile was proud and happy.

"All I ever get's the answerphone too," she complained, coming back. "It's been the same all week. There's a storeman there *and* a secretary. Why don't they switch off the machine and answer the phone for themselves? They're supposed to have been there since nine."

"Can't you reach one of them at home?"

"Aitken just *will* hire these way-out people!" she protested, shaking her head. "He calls them his Odd Couple; *she's* a retired librarian or something, *he's* ex-army. They live in a cottage in the moors and don't talk to anyone except their goats. Which is why he hires them. Honestly."

"And no telephone?"

She had placed herself at the window again, bare feet apart. "Water from the well," she said indignantly. "No mains, no phone, no nothing. You're absolutely *certain* he didn't say the store, aren't you? I don't mean to be stupid or rude or anything, but he just never, *never* has business people here."

"Where's he been travelling?"

"Ankara. Baghdad. Baku. You know how he is. Once he gets on a scent there's no stopping him."

She drummed her fingertips on the window.

"It's his Muslim side," she said. "Keep the women out of it. How long have you known him?"

"Six years. Seven maybe."

"I just wish he'd talk about the people he meets. I'll bet some of them are really, really interesting."

A taxi came up the hill and drove past without slowing down. It was empty.

"I mean what's he *pay* them for?" she protested in exasperation. "Two grown-up zombies sitting on their backsides listening to a machine. I'm just so *sorry* for you. Aitken'll kill them, he really will."

"Oh dear."

"He has this really *ridiculous* superstition thing about not telling me which plane he's on, too," she said. "He thinks they'll blow him up or something. I mean he's so *spooky* sometimes. I wonder—you know, am *I* going to be like *him*, or is *he* going to be like *me*?"

"What car does he drive?"

"A Merc. Metallic blue. Brand-new. Two-door. It's his pride and joy. It's your deal that paid for it," she added.

"Where does he leave it when he goes abroad?"

"At the airport sometimes. Sometimes at the store. Depends."

"He's not with Terry, is he?"

"Who?"

"Sort of half partner of mine and Aitken's. Terry Altman. Amusing chap. Talks a lot. Got a beautiful new girlfriend called Sally. Sally Anderson. But her friends call her Emma for some reason."

"If they're business, forget it."

I stood up. "Look. There's been a muddle. Why don't we abandon this, and I'll go down to the store and see if I can rouse the secretary. If I find anything out, I can give you a ring. Don't worry. I've got the address. I'll just wander down the hill and get a cab."

I took my shoes from the rack and laced them up. I stepped into the sunlight. A knot had formed in my gut, and there was a singing in my ears.

12

THE HILLS darkened as I drove, the roads grew steeper and smaller, the rock peaks of the hilltops were blackened as if burned. Stone walls enclosed me, and I entered a village of slate roofs, crumbling walls, old car tyres, and plastic bags. Piglets and hens wandered in my path, inquisitive sheep eyed me, but I saw no human soul. My ordnance survey map lay open on the passenger seat beside Ockie's list of Aitken May's addresses.

The stone walls gave way, and I was flying over wide valleys patched with sun and crossed with streams. Chestnut horses grazed in perfect rectangular meadows. But in my apprehension everything was too late, and I sensed not pleasure but despair. Why had I never played here as a child, walked here as a boy? Run in that field, lived in that cottage, made love beside that stream? These colours, why had I never painted them? Emma, you were all these hopes.

Pulling up in a lay-by, I consulted the map. From nowhere an old man appeared at my car window, and his gnarled face reminded me of the groundsman at my first boarding school.

"Past yonder reservoir . . . turn right at t'gospel hall . . . go on till th' sees t'mill in front o' thee . . . then keep on going till th' can't go no further. . . ."

I drove over humpbacked hills into a plantation of blue conifers that turned green, then polka dot. I scaled the first hump and saw Larry in his broad hat standing at the roadside with one arm raised to stop me and his other arm round Emma, but they were just two travellers with a dog. I scaled the second and saw them in my driving mirror, giving me the finger. But my fears were worse by far than these anxious fantasies. They were composed of the uncompleted warnings still ringing on the path behind me. *A week*, Julie had said. *All I ever get's the answerphone. . . . It's been the same all week.*

A gospel hall loomed at me. I turned right as the old man had instructed and saw the wrecked mill, a monster with its eyes put out. The road became a track; I crossed a ford and entered a rural slum of rotting cauliflowers, plastic bottles, and the collected filth of tourists and farmers. Hard-jawed children watched me from the threshold of a tin shed. I crossed a second stream or the same one, skirted the stone face of a quarry, and saw a glitter-paint orange arrow and the words HARDWEAR WHOLESALE ONLY stencilled below it. I followed the arrow and discovered that I had descended further than I realised, for a second valley now opened before me, its lower slopes heavy with trees, and above the trees squared green fields and brooding moors, their tops cut off by cloud. Another arrow pointed me towards a wooden gate. A yellow sign said private road. I pushed the gate open, drove through, closed it behind me. A sign said: HARD-WEAR STRAIGHT ON (TRADE ONLY).

Barbed wire ran either side of the track. Tufts of sheep's wool clung to the barbs, white cattle grazed among the rocks. The track led uphill. I followed it and saw at three hundred yards' distance a chain of stone farm buildings of no merit, some with windows, some without, and together resembling a freight train with the tallest cars at the left, and tailing to a run of chicken houses and pigsties. The track led over a white bridge and an island of brown marshland to reappear before the main entrance. A sign said: INVITED VISITORS. An orange arrow pointed directly at the house.

I crossed the bridge and saw a blue Mercedes parked in the front drive, its bonnet towards me. Metallic, she had said. But I couldn't tell whether the blue was metallic or not. Two-door, she had said. But the car was facing me, and I couldn't count the doors. Nevertheless my heart beat faster in spite of my forebodings. Aitken May's here. He's back. In the house. With them. Larry's here too. Larry came north despite the warning: when did Larry ever heed a warning? Then he went to Paris to find Emma.

I drew near to the house, and a curtain of white cloud rolled off the hill to prevent me entering, then rolled over me and down the track. There were two other cars, one a Volkswagen Golf, the other a battered grey Dormobile, with a triangle of faded red flag on the aerial and flat tyres. The Volkswagen was parked on the far side of the forecourt. The Dormobile stood forlornly in the hay barn, which seemed to be its final resting place. I saw now that the Mercedes had two doors, that its paintwork was indeed metallic, and that its windows were coated with grime. *It's your deal that paid for it*, Julie had said. I saw the telephone aerial and remembered the proud, not quite English voice: "Hullo, Sally, this is Hardwear, calling from the *car*. . . ."

Parking my red Ford, I was faced with a problem I should have solved already: to take the briefcase with me or leave it in the car? Keeping my back to the house and using the open door for cover, I fished the .38 revolver from the briefcase and jammed it once more in my waistband. I was getting a little too used to it. I locked the briefcase in the boot. Passing the blue Mercedes, I brushed my knuckles against the bonnet. It was stone cold.

THE FRONT entrance to the house was protected by a storm porch of quarried black stone. The door was painted green. The doorbell was linked to an intercom. Beside the bell was a brushed-steel plate with numbers on it. Either you rang the bell or you punched in the combination. The door had an eyehole and strips of stained-glass window either side of it, but the glass had no luminosity, and I guessed it was boarded on the inside. A curled visiting card read: "Aitken Mustafa May, BADA, Oriental Carpets, Objets d'Art, Chmn, The Hardwear Company, GmbH." I pressed the bell and heard it ring inside the house: one of those sleigh-bell chimes that are supposed to calm spirits but drive them to the brink. I rang a second time, my eyes fixed upon the Volkswagen. This year's registration. Local licence plates, like the Mercedes. Blue, like the Mercedes. And its windows, like the Mercedes, coated with grime and weather. When Aitken's ship came home, everyone got a new car, I decided. *Are you the big, big buyer? The one that's going to make us all mountainously rich?* No, that's my friend, actually: the one with thirty-seven million stolen pounds to spend on carpets from the Caucasus.

I pressed the bell three times. Rather than listen to any more sleigh bells, I walked along the front of the house in search of another door to try, but there wasn't one, and the windows gave onto a narrow corridor of white-painted brick. And when I tap-tapped on the glass, no smiling, friendly face appeared to welcome me, not even Larry's.

I walked round to the back, picking my way through the remains of an old timber mill: rusted circular saws, cumbersome engines with frayed belts, a pile of sawn logs that lay as they had fallen years ago, a rusted axe, heaps of sawdust overgrown with weed and lichen, all abandoned as if at a single summons. And I wondered what it was about this place that, however many years ago, a sawyer and his mates should have stopped sawing and fled, leaving everything exactly as it was now; and that Aitken Mustafa May and his storeman and his secretary had abandoned their nice new cars and followed him.

Then I saw the blood, or perhaps I had seen it already and was finding other things to think of: one patch of unisex blood, Emma's or Larry's equally, one finely fretted island about a foot long and six inches wide, congealed, lying across the sawdust; but so rich, so assured, that as I stooped to it I perceived it first as solid rather than liquid, and was half inclined to pick it up—until I saw my hand recoil and fancied Emma's pale dead face staring up at me through the sawdust. I delved. The sawdust turned out to be common sawdust all the way to the ground.

But no gruesome trail, no telltale drips or stains led the keen-eyed detective to the next clue. There was the patch of blood, and it lay on the pile of sawdust, and the sawdust lay five paces from the back door. And between the sawdust and the back door I made out a lot of busy footprints in both directions, not unisex this time but distinctly male: either track shoes or just standard flat-soled shoes with nothing special to distinguish them. But still emphatically male, and going back and forth enough times and with enough male haste and vigour to establish an oily river of churned mud, ending at the island of poured blood that seemed so determined to remain separate from the sawdust it had settled on.

Or perhaps the river did not end there after all. For beyond the pile of sawdust I now saw the tyre tracks of two single wheels acting in tandem. They were too narrow for car wheels, but they would have been all right for a motorbike, except that there was only one wheel to each track and therefore—my mind had decided to travel slowly now, being mostly occupied with the possible ownership of the pool of blood—and therefore something more in the nature of a farm vehicle.

A trailer? The sort of carriage that pulls a sailing boat down busy roads and holds up bank holiday traffic on its way through Somerset? A gun carriage? A funeral carriage? *That* sort of trailer? As to where it had gone, that was anybody's guess, because after a few yards the tracks mounted a concrete path and thereafter held their peace. And the concrete path led nowhere at all: for another white, fresh, hard-edged cloud was already rolling down the hill.

The back door was locked, which first frustrated me, then quickly made me angry, although I knew perfectly well that of all the useless emotions I might have given way to—grief, despair, frustration, terror—anger was the least productive and the least adult. I had actually started towards the cars with the intention of taking a methodical look at them, when my anger stopped me in mid-stride and yanked me round and made me attack the locked door. I beat on it with my fists. I shouted, "Open up, damn you!" I shouted, "Larry! Emma!" I hurled myself several times against it, with little effect on the door or, more remarkably, my shoulder. I had the immunity that comes of heedlessness. I shouted, "May! Aitken May! Larry, for Christ's sake! Emma!" I remembered the rusted axe beside the log pile. A more adept spy would have shot the lock out with the .38, but I wasn't feeling adept, and in my distraction I didn't really consider whether the door was locked. I simply hit it, rather as I had lashed out at Larry, but with an axe.

My first blow caused a decent split and sent a squadron of rooks protesting into the cloud: which surprised me because the trees round the house were sparse and mostly dead, except for a row of hideous windburned macracarpa that seemed to have grown and died at the same time. My second blow missed both the door and my left leg by fractions of an inch. But I swung back the axe and struck again. A fourth heave, and the door exploded like paper. I flung the axe through the opening and stepped after it, roaring "Get out!" "Stand back!" and "Bastards!" in another furious expulsion of air and tension. But perhaps that was just my way of whistling up my courage, because when I looked down at my feet I saw that they were isolated in a lake of blood, in shape very like the first, but larger. And this must have been what my eye had chosen to see before everything else in the raftered farmhouse kitchen: the smashed crockery, the cutlery and pots hurled over the flagstone floor, the splintered chairs and over-turned table, and the tree, the unmistakable outline of a tree, drawn or, more accurately, painted on the whitewashed brickwork above the smashed kitchen range. A chestnut perhaps, or a cedar—certainly a tree that spread. And the blood still dripping down from it as it had dried, like so many cones or spikes. The Forest was watching.

Ossetian Ku Klux Klan, I heard Simon Dugdale say. *Shadowy mob, fed and watered by the KGB . . .*

But I allowed myself to study these things only after I had seen the blood at my feet. And when I had studied enough of them to draw the necessary conclusions, I pulled the gun from my waistband—more, I suspect, to protect me from the dead than from the living—stepped into the corridor, and *sashayed* down it, as the trainers say, keeping my left forearm raised across my face and shouting, "Aitken Mustafa May. Come out! Where are you?" because although I knew very well that the names I should be shouting were still "Larry" and "Emma," I dreaded finding them, which was why I had my left hand up to fend off the sight I feared the most.

I was wearing good brown country shoes by Ducker's of Oxford, handmade and rubber-soled but not a lot of bend in them. Glancing over my shoulder, I saw a trail of sticky brown imprints on the dusty parquet floor and realised that while the ownership of the blood was an open question, the prints were unquestionably my own. I sashayed past a closed door and another, shouting, "Hullo, hullo, who's in there?" And then, peremptorily, in my six-acre voice: "May! *Aitken* May!" But the silence that followed these outbursts was more ominous than any answer could have been, and I'm afraid I thought of it as the silence of The Forest.

I passed another window and saw grazing white cattle, marshland, and the bridge, and was grateful to be restored to nature. I passed a third closed door but kept going, determined to launch my reconnaissance from the front entrance rather than by axe through the back door. Also I am right-handed, and if I was going to behave like a middle-aged storm trooper, I preferred to attack doors that were on my left side, holding the gun in my right. That might not be how they do it at training school or in films, but it was what came naturally at my age, and I was damned if I was going to give both hands to the gun.

Age was concerning me a lot just now, the way it used to concern me each time I went to bed with Emma: Am I up to this? Am I too old for my passions? Wouldn't somebody younger do it better? I had reached the entrance hall. Go cold, Cranmer. Walk, don't run.

"Anyone around?" I called in a more conciliatory tone. "It's Cranmer. Tim Cranmer. I'm a friend of Sally and Terry."

Soft chairs. A coffee table, a pile of dog-eared magazines from the fine-rug and antiques trades. A counter with a home telephone exchange and answering machine: the still-functioning answering machine. A woman's umbrella, unfurled, drying in the umbrella stand, though it was dry. Was it raining that day? What day? Remember the footprints in the mud outside the back door.

On the wall, Asian embroideries and a poster of jet fighters tearing across the desert at low altitude. On the table, three used teacups and one ashtray in the shape of a miniature car tyre, overflowing with untipped cigarette stubs. The tea dregs thick black, no milk or sugar. Russian tea? It would have been sweet. Asian tea? It would have been weak. Tea from the great barrier between the two, perhaps. And Russian cigarettes like Larry's.

About to address the first door, I paused to listen for a footfall, or a car coming down the track, or a postman's knock on the front door and a cheery call of "Anyone at home?" The country is never silent, as I knew, but I heard nothing to increase my alarm. I turned the handle without testing it and shoved it away from me as hard and fast as I could. I hurled myself after it in the forlorn hope that if anyone was inside, I would surprise them if they weren't dead. But the surprise had happened already, because the room had been systematically devastated. Desk drawers had been turned upside down and stamped on. Fax machines and copiers clubbed out of recognition. The desk chair sliced so viciously that its entrails hung free of its skin. Filing cabinets flung facedown to the floor and beaten head to toe. Curtains shredded with sweeping knife thrusts. The very sex of the room's missing occupant a mystery until my researches slowly revealed the absence of a woman: a fragment of a fake-leather shoulder bag, not Emma's taste at all; a crumpled face tissue stained with nothing worse than a cheap lipstick that Emma would never have worn; the lipstick itself, crushed flat; face powder scattered like human ash; a lady's money purse with coins to fit a parking machine; a Volkswagen key with remote-control locking switch, smashed.

And a pair of shoes. Not mud-caked buckskin or the waif's black lace-up boots that Emma favoured, but decently polished nearly-new women's low-sided brown shoes of a sort to kick off when you've been slogging at your desk all day and are in need of a bit of Christian air round your poor old feet, size five. Emma was size three.

There had once been two doors linking Aitken Mustafa May's secretary to her master. They had been set about ten inches apart and upholstered in a vile green plastic, buttoned. But whatever privacy May had hoped to derive from this arrangement, it had been rudely disturbed, for the first door had been reduced to matchwood and the second flung giddily across his desk, awakening images of some mediaeval torture in which the victim was stretched flat and a board laid on top of him and he was pressed to death by the literal weight of his misdoings: in this case, by heaps of magazines for would-be freebooters and mercenaries and shooters; arms catalogues, inventories, and price lists from potential suppliers; and shiny photographs of tanks, artillery pieces, heavy machine guns, rocket launchers, battle helicopters, and torpedo boats.

Stepping fastidiously amid the chaos, I was struck by the deliberation of the intruders. It was as if every idolatrous symbol must be methodically sought out and destroyed—and some symbols that were not, to my knowledge, idolatrous at all, such as the washbasin in the adjoining bathroom, and the glass shelving flung into the bathtub, and the curtains stuffed into the lavatory bowl.

But the greatest defilements had been reserved for the things Aitken Mustafa May loved the most: the photographs of his children, who seemed to be many and by different women; the Mercedes paperweight, property of a proud new owner; the bronze figurines and ancient ceramic pots; or the jacket of his brand-new dark-blue lightweight suit by Aquascutum, parts of which were still draped over the back of his chair; or the illuminated Koran, desecrated by heaves so powerful they had sliced through the table it was lying on; or the picture of Julie, taken, I imagined, by the same photographer who had posed them on the sunlit log, but here she was to be seen in a bathing suit, standing on the deck of what was supposed to be a Caribbean cruiser, leaning into the camera with her smile. And the discreet trophies of his other life, such as the brass shell case cut down to make a flower vase and the silver-plated armoured personnel carrier inscribed to him from a grateful but anonymous buyer, both flattened.

I retraced my footprints down the corridor. The kitchen door was still open, but I passed it without a look. My gaze was fixed straight ahead of me, where a different door, this time of steel, barred my advance. A bunch of keys hung from the keyhole, and as I made to turn the key that was already in the lock, I noticed the keys to Aitken May's Mercedes nestling among them. I dropped the bunch into my pocket, stepped over the steel threshold, and, by the daylight coming through the open doorway behind me, saw that the corridor was now brick-lined and that sandbags filled the boarded windows. I remembered the outside aspect of the house and knew I was in the second freight car. I was still making this discovery when I went blind.

Struggling for sanity, I concluded that the steel door behind me had swung shut, either of its own free will or because somebody had pushed it, and that I would therefore do best to search for a light switch, though I doubted whether any electrical system could have survived so much destruction. But I remembered the answering machine and took heart. And my optimism was rewarded, for, feeling my way along the brickwork, I discovered to my joy the line of an external electrical wire. Returning the gun to my waistband—for what could I shoot in pitch darkness?—I followed the wire's path with my fingertips, and suddenly there before me in glorious Technicolour was a bulbous green light switch, not six inches from my eyes.

I was in an indoor firing range. It ran the distance of the buildings, perhaps a hundred feet. At its end, under stark downlights, stood man-sized targets of unabashed racist implication: grinning Negroid or Asiatic ogres clutching submachine guns across their chests, one knee lifted as they cleared whatever they had just bayonetted, their uniforms dappled green and ochre, their steel helmets tipped saucily awry to suggest a lack of discipline. The place where I stood was the firing area: there were sandbags to stand or kneel behind, and metal forks to rest your firearm, and telescopes if you wished to study the target, and armchairs if you didn't.

And just a few yards beyond the firing area, hauled into the centre of the range and obstructing it for any serious-minded user, stood an armourer's workbench with blood on it. And round the feet of the workbench and on the floor, more blood. Which accounted for the smell I had been noticing but had attributed to gun oil and old cordite fumes. But it wasn't either of these things. It was blood.

Slaughterhouse blood. And this tunnel was where the slaughter had taken place, this soundproofed bunker devoted to the profitable entertainments of destruction. This was where the victims had been dragged, one shoeless, one without his jacket, and a third—as I now feared from the sight of the brown cotton overall hanging from a nail above a row of workman's tools—without his storeman's overalls. This was where they had been cut up at leisure, in the seclusion of this artificial silence, before being carried by men in plain shoes or track shoes through the kitchen and across the pile of sawdust to whatever it was that had two wheels and was waiting for them.

Oh, and on the way someone had stopped to paint a tree. Tree as in Forest. Tree as in blood.

THE KEYS to both the Mercedes and the Volkswagen were in my pocket. My legs were leaden, my head was full of images of seven-day-old bodies in car boots. But I was running, because I had to do it quickly or not at all. The Mercedes was locked, and when I turned the key in the passenger door a howl went up and the white cows lifted their heads and stared at me, and a black-faced sheep in the adjoining field baahed long after I had switched the noise off. The interior of the car smelled of newness. A pair of pigskin driving gloves lay hand in hand beside the treasured car phone. A string of worry beads hung from the driver's mirror; a copy of *The Economist* from eight days ago, unopened, lay on the passenger seat.

But no bodies.

I took a deep breath and unlocked the Mercedes boot. It rose automatically, and I helped it the rest of the way. One overnight bag, part of a fitted set. A black hide attaché case, so slim it was no more than a man's vanity case. Key-locked. Examine later. I thought of transferring them to the red Ford but on second thought left them where they were. I moved to the Volkswagen and with a handkerchief wiped the muck from the window. I peered inside. No bodies. I unlocked the boot and raised the lid. A new tow rope, a can of antifreeze, a bottle of windscreen wash, a foot pump, a fire extinguisher, foot mats, a pullout radio. No bodies. I started towards the battered grey Dormobile and stopped dead, for now I saw for the first time what till now it had concealed: an old pony cart with a bridle shaft and rubber tyres half buried in the hay. And winding up the hill, the unmistakable tracks of the same tyres in rough grass. And at the end of the tracks, a granite hut with a slate roof and one dead tree beside it, perched on the side of the hill just beneath the line of receding cloud. I was standing about fifteen feet from the pony cart when I saw it, and somehow I covered the distance and pulled away the hay. Blood was smeared over the old coachwork and upholstery. I walked to the back of the Dormobile and seized the door handle and twisted it as if I wanted to break it off, which perhaps I did. The handle gave way suddenly. I pulled back both doors at once, but all I found was sacks and rats' mess and a pile of old erotic magazines.

I started up the hill, half running, half walking. The grass was tufted and knee-high like the grass at Priddy, and after three steps my trousers were soaked through. A stone wall jogged at my side. Lone bare trees, split from their bark by lightning and silvered by the sun and rain, poked their thin fingers at me. Twice I stumbled. A barbed-wire fence enclosed the hut, but it was parted where the tyre tracks passed through it. The hut was rectangular, no more than twelve feet by eight, but at some point in its life a crude extension had been added, of which only a wooden skeleton survived. The cloud had vanished. From either side of the valley black peaks glowered down at me, their bracken flanks stirring with the wind.

I was searching for a door or window, but a first tour of the perimeter yielded nothing. I looked again at the tracks and saw that they had stopped on the uphill side of the hut, short of a point in the wall where a door had once been, for the stone lintel and wood frame were still legible, though the opening had been filled with random granite stonework and plaster. And I saw a patch of churned and trampled mud at the foot of the doorway, and footprints leading to and from the tyre tracks: the same male footprints I had seen outside the kitchen door. I saw no blood, but when I took a coin from my pocket and dug into the plaster, it was softer than the plaster in the wall outside the doorframe.

And here I had a second intimation concerning the intruders: that they were not only desecrators and men of the knife, but men of the rough country too, outdoor men, accustomed to the dour life. All this I was telling myself as I prodded inexpertly at the plaster with a bit of old iron. I prodded until I could prise, and having prised, looked in. Then I tore my face away and retched as the stench poured out at me, because by then I had seen by the single shaft of light three bodies with their hands tied above their heads, and their mouths open in the same silent chorus. But such is our egotism in crisis that in the very midst of my revulsion I was still able to offer a wordless Allelujah of relief that neither Emma nor Larry was of the company.

HAVING replaced the stones as best I could, I walked slowly down the hill, my soaked trousers chafing my legs. In the presence of death we cling tenaciously to banalities, which no doubt was why I returned to the reception room and, as a matter of routine, extracted the incoming sound cassette from the answering machine and crammed it into my long-suffering pocket. From there I passed from room to room, retracing my steps and considering what else I should take with me, and whether it was worth my time trying to remove the evidence of my presence. But my fingerprints were everywhere, my footprints too. I took another long look at May's office. I patted what was left of his suit jacket and rummaged among the debris of his desk. No wallet. No money. No credit cards. I remembered the black attaché case.

Returning at a slow pace to the Mercedes, I hunted through May's bunch of keys until I came to a thing that was no more than a tiny chrome-coated can opener. I unlocked the attaché case and found inside a file of papers, a pocket calculator, a German fountain pen and matching propelling pencil, a fat British passport in May's name, traveller's cheques, U.S. dollars, and a folder of air tickets. The passport was of the same type as Bairstow's: blue-bound, ninety-four pages, exotic visas, entry and exit stamps galore, ten years' validity, height 1 metre 70, born Ankara 1950, issued 10 Nov 1985, expires 10 Nov 1995. The fresh-faced photograph of the bearer on page three had little in common with the middle-aged gentleman bestriding the log with his loved one. And none at all with the bound and mutilated corpse in the hut. The air tickets went to Bucharest, Istanbul, Tbilisi, London, and Manchester, so his girl had been wrong about Ankara and Baku. Only the Bucharest flight was booked, and he had already missed it. The remainder of his journey, including the homeward leg, remained open.

I put everything back into the attaché case, fetched my own luggage from the red Ford, restored the .38 to my briefcase, and loaded them into the boot of the Mercedes. I was making a choice between two hot cars: the Ford, which together with the person of Colin Bairstow might or might not be on every policeman's wanted list; and the blue Mercedes, which, from the moment the bodies were discovered, would be the hottest car in the country, but until then nothing. And after all: if seven days had passed already, why not an eighth? Aitken May, as far as anyone knew, was abroad. He collected his mail from a postbox in Macclesfield. No postman had occasion to come here. And how long would it take anyone to notice that the Odd Couple were absent from their remote cottage on the moors?

Parking the Ford out of sight between the Dormobile and the pony cart, I hauled down a bale of hay and spread it over the roof and bonnet. Then I drove across the white bridge, knowing that every hour that I delayed was likely to be my last.

EMMA WAS talking to me again. Insistently. I had never heard this tense, commanding voice from her before.

"Hardwear," said the first message. "This is Sally. Where are you? We're worried about you. Call me."

"Aitken. It's me again. Sally," said the second. "I've got a very important message for you. There's a bit of trouble on the way. Call me, *please.*"

"Hardwear, this is Prometheus again," said the third. "Listen. Terry can't make it. Things have changed. Please, when you hear this, wherever you hear it from, drop everything and *phone*. If you're away from work, stay away. If you have family, take them on holiday. Hardwear, talk to me. Here's the number in case you've lost it. Cheers. Sally."

I switched off the tape.

I WAS in a state of horror deferred. The moment I allowed myself to sink through the thin ice of my composure, I was lost. Whatever doubts I might have had about my errand were swept away. Larry and Emma were at terrible risk. If Larry was dead, Emma was in double jeopardy. The fire I had kindled in him half a life ago, and stoked for as long as it had served us, was out of control, and for all I knew, its flames were lapping at Emma's feet. To bare my soul to Pew-Merriman would be to compound my guilt and achieve nothing: "They're worse than thieves, Marjorie. They're dreamers. They've enlisted in a war that nobody's heard of."

I had two passports, one for Bairstow, one for May. I had luggage for May and Bairstow, and I was driving May's car. In my head I set to work testing combinations of these blessings. Bairstow's passport was a liability, but only within the United Kingdom, since I could not imagine the Office, with its congenital terror of exposure, would risk passing Bairstow's name to Interpol. May's passport was in better health than its owner, but it was still May's, and our features were comically dissimilar.

Ideally I would have liked to replace the third page of May's passport—which carried the photograph but no personal particulars—with the third page from Bairstow's, thus giving the bearer my face. But a British passport lends itself badly to adaptation, and vintage models such as May's and Bairstow's are the worst. No page exists in isolation of any other. Sheets are concertina'd, then stitched into the binding with a single piece of thread. The printer's ink is water based and runs the moment you start to fiddle with it. Watermarks and colour gradations are impressively complex, as the resentful white-coated instructors of the Office forgery section never tired of telling us: "With your British passport, gentlemen, you do better to suit your man to the document rather than the document to your man," they would intone, with a venom more commonly associated with army sergeants addressing officer cadets.

Yet how could I suit myself to May's passport when it gave him a height of one metre seventy—even allowing for his raised heels—and my own height was a metre eighty-three? A black beard, a slight darkening of the complexion, blackened hair—these, I supposed, were all more or less within the reach of my inexpert skills. But how on earth was I supposed to reduce my height by thirteen centimetres?

The answer, to my joy, was the Mercedes driver's seat, which, by the depression of a button on the inside of the door, turned me into a dwarf. And it was this discovery that, an hour out of Nottingham, persuaded me to pull in at a roadside café, take the travel agent's luggage labels from May's folder of tickets, write May's name and address on them, and substitute them for the Bairstow labels on my own luggage; then book myself and the Mercedes in the name of May a passage on the ferry from Harwich to the Hoek of Holland, sailing at nine-thirty that night; and, having done all this, to consult the yellow pages for the nearest theatrical costumier and supplier, who turned out unsurprisingly to be in Cambridge, not fifty miles away.

In Cambridge also I bought myself a lightweight blue suit and gaudy tie of the sort May appeared to favour, as well as a dark felt hat, a pair of sunglasses, and—since this was Cambridge—a secondhand copy of the Koran, which I placed, together with the hat and glasses, on top of the attaché case on the passenger seat, in a position best suited to influence the casual eye of an alerted immigration officer leaning through the window of my car in order to compare me with my passport.

I now encountered a dilemma that was new to me and which in happier circumstances I would have found diverting: where can an honest male spy spend four hours altering his appearance, when by definition he will enter the place as one person and leave it as another? The golden rule of disguise is to use as little of it as possible. Yet there was no getting round the fact that I would have to rub a darkening agent into my hair, lower the English country tone of my complexion, not forgetting my hands, paint mastic on my chin, and provide myself, strand by strand, with a greying black beard which I must then lovingly trim to Aitken May's flamboyant taste.

The solution, after a reconnaissance of the environs of Harwich, turned out to be a single-storey motel whose cabins gave directly onto numbered parking bays, and whose unpleasing male receptionist required payment in advance.

"Been on long?" I asked him conversationally as I counted out my thirty pounds.

"Too bloody long."

I was holding an extra five pounds in my hand. "Shall I see you tonight? I'm catching the ferry."

"I'm off at six, aren't I?"

"Well, here, have this," I said generously: and for five pounds established that he would not be there to see me in my new persona as I left.

My final act before leaving England was to have the Mercedes washed and polished. Because when you are dealing with official minds—I used to teach—if you can't be humble, then at least be clean.

FRONTIER posts have always made me nervous, those of my own country the most. Though I count myself a patriot, a weight rolls off my shoulders each time I leave my homeland, and when I return I have a sense of resuming a life sentence. So perhaps it came naturally to me to play the outgoing passenger, for I entered the queue of cars with a good heart and advanced cheerfully towards the immigration post, which was manned, if that was the word, not by a posse of officers provided with a description of me, but by a youth with a white peaked cap and blond hair to his shoulders. I flapped May's passport at him. He ignored it.

"Tickets, mate. Bill-etti. Far-carton."

"Oh, sorry. Here."

But it was a wonder I could speak to him at all, for by then I had remembered the .38. It was nestling, together with sixty rounds of ammunition, not four feet from me, on the floor of the passenger seat in Bairstow's bulky briefcase, now the property of Aitken Mustafa May, arms dealer.

ON DECK a fierce night wind was blowing. A few hardy passengers huddled among the benches. I staggered towards the stern, found a dark patch, leaned over the rail, and, in the classic pose of a seasick passenger, allowed first the gun and then the ammunition to slip into the blackness. I heard no splash, but I could have sworn I smelled the grassy smells of Priddy racing past me on the sea wind.

I returned to my cabin and slept so deeply that I had to dress in a hurry to reach the Mercedes in time and consign it to a multistorey parking garage in the docks. I bought a phone card and from a public call box dialled the number.

"Julie? It's Pete Bradbury here from yesterday," I said, but I had barely got even this far before she cut in on me.

"I thought you said were going to ring me," she burst out hysterically. "He *still* hasn't come back, I'm *still* getting the answering machine, and if he's not home tonight I'm putting Ali in the car and I'm going out there first thing in the morning and—"

"You mustn't do that," I said.

A bad pause.

"Why not?"

"Is there anyone with you? Apart from Ali? Is there anyone with you in the house?"

"What the hell's that to do with you?"

"Is there a neighbour you can go to? Have you got a friend who will come round?"

"Tell me what you're trying to tell me, for Christ's sake!"

So I told her. I had no tradecraft left, no tactical aids. "Aitken's been murdered. All three of them have. Aitken, his secretary, and her husband. They're in the stone hut on the hill above the store. He dealt in arms as well as carpets. They got caught in the crossfire. I'm very sorry."

I had no idea anymore whether she was hearing me. I heard a shout, but it was so shrill it could have been the child. I thought I heard a door open and shut and the sound of something crashing. I kept saying, "Are you there?" and getting no answer. I had a picture of the receiver swinging on its cord while I talked to an empty room. So after a while I rang off, and the same evening, having removed my beard and restored my hair and skin to something of their former colour, took the train to Paris.

DEE'S A saint, she is saying from the window of my bedroom.

Dee took me in when I was down-and-out, she is saying as we stroll together on the Quantocks, her two arms locked round one of mine.

Dee put me back together again, she is reminiscing drowsily into my shoulder as we lie before the fire in her bedroom. *Without Dee I would never have made it out of the gate. She's been mother, father, chum, the whole disaster for me.*

Dee gave me back to life, she is saying, between earnest discussions of how we can be most useful for Larry. *How to make music, love, how to say no . . . Without Dee I would have died. . . .*

Until bit by bit my agent-runner's pride takes exception to this other controller of her life. I wish Dee forgotten and discourage further talk of her—this Dee of the fabulous empty castle in Paris, nothing in it except a bed and a piano—this Dee whose aristocratic name and address are lovingly illuminated in Emma's pop-up book: alias the Contessa Ann-Marie von Diderich, with an address on the Île St.-Louis.

13

WET CHESTNUT leaves stuck to the cobbled pavement. This is the house, I thought, staring up at the same high grey walls and shuttered windows that I had pictured in my dreams. Up there in the tower is where Penelope sits, weaving her shroud, and remains faithful to her Larry in his wanderings, accepting no substitutes.

I had watched my back for hours. I had sat in cafés, observed cars, fishermen, and cyclists. I had ridden on the metro and in buses. I had walked through classical gardens and perched on benches. I had done everything that Operational Man could think of to protect his unfaithful mistress from Merriman and Pew, Bryant and Luck, and The Forest. And my back was clean. I knew it was. Though the experts say you never know for sure, I knew.

A wrinkled old woman opened the door to me. She wore grey hair knotted behind her and the coarse blue-black tunic of a menial. And wooden therapeutic sandals over lisle stockings.

"I would like to see the Contessa, please," I said severely in French. "My name is Timothy. I am a friend of Mademoiselle Emma."

I could think of nothing to add, and for a while neither apparently could she, for she remained on the threshold, tilting her head and screwing up her eyes as if to get me into focus, until I realised she was measuring me minutely, first my face, then my hands and shoes, and then my face again. And if what she saw in me was an uncomfortable mystery to both of us, what I saw in her was an intelligence and a humanity that were almost too powerful for the rumpled little frame that was obliged to accommodate them. And what I heard, faintly from upstairs, was the sound of a piano playing, whether live or recorded was anybody's guess but mine.

"Kindly follow me," she said in English, so I walked behind her up two flights of stone steps, and with each step the sounds of the piano grew a little louder, and I began to feel a sickness of recognition that was like a giddiness from altitude, so that the views of the Seine through the windows at each half-landing were like views of several different rivers at once, this one fast-flowing, another calm, and a third strict as a canal. Brown-skinned children watched me from a doorway. A young girl in the bright cottons of Arabia flitted past me on her way downstairs. We reached a high room, and here through the long window the rivers joined together and became the Seine again, with appropriate anglers in berets, and lovers arm in arm. In this room the music was much fainter, though my recognition of it was no less, for it was some obscure Scandinavian piece that Emma used for her finger exercises at Honeybrook before the Hopeless Causes took her over. And this morning she was still sticking on the same little phrases, replaying them over and over till she had them to her satisfaction. And I remembered how, where others might have tired of this constant repetition, I had always been deeply taken by it, empathising with her, trying almost physically to help her over every hurdle, however many shots it took, because that was basically how I had seen my role in her life: as her conductor and devoted audience, as the fellow who was ready to pick her up each time she fell.

"I am called Dee," the woman said, as if accepting that I was unlikely to offer much in the way of conversation. "I am Emma's friend. Well, you know that."

"Yes."

"And Emma is upstairs. You hear that."

"Yes."

Her accent was more German than French. But the lines in her face were of universal suffering. She had sat herself stiffly in a tall chair and was holding its arms like a dowager. I sat opposite her on a wooden stool. The floorboards were bare and ran directly from her feet to mine. There were no carpets, no pictures on the walls. In a room not far off, a telephone was ringing, but she paid it no attention and it stopped. But soon it began ringing again, as I suspected it rang most of the time, like a doctor's.

"And you are in love with her. And that is the reason why you are here."

A diminutive Asian girl in jeans had appeared in the doorway to listen to us. Dee said something sharp to her, and she pattered off.

"Yes," I said.

"To tell her that you love her? She knows it already."

"To warn her."

"She is warned. She knows she is in danger. She is content. She is in love, though not with you. She is in danger, but his danger is greater than hers, therefore she is not in danger. It is all quite logical. Do you understand?"

"Of course."

"She has ceased to find excuses for loving him. You must not ask for them, please. It would be degrading for her to apologise any more. Please do not require it of her."

"I don't. I won't. That isn't why I came."

"Then we must ask again: why did you come? Please—it is honourable not to know! But if you should discover your motives when you see her, kindly consider her feelings first. Before she met you, she was a shipwreck. She had no centre, no stability. She could have been anyone. Like you, perhaps. All she wished was to climb into a shell and live the life inside it. But now it is over. You were the last of her shells. Now she is real. She is defined. She is one person. Or feels she is. If she is not, then at least the different people in her are going in the same direction. Thanks to Larry. Perhaps it is also thanks to you. You look sad. Is that because I mention Larry?"

"I didn't come for her thanks."

"Then for what? For an obligatory scene? I hope not. Perhaps one day you also will be real. Perhaps you and Emma were very similar people. Too similar. Each wished the other to be real. She is expecting you. She has been expecting you for some days now. Are you safe to go alone to her?"

"Why should I not be?"

"I was thinking of Emma's safety, Mr. Timothy, not yours."

She returned me to the staircase. The piano playing had stopped. The little girl was watching us from the shadows.

"You gave her a lot of jewellery, I believe," Dee said.

"I don't remember that it did her any harm."

"Is that why you gave it to her—to save her from harm?"

"I gave it to her because she was beautiful and I loved her."

"You are rich?"

"Rich enough."

"Perhaps you gave it to her because you *didn't* love her. Perhaps love is a threat to you, something to be paid off. Perhaps it is in competition with your other ambitions."

I had faced Pew-Merriman. I had faced Inspector Bryant and Sergeant Luck. Facing Dee was worse than any of them.

"You have one more flight to climb," she said. "Have you decided what you came for?"

"I'm looking for my friend. Her lover."

"So that you may forgive him?"

"Something like that."

"Perhaps he must forgive you?"

"What for?"

"We human beings are dangerous weapons, Mr. Timothy. And most dangerous where we are weak. We know so much about the power of others. So little about our own. You have a strong will. Perhaps you did not know your own strength with him." She laughed. "Such an inconstant man you are. One minute you are looking for Emma, the next you are looking for your friend. You know what? I don't think you wish to *find* your friend, only to *become* him. Be careful with her. She will be nervous."

SHE WAS. So was I.

She stood at the end of the long room, and it was a room so like her side of the house at Honeybrook that my first thought was to wonder why she had ever bothered to change it. It had the attic look she liked, with a high-timbered ceiling rising to an apex, and the views she liked, down to the river at either end. An old rosewood upright piano occupied one corner, and I supposed it was the sort of piano she had coveted in the Portobello Road at the time I had bought her the Bechstein. In another corner she had a desk—not a kneehole but more in the style of her prosaic desk in Cambridge

Street. And on the desk stood a typewriter, and over it and on the floor lay a re-creation of the papers I had plundered. So that there was a look of proud resurgence about them, as if they had valiantly regrouped after a frightful pounding. If a tattered flag had flown from them, it would not have been surprising.

She had her hands at her sides. Black half-gloves as on the day we had first met. She was wearing a crushed linen smock, and it had the appearance of a habit: of a deliberate renunciation of the flesh; and of me. Her black hair was bound in a ponytail. And the improbable effect of this was that I desired her more urgently than ever before.

"I'm sorry about the jewellery," she began in a sort of lurch.

Which hurt me, because I didn't want her thinking, after everything that I had been through on her account—the anguish and the battering and the deprival—that I had any concern left for something as trivial as jewellery.

"So Larry's all right," I said.

Her head flung round eagerly, eyes wide with anticipation. "All right? What do you mean? What have you heard?"

"I'm sorry. I just meant in general. After Priddy."

Belatedly she understood my point. "Of course. You tried to kill him, didn't you? He said he hoped all his deaths would be so comfortable. I hate him talking like that, actually. Even joking. I don't think he should. Then of course I tell him, so he does it again, just because he's been told not to." She shook her head. "He's incurable."

"Where is he now?"

"Out there."

"Out where?" Silence. "Moscow? Back to Grozny?" More silence. "I suppose that's up to Checheyev."

"I don't think anyone moves Larry around like dry goods. Not even CC."

"I suppose not. How do you get hold of him, actually? Write? Call? What's the drill?"

"I don't. Nor do you."

"Why not?"

"He said that."

"Said what?"

"If you came after him, asking for him, not to tell you even if I knew. He said it wasn't that he didn't trust you. He was just worried that you might love the Office more. He won't phone. He says it's not safe. Not for him, not for me. I get messages. 'He's all right. . . .' 'He sends love. . . .' 'No change. . . .' 'Soon. . . .' Oh, and 'Miss your beautiful eyes,' of course. That's practically standard."

"Of course." Then I thought I'd better tell her in case she didn't know. "Aitken May's dead. His two helpers were killed with him."

Her face turned abruptly from me as if I had slapped it. Then her whole back turned on me.

"The Forest killed them," I said. "I'm afraid your warning came too late. I'm sorry."

"Then CC will have to find a substitute," she said at last. "Larry will know somebody. He always does."

She had her back to me still, and I remembered that she had always found it easier to talk that way. She was staring out of the window, and the light of the window showed me the shape of her body through her smock, and I was desiring her so strongly that I hardly dared speak, which I supposed was something to do with the sexual chemistry between us: that by the nature of our misalliance we had made love as strangers, thus ensuring that the erotic charge between us was always extraordinarily strong. And I wondered whether her desire matched my own the way it had always seemed to in the good times, and whether she was half expecting me to take her here and now, just turn her into me and topple her to the floor, while Dee sat downstairs, listening for fair play. And I remembered the kiss she had given me at the Connaught, which had woken me from my hundred-year sleep, and how her instinctive ingenuity as a lover had taken me to regions I had not known existed.

"So how's everybody at Honeybrook?" she said, as if vaguely remembering the place.

"Oh, fine, actually. Yes, great. And the wine looks better and better. . . ."

And because partly I was thinking of her as somebody being brave in hospital—too much emotional matter could be harmful—I made up some stuff about the Toller girls, saying they were bouncier than ever and sent lots of love; and some other stuff about Mrs. Benbow respectfully wishing to be remembered; and about Ted Lanxon's cough sounding a lot better, although his wife was still convinced it was cancer, never mind the doctor insisted it was just a light bronchitis. And she received all this as the welcome news it was intended to be, nodding out of the window and saying artificial things like "Oh, *great*" and "That's *really* nice of them."

Then she asked me brightly what plans I had, and whether I had thought of travelling for the winter. So I made up some plans for the winter. And I couldn't remember a time when small talk came so readily to me, or to her, so I supposed we were both enjoying the relief that comes over people when they discover that, after the awful things they have done to each other, they are both upright and healthy and functioning and, best of all, free of one another. Which might, in other circumstances, have been grounds for making love.

"What will you do when he comes back, both of you?" I asked. "Make a home or something? I never really thought of you with children."

"That's because you thought I was a child," she replied. After the small talk we had graduated to big talk, and the atmosphere had tautened in consequence.

"Anyway, he may not come back," she added in a proprietorial voice. "I may go out there. It's God's last good acre, he says. It won't all be fighting. It'll be riding and walks and wonderful people and new music and all sorts of things. The trouble is, it's the anniversary of the great repression. Things are frightfully tense. I'd be a drag on him. Specially with the way they treat women down there. I mean they wouldn't know what to do with me. It isn't that *I* mind everything being frightfully primitive and basic, but Larry would mind for me. And that would distract him, which is the absolute last thing he needs. Just at the moment."

"Of course."

"I mean he's practically a sort of general to them. Particularly on the logistical front—how to get stuff through, and pay for it, and train people to use it, and so on."

"Of course."

She had evidently heard something in my voice that she thought she recognised and didn't like. "What do you mean? Why do you keep saying *of course?* Don't be so smooth, Tim."

But I wasn't being smooth, or not consciously. I was remembering my other conversations with Larry's women: "He's bound to be back soon . . . well, you know what Larry is. . . . I'm sure he'll phone or write." And sometimes: "I'm afraid he rather thinks that your relationship has run its course." I was reflecting without fuss that although Larry's love for Emma had undoubtedly been a great passion while it lasted—and for all I knew it was lasting still—actually I had loved her more than he had, and with greater risk. The reason being that women came to him naturally; he just had to reach out for them, and they hopped onto his hand. Whereas Emma for me had been the one, the only one, though it had never been easy to explain this to Larry, least of all on Priddy. And the sum of my contemplations was that I found myself hunting for some clearer sign from him that he loved her, beyond just saying, "Weave and wait for me." And since I couldn't think of one, my next-best thing was to encourage her to go and find him before his ardour fixed on someone different.

"It just occurred to me . . . well, you know this anyway, but there are a lot of people in England looking for you both—not just in England. I mean they're pretty angry. Police and people. I mean thirty-seven million isn't the sort of sum that anybody leaves under the plate, is it?"

She granted me a small laugh.

"So I mean the Caucasus might make rather good sense, in a way. Even if you have to sort of tough it out with the other women, so to speak, and don't get to see that much of Larry. For a time, at least. Till things have died down."

"You mean from a *practical* point of view," she suggested, raising her voice slightly in challenge.

"Well, it's not always the worst point of view, the practical one. The irony is, you see, I'm in the same boat."

"You *what?* Nonsense, Tim. Why?"

"Well, the powers that be have lumped me in with your operation, I'm afraid. They think I'm part of it. With the result that . . . well, I'm on the run too."

"How *utterly* ridiculous. Just tell them you're *not* part of it." She was cross that I should aspire to the heights of their shared criminality. "You're terribly persuasive when you want to be. Your signature isn't on anything. You're not Larry. You're you. I never heard *anything* so absurd."

"Well, anyway, I just thought I'd wander for a bit," I said, feeling obliged for some reason to persist with this futuristic account of myself. "Stay out of England. Out of harm's way. Let things die down."

But it was already clear that she wasn't faintly interested in my future.

"And it wasn't all a wicked Kremlin plot; we know that now," I said conversationally, like someone determined to look on the bright side. "I mean you and Larry and CC—setting me up somehow, using Honeybrook as a safe house or something. I had these awful conspiracy theories when I was low. It was such a relief to discover they were nonsense."

She shook her head, pitying me, and I knew it was a relief to her to discover that I was once more beyond the pale. "Tim. *Honestly*, Tim. *Really*."

I was at the door before she realised I was saying goodbye. I considered other things to say—nice things: "I'll always be there if you want me," for instance, or "If I find him I'll give him your love"—but if I had a sense of anything, it was of my irrelevance, so I said nothing. And Emma at the window seemed to have reached the same decision, for she remained looking out as if she were expecting Larry to come striding towards her down the riverbank, wearing one of his hats.

"Yes. So goodbye," she said.

CONTACT Sergei, who is arranging to post this letter for me, I read as I lay sleepless. *Phone him* in English only *at the number you know* . . . In Zorin's world, it was wise to have a Sergei.

I dialled the number in Moscow, and at the sixth attempt it rang. A man's voice answered.

"This is Timothy," I said in English. "Peter's friend. I would like to speak to Sergei."

"Sergei is speaking."

"Kindly tell Peter I'm on my way to Moscow. Tell him to leave word with a friend of mine named Bairstow. He'll be staying at the Luxor Hotel a few days from now." I spelled Bairstow, then added Colin for good measure.

"You will receive a message, Mr. Timothy. Please do not call this number again."

FOR THE three days while I waited for my visa I visited art galleries, ate meals, read newspapers, and watched my back. But I saw and tasted nothing. By day I remembered her with fondness. She was family, an old friend, a rash act long forgiven. But by night visions of mutilated corpses alternated with images of Emma dead in forest pools. Bloodstained heaps of sawdust rose in Caucasian mountain ranges round my bed. I traced the causality of everything that had happened to me in my life till now and saw Emma as the consummation of its failure. I remembered all my avoiding and pretending. I looked back on everything I had valued, the shelter and ease that I had taken for granted, the prejudices I had unthinkingly adhered to and the nimble ways in which I had escaped the import of my self-perceptions. Seated at my bedroom window, watching the old city brace itself for winter, I realised also, without any great sense of revelation, that Emma was dead: which was to say that from the moment it was clear to me that she had no use for my protection, she was as remote from me and as faceless as any passerby out there on the pavement.

Emma was dead because she had killed me, and because she had returned herself to the half-world where I had found her, feet sinking in the mud, eyes fixed on the impossible horizon. Larry alone survived. Only by going after Larry could I fill the pit that for so long had done duty for my soul.

14

THERE was no message from Sergei.

Tsarist chandeliers lit the vast hall; plaster nymphs cavorted in a rainbow fountain, their shiny torsos reflected to infinity by a carousel of gilt-framed mirrors. A cardboard dancing girl recommended the casino on the third floor, imitation air hostesses told me to enjoy my day. They should have told it to the muffled beggarwomen outside on the street corner, or the dead-eyed children hovering purposefully at the traffic lights and in the filthy underpasses, or the twenty-year-old wrecks in doorways, sleeping upright like the dead; or the defeated armies of pedestrians hunting for a morsel of the dollar economy to buy with their evaporating roubles.

But there was still no message from Sergei.

My hotel was ten minutes' walk from the real Lubyanka, in a pitted dark street where the paving stones chimed like metal when I stepped on them and yellow mud oozed between them as they sank. The guard on the front door was six strong: one hard-eyed sentry in a blue uniform to man it from outside, two plainclothes boys to cover arriving and departing cars; and inside the lobby a second trio, in black suits, all so solemn that I could have taken them for a bunch of undertakers, measuring me for my coffin with their head-to-toe stares.

But they had no message from Sergei.

I walked the wide streets, analysing nothing, alert to everything, knowing I had no shelter left to scurry to, no reassuring telephone number to call if I was in trouble, that I was naked, living under a false name in what all my life had been enemy territory. Seven years had passed since I had last been here, disguised as a Foreign Office flunkey on a two-week administrative errand to the embassy, in reality to hold secret meetings with a Party technocrat with wares to sell. And though I had spent some anxious moments smuggling myself in and out of cars and darkened doorways, the worst I had faced was exposure, and an undignified retreat to London, and a couple of inaccurate lines in the newspapers, and a wry smile from colleagues in the senior officers' bar. If I had had a vision of myself, as I looked down upon the unhappy souls around me, it was as the clandestine emissary of a superior world. No such ennobling visions consoled me now. I was part of them, propelled by my past as they were, ignorant of my future. I was a fugitive, homeless and stateless, a small nation of one.

I walked, and wherever I looked the madness of history answered me. In the old GUM building, once host to the world's most unwearable clothes, burly women of the new Russian rich sampled dresses by Hermès and scents by Estée Lauder, while their chauffeur-driven limousines waited in line outside, bodyguards and chase cars in attendance. Yet glance up and down the street, and there were the skeletons of yesterday dangling from their grimy gibbets: iron quarter-moons with the rusting stars of Soviet triumphalism trailing from their tails, hammers and sickles carved into crumbling façades, fragmented Partyspeak scrawled in drunken tracery against the rain-swept sky. And everywhere, as evening gathered, the beacons of the true conquerors flashing out their gospel: "Buy us, eat us, drink us, wear us, drive us, smoke us, die of us! We are what you get instead of slavery!" I remembered Larry. I was remembering him a lot. Perhaps because remembering Emma was too painful. "Workers of the world unite," he would say when he wanted to taunt me. "We have nothing to sell you but our chains."

I let myself into my room and saw a brown envelope staring at me from the luxurious pillows of my king-sized bed.

"You will please come to this address tomorrow at 1.30 p.m., the seventh floor, room 609. You will bring a bunch of flowers. Sergei."

IT WAS a narrow house in a narrow, filthy street on the eastern edge of town. Nothing gave away its function. I had brought a bunch of pinks with no smell, wrapped in newspaper. I had travelled by metro, deliberately changing more often than I needed. I got off one stop early and walked the last half mile. The day was sullen. Even the birch trees in the boulevards looked dark. There was nothing on my back.

It was number sixty, but you had to work that out for yourself from the buildings either side, because there was no sixty on the door. A black Zil was parked in front of the drab entrance, and two men sat in it, one of them the driver. They stared at me and at my flowers, then stared away. Luck and Bryant, I thought, Russian style. I stood on the step, and as I rang the bell a camphorous stench came at me through the gap between the poorly fitted doors, and I remembered the stench that had come at me when I unlocked Aitken May's tomb. An old man admitted me; a white-clad woman at a desk paid me no attention. A man in a leather jacket was sitting on a bench. He studied me over his newspaper, then resumed his reading. I was in a high, dilapidated hall with marble pillars and a broken lift.

The stairs were of polished stone and uncarpeted. The sounds were just as hostile: hard heels on ceramic, trolleys warbling, and the harsh voices of old women calling above the murmurs of their patients. A place of former privilege, now fallen on hard times. On the seventh floor, a stained-glass canopy lit the stairwell. A bearded little man with spectacles stood shyly beneath it, wearing a black suit and clutching a bunch of gold lilies.

"Your friend Peter is visiting Miss Eugenie," he told me all in a rush. "His protectors have allowed him half an hour. Please be brief, Mr. Timothy." And he handed me the lilies to take with me.

My friend Sergei is a card-holding Christian, Zorin had confided to me. *If I keep him out of prison, he'll get me into heaven.*

MISS EUGENIE was a thin white ridge in the grimy sheets that covered her. She was tiny and yellow and breathed in rasping sips, and Zorin the soldier sat to attention over her like her one-man guard of honour, his shoulders back, his chest thrown out for the medals that he ought to have been wearing. His craggy features were carved in grief. While he watched me I ran water into a glass jar and put the flowers in it, then squeezed myself along his side of the bed till I was able to grasp his outstretched hands. He rose, and with his handshake drew me to him like a wrestler for the embrace, left side, right side, and a kiss, before releasing me to sit across the bed from him on what seemed to be a milking stool.

"Thank you for coming, Timothy. I am sorry to be inconvenient."

He took up Miss Eugenie's hand and held it for a moment. She could have been a child or an old man. Her eyes were closed. He replaced her hand on her breast, then moved it to her side for fear it would weigh too heavily on her.

"She is your wife?" I asked.

"She should have been."

We stared awkwardly at one another, neither able to speak first. There were yellow rings under his eyes. Perhaps I looked no better.

"You remember Checheyev," he said.

The ethic of our trade required that I search my memory.

"Konstantin. Your embassy culture vulture. Why?"

He gave an impatient frown and glanced at the door. He was speaking English quickly but in a low voice. "Culture was his cover. I think you know that very well. He was my number two in the residency. He had a friend called Pettifer, a bourgeois intellectual Marxist. I think you know him too."

"Distantly."

"Let's not play games today, Timothy. Zorin has no time, neither has Mr. Bairstow. This Pettifer conspired with Checheyev to steal enormous sums of money from the Russian government, using the London embassy as a front. You will recall I had commercial rank. Checheyev forged my signature on certain documents. The sum they stole exceeded all sanity. It could be as much as fifty million pounds. Do you know all this?"

"Rumour has reached me," I said, and was reminded how, at fifty-five, Zorin still spoke the elaborate English of his spy school, full of pedantry and old-fashioned idiom; and how, listening to him in the safe house in Shepherd Market, I used to picture his tutors as wispy old Fabians with a passion for Bernard Shaw.

"My government wants a scapegoat. I have been selected. Zorin conspired with the blackarse Checheyev and the English dissident Pettifer. Zorin must be brought to trial. What part has your former service played in this?"

"None."

"Your word?"

"My word."

"So you know of this matter. They have consulted you."

The speed and intensity of his questions, and the gravity with which he put them, persuaded me to set caution aside.

"Yes," I said.

"To seek your advice?"

"To question and accuse me. They are casting me in a similar role, as your accomplice. You and I had secret talks, therefore we must be thieves together."

"Is this why you're Bairstow?"

"Yes."

"Where is Pettifer?"

"Here perhaps. Where's Checheyev?"

"My friends tell me he has vanished. Maybe he's in Moscow, maybe the mountains. The idiots looked high and low for him; they pulled in some of his people. But the Ingush don't interrogate easily." His features cracked into a grim smile. "None has so far come up with a voluntary statement. Checheyev's a clever guy, I like him, but in his heart he's a blackarse, and we're killing blackarses like flies. He stole the money to help his people. Your Pettifer assisted him—for money, for who knows? Maybe friendship, even."

"Do the idiots also think that?"

"Of course they don't! So idiotic they are not!"

"Why not?"

"Because they refuse to countenance a theory of their own incompetence!" he retorted, keeping his voice low with difficulty as his pressed-in anger broke free. "If Checheyev was an Ingush patriot, they should never have sent him to London. Do you think the Kremlin wants to advertise to the world the national aspirations of a tribe of savages? Do you think they want to tell the blessed fraternity of international bankers that a blackarse can sign himself a cheque for fifty million pounds across the counter of a Russian embassy?"

Eugenie was coughing. Cradling her in his great arms, he sat her upright and gazed with desolation into her face. I don't think I ever saw such an expression of pain and adoration etched in such unlikely features. She gave a soft, apologetic cry. On his nod, I puffed up her pillows. He laid her gently back on them.

"Find Checheyev for me, Timothy," he ordered. "Tell him to shout it to the world, declare his cause, say he is a good man, say what he's done and why. And while he's about it, he can tell them Volodya

Zorin is innocent and so are you. Tell him to move his black arse before the idiots put a bullet in my neck."

"Find him how?"

"Pettifer was your agent, for Christ's sake! He wrote to us. To *us*. To the KGB, or whatever they call us these days. He made a full confession of his crimes. He told us he belonged to you first and only afterwards to us. But now he wishes to be no one's man but his own. Not yours, not ours. Unfortunately, the idiots have his letter, so it will never see the light of day. All he's done is make a target of himself. If the idiots can kill Pettifer as well as Checheyev, they'll be delighted." He drew an English matchbox from his pocket and laid it on the bed before me. "Go to the Ingush, Timothy. Tell them you're Pettifer's friend. He will confirm it. So will Checheyev. Those are the telephone numbers of the known ringleaders of the movement here in Moscow. Tell them to take you to him. They may. They may kill you first, but that won't be anything personal. A blackarse is a blackarse. And if you meet Checheyev, cut his balls off for me."

"There's one problem."

"There's hundreds. What the hell?"

"If I were your masters—and if I wanted to catch Checheyev—and if I had you as my prisoner—what you have just suggested to me is exactly what I'd be telling you to say to Cranmer when he walked into this room." He started to protest, but I spoke through him. "Then I'd wait for Cranmer to lead me to Checheyev. And to his friend Pettifer, naturally—"

With a suppressed growl of fury, he cut me short. "Do you think I wouldn't do that if it was there to do? Jesus Christ! I would go to the idiots myself. 'Listen, idiots! Cranmer the British spy is coming to see me! He's soft in the head. He thinks I'm his friend. I've lured him. Let me direct him to the Ingush. We'll trace him together, like a stain in the water, till we reach the well! Then we'll smash their rebel scum to pieces and send their British spymasters to hell!' I would do all of it and more if it would give us back our dignity and standing in the world. All my life I believed in what we did. 'Well,' I said, 'we make mistakes, we take wrong roads, we are human beings, not angels. But we are the right side. Man's future is safe with us. We are the moral instruments of history.' When the perestroika came, I supported it. So did my Service. 'But *gradually*,' we said. 'Spoon-feed them. A little freedom at a time.' They didn't want spoon-feed. They kicked over the bucket and ate the whole meal at once. And what are we now?"

He was staring at Eugenie. He seemed to be talking to her also, for his voice had fallen and he spoke quite tenderly.

"So we shot people," he said. "A lot of people. Some were good men and shouldn't have been shot. Others were lousy bastards and should have been shot ten times. So how many people has God killed? For what? How many does He kill unjustly every day, without reason, or explanation, or compassion? And we were only men. And we *had* a reason."

About to leave the room, I looked back. He was bending over her, listening tensely to her breathing, his great face wet with tears.

THERE were two telephones in my room, red and black. The red, according to the glossy leaflet, was my Personal Direct Line to All the World. But it was the black that, somewhere around two in the morning, tore me from my wakeful slumbers.

"You are Mr. Bairstow, please?" A male voice, speaking precise but accented English.

"Who's speaking?"

"Issa is speaking. What do you wish from us, please, Mr. Bairstow?"

Issa from Emma's answering machine in Cambridge Street, I thought. "I'm a friend of Misha," I said.

I had said it already, over two days, from call boxes and cafés to answerphones and curt intermediaries, in my hand-pressed Russian, as Larry called it, using the numbers Zorin had given me: I am here, I am Bairstow, I am a friend of Misha, it is urgent, please contact me, here is the telephone number of my hotel. And it came a little strangely to me, I'll admit, to hear myself performing, if only in part, as Zorin's agent.

"Who is Misha, please, Mr. Bairstow?"

"Misha is an English gentleman, as I am, Issa," I replied breezily, since I did not wish our conversation to sound conspiratorial to the twenty other people listening.

Silence while Issa digested this.

"What is the occupation of Misha, please, this man?"

"He deals in carpets. He buys carpets abroad and has them delivered to his special customers." I waited, but nothing came back. "Unfortunately, the particular exporter that Misha has been using for his deliveries—" But I got no further before Issa cut me short.

"What is your business in Moscow, please, Mr. Bairstow?"

"Friendship. I have important personal messages for Misha."

The line went dead. Like Larry, few Russians say goodbye on the telephone. I stared into the darkness. Ten minutes later the phone was ringing again. This time Issa was speaking to the accompaniment of crackling voices in the background.

"How is your first name, please, Mr. Bairstow?"

"Colin," I replied. "But people who know me well sometimes call me Tim."

"Tim?"

"Short for Timothy."

"Colin Timothy?"

"Colin *or* Timothy. Timothy is like a nickname." I repeated "nickname," using the Russian word. I repeated "Timothy," in English, then in its Russian version.

He disappeared. Twenty minutes later he was back.

"Mr. Colin Timothy?"

"Yes."

"It is Issa."

"Yes, Issa."

"A car will wait outside your hotel. It will be a white Lada. The numbers of this car"—he put his hand over the mouthpiece as if to confer with someone—"the numbers are 686."

"Who will be in it? Where will it take me?"

The voice became an order, and an urgent one, as if he himself were receiving orders as he spoke to me. "It is outside your hotel now. The driver is Magomed. Come immediately, please. Come now."

I flung on my clothes. The corridor was holding an exhibition of appalling paintings of happy Russian peasants dancing in snow-filled forest glades. In the casino, two sullen Finns were playing against a roomful of croupiers and hostesses. I stepped into the street. A flurry of girls with their pimps advanced on me. I shouted "no" at them more vehemently than I meant to, and they recoiled. Flakes of sleet mingled with the icy rain. I had no hat and only a thin mackintosh. Did the Herr require a taxi? the doorman asked in German. The Herr didn't. The Herr required Larry. Steam was pouring from the drain covers in the cobble. Figures slipped among the shadows across the street. A Lada stood parked between two lorries in the centre of the road, not white but green, and the numbers 688, not 686. But it was a Lada, and this was Moscow, where precision was a variable quantity. A very broad, twinkly man no more than five feet tall was holding open the passenger door, smiling at me. He wore a fat skullcap with a tassel hanging from the crown, a tracksuit, and a padded waistcoat, and he had a jester's sadness. A second man lurked in the shadows of the back seat, his gaunt face barely legible under the brim of his hat. But his pale-blue shirtfront had caught a ray of light from the street lamp overhead. And because in tense moments one sees either everything or nothing, I observed that his shirt had no collar in the Western sense and was of a heavy, hand-loomed material, high at the neck and fastened with toggles of plaited cloth.

"Mr. Timothy?" the jester asked. He shook my hand. "My name is Magomed, sir, after the Prophet," he announced in a Russian as stately as my own. "I regret that most of my friends are dead."

I climbed into the passenger seat, wondering whether he was telling me that my friend was as well. He closed the door on me and reappeared at the front of the car to fit the windscreen wipers into their sockets. Then he alighted neatly in the driver's seat beside me, though he was too wide for it. He turned the ignition once, then several times. He shook his tasseled head like a man who knew that nothing ever really worked, and turned the key again. The engine fired and we set off, weaving between the potholes in the road, and I saw that Magomed was doing what I hoped he would do: he was watching his rear mirror all the time.

The man behind us was mumbling into a cell phone in the language I couldn't understand. Occasionally he broke off to give Magomed directions, only to countermand them moments later, so that our journey became a series of repeated false spurts and hasty realignments until we hurtled gratefully to a halt behind a row of limousines and their minders. Wiry young men in mink hats, roll necks, and cowboy boots stepped forward from a doorway. One carried a machine pistol and had a gold chain round his wrist. Magomed asked him a question, waited, and received a thoughtful answer. He cast a leisurely glance up and down the road, then dabbed at my elbow in the way we steer the blind. Magomed entered an alley between two warehouses held apart by girders. He walked widely, his huge chest forward and head back, his hands curled ceremoniously at his sides. Two or three boys followed us.

We passed under an arch and down a steep flight of stone steps to a red iron door with a bulkhead light burning above it. He rapped a tattoo, and we waited while the rain poured down our necks. The door opened, and a cloud of cigarette smoke engulfed us. I heard the pulse of rock music and saw a mauve brick wall hung with the white faces of Magomed's dead friends. The mauve turned orange, and I made out dark-clad bodies beneath the faces, a glint of weaponry, and hard hands ready to engage. I was facing a detachment of seven or eight armed men in flak jackets. Grenades hung from their belts. The door behind me closed. Magomed and his friends had gone. Two men marched me along a crimson corridor to a darkened observation balcony that looked down through smoked glass onto Moscow's rich, reclining in the plush alcoves of a nightclub. Slow waiters moved among them, a few couples danced. On foreshortened pillars, naked go-go girls rotated mindlessly to the rhythm of rock music. The atmosphere was about as erotic as an airport waiting room, and as tense. The balcony turned a corner and became a projection room and office. A stack of Kalashnikovs stood against the wall beside boxes of ammunition and grenades. Two boys manned the observation window, a third held a cell phone to his ear and watched a bank of television monitors showing the alley, the parked limousines, the stone stairway, and the entrance lobby.

In a far corner a bald-headed man in underclothes was handcuffed to a chair. He was slumped forward, crouching in a mess of his own blood. At a desk not four feet from him sat a pudgy, industrious little man in a brown suit, passing hundred-dollar bills through an electronic money-detector and totting up his findings on a wooden abacus. Occasionally as he counted he shook his head or lowered his spectacles and peered over the top of them at a ledger. Occasionally he paused to take a portentous gulp of coffee.

And presiding over the room, surveying each part of it with steady, expressionless glances, stood a very athletic man of about forty, in a dark-green blazer with gold buttons, and on his fingers a line of gold rings, and on his wrist a gold Rolex watch enriched with diamonds and small rubies. He was broad-faced as well as broad-shouldered, and I was aware of the muscles in his neck.

"Are you Colin Bairstow they call Timothy?" he demanded, in the English I recognised from the telephone.

"And you are Issa," I replied.

He murmured an order. The man on my right put his hands on my shoulders. A second placed himself behind me. I felt their four palms explore my upper body, front and back, my crotch, thighs, ankles. They took my wallet from the inside pocket of my jacket and handed it to Issa, who accepted it in his fingertips as if it were unclean. I noticed his cuff links: big as old pennies, and engraved with what appeared to be wolves. After my wallet, the men gave him my fountain pen, handkerchief, room key, hotel pass, and loose change. Issa laid them fastidiously in a brown cardboard box.

"Where is your passport?"

"The hotel takes it from you when you check in."

"Remain in this position."

From the pocket of his tunic he extracted a small camera, which he trained on me at a yard's range. It flashed twice. He walked round me with slow proprietorial steps. He photographed me from both sides, wound the film through the camera, shook it into his palm, and handed it to a guard, who hastened from the room with it. The man in the chair let out a choked cry, put back his head, and began bleeding from the nose. Issa murmured another order; two boys unlocked the handcuffs and led the man down the corridor. The brown-suited beadle continued passing hundred-dollar bills through his machine and noting them on the abacus.

"Sit here."

Issa sat himself at a desk. I sat the other side. He fished a sheet of paper from his pocket and unfolded it. He set a pocket tape recorder between us, reminding me of Luck and Bryant at the police station. His hands were large and adept and mysteriously elegant.

"What is the full name of the man you call Misha?"

"Dr. Lawrence Pettifer."

"What are the aptitudes of this man?"

"I'm sorry?"

"His skills. His accomplishments. What is wrong with *aptitudes?*"

"Nothing. I didn't understand you for a moment. He's a student of revolution. A friend of small nations. A linguist. Like yourself."

"What else is this man, please?"

"A former agent of the KGB but in reality an agent of the British Secret Service."

"What is the official situation in Britain regarding this man?"

"He's a fugitive. The British suspect him of stealing a large sum of money from the Russian Embassy. So do the Russians. They're right. He did."

Issa studied the paper before him while at the same time holding it out of my sight. "When was your last meeting with the man Misha?"

"On September eighteenth of this year."

"Describe the circumstances of this meeting."

"It occurred at night. At a place called Priddy, high up in the Mendip hills in Somerset. We were alone."

"What was discussed?"

"Private matters."

"What was discussed?"

There is a Russian bureaucratic snarl I had occasionally called upon to good effect, and imprudently I called upon it now.

"Don't you talk to me as if I were a peasant. If I tell you it was private, it was private."

I had been slapped at school, too often. I had been slapped by women, though they were never allowed a second bite. I had boxed. But the two slaps that Issa dealt me as he leaned across the desk were like colours I'd never seen and sounds I'd never heard. He hit me with the left hand, then with the right hand almost simultaneously, and the right hand felt like an iron pipe because of the line of gold rings at the stem of each hard finger. And while he hit me I saw between his hands his brown marksman's eyes fixed on me so steadfastly that I was afraid he was going to go on hitting me till I was dead. But at a summons from across the room he stopped and, pushing aside the accountant, grabbed the cellular telephone that was being proffered to him by the boy at the television monitors. He listened, handed back the phone, and turned in question to the accountant, who shook his head, still counting hundred-dollar bills.

"They're jokers," the accountant complained in Russian. "They call it a third, and it is not even one-tenth of a third. It is not enough to pay their dues; it's not enough to feed a mouse. They are such stupid robbers you wonder how they became crooks."

With a skip of his elbows he scooped up the money, presented it to Issa, executed a few quick flicks of the abacus, seized a ruler and a red pencil and drew a line through each of four pages of the ledger, removed his spectacles and placed them in a steel case and posted the case in an inside pocket of his brown suit. At once the whole party of us—accountant, fighters, Issa, and myself—were hastened down the crimson corridor to the lobby. The iron door stood open, the stone staircase beckoned, armed boys were flitting everywhere, fresh air washed over me like a draught of freedom, last stars winked from a pale morning sky. A long car was drawn up at the top of the steps. Magomed's gaunt companion was installed in the driving seat, gloved hands on the steering wheel. At the rear door stood Magomed himself, holding a dotted head scarf, which, with all the deftness of a nurse, he proceeded to bind round my eyes.

I'm passing through the looking glass, I told myself, as the blackness engulfed me. I'm drowning in Priddy Pool. I'm a Berkeleyan. I can't see, therefore I can't breathe. I'm screaming, but everyone's deaf and blind. The last thing I saw was Issa's elegant Italian shoes as Magomed slowly pulled the blindfold tight. They were of woven strips of brown leather and had buckles of gold chain.

WHAT DO they want?

Who are we waiting for?

Something has gone wrong. Plans are being revised.

I dreamed I was going to be shot at dawn, and when I woke it was dawn and I could hear footsteps and soft voices outside my door.

I dreamed that Larry was sitting on my bed, staring down at me, waiting for me to wake up. I woke and saw Zorin stooped over me, listening to my breathing, but it was only my young guards bringing me my breakfast.

I heard Emma playing Maxwell-Davies in the church at Honeybrook.

MY CELLAR was a fitness club with ancient gymnasium apparatus shoved against the wall and a notice on the door saying CLOSED FOR REPAIR. It was situated beneath a monstrous slab apartment block one hour's blindfold drive from metropolitan Moscow, at the end of a bumpy gravel road amid smells of garbage, oil, and rotting trees, and it was the unfittest place on earth or under it. The humid air stank, water dripped and gurgled all night long from pipes that ran along the ceiling and down to the cracking concrete floor—pipes for sewage, pipes for hot water and drinking water, pipes for heating, and pipes that were ducts for electricity and telephone, and small grey rats, mostly on their way to somewhere else. To the best of my arithmetic, I stayed there nine days and ten nights, but time was irrelevant because when you are first imprisoned, years go by without your wristwatch advancing more than a few seconds, and the distance between two meals is a march across the entire desert of your life. In one night you sleep with every woman you've known, and when you wake it's still night and you're still shivering alone.

MY CELLAR had no windows. The two grilles high in the wall that were supposed to provide ventilation had long been screwed shut. When I clambered onto a rat-eaten vaulting horse and examined them, I found that their iron frames were welded together with rust. For the first day the stench of my cell was unbearable, by the second day it bothered me a little less, and by the third it had disappeared, and I knew I was part of it. But the smells from above me were a constant theatre of the senses, from sunflower oil and garlic and onion and roasting lamb and chicken to the universal fug of large families in tiny crowded rooms.

"*BASHIR Haji!*"

I woke with a great shudder to the cry uttered in marvel or agony by my guards at dead of night.

First their field telephone had rung. Then this tortured or delighted cry.

Were they celebrating him?

Were they declaring him their creed, shouting his name to the hilltops?

Were they calling down curses on him? Lamenting him?

I lay awake, waiting for the next act. None came. I fell asleep.

.   .   .

A PRISONER of the Ingush may be lonely, but he is never alone.

A childless man, I was inundated with children. They ran over my head, jumped on it, beat it, laughed at it, and screamed at it, and their mothers screamed back at them. Now and then a loud smack was followed by a bitter, breathless silence, and more screaming. I heard dogs howling, but only from outside the building. While I craved to be let out, the dogs demanded to be let in. I heard cats from everywhere. I heard the pompous boom of television sets switched on all day. I heard Mexican soap opera dubbed into Russian, and an urgent announcement interrupting it, reporting the crash of yet another financial company. I heard the slap of washing, the skirmishing of men in anger, men drunk, women in outrage. I heard weeping.

For music I had cheap Russian disco and mindless American rock, punctuated by something altogether deeper and more welcome: a slow, soft-throated rhythmic drumbeat, agitated and insistent, urging me to get up, brave the day, strive, attain. And I knew it was Emma's kind of music, grown in the home valleys and mountains of the exiles who listened to it. And at night, when most of these sounds were asleep, I heard the steady flow, as old as the sea, of gossip round campfires.

Thus I had in every sense the impression of having joined an underlife, for my hosts were themselves far from home and despised, and if I was their prisoner, I was also accorded the privileges of an honoured guest. When my guards led me to my daily wash, fingers to the mouth to command my silence, dark scowls as they spirited me through the entrails of the building to the tiny lavatory with its freshly torn pieces of unintelligible newspaper, I felt as much their accomplice as their ward.

I AM LISTENING to Pettifer on fear. It is not a long dissertation, certainly not a Sunday seminar. Our hotel is in Houston, Texas, and he has just spent ten days in a Cuban gaol on a trumped-up charge of possessing drugs—but in reality, he suspects, to provide the security police with an opportunity to take a closer look at him. First they wouldn't let him sleep. Then they gave him a night and a day without water. Then they spread-eagled him to four rings on a wall and invited him to admit that he was an American spy.

"Once I got my dander up, it was great," Larry assures me, lounging beside the hotel pool, studying the passing bikinis while he sucks at the straw of his piña colada. "I told them that of all the insults they could heap on an English gentleman, accusing him of being a Yanqui spy was the lowest. I said it was worse than telling me my mother was a whore. Then I told them that their mothers were whores, at which point, more or less, Rogov barges in and tells them to take me down and give me a bath and let me go."

Rogov is the KGB head resident in Havana. It is my secret conviction that Rogov ordered the interrogation.

I ask the impossible question: What was it like? Larry affects to be surprised.

"After Winchester? A piece of cake. I'll settle for a Cuban prison over House Library any day. Hey, Timbo"—nudging my arm—"how about her? Cut out for you. Ugly and willing. No threat."

I HAD two guards, and they had no other life but me. They did everything together, whether it was night or day. Both had that tipping walk I had noticed in their comrades at the nightclub. Both spoke the gentle Russian of the south, but as a second language or perhaps by now a third, for they were first-year students in Muslim Studies at the Islamic University in Nazran, and their subjects were Arabic, the Koran, and the history of Islam. They declined to tell me their names, I supposed again on orders, but since they were also forbidden by their faith to lie, for those ten days they had no names at all.

They were Murids, they told me proudly, devoted to God and their spiritual masters, committed to a discreet and manly life in the search for sacred knowledge. Murids, they said, were the moral heart of the Ingush cause and of the military and political opposition to Russia. They were pledged to set an example of piety, honesty, bravery, and self-deprivation. The bigger and more studious—I gave neither more than twenty—came from Ekazhevo, a large village on the outskirts of Nazran; his diminutive comrade was from Jairakh, high in the mountains close to the Georgian Military Highway at the southern extremity of the disputed Prigorod region, which they told me constituted half of traditional Ingushetia.

All this on the first day, while they stood shyly at the far end of my cell, dressed in bomber jackets and clutching machine pistols, watching me eat a breakfast of the same strong black tea I had found in Aitken May's waiting room, with a piece of precious lemon, and bread

and cheese and hard-boiled eggs. Meals were from the start a ceremony. My Murids took turns to carry the tray, and great pride in their
munificence. And since I quickly noticed that their own fare was less
lavish—consisting, as they told me, of provisions they had brought
from Nazran so that no dietary laws were breached—I made a show of
eating mine with relish. By the second day, the cooks themselves
started to appear: straight-eyed women in head scarves, who peered in
at me from the cover of the doorway, the youngest the most modest,
the older ones quizzing me with sparkling eyes.

Only once, through a misunderstanding, did I savour the less
sociable side of our relationship. I was lying on my bed dreaming,
and my dreams must have taken a violent turn, for when I opened my
eyes and saw my two Murids staring down at me, one proudly bearing a cake of toilet soap and towels, the other my evening meal, I
sprang up with a warlike shout, only to have my feet swept from
under me and, as I started to struggle to my feet, the oily muzzle of a
pistol pressed into my neck. Alone again, I heard their field telephone crackle and the sound of their quiet voices as they reported the
event. They returned to watch me eat my meal, then removed the
tray and chained me to my bed.

For my salvation I abandoned all resistance of body and mind.
Supine and inert, I convinced myself that the greatest freedom in the
world was to have no control over one's destiny.

Yet in the morning, when my guards released me, my wrists
were bleeding and my ankles so swollen that we had to bathe them
in cold water.

MAGOMED arrived with a bottle of vodka. His eyes were rimmed with
red, and his round face under his skullcap was dark with stubble.
What was saddening him? Or were his smiles always as sad as this? He
poured the vodka but drank none himself. He enquired whether I was
content. I replied, "Royally." He gave a distant smile and repeated:
"Royally." We discussed in no particular sequence the writers Oscar
Wilde, Jack London, Ford Madox Ford, and Bulgakov. He assured me
that it was rare for him to engage in civilised conversation and asked
whether such discussion was available to me in England.

"Only with Larry," I replied, hoping I might draw him.

But his reply was another sad smile, which neither acknowledged Larry's existence nor denied it. He asked how I was getting along with my Murids.

"They are polite?"

"Perfectly."

"They are the sons of martyrs." The sad smile again. "Perhaps they think you are the instrument of God's will."

"Why should they think that?"

"There is a prophecy, widely believed in Sufist circles ever since the nineteenth century when the Imam Shamyl sent letters to your Queen Victoria, that the Russian Empire will one day collapse and the North Caucasus, including Ingushetia and Chechenia, will come under the rule of the British sovereign."

I received this information gravely, which was how he had imparted it.

"Many of our elders are speaking of the English prophecy," he went on. "If the collapse of the Russian Empire has now come about, they ask, when will be the second sign?"

A fluke of memory reminded me of something Larry had once told me: "And did I not read," I said artfully, in phrases as carefully weighed as his, "that Queen Victoria provided the Imam Shamyl with weapons in order to help him vanquish the Russian oppressor?"

"It is possible," Magomed conceded, without much interest. "The Imam Shamyl was not of our people and is consequently not the greatest of our heroes." He passed his thick palm first across his brow and then his beard, as if he wished to cleanse himself of an unfortunate association. "There is also a legend that the founders of the Chechen and Ingush nations were suckled by a she-wolf. The story may perhaps be familiar to you in a different context."

"It is," I said, remembering the wolves engraved on Issa's gold cuff links.

"More practically, there has always been a view among us that Great Britain could moderate the Russian determination to enslave us. Do you consider this to be another of our empty dreams, or may we hope that you will speak for us in the councils from which we are excluded? I ask you this in all seriousness, Mr. Timothy."

I had no reason to doubt him, but I was hard put to provide him with an answer.

"If Russia breached her treaties with her neighbours . . . ," I began awkwardly.

"Yes?"

"If the tanks ever rolled into Nazran as they rolled into Prague in '68—"

"They have already done so, Mr. Timothy. Perhaps you were asleep at the time. Ingushetia is a country under Russian occupation. And here in Moscow we are pariahs. We are neither trusted nor liked. We are the victims of the same prejudices that prevailed in tsarist times. Communism brought us nothing but the same. Now Yeltsin's government is full of Cossacks, and the Cossacks have hated us since the dawning of the earth. He has Cossack generals, Cossack spies, Cossacks in the committees charged with deciding our new frontiers. You may be sure they will trick us at every turn. The world has not altered for us one centimetre in the last two hundred years. We are oppressed, we are stigmatised, we resist. We strenuously resist. Perhaps you should tell this to your queen."

"Where's Larry? When can I see him? When will you let me out of here?"

He was already rising to leave, and at first I thought he had decided to ignore my questions, which to my regret had a note of desperation not consistent with good bearing. Relenting, he gave me a solemn embrace and gazed fiercely into my eyes and muttered something I could not understand, though I feared it was a prayer for my protection.

"Magomed is the master wrestler of all Ingushetia," said the elder Murid proudly. "He is a great Sufi and a doctor of philosophy. He is a great warrior and spiritual master. He has killed many Russians. In prison they tortured him, and when he came out he couldn't walk. Now he has the strongest legs in all the Caucasus."

"Is Magomed your spiritual master?" I asked.

"No."

"Is Bashir Haji?"

I had foundered against the wall of forbidden topics. They fell quiet, then withdrew to their cubicle across the corridor. Thereafter I heard a deep silence, broken only by the occasional murmur. I assumed that the sons of martyrs were at prayer.

.   .   .

ISSA APPEARED, looking vast in a brand-new bulky leather jacket, very shiny, and bearing my suitcase and attaché case from the hotel. He was accompanied by two of his armed boys. Like Magomed, he was unshaven and wore a harrowed, serious expression.

"You have a complaint?" he demanded, bearing in upon me so fiercely I assumed he was going to slap me again.

"I am being treated with honour and respect," I returned, equally aggressively.

But instead of hitting me, he took my hand and drew me to him in the same single embrace that Magomed had bestowed on me, and gave me the same confiding pat across the shoulder.

"When will I leave here?" I asked.

"We shall see. One, three days. It will depend."

"What on? What are we waiting for?" My conversations with the Murids had emboldened me. "I have no argument with you. I have no evil designs. I am here on an errand of honour to see my friend."

His glower unsettled me. His stubble, his ravaged eyes, gave him the appearance of someone who had seen dreadful things. But he offered me no answer. Instead he turned on his heel and left, followed by his fighters. I opened my suitcase. Aitken May's papers were missing, so was Emma's pop-up address book. I wondered whether Issa had paid my hotel bill and, if so, whether they had used Bairstow's cancelled credit card.

I AM HEARING Pettifer on the long-distance loneliness of the spy. Half of him is complaining, half content. He is comparing his existence with rock climbing, which he loves.

"It's one bloody great overhang in the dark. One minute you're proud to be on your own. The next you'd give anything for a couple more blokes on the rope. Other times you just want to pull your knife out, reach up, cut the rope, and get some sleep."

As EACH day passed, my most diverting hours—and most informative—were those I spent in dialogue with my Murids.

Sometimes without embarrassment they would pray before me, after they had prayed alone. They would come into my room wearing their skullcaps, sit down, and, turning away from me, close their eyes and pass each bead reverently from hand to hand. A Murid, they explained, never took a bead in his fingers without invoking the name of God. And since God had ninety-nine names, there were ninety-nine beads, which meant that ninety-nine was the minimum number of invocations. But certain Sufi orders—they implied their own—required the invocation to be repeated many times. A Murid had his loyalty tried and tested in many different ways before he was accepted. The Murid hierarchy was intricate and decentralised. Each village was divided into several quarters, each quarter had its own small ring, headed by a Turqh, or ringleader, who was in turn subordinate to a Thamada, who was in turn subordinate to a *vekil*, or deputy sheikh. . . . Listening to them, I felt a certain kindred sympathy for the wretched Russian intelligence officer charged with the impossible task of penetrating their organisation. My Murid guards performed their five obligatory prayers of the day, on the prayer mats they kept in the cubicle. The prayers they offered in my presence were supplementary prayers, addressed to certain holy men and special causes.

"Is Issa a Murid?" I asked, and my question produced hilarious laughter.

Issa is *very* secular, they replied amid renewed laughter. Issa is an excellent crook for our cause! He is providing us with financial support from his rackets! Without Issa we would have no guns! Issa has many good friends in mafia; Issa is from our village; he is the best shot with a rifle in the whole valley, the best at judo and football and . . .

Then the quiet again, while I contemplated Issa in his new persona as Checheyev's accomplice and perhaps mastermind behind the theft of thirty-seven million Russian pounds . . .

My urge to question them was nothing beside their intense curiosity about myself. Scarcely had they set my tray before me than they were seated at my table, firing their latest batch of questions:

Who were the bravest of all the English? they wished to know. Who were the best warriors, wrestlers, fighters? Was Elvis Presley English or American? Was the Queen absolute? Could she destroy villages, order executions, dissolve Parliament? Were English mountains high? Was Parliament only for elders? Did Christians have secret orders and sects, holy men, sheikhs, and imams? Who trained them to fight? What weapons did they have? Did Christians slaughter their animals without first bleeding them? And—since I had told them that I lived a country life—how many hectares did I own, how many head of cattle, sheep?

My personal situation perplexed them endlessly. If I was a man like a man, why did I have no wife, no children to bless me in my old age? In vain I explained to them that I was divorced. Divorce for them was a detail, the adjustment of a few hours. Why had I no new wife to give me sons?

Wishing to be repaid by a similar frankness, I answered them with the greatest care.

"So what brings you both to Moscow? Surely you should be in Nazran, studying?" I asked them one evening over endless cups of black tea.

They consulted each other, debating who should have the honour of the first reply.

"We were selected by our spiritual leader to guard an important English prisoner," the boy from the valley declared in a rush of pride.

"We are the two best warriors in Ingushetia," said the boy from the mountains. "We are without rivals, the bravest and best fighters, the hardiest, the most loyal!"

"And the most dedicated!" said his friend.

But here they seemed to remember that boasting was against their teaching, for they put on serious faces and spoke softly.

"We came to Moscow to accompany a great sum of cash for an acquaintance of my uncle," said the first boy.

"The money was stuffed inside two beautifully embroidered cushions," said the second. "This was because Caucasians are searched at airports. But the foolish Russians did not suspect our cushions."

"We believe that the cash we escorted was counterfeit, but we cannot be sure of this," said the first earnestly. "Ingushetians are fine forgers. At the airport a man identified himself to us and drove our cushions away in a jeep."

For a while they lost themselves in a tense discussion about what they would buy with the money they had earned by this service: a stereo, some clothes, more gold rings, or a stolen Mercedes car smuggled in from Germany. But I was in no hurry. I could wait my chance all night.

"Magomed tells me you are the sons of martyrs," I said, when this topic had run its course.

The mountain boy became very still. "My father was blind," he said. "He earned his living by reciting the Koran by heart. The Ossetians tortured him in front of the whole village, then the Russian soldiers tied his hands and feet and crushed him with a tank. When the villagers tried to retrieve his body, the Russian soldiers fired their guns at them."

"My father and my two brothers are also with God," said the valley boy quietly.

"When we die we shall be ready," said his friend, with the same stillness with which he had spoken of his father. "We will avenge our fathers and brothers and friends, and we shall die."

"We are sworn to fight the *gazavat*," said his comrade, with similar intensity. "It is the holy war that will free our homeland from the Russians."

"We must rescue our people from the injustice," said the mountain boy. "We must make our people strong and devout so that they cannot be preyed upon by infidels." He stood up and, reaching behind him, drew out a curved dagger, which he offered me to hold. "Here is my *kinjal*. If I have no other weapon and I am surrounded and I have no ammunition, I shall run out of my house and strike dead the first Russian I see."

It was some while before the fervour passed. But the word *infidel* had given me the chance I had been waiting for all evening.

"Can an infidel ever be the subject of a Murid's prayers?" I asked.

The boy from the valley clearly regarded himself as the more dependable spiritual authority. "If the infidel is a man of high esteem and morals, and this man is serving our cause, a Murid will pray for him. A Murid will pray for any man who is the instrument of God."

"Could an infidel of high esteem and morals make his life among you?" I enquired, privately wondering how Larry would take to this description.

"If an infidel is a guest in our household he is called *hashah*. A *hashah* is a sacred trust. If he is harmed, the offence will be the same as if the tribe that protected him was harmed. A blood feud will be called to avenge the *hashah*'s death and clear the honour of the tribe."

"Does such a *hashah* live among you now?" I asked—and while I waited for their answer—"an Englishman perhaps? A man who serves your cause and speaks your language?"

For a wonderful moment I really believed that my patient strategy had paid off. They glanced excitedly at each other, their eyes fired; they spoke back and forth in hushed, breathless sentences filled with unintelligible promise. Then gradually I realised that what the mountain boy would love to tell me, his friend from the valley was ordering him to keep to himself.

The same night I dreamed of Larry as a latter-day Lord Jim, the enthroned monarch of all the Caucasus, and Emma as his somewhat startled consort.

THEY CAME for me at dawn, when executioners come. First I dreamed them, then they were true. Magomed, his gaunt companion, and two of the boys who had watched me being slapped at the nightclub. My Murids had disappeared. Perhaps they had been recalled to Nazran. Perhaps they wished to distance themselves from what was about to happen. An astrakhan hat and a *kinjal* lay on the foot of my bed, and they must have put them there while I slept. Magomed's stubble had become a full beard. He wore a mink hat.

"We shall leave at once, please, Mr. Timothy," he announced. "Please prepare yourself for a discreet departure."

Then he spread himself expansively in my armchair like a master of ceremonies, the aerial of a cell phone poking from his padded waistcoat, while he watched his boys hasten me through my packing—the *kinjal* to my suitcase, the astrakhan hat to my head—and kept his ear cocked to the corridor for suspicious sounds.

Magomed's cell phone peeped; he murmured an order and tapped me on the shoulder as if starting his champion on a race. One boy grabbed my suitcase, another my attaché case; each held a machine pistol in his spare hand. I stepped after them into the corridor. Icy air greeted me, reminding me of my thin clothes and making me grateful for the hat. The gaunt man hissed, "*Fast*, damn you," in Russian and gave me a prod. I climbed two short staircases, and by the time I reached the second, snow was flying down the steps at me. I scrambled through a fire exit onto a snow-clad balcony manned by a boy holding a pistol. He waved me down an iron ladder. I slipped and caught my lower spine a painful blow. He shouted abuse at me. I swore back at him and stumbled forward.

Ahead of me I made out the boys with my luggage, disappearing behind a screen of driving snow. I was in a building site amid mounds, trenches, and parked tractors. I saw a row of trees and beyond the trees a huddle of parked cars. Snow poured into my shoes and grasped my calves. I slid into a trench and dragged myself free of it with my elbows and fingers. Snow blinded me. Wiping it away, I was amazed to glimpse Magomed leaping ahead of me, half clown, half deer, and the gaunt man at his heels. I struggled on, using the footprints prepared for me. But the snow was so deep that each time I landed I sank deeper into the Priddy mire, flailing and falling from one trough to the next.

Magomed and his companion were hanging back for me. Twice they yanked me to my feet by brute force; until with a roar of frustration Magomed scooped me up in his arms and wafted me across the snow and between the trees to a four-track van, its rear half covered in a tarpaulin. As I scrambled into the cab I saw the second of the two boys from the nightclub worm his way under the tarpaulin. Magomed took the wheel, the gaunt man sat himself the other side of me, a Kalashnikov between his knees and spare magazines of ammunition at his feet. The truck's engine howled in protest as we barged the drifts aside. Through a snow-caked windscreen, I took my leave of the ghostly landscape I had only now set eyes on: blackened apartment houses stolen from old war films; a smashed window with hot air belching out of it like smoke.

We sidled onto a main road; lorries and cars bore down on us. Magomed slapped his hand on the horn and kept it there while he forced a gap. His companion to my right watched every car that overtook us. He had a cell phone, and I guessed from the laughter and head turning that he was talking to the boys under the tarpaulin. The road tipped, and we tipped with it. A bend lay below us. We approached it confidently, but our van, like a stubborn horse, refused and glided straight on, mounting what was evidently a verge, then rolling gracefully onto its flank in the snow. Magomed and three of the men were on their feet beside it in a moment. In perfect unison they righted the van, and we were off again before I had time to be alarmed.

Now dachas lined the road, each fretted gable fat with falling snow, each tiny garden draped in its white dust sheet. The dachas ceased. Flat fields and pylons skimmed past us, followed by high walls and three-metre razor-wire fences that guarded the palaces of the superrich. Now, to a kind of common relief, we were in forest—part pine, part shedding silver birch—nosing our way down a pencil-straight track of virgin snow that took us past felled logs and the burned-out wrecks of mysteriously abandoned cars. The track narrowed and grew darker. Clouds of frosted mist rolled over the bonnet of the van. We reached a clearing and stopped.

At first Magomed kept the engine running so that we could keep the heater on. Then he switched it off and wound down his window. We smelled pinewood and washed air, and listened to the furtive plops and flurries that are the language of the snow. My overcoat, soaked from falling, was wet and cold and heavy. I began worrying about the men under the tarpaulin. I heard a whistle, three soft notes. I glanced at Magomed, but the holy man's eyes had closed and his head was tilted backward in meditation. He held a green plastic grenade in his hand and had put his little finger through the loop. It was evidently the only finger that would fit. I heard a second whistle, one note. I looked at the trees to left and right of me, then up and down the track, but saw nothing. Magomed gave a whistle in return, two notes. Still nobody moved. I turned to look again at Magomed and saw, framed in the window beside him, the half-bearded face of Issa peering in.

ONE MAN stayed with the van, and as the rest of us set off I heard it drive away and saw billows of snow run after it down the road. Issa led, Magomed walked alongside him, in the manner of a hunting pair, each with his Kalashnikov covering the forest to his side of the path. The gaunt man and the two boys took the rear. Magomed had given me kapok gloves and strap-on overshoes which allowed me decent progress through the snow.

Our party was descending a steep bank. The trees above us joined in a dense arch; the sky glinted through it in pale shards. The snow gave way to moss and undergrowth. We passed tipped rubbish and old tyres, then carved effigies of deer and squirrels. We entered a clearing filled with tables and benches, and on the further side of it a row of wooden huts. We were in an abandoned summer camp. An old brick shed stood at its centre. On the padlocked door, the word CLUB was stencilled in military paint.

Issa went forward. Magomed stood under a tree with his hand raised, commanding the rest of us to remain where we were. I glanced upward and saw three men posted above us on the hillside. Issa rapped a signal on the door, then a second. The door opened. Issa nodded to Magomed, who beckoned me to his side at the same moment that the gaunt man gave me an unloving push.

Magomed fell back, ushering me ahead of him. I entered the hut and saw at the far end of the room one man seated alone on a makeshift stage, his dark head sunk despairingly in his hands. A tattered backdrop portrayed heroic farmworkers with shovels, digging their way to victory. The door closed behind me, and at the sound he raised his head, as if woken from a sleep, and turned to stare at me. And I recognised by the light from the snowed-up windows the harrowed, bearded features of Konstantin Abramovich Checheyev, looking ten years older than his last clandestine photograph.

15

"YOU ARE Cranmer," he said. "Larry's friend. His *other* friend. Tim, his great British spymaster. His middle-class destiny." His voice was drugged with exhaustion. He passed a hand across his jaw, reminding me of the Murids. "Oh, Larry told me all about you. Just a few months back, in Bath. 'CC, are you sitting comfortably? Well, take a big gulp of Scotch—I have a confession for you.' I was amazed he had anything left to confess. You know that feeling?"

"Too well."

"So he confessed. And I was shocked. I was a fool, of course. Why be shocked? Merely because I betrayed my country, why should I expect him to betray his? So I swallowed some more whisky and wasn't shocked anymore. It was good whisky. Glen Grant from Berry Brothers and Rudd. Very old. Then I laughed. I'm still laughing now."

But neither his ravaged face nor his flattened voice suggested it, for I never saw a man so degenerated by exhaustion and, as I read it, self-hate.

"Who's Bairstow?" he asked.

"An alias."

"Who provided his passport?"

"I stole it."

"Who from?"

"My former Office. For an operation some years ago. I kept it back for my retirement."

"Why?"

"As an insurance policy."

"Against what?"

"Misfortune. Where's Larry? When can I see him?"

The hand again, passed across the jaw, this time in a brusque gesture of disbelief.

"Are you seriously trying to tell me you are here on private business?"

"Yes."

"No one sent you? No one said, Bring us Pettifer's head, we will reward you? Bring us both their heads and we will reward you twice? You are seriously only one person here, looking for your friend and spy?"

"Yes."

"Larry would say bullshit. So I say it too. Bullshit. We are not much given to swearing in my country. We take insults too seriously for swearing to be safe. But bullshit all the same. Double bullshit."

He was sitting at a table with one foot forward, a solitary figure on the stage, staring away from me at the workers on the wall. A lighted candle stood on the table. Others burned at intervals along the floor. I saw a shadow move and realised we were not alone.

"How is the great and good Colonel Zorin?" he asked.

"He's well. He sends greetings. He asks that you make some public declaration that you stole the money for your cause."

"Maybe they both sent you. The British and the Russians. In the great new spirit of *entente*."

"No."

"Maybe the world's only superpower sent you. I like that. America the great policeman: Punish the thieves, quell the rebels, restore order, restore peace. There will be no war, but in the struggle for peace not a stone will remain standing. You remember that very funny joke from the Cold War?"

I didn't but said yes.

"The Russians are asking the West for peacekeeping money. Did you hear that joke also?"

"I believe I read something of the sort."

"It's true. A real-life joke. And the West is giving it. That's an even better joke. For the purposes of peacekeeping in the former Soviet Union. The West supplies the money, Moscow supplies the troops and the ethnic cleansing. The graveyards are full of peace, everybody's happy. How much are they paying you?"

"Who?"

"Whoever sent you."

"Nobody sent me. Therefore nothing."

"So you're freelance. A bounty hunter in the spirit of free enterprise. You are here to represent market forces. How much are we worth on the open market, Larry and Checheyev? Do you have a contract? Did your lawyer negotiate the deal?"

"Nobody's paying me, nobody sent me. I'm not taking orders from anyone, I'm not reporting to anyone. I came under my own power to find Larry. I'm not proposing to sell you. Even if I could. I'm a free agent."

He dragged a flask from his pocket and took a pull from it. It was dull and battered by use, but in design it was the same flask that Zorin had given me, with the same garish red insignia of his former service.

"I hate my name. My dirty, bloody name. If they had stamped it on me with a hot iron, I would not hate it more."

"Why?"

" 'Hey, blackarse, how do you like Checheyev?' 'No problem,' I say. 'It's a nice name. It's a blackarse name, but it's not *too* black. Got a nice ring to it.' Any other Ingush, you call him a blackarse to his face, he kills you. But me? I'm a concession man, a comedian. Their white nigger. I use their insults before they do. 'So how about Konstantin?' they ask. 'No problem,' I say. 'Great emperor, big lover.' Wasn't till they got to the patronymic that they had their fun. 'Hey, blackarse, maybe we should make you a bit of a Jew,' they say, 'lead them off the scent. Abraham had a lot of sons. One more he won't notice.' So I'm a blackarse, and I'm a Jew, and I'm still smiling."

But he wasn't. He was in furious despair.

"What will you do if you find him?" he asked, wiping the neck of his flask on his sleeve.

"I'll tell him he's embarked on a trail of disaster and dragged his girl with him. I'll tell him that in England three people have already been murdered—"

He cut me short. "Three? *Three* already! A disaster? Remember that joke Stalin liked? Three people dead in a ditch after a motor accident, that's a national tragedy. But a whole nation deported and half of them exterminated, that's a statistic. Stalin was a great guy. Better than Konstantin."

I kept talking determinedly. "They've committed grand larceny, they've got themselves up to the neck in illegal arms dealing, they've placed themselves outside the law—"

He had risen and, with his hands behind his back, was standing centre stage. "What *law?*" he demanded. "What law, please? What *law* has Larry broken, please?"

I was losing patience. The cold was making me desperate.

"Whose *law* do you throw at me? British law? Russian law? American law? International law? United Nations law? The law of gravity? The law of the jungle? I don't understand whose law. Is that why they sent you—your Office—my Office—the sensitive and altruistic Colonel Zorin: to preach to *me* about the law? They've broken every law they ever made! Every promise to us: broken! Every pat on the back for the last three hundred years: a lie! They're killing us, in the villages, in the mountains, in the towns, in the valleys, and they want *you* to talk to *me* about the law?"

His anger kindled my own. "Nobody sent me! Do you hear me? *I* found the house in Cambridge Street. *I* heard that you'd been visiting Larry in Bath. *I* put it all together. *I* went north and found the bodies. Then *I* had to leave the country!"

"Why?"

"Because of you. CC. And your intrigues. And Larry's intrigues. And Emma's. Because I was suspected of being CC's accomplice. I was about to be arrested, like Zorin. Because of you. I need to see him. I love him." As a good Englishman, I hastened to qualify this. "I owe him."

A stirring in the shadows, or perhaps a wish to escape the intensity of his fury, caused me to glance round the shed. Magomed and Issa were seated by the door, their heads close together while they watched us. Two other men guarded the windows, a third was making tea on a primus. I looked back at Checheyev. His exhausted gaze was still fixed on me.

"Perhaps you haven't got the clout," I suggested, thinking I might taunt him into action. "Should I talk to somebody who can say 'yes' instead of 'no'? Perhaps you should take me to your Chief Leader. Perhaps you should take me to Bashir Haji and let me explain myself to him."

Speaking this name, I felt a tensing in the room, like a tightening of the air. Out of the corner of my eye I saw a sentry at the window turn his head and the barrel of his Kalashnikov swing gently round with him.

"Bashir Haji is dead. Many of our people were killed with him. We don't know who. We're in mourning. Tends to make us bad-tempered. Perhaps you should be in mourning too."

A TERRIBLE tiredness had descended over me. The cold seemed not worth fighting anymore. Checheyev had leaned himself in a corner of the stage, his hands deep in his pockets, his bearded head sunk inside the collar of his long coat. Magomed and Issa had lapsed into a kind of trance. Only the boys at the windows seemed to be awake. I tried to speak, but there was no breath in me. But I must have spoken all the same, for I heard Checheyev's answer, either in English or in Russian.

"We don't know," he repeated. "It was a village high up. First they say twenty dead, now they say two hundred. The tragedy is becoming a statistic. The Russians are using stuff we've never seen before. It's like air guns against stealth bombers. You don't even get the bullet in the air before they've fried you. The people around are so scared they don't know how to count anymore. Want some?"

He was offering me the flask. I took a long pull.

SOMEHOW it was dusk and we were seated round a table, waiting to go on a journey. Checheyev sat at the head, I sat beside him, mystified by my feelings.

"And all those fine subsources he had," he was saying. "You invented them?"

"Yes."

"You personally? Your own professional ingenuity?"

"Yes," I said.

"Not bad. For a middle-class destiny, not bad. Maybe you're more of an artist than you know."

I had a sudden sense of Larry's proximity.

MAGOMED was squatting to an army radio set. It spoke only occasionally, in a furtive staccato. Issa had his hands folded over his

Kalashnikov. Checheyev sat with his head in his hands, peering into the gloom with eyes half closed or half open.

"You'll find no Islamic demons here," he said in English, as much to himself as to me. "If that's what they've sent you for, forget it. No fundamentalists, no crazies, no bomb throwers, no dreamers of the great Islamic superstate. Ask Larry."

"What's Larry doing for you?"

"Knitting socks."

He seemed to drop off for a while.

"You know another joke? We're peaceful people."

"The casual observer could be excused for not noticing this, however."

"We had Jews among us for hundreds of years. Ask Konstantin Abramovich. They were welcome. Just another tribe. Another sect. I don't mean that we should be thanked for not persecuting them. I'm telling you we are peaceful people with a lot of peaceful history that we don't get any marks for."

We enjoyed an agreed respite, like two tired boxers.

"Did you never suspect Larry," I asked him, "deep down?"

"I was a bureaucrat. Larry was prime beef. Half the stupid Praesidium was reading his reports. You think I wanted to be the first to go in there and tell them, He's bad, and he's been bad for twenty years—me, a blackarse, on sufferance?"

He resumed his meandering. "Okay, we're a pugnacious lot of savages. Not as bad as Cossacks. Cossacks are the pits. Not as bad as Georgians. Georgians are worse than Cossacks. Not as bad as Russians, for sure. Let's say the Ingush have a selective approach to right and wrong. We're religious—but not so religious we aren't secular." His head fell forward, and he lifted it sharply. "And if some crazy policeman ever tried to enforce the criminal code among us, half of us would be in gaol, and the other half would be standing in the street with Kalashnikovs, getting us out." He drank. "We're a bunch of unruly mountaineers who love God, drink, fight, boast, steal, forge a little money, push a little gold, wage blood feuds, and can't be organised into groups of more than one. Want some more?"

I again took the flask from him.

"Alliances and politics, forget them. You can make us any promise you like, break it, and we'll believe you again tomorrow. We've got a diaspora no one's heard of and suffering you can't get on television even with a special aerial. We don't like bullies, we don't have hereditary peerages, and we haven't produced a despot in a thousand years. Here's to Konstantin."

He drank to Konstantin, and for a while I thought he was asleep, until his head lifted and he stabbed his finger at me.

"And when you Western whitearses decide it's time for us to be crushed—which you will, Mr. Timothy, you will, because no compromise is beyond your English grasp—part of you will die. Because what *we* have is what you used to fight for when you were men. Ask Larry."

The radio gave a shrill yell. Magomed sprang to his feet; Issa spoke an order to the boys at the windows. Checheyev walked me towards the door.

"Larry knows everything. Or he did."

A BUS conveyed us: Magomed, Issa, two Murids, Checheyev, and myself. An army bus with small steel windows, and kit bags that weren't ours on the roof. And a shield at the front and back that said it was bus 964. A fat man in army uniform drove us, the Murids sat behind him in their flak jackets, their Kalashnikovs held low in the aisle. A few rows back from them sat Magomed and Issa, whispering like thieves. The fat man drove fast and seemed to take pleasure in edging cars off the icy country road.

"I was a clever boy for a blackarse," Checheyev confided to me, half-heartedly pushing his battered flask at me and taking it away again. We were sitting on the bench seat at the back. We were speaking English and nothing but English. I had a feeling that as far as Checheyev was concerned, Russian was the language of the enemy. "And you were a clever boy for a whitearse."

"Not particularly."

By the blue light inside the bus, his haggard face was a death mask. His cavernous eyes, fixed upon me, had a violent dependence.

"You ever suspend your intellect?" he enquired.

I didn't answer. He drank. I changed my mind and drank too, suspending my intellect.

"You know what I said to him when I got over the shock? Larry? After he told me, 'I'm Cranmer's child, not yours'?"

"No."

"Why I started laughing?"

He laughed now, a choking, arid laugh.

" 'Listen,' I told him. 'Until October '92, I forgot how much I hated Russians. Today, anybody who spied on Moscow is my friend.' "

LARRY's dead, I thought. Killed with Bashir Haji. Shot while escaping his middle-class destiny.

He's lying in the water, faceup or facedown, it doesn't matter anymore which.

He's a tragedy, not a statistic. He's found his Byronic death.

CHECHEYEV was delivering another mordant monologue. He had drawn his collar high around his face and was talking at the seat in front of him.

"When I came home to my village, my friends and relations still liked me. Okay, I was KGB. But I wasn't KGB back home in Ingushetia. My brothers and sisters were proud of me. For my sake, they forgot they hated the Russians." He made a grim show of enthusiasm. " 'Maybe it wasn't the Russians who deported us to Kazakhstan,' they said. 'Maybe they never shot our father. And look here, didn't they educate our great brother, turn him into a Westerner?' I hate that kind of sweetness. Why don't they listen to the damn radio, read the damn papers, grow up? Why didn't they throw rocks at me, shoot me, put a knife in me—why didn't they scream damn traitor at me? Who wants to be loved when he's betraying his own people? You got an idea on that? Who did *you* betray? Everyone. But you're English. It's okay."

He was excited: "And when the great Soviet Empire fell on its white arse, you know what they did, my friends and relations? They comforted me! They told me don't worry! 'This Yeltsin, he's a good fellow, you'll see. Now that we haven't got Communism, Yeltsin will give us justice.' " He drank again, whispering some insult at himself as he did so. "You know what? I'd told them the same stupid story when Khrushchev came to power. How many times can you be that kind of idiot? You want to hear them. Zorin. All the Zorins. Sitting in the canteen. Dropping their voices when the white nigger comes too close. The Soviet Empire not even dead in its grave, and the Russian Empire already climbing out. 'Our precious Ukraine, gone! Our precious Transcaucasia, gone! Our beloved Baltics, gone! Look, look, the virus is moving south! Our Georgia, going! Nagorno Karabakh, going! Armenia, Azerbaijan, going! Chechenia, gone! The whole Caucasus, going! Our gateway to the Middle East, going! Our route to the Indian Ocean, going! Our naked southern flank exposed to Turkey! Everybody raping Mother Russia!' " The bus slowed down. "Pretend you're asleep. Put your head forward, close your eyes. Show them your nice fur hat."

The bus stopped. A draught of icy air ripped through it as the driver's door slammed open and Checheyev pushed past me. From beneath lowered lids I saw a figure in a long grey overcoat step aboard and grasp Checheyev in a swift embrace. I heard confidential murmurs and saw a fat envelope change hands. The overcoat departed, the door slammed shut, the bus eased forward. Checheyev remained standing at the driver's side. We passed a barracks and a floodlit football field. Men in tracksuits were playing six-a-side in the snow. We passed a canteen and saw Russian soldiers eating under fluorescent lighting. They were enemy to me in a way they had never been before. Our driver advanced at a leisurely pace, nothing guilty, nothing rushed. Checheyev remained at his side, one hand in his pocket. A checkpoint came towards us. A red-and-white boom blocked our path. The two Murids laid their Kalashnikovs across their knees. The boom rose.

Suddenly we were careering towards the dark side of the airfield, following black tyre tracks in the snow. Any moment, I was certain, we would feel the wincing of the bus as bullets began to strike it. A battered twin-engined transport plane appeared suddenly in our headlights, doors open, gangway in place. Our bus skidded to a sideways halt, and we jumped into the freezing night, no bullets pursuing us. The plane's props were turning, its landing lights switched on. In the cockpit, three white faces were yelling at us to get a move on. I scurried up the rickety steps and from old habit memorised the registration number on the fin, then thought myself a bloody fool. The belly of the plane was bare except for a stack of brown cardboard boxes strapped with webbing, and steel crates for seats lashed to the side bars. We taxied a few yards, climbed, the engine cut and we sank again, and I saw by a stray shaft of moonlight three onion domes of a church rising at me from a hillside, the largest gilded, the other two encased in scaffolding. We climbed again and banked so steeply that I wondered whether we were upside down.

"Did Magomed give you that crap about the English prophecy?" Checheyev yelled as he flopped beside me and handed me the flask.

"Yes."

"Those chickenheads will believe anything."

Larry, I thought. Your kind of journey. *Fly to Baku, sneak up the coast a bit, turn left, piece of cake.* The danger consoled me. If Larry survived this journey, he survived everything.

CROUCHED on his steel crate, Checheyev was talking about the autumn of two years ago.

"We thought the Russians wouldn't shoot. This isn't happening to us. Yeltsin's not Stalin. Sure he isn't. He's Yeltsin. The Ossetians had tanks and helicopters, but the Russians came along all the same, to make sure no Ossetians got hurt. Their propaganda machine was great. Ingush were bloodthirsty savages, the Russians and Ossetians were good cops. I really felt I knew the great scholars who were writing it. The Ossetians shot the daylights out of us, and the Russians stood around and laughed while sixty thousand Ingush ran for their lives. Most of the Russians were Terek Cossacks, so they knew a good joke when they saw one. The Russians had brought up extra Ossetians from the south who'd already been ethnically cleansed by the Georgians, so they knew how to do it. The Russians sealed off the region with tanks and declared military rule in Ingushetia. Not in Ossetia, because Ossetians are civilised guys, old Kremlin clients, Christians." He drank and again handed me the flask. I waved it away, but he didn't notice.

"That was when you reconverted," I suggested. "Came home."

"The Ingush appealed to the world, and the world was too damn busy," he went on, as if he hadn't heard me. He recited the world's reasons for being busy: " 'Who the hell are the Ingush? Hey, that's the Russians' backyard, isn't it? Hey, listen, all this fragmentation's going too far. While *we*'re pulling down the *economic* borders, these ethnic crazies are putting up *national* borders. They're dissidents, aren't they? They're Muslims, aren't they? *And* criminals. I mean forget *Russian* criminals, these blackarses are the real thing. Don't they know that justice is for big guys? Best let Boris handle it.' "

The plane's engines faltered and resumed on a lower note. We were losing height.

"We could solve it," he said. "Six months. A year. No problem. There'd be fighting. A few heads would end up a little bit further from their bodies. Some old scores would be settled. Without the Russians round our necks we'd solve it."

"Are we landing or crashing?" I asked.

I have a recurrent nightmare of being in a plane at night, hurtling between buildings down a road that gets narrower and narrower. I was having it now, except that this time we were hurtling between light towers towards a black hillside. The hillside opened, we shot into a tunnel lit by cat's-eyes, and the cat's-eyes were above us. To either side of us ran red and green lights. Beyond them lay a sallow concrete playground with parked fighter planes, fire engines, and fuel lorries behind high wire netting.

Checheyev's reflective mood had left him. Even before we came sidewinding to a halt, he sobered. He opened the fuselage door and peered out, while the two Murids stood behind him. Magomed pressed an automatic pistol into my hand. I entrusted it to my waistband. The secular Issa took the other side of me. The crew were staring tightly ahead of them. The plane's engines roared impatiently. From the misty recesses of the bunker a pair of headlights flashed twice. Checheyev dropped to the tarmac, we followed, fanned out, and formed an arrowhead, of which the Murids made the wings and Checheyev the point. We trotted forward, the Murids sashaying with their Kalashnikovs. Two grimy jeeps were waiting for us at the foot of a long ramp. As Magomed and Issa grabbed an elbow each and spirited me over the tailboard of the second jeep, I saw our bloated little transport plane taxiing for takeoff. The jeeps cleared the ramp and raced down a tarmac road past an unmanned checkpoint. We reached a roundabout, bumped across a beaten down traffic island, and keeled left onto what in these parts I took to be a main road. A sign in Russian said Vladikavkaz 45 kilometres, Nazran 20. The air smelled of dung and hay and Honeybrook. I remembered Larry in his strat and peasant's smock, picking grapes and singing "Greensleeves" to the delight of the Toller girls and Emma. I remembered him belly up or belly down. And thought of him alive again after I had killed him.

·   ·   ·

OUR SAFE house was two houses inside a white-walled courtyard. There were two gateways—one to the road, one to open pasture. Beyond the pasture, foothills patched with shadow by the moon lifted into a star-filled sky. Above the hills rose mountains and more mountains. The lights of distant villages twinkled among the foothills.

WE WERE in a living room with mattresses on the floor and a plastic-topped table at the centre. Two women in head scarves were setting out food, I guessed a mother and her daughter. Our host was a stocky man in his sixties, who spoke gravely while he grasped my hand.

"He says you are welcome," said Checheyev without his custom-ary cynicism. "He says he's greatly honoured by your presence here and that you should sit beside him. We can fight our wars for our-selves, he says. We don't need outside help. But when the English lend us their support, we are grateful and we thank God. He means every word, so smile and look like an English king. He's a Sufi, so we don't question his authority."

I sat beside him. The older men took their places at the table, while the young remained standing and the women served pita loaves, fried beef in garlic, tea. A photograph of Bashir Haji hung on the wall. It was the photograph from Cambridge Street, except that it had no inked inscription across the corner.

"The village was attacked at night," Checheyev said, translating our host's words while the young men listened in respectful silence. "The village has been deserted for years, ever since the Russians knocked down the houses and drove the inhabitants into the valley. In the old days we could always take refuge in the mountains, but today they have technology. They fired rockets, then they landed helicopters. Russians or Ossetians, probably both." He added his own aside: "Ossetians are bastards, but they're our bastards. We'll deal with them in our own way." He resumed his translation. "People in nearby villages say they heard sounds like thunder and saw flashes in the sky. *Silent* helicopters, he says. That's just peasant talk. Anyone who could invent a silent heli-copter would own the world." Hardly a change to his voice, or to the pace of his delivery, but the words became an aside of his own: "The Sufis are the only outfit round here that're capable of taking up the Russian challenge. They're the keepers of the local conscience. But when it comes to guns and training, they're turtles on their backs. That's why they need Issa, and me and Larry." He resumed his taste of translation: "A woman was attending the funeral of her mother ten kilometres away. When she got home she found everybody dead, so she turned round and walked back to the village where she'd buried her mother. Next day a group of men set out. They washed whatever they could find of the bodies, said the words over them, and buried them, which is our custom. Bashir had been tortured with knives, but they recognised him. Our host says we were betrayed."

"Who by?"

"He says a traitor. An Ossetian spy. That's all he knows."

"What do you think?"

"With satellites? Spook cameras? Spook listeners? I think the whole trash of modern technology has betrayed us." I had opened my mouth to ask him but he anticipated my question. "No other identifications have been made. It's not polite to grill him."

"But surely . . . a European man . . ."

But as I said this I remembered Larry's wayward black forelock, no different from the forelocks round me, and his skin that went brown in the sun where mine went pink.

Magomed was saying a prayer to take to bed. " 'We shall kill every one of them,' " Checheyev translated, while our host led a soft chorus of approval. " 'We shall find out the names of the helicopter pilots, and of the men who planned the operation, and of the man who commanded it, and of the men who took part in it, and with God's help we shall kill them all. We shall go on killing Russians till they do what Yeltsin said they would do: take their tanks and guns and helicopters and rockets and soldiers and officials and spies to the other side of the Terek River and leave us to settle our differences and govern ourselves in peace. That is God's will.' You know something?"

"Nothing."

"I believe him. I was an idiot. I took a holiday from who I was. It lasted twenty years. Now I've come home and I wish I'd never been away."

OUR GUEST room was the House sick bay in a measles epidemic at Winchester: beds pushed against the walls, mattresses on the floor, and a bucket to pee in. A Murid stood at the window, watching the road while his comrade slept. One by one my companions dropped off to sleep around me. Sometimes Larry spoke to me, but I preferred not to hear his words because I knew them too well. Just you stay alive for me, I warned my agent. Just damn well stay alive, that's an order. You're alive for as long as I don't know you're dead. You've survived death once. Now do it again, and keep your big mouth *shut*.

Hours passed, I heard cockerels and the bleating of sheep as a faltering muezzin sang over a loudspeaker. I heard the shuffle of cattle. I got up and, standing beside the Murid at the window, saw the mountains again, and the mountains above the mountains, and I remembered how Larry in a letter to Emma had sworn to throw down his *bourka* and fight his ground here on the road to Vladikavkaz. I watched women driving buffaloes through the courtyard in the darkness before dawn. We breakfasted quickly, and on Checheyev's insistence I gave ten dollars to each child, remembering the black boy who had followed me in Cambridge Street.

"If you're proposing to fulfil the English prophecy, you'd better leave a good impression," Checheyev said drily.

It was still dark. We drove first on the main road, then up a widening valley until the road became a field strewn with boulders. The jeep in front stopped, and we stopped beside it. By our headlights I saw a footbridge over a river and at the side of it a steeply rising grass track. And on the riverbank, eight horses already saddled, and one old man in a high fur hat and boots and breeches, and one slender mountain boy with eyes that heard us coming. I remembered Larry's letter to Emma and, like Negley Farson, begged to be allowed to take the Caucasus into my protection.

THE BOY set out first, accompanied by one of the Murids. We waited for the sounds of their hoofs to disappear into the darkness. Our guide went next, then Checheyev, then myself. Issa, Magomed, and the second Murid made up the tail. To the pistol that Magomed had given me he now added a holster and an ammunition belt with metal loops on it for grenades. I wanted to refuse the grenades, but Checheyev angrily commanded me: "Take the damn things and wear them. We're close to the Ossetian border, close to the military highway, close to the Russian camps. This isn't Somerset, right?" He swung back to our old guide, who was murmuring in his ear. "He says talk quiet and don't talk unless you have to. Don't shoot unless you have to, don't stop unless you have to, don't light a flame, don't swear. Can you ride a horse?"

"I could when I was about ten."

"Don't mind the mud or the steep places. The horse knows the way; the horse will do the work. Don't lean. If you're scared, don't look down. If we're attacked, nobody surrenders. That's the tradition, so kindly observe it. We don't play cricket here."

"Thanks."

Whispering from the guide, then grim laughter from both of them.

"And if you want to piss, save it till we've killed some Russians."

We rode for four hours, and if I hadn't been so fearful of what awaited me, I would have been more fearful of the journey. Within minutes of our departure we were looking down on the lights of villages thousands of feet below us, while the black mountain wall brushed past our faces. But in the broken bodies that I saw ahead of me I was witnessing an extinction of my life more absolute than anything that might happen to me on my way to them. The sky lightened, black peaks appeared among the clouds, snowcaps rose above them, and my heart lifted in mystical response. Rounding a bend, we came on herds of black, thick-coated sheep perched precariously on the slopes below us. Two shepherds huddled under a crude shelter, warming themselves before a fire. Their shadowed eyes took the measure of our guns and horses. We entered a forest of trees veiled in lianas, but the forest was to one side of us and on the other lay the chasm of the valley, full of swirling dawn mist and the sigh of wind and the scream of birds below. And since I have little head for heights, I should have swooned with each new sight of the precipice between my horse's slithering feet, and of the tiny, winding valley floor, and of the crumbling ridge of stone, inches broad and sometimes less, that was my only hold upon the mountain face, and at the unearthly and mysteriously graceful sounds of waterfalls that were as much to breathe and drink as hear. But the survival I craved was Larry's, not mine, and the lucid, unencompassable majesty of the mountains drew me upward.

The weather changed as wildly as the landscape; giant insects hummed around my face, nudged my cheeks, and danced away. One moment friendly white clouds drifted sweetly across the blue alpine sky, the next I was cringing in the lee of enormous eucalyptus trees in a vain effort to escape onslaughts of torrential rain. Then it was a sweltering June day in Somerset, with scents of cowslip and mown grass, and warm cattle from the valley.

Yet these unheralded changes acted on me like the moods of a loved and volatile friend, and sometimes the friend was Larry, and sometimes Emma. I will be your champion, your friend, your ally. I will be the facilitator of your dreams, I whispered in my heart to the passing crags and forests. Just let Larry be alive for me when I come over the brow of the last hill, and whatever I have been I will never be again.

We were in a clearing, and the old guide had ordered us to halt and bunch together under an overhanging cliff. Stinging sunlight burned our faces; birds screamed and wheeled in delight. Magomed had dismounted and was busying himself with his saddlebag while he kept watch up the track. Issa sat with his back to him, his gun held across his chest as he covered the route we had ascended. The horses stood with hung heads. Out of the trees ahead of us rode the mountain boy. He murmured to the old guide, who touched the brow of his tall fur hat as if he were placing a mark on it.

"We can ride on," Checheyev said.

"What was holding us up?"

"Russians."

AT FIRST I didn't realise we had entered the village. I saw a wide plateau like a sawn-off mountain, but it was covered in smashed stones that reminded me of the view of the Beacon from my priest-hole at Honeybrook. I saw four crumbling towers with blue cloud rolling over them, and in my unfamiliarity I supposed them to be ancient furnaces—a notion that was given force by the sight of scorch marks, which I took to be evidence of charcoal burning, or whatever else might have been burned a hundred or so years ago in stone furnaces on godforsaken mountaintops eight thousand feet above sea level. Then I remembered reading somewhere that the region was famous for its ancient stone watchtowers; and I remembered Emma's drawing of herself and Larry gazing from the upper windows.

I saw dark figures dotted across the landscape, but I dismissed them first as shepherds with their flocks, then as gleaners of some kind, for as we drew nearer I noticed that the figures had a tendency to stoop and rise and stoop again, and I imagined them using one arm to pick whatever they were picking, and the other to keep it safe.

Then I heard above the wind—for the wind in this open wilderness was coming on fiercely—an insistent, high-pitched nasal whine, rising and falling, which I attempted to ascribe to whatever mountain animals might be at home here, some wild breed of sheep or goat; jackals, perhaps wolves. I glanced behind me and saw a black knight in broad armour, but it was only the silhouette of Magomed's great bearded bulk, for the horse they had given him was taller than mine by several hands, and Magomed was wearing a sheepskin hat of the region, wider at the top than at the bottom, and to my astonishment he had donned a traditional wide-shouldered *cherkesska* with loops for ammunition across the chest. And his Kalashnikov protruded like a great bow from his shoulders.

The wailing grew louder. A chill passed over me as I recognised it for what it had been all along: the keening of women mourning the dead, each for herself and each in strident discord with the others. I smelled wood smoke and saw two fires burning halfway up the slope ahead of me, and women tending them, and small children playing round them. And wherever I looked, I hoped desperately for a familiar pose or gesture: Larry's unmistakably English stance, one leg struck forward, hands thrust behind his back; or Larry punching away his forelock while he gave an order or scored a debating point. I looked in vain.

I saw smoke plumes rise until the wind bent them back down the hill at me. I saw a dead sheep hanging head downward from a tree. And after the wood smoke, I smelled death and knew we had arrived: the sweet, sticky smell of blood and scorched earth opened to the sky. The wind blew stronger with each step that we advanced, and the keening grew louder, as if wind and women were in league with each other, and the harder the wind blew, the more sound it drew from the women. We were riding in single file, Checheyev leading and Magomed close behind me, granting me the solace of his proximity. And behind Magomed rode Issa. And Issa the great secularist and swindler and *mafioso* had put on his ceremonial clothing for the occa-

sion, for he was wearing, as well as a tall hat, a heavy cloak that made
a pyramid of his upper body but did not quite conceal the gold buttons of his green blazer. Like Magomed's, his fierce eyes were darkened by the browline of his hat, and by his beard of mourning.

I began to identify the functions of the figures among the rubble.
Not all wore black, but every head was covered. At the edge of the
plateau, at a spot equidistant from the two furthest watchtowers, I
made out crude, elongated piles of stones in the form of coffins
raised from the ground and tapering towards the top. And I saw that
as the women moved among them, they stooped to each in turn and,
while crouching, placed their hands on the stones and talked to whoever lay inside. But with discretion, as if they must not wake them.
The children kept their distance.

Other women pared vegetables, fetched water for the cauldrons,
cut bread and set it on makeshift tables. And I realised that those who
had arrived before us had brought offerings of sheep and other food.
But the largest group of women was segregated and tightly packed
together inside what seemed to be a ruined barn, and it was they who,
with the arrival of each new delegation of mourners, wailed in misery
and outrage. At a distance of perhaps fifty yards from the barn, and
down the slope from it, stood the remains of a courtyard surrounded
by charred fencing. A finger of roof hung over it, a form of doorway
led to it, though there was neither door nor lintel and the walls
around were so pierced with high-velocity shell holes that they were
defined as much by what wasn't there as by what was.

Nonetheless with each new arrival men entered by this doorway,
and once inside, they greeted other men, shook hands, embraced and
faced each other and prayed, then sat and talked and came and left
with the gravity of centuries, and like Magomed and Issa, they had
dressed themselves for ceremony: men in tall sheepskin hats and
1920s breeches, men in broad Caucasian belts and knee boots and
gold watchchains, men in skullcaps with white or green bands, men
with their *kinjals* at their sides, holy men with beards, and one old man
resplendent in his *bourka*—the great felt cape more like a tent than a
coat, where by tradition his children can hide themselves from storms
or danger. But look as I might, I saw no tall Englishman with an errant
forelock and an easy grace and a taste for other people's hats.

Checheyev had dismounted. Behind me, Magomed and Issa leapt
lightly to the ground, but Cranmer after too many years on foot was

welded to his saddle. I tried to wrestle free, but my feet were locked in the stirrups—until Magomed, once more coming to my aid, first lifted me in the air, then tipped me into his arms and set me on my feet, then righted me again before I fell. Young boys took our horses.

We entered the courtyard, Checheyev leading and Issa at my side, and as we entered I heard them offer a salaam in Arabic and saw the men who were sitting before us rise, and those who were already standing brace themselves as if called to order, until all stood before us in a half circle, the oldest to the right of us; and of those before us, it was the man on our left, a giant of a man in a tunic jacket and knee breeches, who took upon himself the responsibility of all of them. And I knew he was the chief mourner and the most afflicted, though his face was set in a grim rejection of grief that reminded me of Zorin with his dying mistress. And I knew that just as there were no greetings here, so there were to be no demonstrations of unmanliness, or unseemly grief, and that it was a time for stoicism and bearing and mystical communion and vengeance, not women's tears.

Checheyev had spoken again, and this time I knew that he had called a prayer, for though no prayer was spoken, all the men around me cupped their hands together in a begging bowl and raised them in oblation and for a minute or so lowered their eyes and moved their lips and muttered occasional and simultaneous amens. After they had prayed they made the washing gesture that I was by now familiar with, as if rubbing the prayer into their faces and at the same time cleansing them in preparation for the next one. As I watched them, I realised I was suiting my own hands to their gestures, partly out of a kind of spiritual courtesy and partly because, just as the landscape had assumed me, so had these people, and I could no longer distinguish between gestures that were familiar to me and others that were not.

From my right an old man said something in Arabic, which was taken up by each man separately, not as words but as a patter of lips endorsed by amens. I heard Issa from close beside me, speaking clear English in his usual voice:

"They are blessing his martyrdom," he said.

"Whose?" I whispered—yet why did I speak so quietly when no one else was lowering his voice?

"Bashir Haji's," he replied. "They are asking God to forgive him and be merciful to him and bless his *gazavat*. They are swearing vengeance. Vengeance is our job, not God's."

Is Larry a martyr too? I was asking. But not aloud.

Checheyev was speaking to the giant, and through the giant to all of them.

"He is saying it is in God's hands that we live and die," Issa translated firmly in English.

There was another moment of muttered quiet, and another washing of the faces. *Who lives?* I begged. *Who dies?* But once more not aloud.

"What else is he saying?" I asked, for by then the word *Larry* had passed through me like a knife, spoken by Checheyev and taken up by everybody in the line, from the giant on the left to the oldest and most venerable on the right. And some were nodding at me and others were shaking their heads and tut-tutting and the giant was staring at me with pursed lips.

"He is telling them you are a friend of Larry the Englishman," said Issa.

"What else?" I implored him, for the giant had spoken some words to Checheyev, and I had heard more amens along the line.

"They are saying that God takes the dearest and the best," Issa replied. "Men and women equally."

"So has God taken Larry?" I shouted, though I was only speaking at their level.

Checheyev had swung round and was addressing me, and I saw both anger and a warning in his wracked face. And I knew that if I had not done Larry the favour of killing him before, I had done it here, in a place further from the earth than Priddy, and closer to the sky.

Checheyev's voice had acquired an operational urgency.

"They expect you to be a man, so speak like a man. Say it in English. To all of them. Let them hear your courage," he said.

So I said it in English to the giant, very loudly, which was completely against my character and training; and to all of those around him, while Checheyev belted out the translation and Magomed and Issa stood behind me. I said that Larry was an Englishman who had loved freedom above everything. He had loved the courage of the Ingush and shared their hatred of the bully. And that Larry would live because he had cared, and that it was those who cared too little who died the death. And that since courage went hand in hand with honour, and both with loyalty, it was necessary also to record that, in a world where loyalty was increasingly difficult to define, Larry had contrived to remain a man of honour even if the necessary consequence of this was to go out and find his death like a warrior.

For it occurred to me as I spoke—though I was careful not to say it in so many words—that if Larry had led the wrong life, he had at least found the right death.

Whether Checheyev translated my words faithfully I never knew. Nor, if he did, how they were received by my audience, for another delegation was arriving and the ritual was already being repeated.

A GAGGLE of small children came with us up the hill, plucking at Magomed's hands as he walked, gazing up in adoration at the great hero and in puzzlement at me. Reaching the barn, Checheyev went ahead while the rest of us stood in the sweeping wind. Here among the women, it seemed, a certain show of emotion was permitted, because as Checheyev returned to us with a white-faced woman and her three small children and declared them to be Bashir's, I saw that his eyes had filled with tears for which the wind was not responsible.

"Tell her that her husband died a martyr's death," he ordered me roughly.

So pretty much I said this, and he translated it. Then he must have told her that I was Larry's friend, because I heard the word *Larry* again. And at the mention of him she seized me in a chaste sideways embrace and wept so much that I had to hold her up. She was still weeping as he took her back to the barn.

A YOUNG man was leading the way. Magomed had found him in the courtyard and brought him to us. Straggling after him, we picked our way through smashed masonry and furniture, past a heap of burned mattresses and a tin bathtub with bullet holes in it. And I remembered a pebble beach in Cornwall called St. Loy, where Uncle Bob sometimes took me on holiday and I collected driftwood while he read the newspaper.

A group of men were slaughtering a sheep, while children watched. They had bound its legs front and back, and now it lay on its side, pointed, I supposed, towards Mecca, because there was fuss about getting its head in the right direction. Then, with a quick prayer and a deft plunge of the dagger, the sheep was killed and its blood was left to pour over the rocks and mingle with whatever blood was there already. We passed a cooking fire and saw bubbling water in a great iron cauldron. We came to the watchtower at the furthest corner of the plateau, and I remembered Larry's passion for rejected places.

The young man who led us wore a long raincoat, but it wasn't green or Austrian, and as we approached the entrance to the watchtower he stopped and, in the manner of a tour guide, raised an arm to the ruined building above us and announced through Checheyev his regret that, as a result of the attack, the watchtower was unfortunately only half its original height. Then he gave a lurid account of the battle, which Checheyev translated but I didn't listen to very much, about how everyone had fought to the last bullet and the last thrust of the *kinjal,* and how God would look mercifully on the heroes and martyrs who had died here and how one day this place would become a holy shrine. And I wondered how that would grab Larry: to be a named ghost in a holy shrine.

Finally we stepped inside, but as so often with great monuments, there really was very little to see, except what had fallen from the upper floors. For the ground floor, being reserved for cattle and horses, was by tradition bare, although Emma's drawing, I remembered, had put a cow in it. A few kitchen saucepans lay about, an oil stove, a bed, a few shreds of clothing. No books, but one would hardly have expected any. Not even, so far as I could see, a radio. So probably after the attackers had shelled the place and shot it up, and made sure by whatever means that everyone including Larry was dead, they looted it. Or perhaps there had been nothing much to loot. I looked for something small for myself as a memento, but really there wasn't anything at all for a man in search of connection to slip into his pocket for a future lonely hour. Finally I hit on a singed fragment of plaited straw, about an inch by two inches and rounded on one side. It was lacquered, and yellowed, and probably it was just a leftover piece of wickerwork—a fruit basket or something of that kind. But I kept it anyway, on the off chance that it was a true fragment of Larry's Winchester strat.

And there was a pile of stones, perhaps to represent a headstone, set apart from the others, respectfully, on its own small mound. The wind lashed over it, hard pebbles of snow had joined the wind, and the pile seemed to get smaller as I stared at it. Cranmer was the box

that Pettifer came in, I rehearsed: but that was because I kept thinking that the grave was my own. Checheyev had found me a couple of
bits of stick, Magomed produced a twist of useful string. With a certain embarrassment, since I had listened to so much of Larry, the
parson's son, inveighing against his Maker, I made an inexpert cross
and attempted to plant it in the mound. I couldn't, of course, because
the ground was iron hard. So Magomed hacked a hole for me with
his *kinjal.*

A dead man is the worst enemy alive, I thought.

You can't alter his power over you.

You can't alter what you love or owe.

And it's too late to ask him for his absolution.

He has you beaten all ways up.

Then I remembered something Dee had said to me in Paris and I
had deliberately chosen not to hear: maybe you don't want to *find*
your friend, but to *become* him.

IN A CLEAR place near the courtyard, a ring of men had started to
dance while they extolled the name of God. Young boys joined them,
the crowd pressed round. Old men, women, and children chanted,
prayed and washed their faces in their hands. The dance grew faster
and wilder and seemed to transcend into a different time and space.

"What will you do now?" I asked Checheyev.

But I must have been addressing the question to myself, because
Checheyev had no doubt what he was doing. He had dismissed our
guide and was leading us at a stiff trot down a narrow path that went
straight over the edge of the plateau and into an abyss. I realised that
we were traversing an overhang more precipitous and alarming than
anything we had negotiated on horseback. Below us, but so far below
as to be another level of the earth and perhaps not attached to it at
all, ran a tiny silver river amid pastoral green fields where cattle
grazed. But here on the mountain face, where the wind howled and
the rock leaned out at us and every foothold was smaller than our
feet, we were in a celestial Hades, with Paradise below us.

We rounded a crag, and another awaited us. We were walking, I
was sure, deliberately and mutely to our deaths. We were taking our
place among the martyrs and heroic infidels. I looked again and saw
that we were standing on a sheltered grass ledge so protected that it

was like a huge chamber of rock with a picture window giving onto the Apocalypse. And in the grass were the burn marks I had noticed on the plateau; and traces of boots and the imprint of heavy pieces of equipment. And the still air inside the chamber smelled once more of burning and exploding.

We passed deeper into the mountain and saw the wreckage of a great arsenal: antitank guns, blown apart and lying on their sides, machine guns with barrels cut in two by clever charges, rocket launchers, smashed. And leading to the abyss, a trail of muddy footprints that reminded me of Aitken May's farm, where the most portable of his carpets had been dragged to the edge and hurled over it for fun.

ON THE plateau, the wind had gone, leaving behind it a cutting alpine cold. Somebody had given me a coat, I supposed Magomed. The three of us stood on the hillside: Magomed, Cranmer, and Checheyev. A bonfire burned in the courtyard below us as men of all ages sat round it and conferred, Issa and our Murids among them. Sometimes a young man sprang to his feet, and Checheyev said he was talking about vengeance. Sometimes an old man waxed impassioned, and Checheyev said he was talking about the deportations and how nothing, nothing had changed.

"Will you tell her?" I asked.

"Who?"

He seemed genuinely to have forgotten her.

"Emma. Sally. His girl. She's in Paris, waiting for him."

"She will be told."

"What are they saying now?"

"They're discussing the virtues of the late Bashir. Calling him a great teacher, a real man."

"Was he?"

"When men die here, we clean our minds of bad thoughts about them. I would advise you to do the same."

An old man's voice was coming up to us. Checheyev translated it. " 'Revenge is holy and cannot be touched. But it won't be enough to kill a couple of Ossetians or a couple of Russians. What we need is a new leader who will save us from being enslaved like animals.' "

"Do they have someone in mind?" I asked.

"That's what he's asking."

"You?"

"You want a whore to run a convent?" We listened and he again translated. " 'Who do we have who is great enough, clever enough, brave enough, devout enough, modest enough—' Why don't they say crazy enough and be done with it?"

"So who?" I insisted.

"It's called *tauba*. The ceremony is *tauba*. It means repentance."

"Who's repenting? What have they done wrong? What's to repent?"

For a while he ignored my question. I had the feeling I was irritating him. Or perhaps, like mine, his thoughts were elsewhere. He took a pull from his flask.

"They need a Murid who has the Sufi knowledge and is trained," he replied at last, still staring down the hill. "That's ten years' work. Could be twenty. You don't pick it up in KGB residences. A master of meditation. A big shot. A classy warrior."

A growl started and became a call. Issa was standing close to the centre of the circle. The glow of the fire lit his bearded cheeks as he turned and signalled up the hill. A few steps below us, Magomed was gazing down at him, the folds of his *cherkesska* gathered round his great back.

Other voices joined Issa's, lending their support. Suddenly it was as if everyone was calling to us. The two Murids burst from the courtyard and ran towards us. I heard Magomed's name repeated till everyone was chanting it. Leaving Checheyev and myself alone, Magomed started slowly down the hill towards the Murids.

A new ceremony began. Magomed sat at the centre of the circle, where a rug had been laid for him. The men, old and young, formed a circle round him, eyes closed while they chanted the same word over and over again in unison. A ring of men clasped hands and began a slow, rotating dance to the rhythm of the chant.

"Is that Magomed speaking?" I asked, for I could have sworn I heard his voice calling above the handclapping and praying and stamping feet.

"He's calling down God's blessing on the martyrs," Checheyev said. "He's telling them there are many battles still to be fought against the Russians. He's damned right."

At which, without another word, he turned his back on me and, as if sick of my Western uselessness or his own, started down the hill.

"Wait!" I shouted.

But either he didn't hear me or he didn't want to, for he continued his descent without turning his head.

With the dark, the wind had fallen. Great white stars were appearing above the mountain crags, answering the fires in the compound. I cupped my hands to my mouth and shouted again: "Wait!"

But the chanting was by now too loud, and he couldn't hear me even if he wanted to. For a moment longer I stood alone, converted to nothing, believing in nothing. I had no world to go back to and nobody left to run except myself. A Kalashnikov lay beside me. Slinging it across my shoulder, I hastened after him down the slope.

Acknowledgements

Academics get a rough time in this book, but that's Larry's fault. My own debt to them is considerable: to Dr. George Hewitt of the School of Oriental & African Studies, and Honorary Consul of Abkhazia; to Marie Bennigsen Broxup, editor of *Central Asian Survey;* to Robert Chenciner of St. Antony's College, Oxford; and to Federico Varese of Nuffield College, Oxford. Major Colin Gillespie and his wife, Sue, of Wootton Vineyard in Somerset make much better wine than Tim Cranmer ever did; John Goldsmith guided me through the corridors of Winchester College; Edward Nowell, master jeweller and antique dealer of Wells, opened his Aladdin's cave to me. All through the writing of this book I was lucky in my choice of friends and strangers alike.

John le Carré
Cornwall, December 1994

A NOTE ON THE TYPE

THIS BOOK was set in Janson, a typeface long thought to have
been made by the Dutchman Anton Janson, who was a prac-
ticing typefounder in Leipzig during the years 1668–1687.
However, it has been conclusively demonstrated that these
types are actually the work of Nicholas Kis (1650–1702), a
Hungarian, who most probably learned his trade from the
master Dutch typefounder Dirk Voskens. The type is an excellent example of the influential and sturdy Dutch types that prevailed in England up to the time William Caslon (1692–1766)
developed his own incomparable designs from them.

Composed by North Market Street Graphics,
Lancaster, Pennsylvania
Printed and bound by R. R. Donnelley & Sons,
Harrisonburg, Virginia
Designed by Virginia Tan